PRAISE FOR KRISTIN WRIGHT

"A fun—and funny—tale of PTA moms and the small-town lawyer mom whose quest for success leads to a moral dilemma. I found myself laughing out loud at the sociopathic PTA mom, Kira."

—Marcia Clark, bestselling author and iconic former LA prosecutor

"Impressive and intoxicating. The women inhabiting this story are bold, clever, complex, and deliciously thorny—quick to show you what they're capable of if you dare underestimate them. This book is a dark delight, and Kristin Wright is an author I'll be closely watching."

—Margarita Montimore, *USA Today* bestselling author of *Oona Out of Order*

"*The Darkest Flower* is juicy, suspenseful, and wickedly fun. With pitch-black humor, a fresh and engrossing voice, and one of the most fascinating characters I've come across, Kristin Wright explores the toxicity of privilege—and its ability to poison people from the inside out. From its attention-grabbing first line to the chilling revelations of its conclusion, this book is a stay-up-all-night read."

—Megan Collins, author of *The Winter Sister* and *Behind the Red Door*

"In *The Darkest Flower*, Kristin Wright takes the legal thriller to a new level when a PTA mom is poisoned (she survives!) and the main suspect is more venomous than the toxin used in the attempted murder. Dark. Twisty. Unforgettable female leads."

—Cara Reinard, author of *Sweet Water*

"*The Darkest Flower* is a fast-paced legal drama that pulls you in from the first page to the last. Like the best fiction, it is about so much more than the plight of its well-drawn characters and the jaw-dropping reveal, as it challenges you to reconsider your own beliefs about the things that matter most—family, friendship, and truth."

—Adam Mitzner, Amazon Charts bestselling author of *Dead Certain*

"*The Darkest Flower* is as much a riveting legal thriller as it is an exploration of modern-day motherhood and privilege. The story shows exactly what happens when the much-feared queen of the PTA gets accused of attempted murder. I couldn't stop reading."

—Kellye Garrett, author of the Detective by Day series and winner of the Anthony, Agatha, and Lefty Awards

"*The Darkest Flower* unfolds with the sinister beauty of a night-blooming poison. Wright has created a character so compelling in her deviousness that you find yourself reading just to find out what she says and does next. Relentlessly suspenseful, grimly humorous, and sneakily challenging, this twisty portrait of the extremes of motherly ambition will stay with you."

—Elly Blake, *New York Times* bestselling author of the Frostblood trilogy

"A twisty and darkly hilarious ride-along, Kristin Wright's timely thriller skewers the deadly sense of entitlement lurking below even the prettiest of facades."

—Mary Ann Marlowe, author of *Some Kind of Magic* and *Dating by the Book*

"Wright's *The Darkest Flower* is a dark, visceral view into the lives of suburban PTA moms. The final twist thrills, leaving you wanting more."

—Roselle Lim, author of *Natalie Tan's Book of Luck and Fortune* and *Vanessa Yu's Magical Paris Tea Shop*

"*The Darkest Flower* is a deliciously nasty drama about the dark side of motherhood, with an antiheroine you'll love to loathe and wicked wit dripping from every line. Clear your schedule, because you won't be able to put this one down until you reach the scandalous and oh-so-satisfying conclusion!"

—Layne Fargo, author of *Temper* and *They Never Learn*

"This is *Big Little Lies* if Cersei Lannister was heading the cast of malicious, impeccably groomed housewives. An addictive page-turner with a twist you won't see coming!"

—Michelle Hazen, author of *Breathe the Sky*

"PTA presidents and poison don't usually mix, but they're the perfect blend in Kristin Wright's fantastic thriller debut *The Darkest Flower*. Wright has created a propulsive legal thriller with plenty of juicy secrets to uncover behind those perfect picket fences. *The Darkest Flower* is *Desperate Housewives* meets *Big Little Lies*, and you won't be able to turn the pages fast enough."

—Vanessa Lillie, Amazon bestselling author of *Little Voices* and *For the Best*

THE DARKEST FLOWER

THE DARKEST FLOWER

KRISTIN WRIGHT

This is a work of fiction. Names, characters, organizations, places, events, and incidents are either products of the author's imagination or are used fictitiously. Any resemblance to actual persons, living or dead, or actual events is purely coincidental.

Published by Thomas & Mercer, Seattle

www.apub.com

ISBN-13: 9781542026345
ISBN-10: 1542026342

Cover design by Shasti O'Leary Soudant

Printed in the United States of America

To all the mothers, who are doing their best
And especially to mine, who is the best.

Look like the innocent flower,
But be the serpent under 't.

William Shakespeare, *Macbeth*

ACCUSATION

CHAPTER ONE
KIRA

I did not poison Summer Peerman with a strawberry smoothie.

I wanted to scream at the absolute injustice of having to put that sentence together but settled for a tiny grind of my perfect teeth while I parked my Volvo. As if I would be part of something so lacking in finesse.

It's true I orchestrated the fifth-grade graduation party, and I did hand Summer that cup of disgusting pureed produce, but I called 911 when she fell to the cafeteria floor gasping and flopping like a prize mackerel. I'd hardly have called so quickly if I'd been the one to spike her smoothie.

Nevertheless, a Neanderthal law enforcement caricature showed up uninvited at my house to threaten me—*me!*—so here I was, outside a law firm. I'd chosen this lawyer through a careful internet search and a hefty dash of intuition. Allison Barton was young, female, talented, and likely desperate to detach herself from the man-shaped pig whose name was on her firm's sign. She was also, by all accounts, well behaved enough to understand where the power would lie in our relationship.

It would lie with me.

Though of course I'd let her believe otherwise for as long as was convenient.

I turned off the engine and swung one Prada sandal onto the blacktop. The office was built of the same brick as the courthouse and sat near enough that it gave the impression of being the runt of the architectural litter. Not exactly basking in that marble-hall-of-justice vibe. A colossal comedown, but it was temporary. For me, it would be temporary.

Society has rules. People expect certain performances from good girls, and I'd always made sure to get a standing ovation for mine. Lucky for me, belonging to the club is half who you are and half doing and saying the right things. Nobody ever wants to know what you actually think. They'll go to some lengths not to find out. You can be two people: shining and perfect on the outside, and any damn way you want on the inside.

A million times, I'd fantasized about death and dismemberment and tire slashing and vandalism, but I'd never indulged. Anyone who says they've never had a malicious thought is lying. I always assumed our criminal system operated pretty much like society: only the actions count, not the thoughts.

Apparently I was wrong.

Inside the office a frumpy secretary glanced up, professional and warm. I hate that kind of person, but I shoved my murky thoughts away and donned my best one-of-the-girls smile, easy as applying a coat of lipstick.

"Hi! I'm Kira Grant, and I'm here for my appointment." I even blew out my cheeks and added a touch of nervous eye widening. The secretary said Ms. Barton was still in with a client, offered me a comfortable chair while I waited, and bustled off to get me a glass of water.

I didn't poison Summer Peerman, but they think I did.

Allison Barton had better be a damn good lawyer.

I do hate it when things don't go the way I plan.

CHAPTER TWO

ALLISON

Books are easier to judge by their covers than people are. Small-town law practice taught me that lesson better than any law professor I ever had.

When Elmer Baker, a silver-haired, twinkly-eyed Keebler elf of a man, came in for his legal consultation two years ago, he cried and told me an upsetting story about how his wife of forty years had racked up massive debt and left him for a man half her age. I signed him up as a client, determined to help him through his divorce.

That was the last time I bought a story like that. I missed the days when I could take people at their word.

"Here's the deal, Elmer," I said to him now. "This only works if we're a team. It's been two years, and you've rejected all my advice. You forged your wife's name on the debts. You're the one cheating. You changed the locks on the house and won't even let her get her underwear. She never had outside employment, at your request, and now she's living off the charity of her brother. You're in for an epic smackdown from the judge. I can't help you. I need you to sign this form agreeing to end our attorney-client relationship."

"What?"

"Here are the names of three attorneys who might be willing to work with you." I handed him a slip of paper.

A full minute passed. Elmer tried the cute and pathetic look that had gotten him on my client list in the first place. Then he switched to sputtering indignation and threats.

I sat silent, unwilling to give him even a single one of my emotions. I missed that, too: getting to show happiness and anger and misery when I felt them.

"Fine," he hissed, narrowing his eyes and completing his transformation from kindly sprite to enraged Gollum. "Don't expect a recommendation from me. Should have known better than to hire a girl. You're weak. Unqualified and bush league. I'll write a review on the computer. I'll call the newspaper."

Internally, I sighed. "That's fine, Elmer. Sign here."

When he was done, I stood and gestured toward the door, then watched him go with satisfaction.

I learned a bit more from every mistake. Too many people thought lawyers existed to serve their worst impulses, as if we were nothing but their conscienceless swords, willing to bend every rule without morals or ethics or any concern for right and wrong. I had a five-year-old daughter. There had to be a way to be both a lawyer and a decent person.

I glanced at my calendar. One more appointment before I could go to lunch. Kira Grant.

All I knew about this appointment was that it had something to do with the poisoning at the elementary school last week. The name wasn't familiar, but then, I didn't know everyone here the way my assistant, Maureen, did. I'd grown up in Northern Virginia and moved to Lynchburg when I married my husband.

Cheating ex-husband, that is. By the time he got caught with a married fellow teacher in the high school chemistry lab, I had a practice here, so I stayed.

So, yeah. I admit I had real trouble dealing with guys like Elmer.

On appointment day, I did my best to fit return phone calls into the cracks. I dialed Emmett Amaro, the assistant commonwealth's attorney

I knew best. We'd gone to law school together and stayed friends even though he was often my adversary.

"Allie. About time you called back. On the Krotow DUI, we'll agree to thirty days, all suspended except for time served."

"Done," I said, relieved to avoid yet another DUI trial. In small towns, lawyers couldn't specialize—I handled criminal defense right alongside divorce and personal injury and estates.

"What are you going to do with all that extra time Thursday morning?" he asked. "I think we should get coffee."

I laughed, knowing he wasn't asking me out on a date. "Your boss would kill you if you used work time to fraternize with the enemy."

Emmett's low chuckle rumbled. "Define *enemy*."

"And besides, I'm not sure what you mean by 'all that extra time,'" I said, going in for the kill. "At best, it would only take ten minutes for you to fail to prove him guilty if we went to trial."

This time he cackled. "Fail? As if."

"Proof's in the offer. I believe you just offered, and I accepted, a plea deal."

Still laughing, he said, "Fine. Yes. We have a deal. Gotta go. I've got court in five minutes."

I hung up, trying to switch gears back to my next appointment.

The elementary school poisoning had been huge local news the previous week. So far nobody at the courthouse knew much about what had happened. This woman might well be able to tell quite a juicy story, though most of my criminal clients were sullen and taciturn. I tried to picture my last criminal client—foulmouthed, chain-smoking, and accused of passing bad checks—at an elementary school event and failed. Come to think of it, though, that woman had had young children in school.

It hadn't really occurred to me before now that my daughter would attend school with the children of my clients.

"Ms. Grant is here, Allison," Maureen said, poking her head through my doorway. "Are you ready?"

"Yup. Send her in."

Maureen paused. "She's not what I expected," she whispered, then disappeared.

I stood to greet the woman who appeared in my office. No, Kira Grant was not what I'd expected. She looked nothing at all like a bad-check client. She wore a fitted, sleeveless silk sweater and expensive linen pants in a community where jeans and T-shirts were the norm. Her heeled sandals were trendy and stylish. She wore a huge diamond ring on her left hand, and her dark-red hair fell in shining waves worthy of a shampoo model or a pop star at the Grammys. Not a molecule of inexpertly applied makeup marred her rose-petal skin.

"Please, sit. You're Kira Grant?"

"Yes, I am. I can't even believe I am in a lawyer's office. Well, a criminal lawyer's office. Oh my Lord." She narrowed her eyes. "You do have experience?"

"Yes. I'm Allison Barton," I said, taking my seat behind my desk. "Our firm is known for criminal defense. I've been in practice six years, most of that doing criminal as well as other areas." That was a bit of an overstatement. The senior partner, my boss, had tried a national-news murder case early in his career and won. It made his reputation and allowed him to hire me as his girl Friday, and afterward, we got all the worst criminals in Lynchburg and five surrounding counties—though I got mostly misdemeanors and a lot of DUIs.

"I tried to get in with Dan—everyone who's everyone knows Dan—but he was booked up, and his secretary assured me I'd be in good hands with you. And that you'd consult with him, of course."

And there it was. As long as Dan ran the firm—and he was only forty and Ironman fit—I'd get the people he shoved off. He took the showy cases, the ones that built reputations and splashed his movie-star face all over TV. I got the rest.

I might consult with Dan, but my pride couldn't bring me to admit weakness to this commanding woman. Increasingly, my pride also kept me from consulting much with Dan. To him, women were attractive appendages. He'd fired a receptionist three years ago because, he told me, he didn't want to look at her "homely" face every morning. He regularly made suggestions for colors I should wear and who should cut my hair. The morning last month when I found a Stila eye-shadow palette on my desk with a bow on top, I fantasized about Thelma-and-Louising myself straight out of Dodge.

"Why don't you tell me why you're here?" I asked, pushing down the familiar resentment and poising my pen over my legal pad.

She blinked, and her mouth worked. "I . . ." It took some time before she could speak. "Last Wednesday we held the graduation party for the fifth grade at the elementary school. I'm the president of the PTA, and my son, Finn, was graduating." The mere mention of her child's name brought a flush of pride to her cheeks. "It was quite a week: Field Day, the awards assemblies, and then the party on the last day of school. So exhausting, but I wouldn't have missed a second of it."

"Yes?" I asked. So far nothing sounded suspicious.

"Well. At the party, right before the children were scheduled to walk to 'Pomp and Circumstance,' the . . . incident happened."

"I saw the story in the news. I assume you're talking about the poisoning."

"Yes. The poisoning. Summer Peerman was poisoned with the homemade smoothies we served at the party. I was at the table, handing them out. I personally gave out dozens of cups to the children, and no one got sick. But she . . ."

I furiously took notes, but I needed her to slow down. "Who is Summer Peerman? Did you know her?"

"Summer is a parent. A friend of mine. Her son, Aidan, is friends with my son." She let out a tense breath and fanned her face with a manicured hand. "Oh my God, I still can't believe it." She closed her eyes.

"So Ms. Peerman drank a smoothie and got sick? I know the news said it was poisoning, but do you know what happened?"

"No, I only know what the news said. And what I saw. Dear God." Kira shivered, shaking away the memory.

"Right, but are they sure it wasn't a heart attack? Choking?"

"The investigator from the sheriff's office who came to my house to question me said poison."

Oh shit. The sheriff's office had already been out to her house. "Whoa. Wait. Are you charged with anything yet?" The news hadn't reported that anyone had been arrested, but it might not have hit yet. "Have you answered any of their questions?"

If she said yes, most likely she'd already said something that would come back to bite her. Most defendants got convicted based on inadvisable cooperation with the police before they talked to lawyers.

"No, to both," Kira said, spreading instant relief. "I'm aware of my rights. That's why I'm here. I think they think I had something to do with it. The investigator acted quite unpleasant. He advised me that if I didn't want to talk to him, I ought to talk to a lawyer. So here I am."

"Has anyone else been charged?"

"No, not according to the PTA Facebook page. But Summer stayed in the hospital for nearly a week—she just got out. She went into cardiac arrest. It nearly stopped her heart. I've heard rumors of some kind of permanent kidney problems. I understand it was too small a dose to kill a person of her size, but my God. What if a child had taken that cup? My son was there that day!" A tear leaked from one eye. She scrubbed at it.

A person of her size? I took a good look at Kira's bony shoulders. My God, indeed. "Did the investigator say what kind of poison it was?"

"He said aconite."

"Aconite? I've never heard of that. Do you know what that is?"

"No. I've never heard of it, either."

I made a note to look it up. "What kind of smoothies were they? Did you make them?"

"No, Brandi Crane wanted to do the smoothies. She insisted. She thinks everyone loves her smoothies, but to be honest, they're awful—she puts beets and spinach and who knows what all in there with the strawberries. She's big on the superfoods. They're a hideous bloody-purple color and have an off taste at the best of times, so it's no wonder Summer didn't taste anything odd."

"Do you know Brandi well?"

"No, we met this year on the PTA. Frankly, we've clashed."

There were two schools of thought on this next question. Some lawyers preferred not to know their clients were guilty. Letting them lie under oath knowing all their statements were false was a no-no under the state bar's ethical rules. I'd rather know, though. I hated the crawly, uneasy feeling of representing a client who might have done bad things I knew nothing about. If she'd poisoned the woman, I didn't want her testifying she didn't. Period.

"Let me ask you straight out: Did you poison Summer Peerman?"

Kira looked horrified. "Of course not! She's one of my best friends!"

"Is there a reason the investigator seemed to think you should get a lawyer?"

She had the grace to look a bit abashed. "Well, I was at the table when Summer took the cup. I handed a cup to her, and she drank, and almost immediately, she started to struggle. It was terrifying. Her son was right there screaming. I called 911."

"So you had an opportunity to poison the cup?" I asked my outrageous question and then stared at her, to watch her reaction.

It was satisfactory. First her eyes widened, but I saw the indignation and shock I was looking for. No furtive eye shifting. No suppressed grins. "I suppose I did, but I. Did. Not. Poison. That. Cup. The very idea."

"Did you help make the smoothies?"

"No. Brandi did that all by herself, at home, the night before. And like I said, I gave out dozens of cups along with several other mothers, and no one else got sick."

"Tell me about Summer. You say you're friends?"

I caught a hesitant eyelash flutter. There was something there. Sadness, maybe, or loss. Something she didn't want to tell me. Interesting.

Her voice gave nothing away. "Yes. Our boys were in the same kindergarten class. Both of them already knew how to read, and Summer and I bonded when we questioned the teacher about whether there'd be extra enrichment opportunities for them." She made the tiniest of grimaces, explained by her next words. "We're both busy, of course—Summer works full-time and I've got a daughter still at home, Fiona. She's five. But we—Summer and I—try to see each other once every couple of weeks. Sometimes I meet her for lunch, or we go out for drinks."

"Is she married?"

"No, not anymore. She and her husband separated when Finn and Aidan were in second grade. They get along fine, as far as I know. I guess you never know for sure, but he wasn't there that day."

I asked for and wrote down the name of Summer's ex-husband. "Does she have any enemies? Who would have a motive to hurt her?"

"Well . . ." Kira brought a delicate finger to her lip. "Summer is so kind. So sweet. She spends time on the weekends, when she's not at Aidan's soccer tournaments, at the food bank. I don't know. Though maybe she made an enemy through her job—she's a social worker. Child Protective Services. You know. An abusive or neglectful parent she took kids from."

"We can check all that out."

Kira bit her lip, somehow managing to emphasize her beauty. "I have to admit, though . . ."

"Yes?"

"Well. I do wonder about Brandi. This is a bit gossipy, but I did hear Summer had some issues with her. She might have a . . . what do you call it?"

"A motive?" I consulted my notes. "Brandi? The PTA mom who made the smoothies?"

"Right. Brandi also has a son, Griffin, the same age as ours. Griffin and Summer's son have played sports together since they were tiny. There was some sort of scuffle between them on the field. Playing time, or something. The parents got involved. Like I said, I only met Brandi this year. She's never been on the PTA before."

"Would playing time on an elementary school sports team be something that would rise to this level?" It seemed ridiculous to me. My daughter, Libby, had just turned five, and her main interest was smearing as much tempera paint on as much square footage as possible. Should I sign her up for sports already? I didn't know if she could catch or kick a ball.

"Oh, it's not related to the school. This is the travel soccer team. I gather the boys are both quite good."

"Okay." I made a mental note to worry about my failure to provide Libby with opportunities for sports-related girl power later. "Do you seriously think Brandi would have a motive to do something like this? Tell me about her."

"She has four kids. Griffin is the youngest. The oldest one is grown and in the military, I think. The two oldest are from her first marriage. The second time, she married . . . up."

The judgment here was unmistakable.

"Up?"

"He's an engineer. She . . . didn't grow up with money."

"I see." I did see. Kira thought Brandi was trash and hadn't tried hard to hide it.

"She . . . I don't know how to say this in a nice way. Brandi overcompensates. She overdoes everything. She can't just serve fresh-squeezed lemonade. She's got to spend hours making smoothies. She can't just put up a Christmas tree at school—she's got to put up a mechanical Santa and all nine reindeer. It's like she's got to prove she's the best mom ever."

"That doesn't add up to murder, though."

"No, of course not."

"So what would be Brandi's motive? A disagreement?"

"Noooo," she said, her brow wrinkling, deep in thought. "I think it goes deeper, but I'm not sure. Things between Brandi and Summer aren't good. Brandi really dislikes her."

"I hate to ask this, Kira, but do you have any criminal record?"

"What? No. Nothing."

"Do you drink? Do drugs?"

"A glass of wine here and there. I don't take any medication."

"Are you employed?"

"Not outside the home, no. I used to be an accountant, though, before the children. They're at the babysitter's right now."

I gestured at her beringed left hand. "And your husband?"

"Miles. He's a dentist in Lynchburg."

Interesting that he hadn't come with her. Or that she hadn't mentioned him until I asked. "Does he know about the visit from the sheriff's office?"

She dropped her gaze, fidgeted with her handbag. Ah. A crack in the perfect life. "He'd gone to work when the investigator came. I didn't want to worry him if there wasn't a reason."

I sat back. "Well, Kira. From what you've told me, you have no motive. You did have opportunity, but no more opportunity than any other PTA parent. Sounds like Summer will survive, so the most serious crime anyone could be charged with is attempted murder, though that's still a felony and plenty serious."

Kira's shoulders relaxed.

I held up a finger. "That's the good news. I'm going by what you've told me. You could have a motive you haven't mentioned to me. You may well be the most hated woman in the PTA." Again, I watched her. An ugly flush rose up her neck. I'd touched a nerve, and she didn't appreciate it. Somehow I guessed she hadn't been voted Miss PTA Congeniality. "You aren't off the hook. Obviously this occurred in a school. Children could have been hurt. They will want to arrest someone. You handed the cup to Summer. You're correct that you're under suspicion if law enforcement has already been out to visit you. You should not talk with them, not at all. If you retain me, I'll investigate the same way the sheriff's office will."

"Yes. I do want to retain you. As long as you're willing to chat with Dan periodically. He's got so much more experience."

I gritted my teeth, agreed, and named a fee—she didn't blink. Before she left, I took down her contact information, the names of the other women who'd worked the refreshment table, and the parents and teachers she remembered being present.

"Okay. I'll let the sheriff's office know I'm representing you as soon as your check clears, and they'll know not to bother you at home anymore."

I stood, reaching out a hand to shake. "You need to tell your husband now."

She smiled sweetly but ignored the hand. "I'll tell him tonight." Kira swept toward the door like a countess who'd finished dictating menus to the cook.

I could do it later just as easily, but it wouldn't hurt her to confront her new reality starting right now.

"And Kira." She turned. "I hope you're not charged, but if you are, a fair warning: your life will change. Nobody, not even the innocent, comes through a criminal prosecution without sustaining some heavy damage."

"Noted," she bit off.

I stared at her for a moment. "I get the sense you like for people to think you're fragile and refined, but I have a feeling there isn't a single fragile thing about you."

Her nostrils flared, but she said nothing.

"If I'm right," I continued, "you'll come through fine."

CHAPTER THREE

KIRA

The absolute audacity.

I gave the receptionist a brief nod and dashed to my car as quickly as I could without actually . . . dashing.

How dare that teenager of a lawyer say the things she said to me? As if I had any reason, any motive, any desire at all to poison Summer, who was at least in the top five of my best friends. And then to imply I wasn't refined? What is the opposite of refined? Uncouth? Surely a person who bought her polyester suit on the sale rack at Belk wasn't presuming to describe me as uncouth.

I didn't spend all my waking hours managing everything down to the last dotted *i* to have a soft-looking, badly dressed, freckly-pale mouse of a girl talk to me with no sense of who I *am*. Besides, she was desperately in need of highlights—and maybe layers—to lighten up that mud-brown hair. Next time she spoke to me so rudely, I would recommend my colorist. And maybe an orthodontist.

Allison Barton had better remember her place, or I wouldn't hesitate to invoke her more well-known boss to keep her in it.

I took a second to calm down before pulling out of the parking lot, sending classical music through the dashboard Bluetooth.

I've always been scrupulously honest with myself, even if not with everyone else—or anyone else, for that matter. I didn't care about classical music. I couldn't keep the composers straight. I just liked thinking of myself as a person who likes classical music.

The babysitter's house was less than a mile from the lawyer's office. At least I could assume Drina had fed them lunch by now.

As Drina swung the door open, Fiona's keening in the background drowned out the television. Oh God, what now? She'd spent an hour this morning crying at the prospect of going to Drina's, and Finn had sulked, too, grumbling because he'd intended to spend this beautiful summer day playing some violent video game Miles bought him. Obviously. What could be more natural than spending your summer vacation inside shooting things?

I shook myself and put on my Happy Mommy face. "Hi, y'all! I missed you!"

"Hey, Mom. We don't have to stop anywhere, do we?" *Ah, Finn. Your expressions of love warm my heart.*

"Mommy!" screamed Fiona, rushing for my arms as if we'd been separated for weeks instead of approximately two hours. "Finn said my book wasn't a real book!"

"Finn?" I raised an eyebrow in question. It took years for me to perfect that move. It looks amazing on me. It's something about the arch of my eyebrow.

"It doesn't have words. Only pictures. It's not a real book."

I cleared my throat. "It is a real book. You've forgotten what it's like to be little."

Fiona's tears had turned to gasping shudders. "See! It is!"

Privately, I had to agree with Finn. Fiona had shown no affinity for the written word. Her affection for this little board book was the first sign I'd seen that she would one day be literate. By her age, Finn had already gobbled up most of the Magic Tree House chapter books. I feared Fiona might, in fact, be dim.

No matter. If she was limited, I would never let anyone pity her. None of these individualized education programs or special accommodations. We would spare no expense to blast everything out of her path.

I picked up Fiona and cuddled her, smoothing her rosy cheeks and rubbing her head through her spectacular sheaf of shining blonde hair. She'd be pretty, at a minimum. In today's world, beauty might take her even further than brains. I kissed her hair in relief.

Over her head I glanced at my son. "Yes, in answer to your question, Finn. We do need to stop somewhere. We're going to buy Ms. Peerman a pie and take it to her. She's been sick." The pie would be my ticket: I needed a few answers from Summer. I'd hardly be the first person to use baked goods as currency.

"Mommy! Can I get a cupcake?" Fiona snuggled into my neck, petting my hair.

She shouldn't eat one—she'd begun a bit of a potbelly—but it would be easier to let her. "Yes, darling. And you, too, Finn. We'll save them for dessert after dinner, all right?"

❧

Thirty indecisive minutes later (Finn opted for the lemon bar, Fiona struggled for ten minutes to choose between yellow frosting and pink), we arrived, crème brûlée pie in hand, at Summer's front door. Her son, Aidan, answered, looking warily pleased to see Finn. Aidan was a tall boy for eleven, fit and strong. My poor little Finn still looked eight, undersized and scrawny.

"How's your mother feeling, sweetie?" I asked.

"We brought her a pie!" Fiona sang out.

"Um, she's doing better." I could have sworn the little brat flared his nostrils at me and blocked the doorway like a club bouncer. "She's watching TV."

From the family room, Summer called, "Come on back, y'all." She sprawled on the sofa, her shoulder-length, straightened hair loose, a blanket over her lap. A *Law & Order* episode went "clung clung" on the TV. Aidan and Finn took off to Aidan's bedroom. Fiona curled into my side. I plucked her onto my lap as I sank into an armchair opposite Summer, making sure my pants didn't wrinkle.

"How are you, really?" I reached out and patted her arm.

Summer turned the volume down and checked to make sure Aidan was out of earshot. "Lucky to be alive, apparently. Five days in the hospital won't be cheap. I didn't realize until a nurse said something near the end that I'd come a couple minutes from flatlining. That stuff stops the heart, they said. They pumped my stomach, and there was all kinds of something called ventricular excitability, and then apparently they're going to have to watch my kidney for the rest of my life. You know I only have one after I donated to my sister. Won't take much to put me on dialysis forever."

"Oh Lord. I'm so sorry this happened to you. What was it again?" I asked.

"Aconite. It's a plant. Also called monkshood, they said, or wolfsbane. It has a pretty flower, but it's really poisonous. You're a gardener. Do you know it?"

"Hmm," I said, desperately waiting for my turn so I could say what I'd been wanting to say. "I don't even . . . Oh God, Summer. I've been going crazy. I handed you that cup. You know I had nothing to do with . . . I'd die if you thought . . ." I touched my fingertip to my eye and came away with a bit of moisture.

"I don't. You wouldn't do something like that," Summer said, shifting to turn more fully toward me. "And besides, if you meant to poison me, you'd have been a lot better at it. You don't do things halfway. Handing me the cup yourself. Amateur hour. Please."

I laughed with her. It was important to know she didn't blame me. I'd gotten the first thing I'd come here for. "You're right. Not exactly the moves of a criminal mastermind. But who did do it?"

Summer made a meaningful glance at Fiona, who stared back, clearly listening.

Right. "Fiona, sweetie, run upstairs and see what the boys are doing, okay?" I lifted her off my lap and set her on the floor.

"Nooo." She clung to my knee.

"Yes, sweetie. Go on upstairs, or no cupcake for you." I gave her a firm pat—well, more like a push—on her behind, and she went.

"I thought about Tammy Cox," Summer said as soon as Fiona's footsteps on the stairs faded.

"Really?" Tammy was not the sort who usually participated much in the PTA, but despite her tattoos and penchant for spaghetti straps in winter, I'd never been able to dislodge her as secretary. We clashed, though I always won, like the time I prevented her from buying two cases of Mountain Dew for the refreshments after the talent show. Not everyone wanted teeth like piano keys. She played up every southern stereotype to annoy me, and I pretended to be annoyed. Tammy and I understood each other. "Why do you think so?"

"Let's say she's not a fan of Child Protective Services."

Aha. That would mean the Department of Social Services investigated Tammy's parenting on a complaint from someone, probably her mother-in-law. I made a mental note to mention Tammy's name to Teen Lawyer. Allison. To Allison. Really, I needed to stop being so juvenile.

Summer clicked off the TV. "Ruthanne was at the table with you, handing out cups."

"Ruthanne? Seriously? You don't think Ruthanne, do you?"

Ruthanne Dillard was even younger than my preadolescent lawyer and the mother of a first grader. She'd shown up at the PTA sign-up table with baked goods the second her daughter arrived for kindergarten registration, practically drooling for any task we'd give her. She wore polka dots and Mommy and Me dresses and headbands, and her every thought was earnest and good-hearted. She'd still be five when she died at ninety. Finn would call her a try-hard—the obvious striving for perfection should embarrass her, but it never had yet.

"I can't imagine why she'd want to hurt me, but she was there."

"She was annoying me is what she was doing," I said, thinking about her endless prattling and preening that day, not to mention the fact that she had to have spent hours carving the cheese cubes on the snack tray into festive shapes.

Summer lifted a tired but inquiring eyebrow.

I rolled my eyes, careful not to create any unsightly forehead lines. "I told her to help pour that disgusting mess of liquid produce into the cups, which she did before everyone came in to get them, but as soon as there were people to coo over, she insisted on trying to hand out cups. Fortunately, we'd poured a whole bunch of them beforehand and had a good thirty or so ready to go."

Summer took that in, showing no surprise. Ruthanne was far too gung ho about the PTA for her own good. She'd criticized the welcome bags we'd made for the kindergarteners the year her daughter started, so this year she'd insisted on doing them herself, filling all eighty bags with packs of sugarless "encourage-mints" and dreadful "friend-ship" drawings. Then she visited every classroom to make sure the teachers knew she'd made them.

Ruthanne still needed to pay her dues and take a Valium—or ten. I'd hide one in her steel-cut oatmeal, but that, at the moment, might be a bit too on the nose. In a year or two, I'd allow her a leadership role, but for now, I had an incoming kindergartener this fall and no intention of allowing someone else to serve as president. "I wondered about Brandi."

Summer waved her hand in a manner I translated as "hogwash" or some other colloquialism. "I guess it's possible, but it seems so bizarre. God. The idea of anyone in the room—anyone we know—doing that is . . . I can't even make my brain go there."

I leaned forward. "No. Think about it. Brandi made the smoothies. She could have put some nasty vegetable in there to cover the taste of whatever you had in yours."

"It didn't taste good, no doubt, but I gulped it down to get it over with. But why would she poison me? Or want to?"

"What about the soccer field thing? You know. Didn't Brandi come at you over some fight Aidan and her son had this spring?"

"Yessss . . . good memory." Summer leaned back, giving me an admiring look. "The boys threw a couple elbows at each other during a game. Nothing major—the kind of thing boys with too much energy do."

"Who started it?"

"I don't honestly know. Brandi went marching right onto the field. Grabbed both kids and yelled. Smacked her own kid hard straight across the face. Wasn't long before the game started up again like nothing happened."

"I can't remember what you said," I prompted. This was juicy and exactly the kind of thing that might help me out. "I know you told me, but maybe it's important now."

"I might have gone off on her a bit after that." Summer shifted on the sofa, in obvious pain.

"Brandi is a classless, high-jumping toad. I can't blame you if you did." One of the things I'd always liked best about Summer was that she was a what-you-see-is-what you get kind of person. Straightforward. Though that characteristic would never describe me, I did have a certain amount of envy for it. "What did you say again?"

"I might have reminded her I work for Social Services, and Social Services doesn't look too kindly on child abuse. I felt bad immediately. I shouldn't have done that."

"Oh, Summer." Exactly what I'd told my lawyer about. They'd have to consider Brandi a suspect. She'd had a public spat with the victim, then made the smoothies. Though I didn't care for Brandi, her son

Griffin was all right. He'd been nice to Finn, and a brainy kid like mine could never have too many jocks for friends. Safer that way.

"But I thought it was fine after that," Summer said. "I didn't report her for a single slap. For the most part I think she does okay with those kids. I apologized after a while, and she choked out some mumbly-ass thing about crossing lines, and we've been civil for the last couple weeks. No way that justifies her trying to kill me."

"Brandi can be vicious. Remember the time she made fun of Linh Nguyen?"

"You mean when Linh mispronounced Dr. Rickman's name?"

"Yes. That." Brandi had cackled away merrily at the sight of the poor woman's face as awareness of her mistake dawned. I took a more serious tone. "And Brandi did say a few things about you after the pancake griddle electrical disaster back in December."

"Like what?"

"Well," I said carefully. "She may have . . . um, implied that your skin tone prevented you from adequately supervising the extension cords for the griddles." Summer was Black, but it took a hard-core racist to think that had anything to do with the fact that we'd blown a fuse by trying to plug in nine billion extension cords.

"That bitch." Summer was also tough, and I admired her ability to shake off insults as I always had. Nothing ever fazed her. She took everything in stride.

"An investigator from the sheriff's office came to my house," I said.

"What?" Summer sat up straighter. "About me? That's ridiculous."

"I went to see a lawyer today, just in case."

"You're serious."

I raised a fingernail toward my mouth, then thought better of it. Manicures took precious time out of my schedule. "Yes. The lawyer—Allison Barton, she's in with Dan MacDonald's firm—said based on what I told her about the investigator, she did think I needed a lawyer."

"Like, as in you'd be charged?"

"Well, noooo. Just that I needed a lawyer. But obviously that was the elephant in the room."

"Oh God, Kira. That's terrible. It's got to be a misunderstanding. They'll figure out who did do it and then it'll all go away. Do you want me to talk to your lawyer?"

"Would you? If she asks, I mean?" Mentally, I clapped my hands. Blunt people never understood how much better it was to make people think things were their idea. It was always worth the extra time to come at things the indirect way.

"Sure. There are a lot of people who could have done it. Tammy, Ruthanne, Brandi. Some other random person I took kids away from once. The list is pretty long." That was true enough. Summer had told stories about people following her from the courtroom to her car or pulling out guns when she arrived, badge in hand, at their houses to remove abused children. "It could even have been some sicko who dropped it in a random cup and had no idea who'd drink it."

"Thanks, Summer. You're a good person."

She gave me a long look I couldn't interpret before her face broke into her usual good-natured smile. "Think nothing of it."

"Well, honey, you need rest, and I've got to get these kids home."

Summer reached out a hand to me. There'd been a time when I didn't have to think about accepting it. "Thanks for the pie, Kira. I'll call you later."

"Call me if you need anything at all," I said, knowing she wouldn't.

I had a lot to tell Allison. I'd made sure the victim was on my side, and our sleepy corner of the world was chock-full of people more likely to have done it than me. That info was well worth the price of the pie.

CHAPTER FOUR

ALLISON

Every Friday afternoon, I packed up all the work I'd have to do at home while I let the TV babysit Libby, sorting my open cases into "stay here" or "go home" piles. I hadn't heard a thing from Kira Grant in a week and a half, so maybe the sheriff's office had homed in on another suspect. I tossed her file on the "stay here" pile. She wouldn't thank me for using up her retainer doing work on her case if she was never charged.

Once, Friday afternoons used to be fun. The weekend spread out in front of me, full of possibilities: free time, sleeping in, parties with wine. On occasion, even sex. All those things were distant memories, sadly enough.

My direct line rang at 4:00 p.m.

"Allison Barton."

"This is Miles Grant."

My mind went blank. The natural depth of his voice had a discordant, panicked high note. "Yes, sir. How can I help you?"

"My wife is Kira Grant. She's been arrested. At home, in front of our children. They've taken her off for fingerprinting. I had to cancel three appointments and dash home. Our son is only eleven, and they left him alone with his sister."

Oh no. I'd let the sheriff's office know I was representing Kira, in the hopes that they would contact me if they were about to arrest her so she could make arrangements for the kids, turn herself in quietly, and get bonded out before her family even knew what was happening. They hadn't called. Arresting her like that did not bode well. Someone was angry.

"I'm sorry, Dr. Grant." He was a dentist, Kira had said. "Are the children okay?"

"Yes, they're fine physically, but it was a bad scene. Fiona is still crying."

I could hear it in the background.

"I'm sorry about that. Kira needs a bond hearing." I checked the clock. Damn.

"Can you get her out today? Please?" I almost missed the tiny hitch in his voice. The poor man sounded devastated.

"I wish I could say otherwise, but I doubt it, Dr. Grant. It's Friday. On occasion, the commonwealth requests arrests on a Friday afternoon on purpose because they know the court can't hold a bond hearing until Monday."

"Until Monday?" Shock raised his voice out of the easy-listening zone. "You've got to be joking."

Unfortunately, I wasn't. Kira would have to stay in the county jail all weekend, and while it wasn't the pen, it wouldn't be much like a Sandals resort, either.

"I wish I were joking, Dr. Grant."

"Call me Miles."

"Miles, then. I'm sorry. I'll make the calls as soon as I hang up and see what I can do for Monday. I can assure you, though, the county jail is not like you see on TV. It's not too bad, and the others there are for the most part not hardened criminals."

He snorted: disbelief, horror, or disgust. I couldn't tell over the phone. Dentists whose wives wore linen probably didn't know many people who spent time in the county jail.

"Well. Let me get to work, then," I said. "Lots to do."

"Thank you. Please call on my cell if you hear anything."

"I will." He gave me the number, and we hung up. Just before the connection severed, I heard another little sigh of despair that shot straight to my heart.

Damn the Commonwealth's Attorney's Office. They'd pulled this crap on purpose. This method ensured the commonwealth could make each defendant, even if ultimately found innocent, serve at least a little time. I felt pretty confident someone had gotten a kick out of the idea of making a nose-in-the-air PTA mom trade her silk and heels for an orange jumpsuit and shower shoes. I picked up the phone.

"Commonwealth's Attorney's Office, this is Hailey." Hailey was the receptionist, had responsibility only for paper organizing, phone answering, and visitor greeting, and did it all with a smile to boot.

"Hey, Hailey. It's Allison Barton. Is Emmett out of court yet?"

"He sure is. Let me transfer you."

Being friends with a lawyer who worked for the commonwealth was touchy, since our jobs required us to confront and antagonize each other on a regular basis. In the courtroom, Emmett was professional, serious, and fair. Outside the court, he had a wicked sense of humor and a taste for craft beer. He might well be my best friend, sad as that was to consider. After my divorce, I'd lost most of our couple friends because my ex, Steve, grew up here and had gone to high school with them.

If Emmett had ordered the arrest, he'd admit to it. If he hadn't, he'd tell me who did.

"Emmett Amaro."

"It's Allison."

There was a pause. He knew about Kira's arrest, knew she'd retained me, and knew I'd be pissed as hell.

"Allie," he said, his voice softening. "You want to know about the Grant arrest, I assume. I didn't order it, in case you were wondering."

I let out my breath in relief while twisting the phone above my forehead so he wouldn't hear it. I had no idea why it mattered that Emmett hadn't done it.

"Then who did? There was no reason. She's not a flight risk. She's got two little kids and no income."

"The order came from On High."

On High referred to Valerie Williams, Emmett's boss, the elected commonwealth's attorney. Valerie had gone to law school late in life after her high school–age daughter had been the victim of a date rape, and she had been an avenging anticrime angel ever since. She was sixty years old, had the kind of deep-bronze skin that made her look forty and a wealth of twisted-up braids, was good to her staff and ruthless in court, and was totally willing to use every trick in the book to stick it to a defendant, all of whom she believed were guilty until proven innocent. She didn't allow her junior attorneys to make decisions.

It drove Emmett crazy to have to ask permission for every little thing. A year or so ago, he'd gone to Valerie and asked for the right to make plea bargain calls on the misdemeanors, at least. She'd told him if he didn't like her style, he was welcome to move on.

"Well. That's not a surprise. Is she handling the case herself?"

Emmett did a diabolical cackle. "No, that would be me."

Dammit. Already, I knew Kira's case would involve unpleasant issues of class, and she gave off a decided whiff of icy hauteur. Somehow, it bothered me that Emmett—and the rest of the courthouse staff—would associate me with her.

"You, huh?" Weird. It had never bothered me before what anyone in the courthouse thought about my clients. Four years ago, I'd tried an armed robbery case with a defendant who overturned a counsel table and told Emmett and the judge both to fuck off in open court. I hadn't even gasped as the bailiff pulled his weapon and dragged my client off to the cell.

"Me." Emmett's voice turned teasing. I could practically see him running his hands through his unruly black hair. "So how are you going to prove the lovely Ms. Grant innocent?"

I curled my fingers in the phone cord. "Uh, you must have slept through that part of law school. I believe it's your job to prove her guilty. I don't have to do a thing unless you actually manage to make your case beyond a reasonable doubt."

"I've been known to stir myself to prove defendants guilty before." He had—and apart from Valerie herself, he was the best attorney they had. Shit.

"Well, I've been known to get a few acquitted." Ugh. Too friendly. Back to business. "I assume you're okay with a bond hearing on Monday morning at nine?"

"How'd you get this case, anyway? Why didn't Dan jump at this one?"

He hadn't answered me. No matter; it's not like I'd forget why I'd called. "Moot point now. She's my client, and she'd like a bond hearing on Monday at nine. So how about it?"

"Let me check the schedule."

"I call BS. You know the schedule. The court hears bond hearings at nine every Monday morning, for exactly this reason. Valerie's dramatic timing isn't new. What's going on?"

"Listen, you'll see when you read the file. This was an attempted murder. She put poison in a drink at an elementary school. Whole row of little paper cups, all in a line for kids to grab. Kids, Allie. Kids like Libby."

It did turn my stomach, but criminal defense was only possible if I focused on my own actions, not the defendant's *alleged* actions. "Nobody else got sick."

"I know, but I don't think that makes it better. Either the Grant lady planned it and targeted the Peerman lady, or she didn't give a shit and played Russian roulette with the lives of ten- and eleven-year-olds."

"You'll have to prove it was her and not someone else. The victim is in the business of taking people's kids away. I expect lots of people hate her. You need a motive for Kira Grant, and you don't have one."

"I'll find one. That's my job." He sounded so certain. And sad, maybe. Why? What did he know?

"Right. Well, my job is to represent her to the best of my ability, starting with giving her the chance to get out of jail as soon as possible. So are we going to do this the easy way or the hard way? Valerie got her piece of flesh. One weekend in jail will freak my client the hell out."

"Yes, we can do a bond hearing. I'm not rolling over, though, Allison, and neither is Valerie. This lady goes to prison."

"Are you kidding me? Is that a threat?"

"No," he said tiredly. "The school board is screaming. The parents want a head on a platter before school starts in August. Valerie is upset about this one. She met with the victim personally. Someone has to pay for this."

"Fine. Then find the real perpetrator and arrest that person. This is ridiculous. Why arrest Kira Grant and not one of the other women in the PTA? They were all working together on the refreshments."

"We have our reasons."

Shit.

"I assume your need for platters and decapitated heads means you won't consider any pleas?"

"I've been told no. No pleas except guilty as charged."

"You don't usually knuckle under to Valerie this easily, Emmett."

The long pause crackled. I'd let my anger get out of control. Most of it was directed at Valerie, who didn't know the meaning of compromise, but some at Emmett for not joking, not acknowledging as he usually did that Valerie could be too unyielding.

"Watch yourself, Allison," he said, an edge of antagonism in his voice that I hadn't heard since Professor Carrasco gave us an obscure single-question exam second year of law school. "I'll see you Monday at nine. Have a good weekend. Tell Libby I said hi."

"Monday." I hung up, frustrated with him, with Valerie, with Kira for being the snooty supermom bitch I normally didn't tolerate but whose tune I'd have to dance to for money for the next few months. Back in law school, they told us we'd be helping people. They didn't mention that we would, more often than not, dislike the people we were helping.

I was frustrated with myself, too. Only rookie lawyers let it get personal. Only a newbie would think that Emmett Amaro failing to joke with me about a case meant anything at all.

With a sigh, I moved Kira's file to the "go home" pile.

❧

"Libby."

Nothing. My little bookworm lay on her stomach on the floor, plowing through the chapter book that should have been too old for her. When she read, she went off somewhere else completely and I had to call her from another dimension.

"Libby. Lib. Liberina. Liberty Bell. Liblibliblib."

"Mommy, I can hear you," she said, through the tangled brown hair spilling like a waterfall around her face. When had I last combed it? "You're being silly."

I stretched. She'd been reading peacefully as I went through a pile of interrogatories. With a guilty start, I noted I hadn't spoken to her for an hour and now it was near her bedtime. Some fun Friday night I'd given her. She needed something that happened outside this room in her life.

"Do you want to play a sport, Libby?"

God love little kids. She rolled over and considered that, untroubled by my non sequitur. "Like softball?"

"Yeah, like softball. I hadn't asked you, but you know I'd sign you up if you want me to, right?"

"No, I don't want to play sports. I want to play the piano."

"The piano?" I looked around in dismay, taking in the sloppy piles of books, the cramped leather sofa, and the battered coffee table. No piano. Not much room in our tiny house to put one, either. "How'd you decide on that, buddy?"

Steve hated it when I called our daughter "buddy." "She's not a boy, Al," he would say, missing the irony completely. Steve no longer got to have opinions on what endearments I called my daughter—one of the silver linings of divorce for sure. He also didn't get to call me Al anymore.

Sometimes I still missed him, though. With a visceral pull of longing, not really for Steve—whose pants had a pathological inability to stay zipped around members of the opposite sex—but for someone. Someone adult, who'd get my jokes and take a little of the burden off and maybe want to see me naked every so often. Libby was a great companion for five years old, but although she was bright for her age, she preferred jokes about farts and still slept with a purple stuffed lion.

"I like piano. Mrs. Crawford plays for us at school. We sing. I want to make people sing, too."

Not a bad life philosophy. "We'll have to see about those lessons, buddy. I think making people sing is a terrific plan. I'll ask Mrs. Crawford on Monday who might be able to teach you." Maybe I could get her one of those portable synthetic keyboards until I saw she was serious about it. Mentally I added up the cost of a keyboard and weekly lessons and sighed. I made decent money, but small-town private practice would never make me rich.

I took Libby upstairs, got her ready for bed, and read her three stories. Then three more. An hour of story time didn't make up for the amount of time I devoted to work, but I tried to pay my debt on the installment plan.

She drifted off near the end of *Bread and Jam for Frances*, and I slipped downstairs to clean up. I took my time lining up all the coffee mug handles as I put them away. The house never felt emptier than it did after Libby went to bed.

I flicked through TV channels, unable to settle on anything. I'd been divorced for a year, separated for two. There was no reason I felt so at loose ends tonight. After two more hours, I gave up on my social media feed, Netflix, and the books I'd gathered around me like a fort. As I refilled the coffee maker for the morning, a wave of longing for human contact hit me out of nowhere, so strong my knees almost buckled. Any human contact at all would do. I reached for my phone. Surely someone would be up at eleven o'clock.

My parents in Florida went to bed at nine. My high school best friend in suburban DC had new twins. I knew better than to take the chance on waking a sleeping baby, or worse, a sleeping mother. My college best friend had moved to London, where it was four in the morning. My law school best friend was . . . my opposing counsel. I couldn't call Emmett on a Friday night at eleven. Definitely not now.

I tossed the phone aside. I could go to bed all defeated and lonely, or I could do something small to change things. Kira's case was the key. If I won it, I could start my own practice and decide what my life would look like. Nothing on Netflix would help with that.

I slid the *Commonwealth v. Grant* case file out from the stack and got to work.

CHAPTER FIVE

KIRA

When I was young, my best friend had a recreation room in the basement of her 1970s-era house. It had the original leprous paneling, shag carpet in a god-awful shade of mustard, and a brown plaid sofa that sagged in the middle. The room had horrified me.

I hadn't seen truly horrifying until I'd seen the "recreation room" of the county jail.

Where—in some nightmarish alternate reality—I was imprisoned.

I sat carefully on a concrete bench, trying not to touch anything. If I ever got out of here, I'd have bedbugs or lice or fleas or an STD. How many meth addicts had worn this disgusting orange onesie before me? And the shoes: slipper things of cheap rubber, but *used*. At a bare minimum, I'd be leaving here with athlete's foot or a contagious cluster of warts on the soles of my feet. I tried to remember how much Clorox I had on hand at home.

Thank God my choices had put me on a different path than these unfortunates. By the barred window, two girls demonstrated dance moves that had never been taught in ballet class. In a corner, an older woman with no teeth and no apparent concern for where they might have gone read an ancient paperback romance novel. Business as usual, I assumed, for the incarcerated.

The surreality of being one of the orange-suited—even for a weekend—sent a wave of nausea through me.

I glanced over at a nearby table where three inmates talked. One young girl, her hair in cornrows, who didn't look a day over seventeen, sprawled all over the tabletop, just as if there weren't *E. coli* or whatever infecting the surface. Another, tattooed up to her ghost-white chin, was laughing as unconcernedly as if she were at a garden party and didn't have nasty dyed-red hair that hadn't been washed in a couple of days. The third I thought might be an actual meth addict: the skin on her sickly-pale face was pitted with sores of some kind. I scooted my rear end farther off the bench. I would do a lot better if I didn't think too much about the hygiene of my fellow prisoners.

I'd made it through one night. It was Saturday. Miles had visited and told me I had a bond hearing set up for Monday, but that meant two more nights in this hellhole. No decent shampoo. No moisturizer. No foundation to cover that tiny age spot near my eyebrow.

So far no one had spoken to me, which was good. I'd seen *Orange Is the New Black*. I sneaked another glance at Tattoo Girl's neck, trying to imagine how she thought she'd ever get a job with that level of bad judgment on display. Then again, she was incarcerated. She had little need for a job.

She caught me looking and exchanged glances with Floppy Child and Meth Head. They shrugged, as if okaying my inclusion.

"Hey. You. Come on over here," Tattoo Girl said, crooking her finger at me.

This was it. Oh God. Did I have it in me to fight off advances with my bare hands? I'd be out of here on Monday. Not enough time for slumming it with the criminal element. I didn't see how I could refuse, though, without drawing unwanted attention to myself.

I joined them at the table, scooting my chair out as far as I dared.

"You're new. What are you in for?" Tattoo Girl asked.

"Someone got sick at a school event. They think I poisoned her, and on purpose."

"Oh, you're the one!" The women exchanged knowing looks. My fame had traveled far.

"Did you do it?" Floppy Child propped herself on her elbows, as if holding herself upright asked far too much of her spine.

Outrage flared. "Of course not."

"So you're innocent, then?" Tattoo Girl said, a shrewd look in her eye.

"Yes."

"Uh-huh." She rolled her eyes while Floppy cackled. Meth Head smiled but didn't comment. Maybe meth rotted vocal cords. I didn't know. I'd only watched a few episodes of *Breaking Bad*, though Miles loved it. "Let me guess. Bond hearing on Monday?"

"How did you know?"

"I've been here a couple times." Tattoo Girl looked pleased at her experience. Floppy Child grinned ingratiatingly. Meth Head stared into space.

"What are you in for, then?" I asked politely, while internally trying to control my *Titanic*-size sense of injustice.

"DUI, third," Tattoo Girl said. "Doing sixty days."

"Accessory," Floppy Child said. "I drove the car for my fiancé. He said he'd kick us out if I didn't. I'm waiting for trial."

I considered Meth Head. She said nothing. I glanced back at Tattoo Girl, clearly the leader of this chapter of People Who Make Criminally Bad Choices.

"Maya is in for drugs," she volunteered. "Also awaiting trial. Caught up in a big ring with her husband and brother-in-law."

Oh, this was not supposed to happen. I shouldn't be here, sitting at a germ-infested table in unspeakable garments talking with three women who'd be lucky to get jobs as janitors in a strip club. My father was the CEO of a moving company in Richmond. He'd made good money, enough for my mother to stay home and participate in the

Junior League. I'd had a car, jewelry, a computer, everything, as long as I kept my grades up. Daddy could be a bit unyielding when it came to academic success. I'd been on the homecoming court, a cheerleader, the prom committee chairman, the perfect recruit to the best sorority at William & Mary, the girl sought after by all the hottest guys. Miles had given me the ring before spring break my senior year of college—and every one of my sorority sisters had swooned. Miles had been quite a ladies' man back then—hair golden as a wheat field, cornflower-blue eyes surrounded by long, lush lashes. He could get any girl to do anything with one flash of his unbelievable white smile. He still could.

I gritted my teeth.

"You got a lawyer?" Tattoo Girl asked.

I supposed I should introduce myself and ask their names, but they hadn't volunteered them and I didn't care enough to remember them. We'd hardly be going out for a girls' night anytime soon. "Yes. Allison Barton of the MacDonald Group. Do you know her?"

"Oh yeah!" Floppy Girl said. "She represented my fiancé in his carjacking last year. Got him off, too. She ain't bad."

"She's good," Tattoo Girl said, eyeing me up and down, not missing my pale-pink manicure. "You'll make her look better. You're rich."

"Well, I hardly think . . ." Oh please. I abandoned the attempt without even trying. Compared to them, I was most definitely rich, and unlike my friends, they wouldn't appreciate efforts on my part to pretend we were all on an equal playing field. "Why? What does that matter?"

I knew why it mattered; I was curious as to why they thought it mattered.

Meth Head let out a snort. Floppy began a rusty giggle that didn't match her childish appearance. And Tattoo Girl laughed in that silent way involving a contorted face and tears at the corners of the eyes.

"You don't look dumb, lady." Tattoo put her hands flat on the table and leaned in. "Being rich means everything. You think it don't make a difference when you come in for that hearing with a lawyer and a nice husband in a tie and all kind of friends with important jobs and shit who'll say you're not a flight risk?" She laughed. "Bond hearing's just for show for people like you. Not me, though. You probably don't have a psycho bitch for a mother. At my bond hearing, Mama came in to say I'd run off if I got bail. She was pissed off because I drank her vodka. She ain't never gonna let me get bond."

I tried to imagine my mother, never without fresh lipstick and a murmured "Bless your heart," sabotaging me over a cheap bottle of alcohol. I failed.

"Yeah," Tattoo Girl continued. "*You* walk into that courtroom and the deputies know you're better and they'll hold out your chair and shit. The lawyers take one look and they know you're one of them. The judge, too. They'll be looking for ways to let you go. Me, they look for ways to keep me in. I bet you rub elbows with all them rich people at the country club or shit like that. They ain't gonna throw you in jail, not you, 'cause if they do, that means it could happen to them. They don't like to think about that shit."

"Well, I hope you're right. I didn't do anything wrong, and I've got two children at home," I said virtuously.

"Yeah, me, too," Floppy said, shocking me. When had there been time since her puberty for this child to have had two children?

"I'd like to get home to them as soon as possible," I said, adding a longing quiver to my voice while chuckling internally at the image of Miles reading Fiona a picture book and disentangling Finn from the Xbox. Not his normal milieu. One weekend away from me wouldn't kill anyone.

"You want some free tips?" Tattoo Girl asked.

"Free tips?" I said.

"Yeah. I'm in a good mood today. You say they think you gave something to some lady to make her sick? You confess to it?"

"Of course not. Because I didn't do it."

"Court ain't about the truth," Tattoo Girl said, reveling in her expertise, "unless they got DNA or confessions or shit. Reasonable doubt, lady. Your lawyer's got to prove reasonable doubt, and that's it. You gotta throw them some red meat. Distractions. Is there a chance some other asshole did it?"

"There are a few others who could have, yes."

"Are they bigger assholes than you?"

I sucked in a breath. Who did she think she was? She hadn't seen *asshole* yet.

Tattoo Girl laughed. "Oh, calm down. We're all assholes. It's a matter of degree. You got any racists you can toss into the mix? That's the best if you got that. Those judges and juries love it when they can blame everything on a racist. This is Virginia. Couple of generations ago, they were out there screaming for segregation and shit. Pointing a finger at a racist lets them off the hook. If you're busy yelling at a racist, you can't be one."

She was not wrong.

I regarded the three of them—teenage mother, drug addict, tattooed jail veteran—then the room as a whole. All the women in my line of sight were poor, members of a marginalized group, substance abusers, or more than one of those things. Women like me didn't stay here long. I'd been aware of this on some level, and Tattoo was right about the reflexive need for the southern educated elite to perform lives of atonement for the region's past. I'd heard enough virtuous hot air at dinner parties to lift a balloon to the moon. I knew for a fact plenty of that atonement was lip service only.

But courtrooms traded in lip service.

I could work with this.

A better woman might hesitate at using the wealth of advantages I had. I should check my privilege, do my own atoning, and bravely get at the back of the line. My mother would.

My father would tell me to do whatever I had to do to keep what was mine.

Fortunately, I'd always been a daddy's girl.

CHAPTER SIX

ALLISON

I made sure to show up at court thirty minutes early. One of Dan's lawyer pals once caught a judge in a bad mood and gave a weak excuse for not being on time, and he spent the next eight hours in the same cell as his client.

Law: the only career where you can be jailed for first-offense tardiness.

Monday mornings at the general district court meant crowds of people waiting for their landlord/tenant cases or medical bill collections, clerks rushing back and forth with files, and deputies ferrying prisoners to the holding cells. In Virginia, the lower courts—what most states call small claims courts or traffic courts—handled bond hearings and preliminary hearings for criminal matters like Kira's.

That meant waiting in the hallway while the overworked judge processed a slew of not-guilty pleas and requests for court-appointed counsel by a parade of impoverished defendants to the unsettling tune of their ankle shackles clanking. The bailiff said it might be a while.

Miles Grant had arrived early as well, crisply dressed in a good-quality suit and a Brooks Brothers tie. It had tiny ship's wheels on an orange field. I wondered if he'd realized it would match his wife's ensemble today.

"I brought tax returns for the last three years. In case the judge thinks I can't afford bond." He collated his papers on his knee nervously. Bless him. And damn, he was good-looking, if a bit pale. I hadn't seen them standing together, but he and Kira must make an eye-catching couple.

"You won't need those. You don't pay cash. If the judge orders bond, you'll visit a bondsman and make arrangements with him. Here are some names." I gave him the little handout card with my firm's name on it, and he tucked it away in his breast pocket.

"Sorry. I've never done this before."

"Of course not. I totally understand. There's no reason to be nervous. I'll ask you questions, and you'll explain that you're willing to post the bond and that she will live with you."

He muttered something, bleak and ugly.

"What did you say, Dr. Grant?"

"Miles. It was nothing. Sorry."

I should let it go, but I was both curious and a little worried. So far I'd seen no evidence of any issues with the way my client would present at trial. Miles seemed to care about her deeply, and all the background she'd given me had checked out. Kira was a stay-at-home mother and had been president of the Wolf Run Elementary School Parent Teacher Association for three years and an active participant for the three years before that. Her son was an excellent student, straight As all the way through fifth grade and perfect scores on two out of three state exams. Her little girl shone like a perfectly pressed angel in the pictures. Miles's dental practice had a good reputation. Their house, a lovely two-story white-wood clapboard with a gracious porch, an emerald lawn, and well-tended flower beds, could have been in a magazine.

It all looked perfect.

"I don't mean to intrude," I said, "but it's my job to know if we have issues before we go in there. Mutters do not usually bode well. Is there something you want to tell me?"

There was a long pause. On the other side of the hallway, a couple argued in angry whispers. I caught the gist: money. It was always about money, or more precisely, the lack of money.

Miles wiped a hand across his mouth. "Sorry. I . . . things have been tense between me and Kira lately. You said I had to tell the judge she'd live with me, and frankly, I'm not sure she wants to live with me."

Oh shit.

"Tense how? For how long? What's the issue? Money?" I asked, glancing at the woman's finger poking at the man's chest.

"It's been about four months now. She thinks I'm cheating on her. That's the main issue."

"Well, I'd say that's a big issue. Are you cheating on her?"

His eyes shuttered over. I'd crossed a line. He'd better get used to this. Lawyers asked questions that crossed lines all the time.

"Miles. If you are, I promise you it will come out anyway. Let's have it."

"I'm not. I swear. I don't know why she thinks I am." He swallowed. "I love Kira."

Okay. Based on his body language, I was 86 percent sure he was telling the truth, but some people were better liars than others. "You said the main issue. What are the other issues?"

"Oh, nothing much. Money, as you say. She spends a lot, and I fuss sometimes. The kids. She thinks I'm not doing enough to make sure Finn gets into a good college."

"Um, Finn is only eleven, right?"

"Right. That's what *I* said. Way too early to worry. But Kira says Finn is unusually gifted and we need to be focused on his future. Kira's dad left money for Finn to go to Yale, if he gets in. Her dad went there. Big alum. The county schools don't send a lot of kids to the Ivy League."

"Finn is an excellent student, I hear."

"He is, but she's always going on about getting him lessons in this and lessons in that and finding him something he can be 'amazing' at for the college applications. That he'll fill out in seven years. Not a big issue, not yet, anyway, before he's even in middle school, but yeah. We're a bit off right now."

"Thank you for telling me." None of that sounded too problematic, if in fact he wasn't actually cheating. I did enough divorce work to know. He'd described the top three things most couples fought over: fidelity, money, and child-rearing. If they had troubles, they weren't unusual troubles, at least.

I glanced at him. He had red-rimmed eyes and nicks where he'd shaved while distracted. I had no doubt whatsoever that cheating or not, Miles Grant loved his wife.

"Will she get a bond?" he asked, his lips tight and tense.

"I think so. We'll see, won't we?"

❧

Kira did not look good in orange, and she knew it. It clashed with the expensive red tones in her hair. She gave Miles a tremulous smile. He'd gone white at the sight of the shackles around her wrists and ankles. She clanked as she shuffled toward us.

"*Commonwealth versus Kira Grant*, bond hearing. Counsel, are we ready?" Judge Pearson heard hundreds of cases in a day and had no time for pleasantries.

Kira yanked on my jacket sleeve. I leaned in.

"Where is Summer? Is she not testifying?"

"The victim? No, of course not."

"Why not?"

"Ms. Barton, did you need a moment?" the judge asked with a degree of acid in her tone.

"No, Your Honor."

"Wonderful. Let's proceed. My docket is an hour behind already." At only ten in the morning, Judge Pearson already looked exhausted.

She pushed back a strand of light-brown hair that had fallen into her eyes. Emmett put down a foot-high pile of files and approached the bench.

"Ready, Your Honor," I said. "I'm representing Ms. Grant."

"Commonwealth is ready," Emmett said, meeting my eyes with a regretful expression that dropped my stomach. He had something I didn't know about, which was of course his job, but it bothered me. He straightened his tie, looking away.

"Your move, Ms. Barton."

I shook off the distracting thoughts. "We call Dr. Miles Grant."

Miles made his way up to the bench to be sworn in. He glanced at Judge Pearson. They were a similar age. Her lips twitched into a partial smile. They probably took debutante dancing lessons together in seventh grade.

In this court, we all stood before the judge in an informal group rather than sitting at counsel tables. Just in time, I refocused on my job: questioning witnesses to show the judge that Kira was a person who shouldn't be in jail.

Miles showed real expertise at making Kira look good: long marriage, wonderful wife, due credit for her devotion to home, children, her mother in a long-term care facility in Richmond, and a wealth of community activities, none of which could survive a single minute without her. He promised to turn over Kira's passport and make sure she appeared for all future court appearances.

During this testimonial, Kira alternated between Helpful Good Girl with her handcuffed hands clasped earnestly and Benevolent Monarch with a haughty nod when Miles got it right. I couldn't decide which was further from reality. Both scared me.

The judge turned to Emmett. He met my eyes, a brief and desolate look. What was going on here? I hated it when I didn't know everything that was going to happen. I also loved the thrill of handling the surprise. Being a courtroom lawyer required a certain amount of tightrope walking.

"Your wife is an avid gardener?" Emmett asked.

"Yes. I said that."

"Do you garden as well?"

"No. I'd kill any plant I touched. She's the green thumb."

"Thank you."

With a glance at me, Miles stepped back. Emmett let him go.

What in the actual hell was that? Summer Peerman had been poisoned by a substance called aconite, which, when I'd googled it, turned out to be a plant people used to keep away pests like deer. Did Emmett have evidence of Kira being connected to it? She gardened, but aconite hardly sounded like the kind of thing that would be found in a suburban yard. I narrowed my eyes.

He wouldn't look at me. Dammit.

He did have evidence of something. Dammit.

It wouldn't matter here, because this hearing had nothing to do with guilt or innocence, but I hated being at a disadvantage. Valerie had a flair for drama, and a secondary benefit of her Friday-afternoon-arrest/first-thing-Monday-bond-hearing scheme was preventing defense attorneys from having time to get up to speed.

I questioned Kira's pastor, who said a lot of marvelous things about Kira's devotion to the church and her lovely soprano in their choir, and her son's swim coach, who said he'd never have been able to get a team in the water without Kira's organization and loyalty. Neither had ever seen, or heard of, any violence on her part. Their testimony was notable for their praise for her actions but not her personality. I didn't think the judge noticed. Emmett let both go with no questions.

Traditionally in these cases, the commonwealth would at this point proffer the evidence they had against the defendant in a dry list of facts. Then they'd argue against bond if they believed there was a flight risk or a danger to the community. No way Emmett actually believed a PTA mom who gardened, organized swim teams, and sang in the church choir presented any danger to the community. Kira was a walking cliché.

Emmett consulted some notes. His hair, black as a crow's wing, thick and shiny and out of control, seemed a living thing. Once, in law school, I saw him coming back from a basketball game with other guys, and he'd taken off his shirt. His skin had a natural coppery tone even in winter. The display took my breath away. Did he still look like that?

Oh my God. What a thing to think about. He was about to tell the judge all the reasons why my client needed to stay in orange sackcloth for the foreseeable future. *Pay attention.*

"Your Honor, the commonwealth believes there is some risk of flight in this matter. The defendant and her husband are people of means. They do have a child enrolled in school, but that school is out for the summer at the moment. The defendant also has access to her father's sizable estate. The defendant herself is not employed and not in need of employment. Beyond flight risk, however, this defendant poses a danger to the community if released. Summer Peerman ingested aconite, a deadly toxin, in a paper cup of fruit smoothie. Aconite ingestion is rare and highly unlikely to be accidental. This incident took place in a school in a room full of eighty fifth graders. Multiple witnesses will testify that Kira Grant last touched the cup prior to handing it to Summer Peerman."

Well, that lined up with what Kira had told me. Tammy Cox, Ruthanne Dillard, and Brandi Crane must be the "multiple witnesses."

"Aconite is a flowering plant known better by its common names: wolfsbane or monkshood. That plant is found in the garden at the Sunnybrook Road residence of the defendant, Kira Grant. Merely touching the plant with bare skin can be toxic. The county investigator discovered a pair of gardening gloves in plain sight on the floor of a porch attached to the house owned by the Grants when he initially went to question Ms. Grant. He asked for consent to take the gloves, and Ms. Grant gave it. Testing showed aconite residue on those gloves."

Emmett fixed his gaze on the judge, and good thing for him, or else the fiery daggers from my eyes would have stabbed him right in his flat, toned gut. Kira grew aconite? In her own yard? And gave consent to the investigator to take her gardening gloves with aconite all over them? Was she stupid? Oh my God. That would just be spectacular—for Emmett. I turned to Kira. She bit her lip but gave nothing else away. My blood pressure rose, and my underarms grew damp.

"And finally, the victim will testify that after the poisoning, Ms. Grant asked her what substance had poisoned her and then claimed ignorance of the plant, despite having grown it in her garden and having handled it recently. As her husband testified, she's a master gardener and he touches no plants. Your Honor, we respectfully request no bond in this matter, and that the defendant remain in the county jail until trial."

At this, Kira hissed in my ear. "What? Did he say Summer is going to testify against me? That is insane. She knows I didn't poison her."

"Apparently there are a number of things we need to talk about," I hissed back at her. My stomach turned. At our first appointment, Kira had told me she'd never heard of aconite as well. Already, there were things I'd missed. "Now let me finish here."

Judge Pearson had heard it all. None of this was at all out of the ordinary for her. "Mr. Amaro, you have no confession, no DNA, and you're a hair away from not even having probable cause. But that's for another day. Bond is set at twenty-five thousand dollars. Any conditions, Mr. Amaro?"

Emmett recovered in less than a second. "Yes, Your Honor. Defendant must surrender her passport. Defendant is not to leave Virginia. Defendant is not to have any contact with the victim or any member of the victim's family. The school system requests she not be present on any school property anywhere within the county, other than to drop off and pick up her own children. She is not to exit her vehicle on school property." He met my eyes. For a second we shared a weird little moment of camaraderie: nobody won here. He wouldn't be able to keep her in jail. I wouldn't be able to keep her happy.

The moment passed.

"What?" squeaked Kira. I put a hand on her arm. I could practically feel the volcano about to blow.

"Any objection, Ms. Barton?" Judge Pearson asked.

"Yes!" Kira hissed.

"No, Your Honor," I said firmly, more to Kira than to the judge. "Thank you."

"All right. I've issued that order. Next!" Judge Pearson put the paperwork aside and gestured at the bailiff to bring in the next unfortunate.

I gave Emmett a look that could kill. He'd ruined my day. He had the courtesy to flush slightly, then turned to retrieve the file for his next case. In one morning in this court, he might try eight or ten cases.

"Your Honor, if I might have a word with my client in the holding room before she's escorted back to jail?"

"Yes, yes. Bailiff."

I turned to Miles. "Go on and see the clerk. Then go visit the bail bondsman. She should be out in a couple of hours." Still white-faced, he left. There'd be an interesting conversation in the Grant household tonight.

In the holding cell, Kira didn't wait more than one second after the heavy door banged shut. "What the hell! Summer turned against me? Against *me*? And now I can't even talk to her? Why didn't you object? Why?"

If only the pastor and the swim coach could see their Miss Proper now. She was spitting nails. "Because those conditions are standard for bond. No contact with the victim. An objection would have made the judge mad and done nothing for you at all."

"And not to go back to the school? Any schools? Are you crazy? I won't be able to meet Finn's new teachers at the middle school. And I practically *live* at the elementary school. I own that school! My daughter starts kindergarten there in August. You'd better get me allowed back there before then!" She sat, the anger having exhausted her. "I cannot believe this."

"My daughter starts kindergarten there in the fall as well."

Kira glared at me. She was not in the mood for motherly bonding.

"Again," I said, softly, "a standard condition of bond."

Fury rose off her in waves.

I didn't give a crap about her fury. I had a little of my own to blow off. "So. I have a couple of questions for you. Monkshood. Wolfsbane. Whatever. You grow it?"

"Yes, I guess so. I'd forgotten. I grow hundreds of things."

"You forgot you grow the murder weapon in your garden?"

"Have you been to my house? Do you know how many plants I have? Gardening is one of the few things I do for myself."

"And you told them to take your gloves? 'Oh, here, Mr. Law Enforcement, please take my gloves so a lab can demonstrate I've touched aconite'? Really?"

"I forgot I'd touched the monkshood with those gloves. I do grow it. I must have been gardening in that spot earlier in the week."

"Well, we might have to tinker a bit with *that* explanation. Good God. Why didn't you tell me about giving them the gloves when we first met?"

Kira's boiling point was always near the surface. "It's your job to handle those difficulties. Are you up to it or not?"

"Why did you tell Summer Peerman you had no idea what aconite was?"

"I don't remember doing that. I don't think I did do that. As I say, gardening is a big hobby for me."

"Well, something happened to cause Summer to switch from supporting you to being a witness for the commonwealth. Any ideas?"

"No."

She'd gone from rage to sulkiness in a matter of minutes. Somehow Kira had lived a life unaccustomed to taking responsibility for things.

"Well. You're out on bond. Follow the conditions or they'll send you straight back to jail. Your preliminary hearing will be in a month or so. It's a formality, but it's where we start seeing how your case is going to look. After that, we'll set a date for the trial. I'd hope to get it on the calendar before the holiday season, if things go right."

"The *holiday* season? As in Christmas? That long?" The "speedy trial" timeline never failed to be an unpleasant shock. *Law & Order* and their hour-long wrap-ups had forever changed defendants' expectations about how fast the system worked.

"Before Thanksgiving, if we're lucky," I said, as patiently as I could. "The wheels of justice, as I'm sure you're aware, turn slowly. I'll spend the summer and early fall interviewing witnesses and getting ready."

"This is all ridiculous."

I almost let her go at that point, but I couldn't bring myself to stay quiet. "I need to ask you again, Kira. No matter your answer, I still represent you and I will still do everything in my power to prevent the commonwealth from getting a guilty verdict. Did you poison Summer Peerman?"

"No. And that's the God's honest truth."

I stared at her for a long moment, and damned if I could spot any lie.

CHAPTER SEVEN

KIRA

Just about the only perk a weekend in jail offers is not having to cook for small children. I'd been home approximately five hours, and I was already girding my loins for the nightly battle over food.

Yes, yes, I know. Perfect mothers cook perfect meals, but I *despise* cooking for my children. Every night I had to marshal all the resources at my disposal not to give in to the temptation to throw frozen chicken nuggets at them and call it a day. Everything I put on their plates looked "funny," or felt "slimy," or was touching something and "ruining" everything. Back when Miles and I were first married, I used to make these incredible meals straight out of Martha Stewart. He'd ooh and aah and eat everything (never gaining a single ounce), and the applause made it worthwhile.

Now, a bit more of my soul died every time I carried the children's plates to the sink, still with more than half the food present and accounted for. Both kids would be digging in the pantry for Goldfish in a matter of minutes.

Few things irritated me more than not being appreciated, and I spent most of my hours doing amazing things no one appreciated. Always a morning person, I woke up every day with new resolve. Today would be the day my mere presence and intrinsic sparkle would make my kids give me those adorable grins and impromptu hugs I saw all the time in TV ads. Today would be the day Miles thanked me for doing the laundry, commented on how delicious breakfast smelled, and said, "I don't know how we'd live without you, hon." Today would be the day that selflessly doing things for other people would bring me abiding satisfaction and a Madonna glow instead of an intense desire to smash plates on the marble counters I kept hospital pristine.

Instead, one of the kids would spill juice at breakfast (cranberry, inevitably, on the marble). Miles would go out the door to work without feeding the dog he'd insisted we get "for the children" again. Finn would stand around staring out the window instead of getting dressed and would make us late. Fiona would scream and throw a fit over what I picked out for her to wear to preschool, forcing me to wrestle her to the ground to shove her plump little legs into her purple polka-dot leggings.

I kept smiling through it all. My smile had burrowed into my DNA until it came as naturally as swallowing. My daddy used to say the ugliest thing in the world was a pretty girl who didn't smile—a waste of God's gift.

I'd bet ten thousand dollars that not a single member of my family had a clue my thoughts weren't always full of rainbows and unicorns. To be totally honest, I doubted any of them even suspected I *had* thoughts. Servile robots generally don't.

"Finn!" I sang for the third time. "It's time for dinner!"

"What've we got, honey?" Miles loosened his tie as he poured drinks for the children.

"*We*," I said, emphasizing the word just enough to help me unclench my fist, "have got salmon."

Plain salmon. I'd have given anything to try the Thai-style peanut salmon, but I could scratch that off the bucket list forever. Miles had one of those peanut allergies that meant we couldn't have peanuts in the house. Neither of my kids had ever even tasted peanut butter. It wasn't rational, but I hated Miles a little bit for that allergy. He'd never mentioned that defect to me before we married. It was a sore point.

"Fish?" Finn said, entering the kitchen. "Eww. Can I have a sandwich?"

"No," Miles said. "Salmon is good for you."

"Mommy, I don't *like* broccoli." Fiona sat on her heels, resting her chin on the cold marble of the island, her nose inches from her colorful plate.

Miles raised his eyebrows at me. We met for the parent sidebar at the far end of the kitchen. "Don't you usually hide the vegetables for her? That's just plain old broccoli."

One death ray glance from me and he shut up. How dare he? To think I'd been fantasizing about receiving praise. Instead, here was Miles, complaining I hadn't done enough. Yes, I usually processed vegetables and hid them in Fiona's food so she'd eat them, but *usually* I hadn't spent the earlier part of the day in jail. Fiona's vitamin-whatever intake wasn't topping my priority list at the moment.

"Broccoli is delicious, and see, it looks like a tree," I said, ruffling both kids' heads as I moved behind them, placing food. They'd better damn well go on to make something spectacular of themselves. This kind of ingratitude was only worth it if I could spend my retirement years taking credit for their glory.

Out of habit, they said the blessing and dug in before I'd even taken my seat. God, the nerve of my family—they behaved as if I were a truck-stop waitress in a pink polyester dress.

"Mommy, why did you go to jail?" Fiona asked, her mouth full, unattractive crumbs of mashed potato falling onto her dress.

A silence fell.

Miles lowered his fork, pressing his lips together. He gave Finn a stink eye. "Hey, Finny. I thought we talked about that?"

Finn stared at his plate. "She was crying and she wanted Mom and I didn't know what to do. I'm sorry."

"Everyone knows, I assume?" I glared at Miles.

"A few people have asked me if you're all right," he said.

So, yes, everyone in the community knew.

"Wonderful," I said. I'd hoped no one would find out I'd actually gone to jail. It hadn't been in the paper yet, it happened over a weekend, and I'd thought Miles would have the sense not to tell anyone. That idiotic fantasy had evaporated into smoke. Fiona had no doubt told her preschool teacher, and she wouldn't stop there. She'd tell everyone she knew and every stranger she saw at Target or the grocery store or the gas station, exactly as she had the time she discovered she possessed a vagina and boys did not.

I set down my fork, shame and anger burning rivers of lava through my veins. "Would you all like a brochure? Shall we consider jail for our next family vacation? Would you like to hear all about it?"

I glared at them. They stared at their plates. "It was disgusting, that's what it was. It was dirty and humiliating and horrifying and easily the worst experience of my life. And I didn't deserve to be there. I don't belong in jail, now or ever." I glared at Miles and Finn. Fiona stuck her thumb in her mouth, her eyes growing huge.

I tried to calm down, but I couldn't. "Is that good enough, or do y'all want the T-shirt, too?"

"Kira. Stop. You're scaring the children. It's not like you," Miles said, getting up to come over to my chair.

"Did you tell Finn he can't see Aidan until all this is over?" I said, waving him off. *Do not touch me.*

"What?" yelled Finn, flipping his head up so fast his glasses slipped to the end of his nose. "Why can't I see Aidan? We were going to go to the pool tomorrow!"

"Not now you're not," I said. "The judge said if I wanted to get out of jail, we couldn't see the Peermans until they find out who put poison in Ms. Peerman's drink."

Fiona peered into her sippy cup. "Is there poison in my drink, Mommy?"

Miles smoothed her hair. "No, sweetie. Your drink is apple juice and there's no poison in it."

"Apple juice? You know she's not supposed to be drinking apple juice, Miles. For God's sake. Calories."

Miles let out an annoyed breath and picked up Fiona to hug her.

"Mom!" Finn said, still on the Aidan thing.

I was so sick of hearing about anyone with the last name Peerman. I hadn't expected it to hurt that Summer had turned against me. I hadn't known her friendship meant anything to me. "Right. No contact with the perfect Aidan Peerman. Judge's orders. If you don't like it, maybe you can write my lawyer a letter explaining how absolutely and totally ridiculous it is that you can't see your friend, who in turn is the son of *my* friend, when some random person decided to do something totally crazy."

Miles put Fiona down. "Finn, can you make sure Fiona has everything she needs? Mom has had a rough time lately. We're going to go for a walk outside. Okay? Finish eating, then take your plates to the sink. Later on, we'll play a video game, okay?"

Somehow, his perfect-father routine turned the rivers of lava into molten rock. Nice. The more he did this comforting-the-children shit, the more certain I got that he was cheating. He'd hired that dental hygienist six months ago, the one who'd won the pageant, the one with the double-D tits and the coin-slot cleavage, the one who could have been my twin when I was in college, and I knew.

Since Sandy joined the practice, Miles had been working late, until 7:00 p.m. sometimes. I knew damn well they always scheduled the last appointment at four thirty, and he didn't spend enough on Novocain to drill anybody that long. Nobody's teeth, anyway. He'd gone in on a Saturday at least four times that I knew of to "look at the books." Please. He must think I had the brain of an amoeba. How on earth could the records of a dental practice require that much review? And they had a bookkeeper/office manager who'd been there ten years or more. That was her job.

A month ago, I'd found an earring back on the floor of his Land Rover, passenger side. I hadn't lost any earring backs. Obviously, I started going through his paperwork after that. The cell phone bill showed a lot of calls to a local number I didn't recognize. When I called it, it went to the voice mail of a breathy-voiced someone named Linda.

Despite my rage at his constant underestimation of me, at the moment I'd follow him outside. It would keep me from yelling at the kids, and maybe I could get some things off my chest. I grabbed a pair of gardening gloves out of habit. I never missed a chance to pull a weed.

Outside, my flower beds were at their peak. Drifts of mop-headed hydrangeas in luxurious white, pink, and blue backed geraniums, hostas, and clematis. I had lilies and roses in every shade of pink and white. Miles had no idea how much work it took to weed and deadhead all that and keep it blooming day after day all summer.

A breeze blew his blond hair across his forehead. Damn, why did he have to be so good-looking? Usually at this time of day he still wore his tie and dress shirt, but today, he'd changed into a polo shirt and wrinkled khakis. A burst of hysterical laughter almost escaped when I imagined him standing in the closet wondering what to wear to pick up your flea-ridden wife from jail. Vineyard Vines, or an old Ralph Lauren?

He reached for a perfect white oakleaf hydrangea flower, then pulled his hand back at the last minute. His face was easy to read. I knew what he wanted to know.

"That's a hydrangea. Not monkshood. It won't kill you to touch it."

"Which is the monkshood?"

I pointed to the tall green spikes barely beginning to bloom at the back of the bed between the pink and white flowering shrubs. Monkshood blooms a long time, and it added height and accents of deep blue-purple to my garden.

"That? I thought it was called delphinium," Miles said. "I mean, I've seen it here for years."

"Delphinium is also tall, but a bit less purple." I pointed to some of the delphinium plantings.

"Why do you grow something so poisonous? Couldn't you stick with the delphinium?"

"Lots of plants are poisonous. Those poinsettias you love so much at Christmas are also poisonous. The monkshood adds some really pretty height and depth at the back of my garden." It did. My beds were carefully curated: no yellow, orange, or red. All my flowers, even the daffodils, were white, pink, purple, or blue. The color scheme went so well with the white clapboard and green tin roof of our house. Photographers had been out numerous times. Once a bride from down the block had nervously asked if she could do her pictures here. I let her.

"It is pretty. I've always thought so." He ruffled the flowers of a blue mophead. Did he know I had to adjust the pH of the soil for that prized blue color? Almost certainly not. I bent to pull a green shoot out of the mulch at the bottom of it. Miles was staring at me when I stood up. "You have on green gloves."

"So?"

"Don't you usually wear flower-print gardening gloves? Blue ones?"

"I have a dozen pairs of gloves, probably. They took my favorite flower-printed gloves when they found them on the porch. These are an old pair," I said, staring at them, their wornness making me mad all over again. "They take everything. Gloves. Peace of mind. My actual freedom."

"Kira, please try not to involve the kids in this. Fiona cried almost all weekend. She missed you desperately. Finn, too. Don't scare them about jail. Please."

"Why? Because you think I'll be convicted and a permanent resident there?" I couldn't help being sour to him, and I needed to at least pretend to like him. *Be sweet, Kira, even if you don't feel sweet,* Daddy would say. *Especially if you don't feel sweet.*

I hadn't felt sweet since about 1991.

"No, of course not. You're not going to jail. You heard the judge today. She said they barely had probable cause. I took that to mean they have a weak case." He fiddled with a leaf, crushing it into green liquid. "Just . . . explain to me why a plant you grow was in Summer's cup? Please?"

Here we go. Did he have to be that annoyingly predictable?

"I hope after sixteen years of marriage, Miles Grant, that you have a higher opinion of my intelligence than that. The fact that it grows in my yard as a prestige plant—and has for years—makes it seriously unlikely I would use it myself. I'd have to know it would be exhibit A against me. You know I'm not that much of a moron. I hope."

"You know I—"

"And besides. We've had dozens of meetings of the Garden Club here and at least five PTA meetings, including one earlier this spring. Every time, the ladies go crazy over my flowers and ask about them. I've probably told ten people over the years about monkshood and that it's poisonous. We don't lock the fence, and we don't use the privacy flood lights. Anyone could sneak in here and get it anytime."

"That's true." Miles ran his hand down my arm to catch my hand. I snatched it away.

The nerve of him. I hadn't let him touch me in three weeks. The first week I'd said I had my period. Even though I'd passed forty, they still came regular as clockwork. The second week I'd said I had a headache. The third week I'd stayed up late reading and managed to wait him out.

So predictable. He'd been forced to stay with the kids all weekend and away from Sandy. Or Linda. Or who-the-hell-ever. No one had taken care of his needs, also as regular as clockwork. Any old port in a storm when a sperm backlog is threatening to burst the dam.

My harbor was closed for the foreseeable future.

I liked sex as much as or more than the next woman, or at least I had once, but I didn't want to give Miles the satisfaction. Literally. "Let's quit with this malarkey. You don't get her at work and me at home."

His hand dropped back, and for a moment he looked like Finn: young and confused.

"I don't know how many times I can tell you I'm not sleeping with Sandy. Or with anyone."

"Please."

"Why do you think I am? I can't understand it, Kira. I am not sleeping with anyone. What has given you that idea?"

Letting him know what evidence I had would hardly benefit me; it would only give him time to find reasonable lying excuses for all of it. Look at me. I'd already learned a few things from that cocky dark-haired prosecutor: let the surprise bombs drop in court. Watch the other lawyer scramble.

Nope. I'd begun making my plans. I'd been to the bank. I'd checked out the title of my house. I'd photocopied all the cell phone records and kept a journal of all the hours he worked and what ridiculous excuses he gave. For the past two months, I'd logged how much time I spent with the kids, driving them, feeding them, reading to them, attending their lessons, while Miles stayed away, doing whatever he did. I'd bagged the earring back in a plastic sandwich bag and hidden it in my nightstand. I wanted the house, obviously. I'd photographed the gardens and made a list of all the tasks I did to maintain the inside.

No, he'd be going. I would keep what mattered: the kids and the house and half or more of his money. I'd planned to make an appointment with Annemarie Collier, the best divorce attorney in Lynchburg, but the damn poison thing messed it all up. Even someone as efficient as I was couldn't realistically expect to stay in the game on two legal fronts.

For now, Miles could stay.

On my terms.

I smiled up at him, the old smile, the sorority girl one. The one that involves wide eyes and eyelash dips and enough blinking to make him think there could be tears of emotion dampening my drought-stricken ducts.

"Okay, Miles. I'll try to get past it. It's hard to believe you're not cheating when . . ." I paused delicately, cast my eyelashes down again. "You know I have trust issues, because of my daddy."

His face pinched in concern. God, he was falling for it. Again.

Daddy cheated up a storm. When I caught him once when I was thirteen with the big-haired floozy who worked behind the hardware store counter, he told me Mama knew about it and didn't do enough to stop him. "Your mama, she don't know how to handle a man. She's happy in her way. I'm happy, Mrs. Sanford here is happy. You be happy, too, darlin'. You're smarter than your mama. You learn how to handle 'em, you'll be fine."

Early in our dating life, I told Miles about this heartwarming scene from my childhood. He thought I told it because of how much my daddy had hurt me. He thought I grieved for Mama. He'd comforted me and wiped away the tears I could still summon on demand. Since then, I'd brought it out whenever I needed a change of subject or some sympathy.

Miles had misunderstood me, and I'd never corrected him. I told the story of Daddy getting caught cheating not because I'd learned that day that Daddy didn't love Mama, but because I admired the hell out of how he took what he wanted from life.

He'd taught me well.

In midsniffle, thanks to that story about Daddy, I thought of something so much more crucial than Miles. I turned on the full waterworks and ran sobbing into the house, straight for my cell phone.

Tom Crawley answered on the first ring. It's good to know people.

"Hello?"

"Tom! This is Kira Grant." Tom went to our church. His wife, Emily, was a dowdy little thing who never opened her mouth except to say "Yes, dear" to her much more important husband. Her family dripped with money, though. Tom depended on it.

Tom was also the features editor of the local newspaper, which served the city and four counties around it. Every single person who might make snap decisions about my case lived in its delivery area. If everyone already knew I'd been arrested, why not get control of the narrative?

"Kira," Tom said, with a certain degree of caution. He would know about jail. He knew everything, damn him. "What can I do for you?"

"So wonderful to catch up, Tom. It's more what I can do for you. I'll cut to the chase. I'm sure the paper is going to run a story on my arrest, yes?"

Tom drew in a long breath. "Well, Kira, it's in the public interest, and I have to—"

"Oh yes, yes, I know. I wanted to offer my help. I can give you some quotes, if that would benefit your reporter."

"You want to . . . to be interviewed?"

"Anything for journalism. Oh, and Tom. Make sure you edit the story personally before it runs. I'd hate for it to imply I wasn't innocent. Which of course I am."

"You know I don't censor my reporters. That would be wrong. Unethical, even."

"We wouldn't want to be unethical, would we?" I could practically hear his discomfort rising over the cell connection. I went with a bubbly yet musing tone. "You know, I think I last saw you up in Charlottesville. I believe you were tucked away in a romantic little booth at the C&O. Let's see. With Emily, right? Oh, wait. No, not Emily. I thought it was, at first. Given how very . . . close you two seemed."

A silence stretched. Tom really was a dear man. He'd get there eventually.

"Okay, Kira. You win. I'll read over the story."

"See that you do. Bye, Tom."

CHAPTER EIGHT

ALLISON

My assistant, Maureen, hung out in my office most mornings. We shared gossip about our kids, about the schools, about the shows we watched on TV.

"Here. Here's a doughnut," she said. "I shouldn't have stopped—diet lasted all of three days this time—but Lord, I needed it. You like vanilla icing, right?"

I took it gratefully, putting it down beside my coffee. Small pleasures. I had a long morning before me of calculating the division of assets in a divorce where most of the division would be their debt. I went to law school because I hated math. Joke was on me.

"Thanks. You've made my day."

Maureen turned to go and almost bumped into my boss, my second visitor before nine thirty.

Dan MacDonald, skin perfectly spray tanned, shirt immaculate and smooth over his spectacularly broad chest, slapped the local paper down onto my desk, nearly upsetting my coffee and squishing a side of my doughnut. Dan hardly ever came into my office. I usually got summoned to his.

At forty, Dan had already been a legend for a decade because of the famous acquittal—in the face of rock-solid DNA evidence—he'd gotten for the man who murdered his pregnant wife and dumped her in a nearby lake. Afterward, so many prospective clients clamored for him to represent them that he'd hired me to take up the slack. Because of his looks and deep voice, he regularly made appearances on local television as a "legal expert." Last year, the Richmond paper had done a splashy feature on him, calling him the "Sexiest Lawyer Alive."

I didn't know about that, but I might have considered a vote for "Most Sexist Lawyer Alive."

As Maureen passed him on his way in, he patted her in an area of her back far too close to her backside. Behind him, she made a truly horrifying face and departed.

"Look at that front page, sweetheart."

The headline read, Poisoned PTA: President in Peril.

Damn.

"This article is practically PR for your client," he said, sitting and fussing with his Italian wool pant leg. "They love her. How is it this Grant lady didn't come see me?"

I let out an internal sigh but gave Dan my best Capable Lawyer face. "She made an appointment and retained me. She did say she'd called you but couldn't get in."

He frowned. "Seems unlikely. You should have let Patty know. Patty would have fit her in."

Oh my God. Dan had at least 150 active client matters at any given time. He owned three BMWs he swapped according to his mood, lived at the lake in a six-thousand-square-foot mansion, had divorced his high school sweetheart right after he made it big while hiding all the money from her, and probably slept under a bedspread made of cash. Nevertheless, he still wanted to handle every case in a thirty-county radius that had any monetary or publicity value, and he pouted like a six-year-old whenever he lost one to a competitor.

Up to this point, he'd never viewed me as a competitor. He kept me in my place in the firm by making sure he got all the personal injury cases with terrible injuries and all the criminal matters with newsworthy felonies. I got the bread and butter that paid for the overhead: the simple wills, the DUIs and bad checks, and all the ugly domestic stuff.

I scanned the article again. My name appeared in paragraph three as Kira's lawyer, which explained Dan's presence in my office. Usually, I only got to read the firm's subscription copy of the newspaper once he finished with it.

"Dan, I could hardly have known what she planned to talk about when she came in. She retained me before she left the office, and a good thing, too. She got arrested over a week ago. I have no idea why it's in the paper now."

"Don't look a gift horse in the mouth." He tapped the paper with a manicured index finger. "You sure you're ready for something like this? This kind of case's gonna be big. You see the alliteration? That's genius. Would look pretty enticing on CNN's website and what-all. There'll be press there."

"I assume so. I think I'll be fine. I've handled felonies before, many times."

He let out his patented sexy growl of a laugh. "Bad checks are felonies, hon, but they don't touch attempted murder by a PTA president. Not the same."

"I'll be fine." *Get your greedy hands off, Dan. My case. Mine.*

"Wellllll, now, be reasonable. You're a busy mom. You're probably pretty tied up with all the shopping and the cooking and the . . . what is it you ladies are obsessed with? Instagram, that's it. I can help out, free up some time for you. Handle some of the hearings. I'll talk to Valerie for you; I'm guessing she wouldn't bother with you. Get her to think about a plea bargain. I'm guessing she's a no on that?" He poked at the peeling faux-wood edge on my desk, pulling it back and making it worse.

Frustration boiled. He did this all the time. Pretended to be helping me out, making time for me to be with Libby, while simultaneously eviscerating my equality as a lawyer. Dan had three teenagers, but his long-time chief assistant, Patty, told me once that he had left all the child raising to his now ex-wife. He'd missed the oldest's high school graduation while attending an out-of-town benefit with a Ford model on his arm.

"Emmett is handling the case. He'll talk to Valerie if a plea looks like a good option down the line."

Dan guffawed. "Honey, you need more coffee if you think that," he said, slapping his muscled thigh. "Emmett Amaro doesn't know his ass from a hole in the ground. Pardon my French in front of a lady. I think we all know who the real lawyers are here. This isn't a practice case you can afford to screw up. Valerie's who we've got to get to."

Real lawyers clearly did not include me. I fought back my temper. I couldn't listen to Dan's snide undermining much longer. At some point I'd blow, and then I'd be lucky to get a job shelving casebooks at the university's law library.

"I will talk to Valerie when the time comes, if necessary. I appreciate your thoughts, Dan. I'm sure I'll need help at some point, and I'll come straight over to get your advice," I said, sugar sweetly, though the saccharine turned sour in my mouth. I hated to grovel, and I'd had hours of intense conversations in my car with myself in which I told Dan in no uncertain terms that he was a misogynist in violation of probably twenty federal employment laws—but I couldn't do it for real yet. Not until I had saved up enough to leave this practice and start up my own.

I wanted this case. Winning it could give me a name and a career. That's how Dan had done it. When he'd won his name-making case, he done it by capitalizing on all the mistakes of Valerie's predecessor, not by actually arguing the guy hadn't killed his wife. His work had been inspired lawyering. I'd taken the job because of it: to learn from him. Oh, I'd learned plenty—just not much about courtroom strategy.

If I won Kira's case, I'd have clients flocking in. I'd be able to rent space near the courthouse and hire Maureen and improve her salary.

Her son was leaving for college next fall, and she was a single mother, too. I'd be able to get Libby a piano if she still wanted one and pay off my law school loans.

"All right," Dan said, his hands in the air. "You call me when it's time for the preliminary. If I'm free, I can come over with you and smooth things with Valerie and the judge. It's all perception. According to this newspaper picture, your lady is hot. Rich and hot. Nobody wants to convict her. You've just got to give them some other option. In fact, see me in my office today after four. We'll consider the possibilities." He stood, giving me a smarmy grin.

"Thanks, Dan. I appreciate the help," I said, with an eye twitching. "I'll do that."

I wouldn't do that. I had court at three thirty, and he'd forget about it. The news coverage was limited to local so far. If it got bigger, he'd be undeniable.

"See you later," he said, brushing some invisible lint off his expensive tie. "Good job signing her up. I'd have hated to see Ed Janeway get this case."

"Right. Thanks."

He left.

Rubbing my temples, I pulled up the financial records I had to review. I hated rolling over and letting Dan think he'd won. I'd never expected to be the kind to do that, and I worried a lot about the example I'd provide for Libby when she got older. I didn't know how to tell her I put up with rank sexism at work and then put up with more so I could provide food for us both to eat. Should I teach her the world is like that, she shouldn't fight back, and she might need to be called "hon" at thirty-one to keep a job?

Like I always did, I swallowed the guilt and visualized every demeaning remark from Dan as another rung in the ladder I'd need to climb over the wall and see the other side.

❧

I successfully dodged Dan and left work at five forty-five, making it to Libby's day care with minutes to spare before incurring late fees. After a deeply unfulfilling meal of fried chicken sandwiches and waffle fries, I turned my beat-up Toyota toward home.

"Did you have a bad day, Mommy?" Libby asked from the back seat.

"No, buddy, just an average day. Why do you ask?"

"You sighed and your head is bent down."

She was right. I'd always assumed since she couldn't see my face from the back seat she'd remain none the wiser about my state of mind.

"You're right. I did."

"I think ice cream will fix it," she pronounced, as if she'd found the cure to polio.

We reached a stoplight. I turned around. Her freckled face lit with hope. Maybe ice cream *would* fix it.

"Okay, Lib, we'll try it. Let's go take the ice cream cure."

Our favorite place only required a U-turn and two more stoplights, and we lucked into a spot right in front. Libby exited the car with her head held high. She was being some sort of royalty. Libby frequently spent time inside her own imagination: I'd taken her out in public as a dinosaur, a ninja, and Dora the Explorer. The time I took her to the pediatrician as a rag doll had been most embarrassing. She swept ahead of me now as if entering a palace.

Inside, only three people waited in line—two teenage girls and Emmett, straight from work in a dress shirt and loosened tie. The tanned hollow of his throat showed through the unbuttoned collar. It seemed risqué, indecent, almost. I hadn't seen Emmett even slightly dressed down since law school. But back then, I thought Steve was the one, and Emmett had . . . what's-her-name. And then the other one. And the one after that.

Without even realizing it, I glanced down. A boring-as-hell brown pantsuit, suitable for a middle-aged insurance broker. With a plain cream blouse. And brown shoes. Damn. Maybe I should rethink choosing my wardrobe to irritate Dan. If I'd tried to look frumpier, I couldn't have succeeded.

Giving myself a mental kick in the ass, I reminded myself Emmett and I were friends only, and, more importantly at the moment, on opposite sides of a case whose profile grew higher every day.

The state ethics rules are strict: no related, married, or romantically involved lawyers on opposite sides of a case, unless the clients agreed, and no client in her right mind would agree to such a thing. Kira never would. Emmett's client was the same Commonwealth of Virginia that had made the rule in the first place.

And what in the hell was causing me to think about Emmett and love lives in any scenario involving me? His reputation preceded him. He dated and broke up with a series of beautiful girlfriends. His social life consisted of bars and benefits and hot new restaurants, and presumably, a regular parade of spectacular bodies through his bedroom door. Mine consisted of three readings of *Owl Moon* and then an illicit handful of potato chips with Netflix.

Libby pulled on my boring brown suit jacket and pointed at the flavors. "I will have chocolate," she said grandly.

I took off the jacket and folded it over my arm, deciding the blouse, although dull, might be a touch less armadillo and a bit more model-type.

Of course Emmett caught me fussing over my clothes. He gave his order (double salted caramel in a waffle cone) and turned. A slow smile started as he beheld Libby in all her paint-daubed pre-K glory. She'd insisted on a blue top with yellow leggings this morning, along with her sparkly pink flip-flops. I let her, because in the mornings I can't accommodate a fight about clothes if there's any hope of getting us both out the door in anything resembling on time.

"Well, you must be Miss Libby Barton," he said, executing a small bow that made me suck back a giggle. He'd noticed her royal bearing.

Libby accepted the bow as if it were her due and inclined her head. She waited, unsure which of her subjects addressed her.

"This is Emmett Amaro, Liberina. You've met him once before, I think. He's a lawyer like me. And a friend," I said, as much to remind myself as for her.

"Oh. Do you have any little kids?"

He considered her question seriously, as if wondering where he'd misplaced them. "No, Miss Barton, I'm afraid I don't. Would you mind if I hung out with you and your mom while you have your ice cream?"

"I guess that would be all right," Libby said. The teenager behind the counter gave Emmett his waffle cone. I ordered Libby's chocolate and my own mint chocolate chip and followed Emmett toward the cash register.

"You are extraordinarily tall," Emmett said to Libby, handing the cashier his credit card. "You must be in seventh grade," he said, brown eyes dancing.

"No! I'm only five!" scoffed Libby, superior intellect exuding from all her pores. She rolled her eyes and ran off to admire the decorated ice cream cakes in the case by the door.

"She's tall like Steve. She starts kindergarten in the fall."

"I don't think I've seen her since that time I ran into y'all at Target, what? A couple of years ago?" He waited while I paid for ours and caught my eye. "She's beautiful."

"Thank you." I didn't know where to look. It had been too long since Emmett and I had talked about anything other than work. In court he was crisp and professional and detached. This Emmett was relaxed, and his voice was warm.

He cleared his throat. "It's always fun to see our names in the paper."

"Yes. Already fielded a call from the Richmond paper, too. They wanted to know if Kira would do an exclusive interview. A chance to tell 'her side of the story.'" The Richmond reporter had talked about her like she was the antihero star of an HBO drama. *She's not your typical criminal defendant,* he'd said. I shuddered.

"Did you agree?"

"No. It's generally a bad idea to let a reporter have free access to a client."

"Dan would have let her," Emmett said through a mouthful of ice cream.

"Oh, I'm sure he would have. He *loved* the local story, that's for sure."

"Oh da—darn," he said, correcting himself in time for Libby, who'd raced up to get her ice cream from me. "I bet he hated that it wasn't about him."

"Yup, you got it in one. He wants to take the case over," I said, performing a twisting maneuver to get the ice cream safely into Libby's hands when she darted under my elbow.

"I hope you told him to go to . . . heck."

"Not in so many words, but I did hold on to it for now."

"Good." He pulled out two chairs at a black iron table and then a third for himself.

I stared at him. "Why? Am I easier to beat?"

His mouth fell open. "No. No, that's not what I meant at all. You aren't easy to beat, and you know it. I meant I don't like having cases with Dan."

"Why?" I sat. Libby, her ice cream already forgotten on an unoccupied table, sagged from the edge of the countertop by her fingertips, watching the technique of the boy scooping ice cream. She never sat if she could help it. A better mother would probably force the issue.

"I don't really want to say bad things about your boss. It feels weird."

I snorted. "Go ahead. I doubt you could top what I've said in my head."

"Okay, then. Dan . . . crosses lines. He can sometimes, um, ignore ethical rules."

"Really?" Nothing I hadn't suspected, but nobody had ever confirmed it to me.

"Once, I had a malicious wounding case with Dan. I spoke to the victim—photos showed a broken nose and a split lip—before the trial. Then Dan caught her in the hallway and took her off into a corner. When the trial started, she said everything the opposite of what she'd told me. Basically denied there'd ever been a crime, denied she'd called the police, denied her husband had touched her. She claimed she'd walked into a door when less than thirty minutes before, she told me her husband had punched her hard enough to drop her, then kicked her in the ribs."

"Oh God. That sounds like Dan. Probably reminded the victim her husband would lose his job, his guns, and his income if he got convicted. I bet she depended on him." Defense attorneys could talk to the victims, if they were willing. They were not, however, supposed to bribe or scare the commonwealth's witnesses into changing their stories.

"How long are you going to stay in that firm with him?" Emmett asked, concern all over his face.

"W-what?"

"You heard me. You're better than that. Valerie said it, too, the other day. Gave you a compliment. She said Dan's a low-down dog."

"I . . . I can't leave, not right now. Not enough money. I mean, I could. I could get another job, but I can't leave Maureen behind. If I left, Dan would fire her, and she lives paycheck to paycheck as it is."

"Oh. Well." He glanced at my forgotten ice cream, now melting. "I should have gotten your ice cream, at least."

"No. You can't. You know that. We probably shouldn't even be sitting here eating it together. Not now that the case is getting coverage. What if someone saw us?"

He let out a long sigh. "We've known each other for years. You got rid of that girl for me, you know, the tall one with the crazy fingernails, back in law school? Surely we can sit and eat ice cream together. We're not talking about the case." He smiled, a bit ruefully. "Much."

"I think we absolutely should be able to eat ice cream like normal people, but now we're 'locally famous,'" I said, making air quotes. "Do you know I've never been quoted in the paper as a lawyer? Not that I know of, anyway."

"I have." Emmett made a face. "A year after law school. I'd tried my first felony. Guy was acquitted and the unbiased news report referred to my courtroom style as 'lackadaisical.'" He sighed. "You're right, though. Valerie would be pissed if she saw us here. Your client, no offense, doesn't look like the sort who'd tolerate it well, either."

"No. She wouldn't." God, he looked good when he brushed his hair off his forehead. My dislike for Kira grew.

"I'd better go, then." Emmett stood. Libby danced over from the counter with a questioning yet regal look on her face. "Well, Miss Barton, I'll have to leave you. Take care of your mother, okay?"

"You may kiss my hand." Libby stuck it out, nose in the air like a duchess.

Emmett obliged, tucking his smile in.

"Now you may kiss the queen's mother's hand."

Our eyes met—mine panicked and glancing around for reporters or Kira, his mischievous and unconcerned. The store was empty except for the two employees. He picked up my hand, sticky plastic spoon and all, and kissed the back of it.

His lips lingered. I could swear it. I knew it, because things blazed that had been cold embers a long time.

"See you later, Allie. After this is over, I'll buy you dinner."

What? Blood rushed to my face and roared in my ears. Still, thank God, my powers of speech didn't desert me. "I believe the speedy trial part is up to your side."

He grinned and, without another word, bowed to Libby and left.

CHAPTER NINE

KIRA

Sitting in traffic didn't do anything pretty to my mood. I'd ditched the children with Miles for the morning and sped joyfully off alone to run errands and attend the Garden Club, but of course I'd pushed it and was a touch late. I glanced idly at the driver of the Honda sedan next to me. Midforties, well groomed, quality sunglasses. I stared at him until he glanced over. Appreciation warmed his face. To reward him, I gave him a Mona Lisa smile and tossed my hair a bit.

I still had it, even if "it" meant the ability to attract an ever-aging and progressively less attractive pool of masculinity. I threw him a flirtatious look as the light turned green. God, I missed the days when I drove around without sippy cups and Goldfish squished into my leather seats. Back then I had a small, sporty car and not this behemoth of a school bus, which, although luxurious, reminded me that MILF was now the best I could do.

Mother. Right. I could multitask. I pushed the button on my steering wheel to activate the Bluetooth phone. "Call Guillaume St. Laurent, on cell."

The dashboard rang as I waited for Lynchburg's premier violin teacher to pick up.

"Hello?"

"Hi, Mr. St. Laurent. This is Kira Grant. Finn Grant's mother. I wanted to confirm the first lesson will be this Thursday at four."

An odd silence stretched.

"Mr. St. Laurent? Are you there?"

"Yes. Yes, I am. And it's St. Laur*ent*," he said, correcting my French accent like some guillotine-bound Parisian nobleman. The unjustified arrogance of him. I knew for a fact he'd grown up in a split-level in Fort Lauderdale.

"Of course. So, four o'clock, right?"

"Ehm. Ms. Grant. I'm so terribly sorry, but I'm afraid I will not be able to teach young Finn after all. My only available slot was Thursdays at four, and I received word only yesterday that one of my most promising students has returned to town unexpectedly. She can be taught only by me."

Au contraire. Whatever this bullshit was, I'd hardly let it pass. "Oh, my dear *monsieur*. This is *très* upsetting," I said, going for a French accent so southernized it was guaranteed to cause Gallic ears to bleed. I made sure to drag out every vowel into three syllables and pronounce every ending consonant. My high school French teacher would die. If she weren't already dead, the old harpy. "*S'il vous plaît,* you said my poor *petit* Finn did the best audition you'd ever heard. *Magnifique, non?*"

Another silence. "I'm sorry, Ms. Grant. I cannot teach him. The slot is no longer available. Your son is *très* talented and I wish him luck in his pursuits."

"It is most distressing to hear you are so unreliable, *monsieur*. Annette Hanks and Jolie Garrett promised me I'd be so pleased," I said, naming two women at the top of the social food chain whose little geniuses sawed away on their instruments once a week for St. Laurent with, no doubt, the mellifluousness of feral cats having an orgy.

"So sorry. I must go. And good luck," he said, hanging up before the last consonant made it out of his mouth.

Guillaume St. Laurent, though hardly Itzhak Perlman, was violin master to all the wealthiest Ivy League–bound kids in the area. Parents tolerated his beret-wearing French affectation for the recommendation on their children's college applications. Damn. Had we not measured up in some way? Possibly because Finn went to public school? Damn. Damn. Damn.

Or else he'd seen my picture in the paper. And not read the article.

I filed away the problem in the back of my busy brain. Maybe Finn could switch from the Suzuki method to bluegrass fiddling. That would stand out on a college application, though perhaps in a worryingly redneck way. Still, well-trained classical violinists had to be a dime a dozen on Yale applications. Ooh. Irish jigs. He could learn to play Irish fiddle. That would set him apart. I'd find him the best teacher of Irish jigs even if I had to wear green, drive him to Roanoke, and buy a case of Jameson as a bribe.

I'd only be about five minutes late to Jeannette Benoit's house for the monthly Garden Club meeting. This was the June meeting, and Jeannette had won the right to host it. The months of March, April, May, and June tended to be hotly contested because they gave us a chance to show off our plantings at their peaks. I spared my monthly moment of pity for Willa Brown, who totally lacked a green thumb and volunteered to host the January meeting every year. We'd stand in the cold, pretend to admire her evergreens, and try to think of something nice to say about dormant shrubs that were common as mud and not even well groomed.

I'd hosted March, my favorite time to show off my carpet of white daffodils and purple crocuses, as well as the flowering dogwoods and redbuds. I always managed to get one of the four peak months because all the ladies knew I had a glorious garden.

Once inside Jeannette's faux-antebellum mansion, I accepted a glass of alcohol-free mimosa from the world's most judgmental gossip, Trudy Ball, and took stock of my surroundings. As usual, every lady present had at least twenty years on me. Everyone wore pastel and matched-set capri pants with appliqué tops. They gestured with languid, beringed hands as they talked and hugged and mingled. A young man sat alone in a corner staring at his glass of orange juice with a bored expression, wearing the khakis of a well-raised southern boy with a gauche short-sleeved button-down. He must be the orchid expert we were to hear from as the "educational" portion of the meeting. He was as out of place as a horseshoe salesman in a car dealership.

I hated orchids—such fussy, high-maintenance flowers. Unnatural, like hairless cats.

I hated Jeannette Benoit more.

"Jeannette!" I squealed in my practiced sorority-girl manner. Jeannette turned away from Nancy Bolling Lewis, who insisted on the use of her full name so no one could forget she descended from Pocahontas. Nancy ranked a close second to Jeannette and the orchids on my internal sliding scale. She blinked at me through crooked glasses with a bedazzled chain.

Usually Jeannette and I, the president and vice president, respectively, of the club, pretended to be the best of friends. Jeannette was my mother's age and liked to provide snippets of life advice for me. I'd accepted and then ignored many a nugget of wisdom, up to and including scenting my sheets with vanilla so Miles would associate me with the comfort of baked goods.

"Kira. So good to see you," Jeannette said, in the exact tone she'd use to greet a Jehovah's Witness at her door.

"We didn't think you were going to make it," Nancy said, squinting.

"Well, you know how it is. The traffic, and Fiona was finishing up the most amazing drawing of a castle. The artistic talent! I couldn't leave until she showed it to me." I put on my best Weary Mom attitude. In actuality, I had no idea what Fiona had done this morning. I'd left them with Miles before they woke.

"Yes, dear. The traffic on Timberlake Road is terrible." Both women stared at me, not helping further. Odd. Usually Jeannette would say something vaguely competitive about Fiona through a boring-as-shit story about her perfect daughter, Lisa. No doubt Lisa, who was in her thirties and "high-up" at Walmart corporate, had won an art scholarship to college she'd never needed. Nancy could be counted on to segue somehow into her "people" and their genealogy and her husband's "people." If she felt especially naughty, she would make a cutting remark about the inferiority of her deceased mother-in-law's genes.

Never before had they stood there and stared at me like I'd sprouted a second, less attractive head.

Being the youngest woman in the Garden Club had, up to this minute, granted me the status of beloved mascot. The ladies were so happy to have a member of the younger generation present they'd forgive me anything. They laughed at all my jokes, complimented my clothes, baked me cookies, gave me long-secret family recipes, and admired the "hunkiness" of my husband. Their years made me feel young and beautiful and made it easier to minimize the slight wrinkle between my eyebrows and the barely perceptible looseness of the skin on my neck. Even now, I flattened my hand over my belly, reassured that it didn't ripple like a pile of mismatched bike tires.

As a rule, I had difficulty liking other women. Women concerned themselves with trivialities, they wholeheartedly believed their husbands were smarter than they were, they let their children—grown or otherwise—walk all over them, and too many of them had never lost the habit of saying everything like it was a question.

But I needed them. They served me, even if they didn't know it. I needed them as a foil. Desperate suddenly, I grasped for straws. "Jeannette. I love those sandals. The silver looks so wonderful with your watermelon motif."

Jeannette looked down over her festive appliqué at her swollen feet, as if noticing them for the first time. She sniffed and exchanged a meaningful look with Nancy, who nodded.

"Kira, we need to talk to you about something. Something serious for the club."

Given that Jeannette's idea about what was serious for the club usually meant deciding between the county extension agent and the gardening columnist for the local paper as a speaker, this didn't worry me much.

"Sure," I said, leaning in helpfully. "What's going on?"

Olivia Mullins entered our tight circle and touched me on the arm. "Oh! I'm so sorry to interrupt, Jeannette, Nan, do you mind if I borrow Kira for a second?"

Nancy opened her mouth but said nothing. Jeannette, looking defeated, said, "Of course not. Go ahead."

Olivia was the closest thing to a real friend I had in the Garden Club. She was some kind of cousin of Miles's mother. She'd been at my baby showers and my wedding. She even sent me a sympathy card when I had a miscarriage before Finn was born. She pulled me into a corner.

"Hon, I'm so sorry to tell you this, but the beach house needs a new roof."

"Your beach house?" In January, Olivia and her husband, John, had offered our family the use of their Virginia Beach house for a week next month. I'd been longing for the trip—a chance to forget all this criminal stuff for a week. And it was even in the same state: the bond restrictions didn't allow me to leave Virginia.

"Unfortunately. A big storm peeled back the metal. There's water damage and a continuing leak problem."

Something in my stomach went sour. I didn't remember hearing about a big storm at Virginia Beach.

"I'm guessing you're saying we'll have to cancel the vacation?"

"Oh, hon, I hate it, but yes. The roofers will be working all the way through July. There's a tarp over it now. And I know the children go back to school in August. It's such a shame. Maybe next year."

I scanned her face. Her age-spotted apple cheeks betrayed no hint of treachery. Her eyes held nothing but regret and the usual concern for me she'd shown since the day I met her at my engagement party.

She was talented at lying, the bitch. I'd give her that.

I'd never believed in coincidences. A year's worth of expensive violin lessons and a week at a friend's beach house had both disappeared in the last hour.

So much for innocent until proven guilty.

Unwilling to let Olivia know I saw through her lie, I gave her a brilliant smile, showing off all the best dentistry a marriage license can acquire. "Oh, hon," I echoed, slight chill on the unaccustomed word, "it's no problem. I'm not sure we were going to be able to go anyway—Finn's decided to switch to Irish fiddle, and we'll be so busy working on settling him in with a new teacher. He told me this morning. It's so good this came up. I hope the repairs aren't too expensive."

I hope the repairs exist. And that they cost you a fucking arm and a leg.

"Oh no. Not too bad. I should return you to Jeannette. I expect she had something important to discuss. I should go see if Arlene is about ready to introduce the lecturer." She nodded toward the young man, who clearly waited for some direction. "He's adorable, and so knowledgeable about orchids. I think he might be a Democrat, though. Such a pity."

"Right," I said, unable to find that concerning at this moment. Or ever. "Yes. It's probably about time to start. Let me go find Jeannette. *So* sorry about the roof, Olivia." I gave her a master-class sympathy face, patted her on the shoulder, and threaded my way through the crowd.

Jeannette's topic might not be as frivolous as usual—I recognized that expression: her funeral propriety face. My funeral, presumably. Nancy, on the other hand, held her knotted hands up high, looking like a particularly avid chipmunk. My mind whirred with ways to combat them. Not like I planned to bow my head and acquiesce to the shaming.

"What is it, ladies? Olivia said things are about to start."

"Kira, we need to talk about your position as vice president. After we hear about the delightful things Andrew has done with orchids, we'll be discussing a new project the club has been asked to take on."

"What project?" I had heard nothing, which in itself irritated me. I preferred to know everything first.

"And of course Jeannette said we'd be delighted to do it," offered Nancy, clearly drooling to volunteer as vice president.

"Do what?" I asked, as politely as possible. Miles hated it when I ground my teeth and spoiled all his work. Not that I cared what Miles thought. I gave them a good grind.

Jeannette drew a breath, puffing up her chest as if about to announce that we'd been selected to take over the White House Rose Garden. "We've been asked to redesign the garden around the sign at Wolf Run Elementary."

I stared at her. Wolf Run was, of course, the school where Finn had just finished fifth grade. The school where Fiona would start kindergarten in August. The school where I'd been PTA president for years.

The school where Summer Peerman had drunk a poisoned smoothie.

It was the prerogative of the PTA president to maintain, or arrange for the maintenance of, the plantings at the sign in front of the school. Currently, they were scrubby Knock Out roses and a murdered crepe myrtle. I'd meant to get to that, but I'd never been able to shake off Ruthanne Dillard's desire to plant liriope as a ground cover. I hated liriope. It was invasive and ugly and had to be divided constantly. We might as well plant kudzu around the sign.

"Wolf Run? Who asked you to do the sign garden?" Dammit. My teeth wouldn't unclench.

"Ruthanne Dillard. She said she's the acting president of the PTA. I assume you know her. Lovely girl. She had an absolutely adorable child. They had the cutest little matching dresses."

I swallowed a lump of bile. "Yes. Ruthanne." Queen of liriope and wearer of pink princess dresses. "Of course."

"Anyway," continued Jeannette. "It would be an honor for us to redesign the plantings. It's been a scraggly old mess for years. You'd think the school would have done something about that years ago."

I said nothing, just stared her down.

She held up her hand for an overcasual examination of her hot-pink fingernails. "Of course the officers of the club are expected to be present at every off-site project. It's a tradition."

I waited for her to show me my coffin. I had a pretty good idea what it would look like.

"And of course, Kira, we understand you're not currently allowed on school property."

That absolute cretinous bitch of a watercress-eating sea cow.

I wanted to stomp on Jeannette's dowdy silver lamé sandals. I wanted to punch Nancy in her overlong First Family of Virginia teeth. I wanted to get on Facebook and post some vaguely threatening non-specifics about Ruthanne and then refuse to tell anyone what Ruthanne had done. But I smiled as if nothing in the world bothered me. "I don't think it will be a problem for me to miss out on that one project. Elaine Prescott missed out the day we did the courthouse gardens."

They exchanged looks. "That . . . that was an oversight. We shouldn't have allowed Elaine to stay on as secretary after, but now . . . of course, she's passed on. But Kira, it simply won't work. Nancy is willing to take over your duties for the time being, until all this . . . unpleasantness is straightened out. I think it would be best." Jeannette glanced at Nancy. "Don't you?"

Nancy nodded. Drool for the glory of the Garden Club vice presidency practically dripped off her hairy chin.

I was badly in need of a miracle, and I got one. My cell phone began to ring. "Ladies, if you'll excuse me. I'll take this outside."

It was only Miles, no doubt wondering where we keep the Cheerios, so I let it go to voice mail as I made my way from the rumpus room, as Jeannette called it, through the more formal front of the house toward the door.

Damned southerners. I knew. I was one. Southerners were never blunt. They hated a mess. They'd stick a knife in you like anyone else, but they'd coat it in butter and make it smell like honeysuckle first. I'd been tarred and feathered and they'd been so sweet about it that I never felt it until I'd been dripping goose down for a country mile.

On impulse, I leaned down and yanked a pair of knitting needles out of the craft bag Jeannette kept beside her "parlor" sofa and stashed them in my bag. The proper ladies of the Seven Hills Garden Club weren't the only people who could stick knives in things.

On the way out the door, I beckoned Trudy Ball over. In a tone of great surprise, I confided to the World's Loudest Mouth that Nancy Bolling Lewis told me she'd been thinking about it and had decided that wealth redistribution actually made a lot of sense. Trudy gasped with delicious shock. I gave her a conspiratorial expression of horror, watched her grab another lady and talk animatedly into her ear, and then, having tossed my apple of discord, made my escape.

Out in the driveway, I called Miles back, rolling my eyes in anticipation as he said hello.

"You should be on your way to swim team practice with the kids. Didn't I say what time you needed to leave?" I said, giving my teeth another good grind as I contemplated his total uselessness.

"Kira. That's why I called. I tried you at Jeannette's, but they said you weren't there. Betsy Liu called from the swim team. She said—"

His tone was dire. I knew immediately. "Let me guess. They don't want me to be team mom anymore?"

The pause told me it was worse. "Well, she did announce herself as the team mom, but that's not what—"

"Betsy Liu is an ungrateful little ferret. If they think I'm willing to step aside, after all I've done for that team, all the swimsuits we've bought and the volunteers I've organized and—"

"That's not all, Kira. Betsy said given everything going on, the team voted and decided it would be best if Finn and Fiona took a break from swim team this summer. They have enough to deal with, she said."

I'd always wondered what it felt like to have your heart stop beating. Now I knew: an instant of liquid nitrogen ice, followed by an almost unbearable rush of white-hot blood as it restarted, different than before. "I'm on my way."

I pulled out my car keys and hit the button to unlock my car at the street, narrowing in on my target: Jeannette's big dove-gray Lexus. I walked over to its side, dropped my keys, jabbed a back tire decisively with one of her own knitting needles, put it back in my bag, and then got in my car.

They'd taken everything. Everything I'd worked for, everything I'd tried to give my children. They'd taken my life and my standing and everything that mattered at all.

I turned up the cheesy pop station that played the songs I'd never admit to liking and drove home.

Enough good girl.

INVESTIGATION

CHAPTER TEN

ALLISON

Reviewing the commonwealth's case file always rubbed me the wrong way. Even though they were required to let me look in order to provide a proper defense for my client, Valerie made it seem like a favor. She didn't allow me to photocopy any of the papers in it or even take a picture with my phone. Which meant I had to devote time to copying the relevant parts by hand onto a yellow legal pad as if I were about to litigate against Atticus Finch in a sweaty pre-AC courtroom.

"Hi, Hailey," I said to the receptionist, wearing my most winning smile, to the extent I had a winning smile. Or a smile. "Emmett said I could look at the Grant file this morning."

"Oh, right. He left it here for you. He should be back from court in twenty minutes or so if you need to ask him anything."

"Thanks." I took the file over to the tiny table they kept for this purpose in the waiting area. Valerie had no doubt instructed Hailey to watch me to make sure I didn't steal a single precious sheet. It was always gratifying to have passed the bar complete with the required background check and ethics exam only to be treated like a potential teenage shoplifter by the county's chief prosecutor.

I opened the folder and flipped through useless pages noting the time and place of the bond hearing. Nothing about a direct indictment of Kira to send her straight to trial. That meant I would need to talk to Emmett to discuss scheduling the preliminary hearing. They definitely had no plans to drop her case.

The prize in these files was the report from the sheriff's office, detailing how they got the case, what they did to investigate it, and what the witnesses said when they spoke to them. At first only EMS had responded to the school when Summer Peerman collapsed, because the symptoms—an irregular heartbeat and chest pain, combined with a numb face—had seemed like a heart attack. Only after a call from the ambulance indicated the extent of the patient's numbness and nausea might mean more than a heart attack did a deputy show up. He recovered the cup Summer had dropped and got the names of witnesses, who all said Summer had drunk the smoothie, then within seconds had clutched her heart. She hit the floor and Ruthanne Dillard had taken charge of Summer's son, Aidan. Brandi and Tammy helped the school principal and some teachers clear the room of celebrating fifth graders and their parents. The initial deputy had noted that the victim was a Black female, and Kira, Ruthanne, Brandi, and Tammy were white.

Kira had called 911, which would help a bit. Surely if she'd done it, she would have delayed.

The sheriff's office appeared to have taken a renewed interest in the case the day after the party, after being notified that the hospital lab tests of the contents of Summer's pumped stomach and the cup had detected the presence of poisonous alkaloids, which they further narrowed to aconite. That made the investigation a criminal one.

I flipped the page and cringed when I saw that the investigator from the sheriff's office who'd visited Summer, Brandi, Tammy, Ruthanne, and Kira was none other than Joey Lucado.

Dammit.

Lucado believed with undying passion in the rightness of law enforcement, the law he enforced, and his own sometimes errant judgment. In his late forties, a red-faced CrossFit fan who never quite managed to get rid of that last twenty pounds, he lived and breathed the fellowship of the cop. Most cops were hard-core believers in justice and worked hard and honestly to bring it about. None of that was a problem.

Lucado, on the other hand, made Valerie look downright sympathetic to defendants. Lucado had never seen a defendant he thought didn't deserve the death penalty and had been rumored for years to be willing to bend the truth in court to achieve the outcome he desired. He exaggerated, found a way to slip in speculation, and remembered things that weren't in his report. Criminal defense lawyers quailed to see his name on their case files.

Shit.

I made laborious notes on what the other PTA women had told him—mostly that they hadn't done anything to the cup Summer drank from, hadn't seen anyone put anything in it, and that they were shocked and horrified by what happened after she drank it—and flipped to his notes about Kira, which I copied in their entirety.

> *Kira Grant, WF, DOB 3/17/1979. Present at home with two children, Finn, 11 and Fiona, 5. She was present at Wolf Run on June 2 at refreshment table. Stated Brandi Crane made drink and she was handing it out to fifth grade and parents at table set up in back of cafeteria. Denied doing anything to mess with cup. Kira handed cup to victim. Described victim and that she clutched her chest. Said she and victim had been friends for a long time and last argued over their sons' grades some years ago. She asked if she was under suspicion and if she needed a lawyer. I said she could feel free to talk to me. She advised would be talking to lawyer. Nothing more.*

Though it didn't sound like Kira had given much away, the notes about an argument worried me. Most likely they'd argued over something like whether everyone deserved an A for a group project when only one bought the poster board, but Lucado tended to find sinister motives for the smallest of things.

I copied everything else useful out of the file and handed it back to Hailey, who tucked it away out of my reach as if I might dive over the counter and steal it back.

"Emmett came in the back door. You can go on to his office if you want."

I thanked her again and wound my way through the maze of tightly packed desks and piles of paper to the tiny office Emmett had earned after three years in a cubicle. He had dark circles under his eyes. I wanted to ask if he was okay, but I couldn't. Not here, where we were officially enemies and the admin he shared with two other attorneys sat outside.

"Hey," he said. He gave me a tired smile and rubbed his scalp, mussing his hair.

A tuft stuck up in one place. A dangerous urge to smooth it made me curl my hands into tight fists by my sides.

"We need to schedule a prelim in the Grant case," I said in my most professional voice.

"Right. Well, as soon as possible, I guess. Three weeks or so? Third week of July? I think I can be ready then."

Preliminary hearings are mostly the commonwealth's to handle. They're required to prove there is probable cause to move the case to the higher court for trial. The burden here would be on Emmett—and Judge Pearson had already told him she thought the commonwealth was weak on probable cause. Still, almost all cases jumped this hurdle and went on to the circuit court. I could attempt to dent Emmett's case, but we both knew it would move on.

"Sure. Three weeks is fine. I'll get Maureen to give you dates. I assume you'll call Summer Peerman as a witness?" The victim frequently, but not always, made an appearance at the preliminary hearing.

Emmett's eyes shuttered. I'd crossed a line. Three weeks ahead he didn't have to tell me the answer to that. He had to do what he could to protect his case from me.

"Sorry. Don't answer that. I'm planning to meet with her either way."

Tense lines appeared at the corners of his mouth. "Allison . . . we're not working on this together, you know. You do what you have to do."

What was happening to me? I'd never shared my plans for a case with a prosecuting attorney before. I needed to get out of here. "Right. See you."

ᢀ

The conference room at the Department of Social Services smelled like despair. Oh, it looked fairly normal—cheap, government-issue foldable tables and plastic chairs, whiteboards covering the walls—but the picture of a flower someone had drawn in blue dry-erase marker on the lowest part of the board had a teardrop next to it.

Summer Peerman sat wearily in the plastic chair, her ID card swinging over her bosom on a lanyard reading **Making a Difference**.

"Is it true the Grant kids got kicked off the swim team?" she asked without preamble.

"Yes, I understand they did. It was couched in different language, but yes."

"People are such assholes. Those are innocent children. How can anyone direct that kind of hatred at kids?"

"Unfortunately things like that happen when there's an accusation like this."

Summer shifted in her seat, clearly uncomfortable. "Look. I agreed to talk to you because I want the court to find the truth. I'm not rooting for one side to win. If Kira did this, then she should go to jail. If she didn't, she needs to be vindicated. So ask away. I'll tell you the same things I told the investigators."

"Great. The truth is what I'm after, too." Well, yes, but that didn't stop me from rooting for one side to win. Mine. "Can you tell me about your job? I assume you've testified in court before?"

"Yes. Many times. I'm a Child Protective Services worker. I receive and investigate complaints of child abuse or neglect. If I find them to be valid, I participate in the court case by testifying on a child's situation, sometimes advocating for the child to be removed temporarily from the parents and placed with extended family or foster parents, and I work with the parents on making changes to allow reunification, if that's possible."

"Have you ever investigated a complaint about the parenting of Tammy Cox, the mother who worked on the refreshments with Kira Grant?"

"I can't answer that. Investigations are confidential." Summer's face gave nothing away. I'd hoped for a clue from her reaction, but she must get asked that kind of question all the time.

She'd put me at a momentary disadvantage. "Right. Had to ask." I consulted my notes to gather myself. I could ask Tammy about Summer. And would, eventually. Maybe I could subpoena the investigation records if Tammy wouldn't talk. "Okay. Can you tell me about your relationship with Kira? How you met, et cetera?"

Her eyes widened. "Oh God. We met years ago. On the first day of kindergarten for Aidan and Finn. The parents attend school with the kids that day. Kira and Miles were the only other set of two parents in the classroom. This was before my divorce. The boys were supposed to draw a picture of themselves for the bulletin board, but Aidan freaked out and wanted to take it home instead. He threw a fit and wouldn't go over to hear a story on the rug with the other kids. Finn made a point of asking him to come with him, and they've been best friends ever since. I went up to Kira and Miles and told them what a nice little boy they had and how grateful I was. We got to talking, and the rest is history."

"The boys are close?"

"Yeah. They're both gifted, and the school didn't have a program for the gifted until second grade, but they were both advanced and so similar that they started one early for the two of them. I don't think it's occurred to them to compete yet—though they will, I'm sure. They seem pretty pleased to have similar interests."

She shifted again. I'd already learned this meant she had something true and straightforward to say. "I know you're here about Kira, though."

"And?" I prodded.

"Before you ask, yes, Kira and I are friends. Close friends, I'd say, as close as possible."

"As close as possible?"

She chose her words before speaking. "Well, we're different. Different kinds of people. And Kira isn't an easy friend. She's not the kind who lets herself relax and be real. Oh, I think she cares about me as much as she cares about anyone, but there's something hidden there. I've never seen her in yoga pants when she's not actually going to yoga. Or in a stained, stretched-out T-shirt. She's always . . . onstage, or something, if you know what I mean."

I did.

"But we've gone to movies together and taken the boys to birthday parties and to the children's museum and drunk a lot of coffee during the playdates when they were small. She was supportive during my divorce. She used to keep Aidan when I needed it. Still does, I suppose, or did, until this stuff. And I kept Finn when she stayed in the hospital having Fiona. That's why . . ."

"Why what?"

"Why I can't wrap my head around the idea that Kira would go out to her yard, pick some poisonous flower, stick it in a cup, and hand it to me. I can't think of a single reason she would want to kill me. Why? What would it do for her? What would she get in exchange for taking a risk like that?"

Summer's calm assumption Kira *might* do something like that if she had a good enough reason made my hands go cold. I didn't doubt her for a second. Sometimes the things we understand instinctively about our friends are even more true than what's passed in words. I refocused on the fact that we didn't have a reason. Summer couldn't think of one, and she'd known Kira for years.

She went on. "We've never really argued or even clashed—like I said, she's the kind to keep the inner feelings hidden. I don't know where she stands politically, or whether she believes in God or only says she does, or even how much she loves her husband. The one thing I know for sure is she'd walk on hot coals for Finn and Fiona. But other than that, she just . . . doesn't talk like that."

I waited, knowing people filled silence.

She picked at a place on her pants where the fabric had worn. "So, honestly, this is going to sound dumb. Kira and I are close, but not close enough that we know each other well enough even after all these years for her to have a reason to kill me. I don't . . . matter to her that much. I can't imagine she thinks about me often enough. Does that make sense?"

I'd had friends like that. I knew in my bones Summer Peerman told the truth. Kira had struck me that way, too.

"So I'm going to assume based on what you just said that you have no reason to think Kira held a grudge against you or had a reason to wish you ill?"

"No. No reason at all. I've been racking my brains, and nothing." She took a long breath and let it out. "Except . . ."

"There's always an 'except,'" I said, smiling. How I hated the "excepts."

"About three weeks before the fifth-grade graduation, Kira stopped speaking to me for a few days. A week, maybe. She and I had what I guess I'd say was our biggest disagreement ever. She'd taken Finn to some violin audition or something, and I kept Fiona. Aidan had gone to his dad's, so I spent a lot of time with Fiona, reading to her. I worked with her on her letters. You know. Because she's going to go to kindergarten soon. Something about the way she stared so hard at the words, at the letters, bothered me. When Kira and Finn came to get her, I told Kira I thought she ought to have Fiona tested for dyslexia."

"How did Kira take that?"

"She blew a gasket. Did the whole lady-of-the-manor thing and told me her kids were her business, and she'd take care of them, and who did I think I was to suggest that Fiona was . . ." Summer paused, her face careful and blank. "Damaged. She used the word *damaged.* As if dyslexia equates to damage. I get it, I guess. In my job, I've seen lots of parents grieve when their kids are first diagnosed with autism or epilepsy or whatever, and then later on they realize they're still the same great kids. Anyway, she didn't speak to me afterward for a while."

"What happened to resolve it?"

"Nothing. One day she started back up as if nothing had happened. I'm assuming she realized Fiona was the same kid she'd always been."

"Do you know if she ever got treatment for Fiona?"

"For dyslexia? No idea. I haven't mentioned the word again."

Kira was undoubtedly fixated on her kids and on perfection and very intelligent herself. I could totally see her freaking out at the idea that her daughter might have a learning disability and be, in her mind, "broken."

"How about the other ladies at the event? The ones serving refreshments. Any issues with them?"

"Ruthanne's harmless. Gung ho on a ten–Red Bulls–a–day level, but harmless. Brandi and I . . ."

"What?"

"Well, Brandi's son Griffin and Aidan were on the same soccer team."

"Tell me about the soccer team. Kira told me you all fought." I poised my pen and schooled my face to reveal nothing.

Summer narrowed her eyes, scanning my face with the expertise born of years of dealing with abusive parents. "You heard about that?"

"Yes."

"Huh. Well. Yes, Brandi and I have known each other since our boys were playing recreation soccer at four. They haven't always been on the same team, but when they are, it's usually a problem. They both want to play the same position: the forward who gets to score the most. They . . . they're like oil and water. They argue. Bump each other. Coach after coach has made one or the other sit the bench. I fuss at Aidan all the time, and he's not blameless. I'm sure I'm biased, but I still think it's Griffin who starts it most of the time. He mouths off on a dime. Shouts instructions to Aidan like Aidan's stupid."

I envisioned some little witch in a ponytail calling Libby stupid. Yeah, that would cause bad blood between the mothers. Idly I wondered if it might be possible for me to avoid youth sports with Libby indefinitely. "And Brandi? What does she do when that's going on?"

Summer let out a derisive snort. "Nothing. She encourages it. You have to understand, Brandi lives for sports. She's the same with all her other kids. Spends every second at the fields, papers her minivan with soccer and football stickers, trashes other kids, yells insults from the sidelines, makes her kids train at home. You know the type. Griffin is a good player, but it's not likely he—or Aidan, or anyone—is headed for the World Cup anytime soon. It would be one thing if I thought she was pushing for college scholarships. That's what I hope for, for Aidan, best-case scenario. But Brandi's oldest didn't go to college at all. She cares about winning."

I did know the type. My ex, for one.

Summer took a deep breath and grimaced. "I shouldn't have said all that. It's not really fair. I don't know what kind of life she's lived. I'm sure she thinks she's supporting her kids, showing her love for them. And she takes care of them. They're clean, well-dressed, decent students. She does participate with the PTA, and that's something."

I had no intention of letting her off the hook. "And things got personal with you and Brandi this spring?"

"Oh God." Summer shifted in her seat again, the lanyard swaying around her neck. "Yes. I'm embarrassed to tell it. I shouldn't have done it."

"What?"

"Well, Griffin got in trouble with the coach and got benched in April. Sat for three games. Aidan played the position. Every game, I watched Brandi get a little more steamed. She couldn't believe Coach Russell really meant to keep Griffin on the bench. Finally, Coach put Griffin back in, at midfield. Midfield is a tough position and doesn't get to score quite as often as forward. The ref blew the whistle, and Aidan and Griffin were elbowing each other. Brandi ran out there and separated them before the ref even saw it, which would have been fine if she hadn't cussed at Aidan. Called him a 'little shit.' Then she walloped Griffin across the face."

"What happened after that?"

"They started up the game again, and the kids played like nothing happened. Brandi came straight over to me and said, loud, all sarcastic, that she guessed I'd paid off the coach to ruin Griffin's season, as if Aidan needed more advantages."

Oh shit. Was that a reference to race? Aidan was Black. "And? What did you do?"

"I told her I'd done nothing of the kind, and I wouldn't need to anyway, because her kids' seasons would be ruined when Social Services came to haul them off for abuse and neglect. She just stood there staring at me, and I couldn't shut up. I told her Griffin would end up in jail along with the rest of his siblings if he kept assaulting people on the soccer field." Summer winced, closing her eyes. "I shouldn't have said it. Tommy, Brandi's oldest, has been convicted of some small-time stuff, and the younger girl hangs with a scary crowd, but Griffin and the older girl are only mouthy. Not criminal."

"Well, everyone says things they regret."

"No. I should have taken the high road. I'm better than that. She's not worth it. I insulted a kid, two kids, and so I joined her down on the low road. I sure as hell shouldn't have threatened her with Social Services action." She looked up. "After that we didn't talk to each other for a month or so. Avoided each other. She mumbled some kind of apology after a while. So did I. We're acting like it didn't happen now." She rubbed the bridge of her nose tiredly.

"I'm going to apologize because there's no way to ask this question in a nonoffensive way. Do you think this argument had anything to do with race?"

Summer sat back and let out a long breath. "I don't know. My guess is Brandi isn't likely a big supporter of Black Lives Matter, but she's so focused on putting her kids forward that she can't see their weaknesses. She reacts in anger." Her expressive face shifted to careful professional blankness. "No, in answer to your question. The argument was about a soccer game."

I scanned her face, looking for any signs she was telling me what she thought I wanted to hear, but she'd walled herself off. No emotion made it through the armor. I pressed on.

"Did you report her for hitting her child?"

"No, I didn't," Summer said, relaxing slightly. "Maybe I should have, but my own behavior wasn't ideal, either. And my mama used to smack me like that when I got out of line."

She clearly had more to say. I waited.

"There's one more thing." Summer squared her shoulders. "Two weeks before school let out, Aidan got awarded the spot on the all-star travel team."

"And Griffin?"

"Griffin didn't make it."

"Did Brandi say anything to you about that?"

Summer closed her eyes. "Yeah. She said for me to enjoy it while I still could."

CHAPTER ELEVEN

KIRA

God, the courthouse depressed me. All linoleum and fluorescent lights and bare-bones benches and no windows. A single step up from the jail decor, really. Anger burned again at the thought that I was now qualified to judge jail interiors. I glanced around the lobby. A sheriff's deputy manned a metal detector, slowly waving the wand over the poor unfortunate souls on their way in, as if it were the line for admission to Hades.

At least Summer Peerman had to blink under the merciless fluorescent glare, too.

I was still stewing over the obnoxious "thinking of you" card Summer and Aidan sent to Finn and Fiona after the swim team debacle, which included a gift card to the movie theater. She had some balls of brass to tell lies about me and then send my children a gift and pretend she cared about them. The pièce de résistance: she knew I wouldn't be allowed to write a thank-you note. I'd have to *owe* her. God. My blood pressure went up ten notches every time I thought about it.

Summer would get to show me the other one of her two faces today. Time for the preliminary hearing.

Knowing this judge was a woman, and, as far as I knew, not a lesbian, I'd worn my most severe tailored suit. For Miles, I wore the

La Perla underwear he liked under it, and I made sure he saw it as I got dressed. I needed him to stay supportive-looking. Allison met us in the hall.

"You look nice. Are you nervous?" she asked.

"A little, I guess." Like hell. *She* ought to be nervous. I didn't have to talk—right to remain silent, and all that—but she did. I knew damn well how important this case had to be to her. Dan MacDonald himself called me to vouch for her and to say he'd be "taking a great interest" in it.

"Well, you don't have to speak. Or you, Miles," she said, patting my husband's shoulder. He looked nervous enough to vomit right there on the gleaming linoleum of the courthouse floor. "This isn't a trial. At the preliminary hearing, the commonwealth has to prove they had probable cause to arrest you and to try you for attempted murder. It's a much lower standard than reasonable doubt, and the vast majority of the time they can prove enough to move the case up to circuit court for trial. Today we'll probably hear from the sheriff's investigator, the victim, and the hospital, most likely. I'll cross-examine them, but you only need to be present. Okay?"

"Okay." I put on my Brave Girl face. Daddy used to love that one.

We entered the courtroom and sat through three other preliminary hearings as I picked at a heretofore-unnoticed crooked seam in my skirt. All three of the other defendants wore jail orange—their lawyers hadn't gotten them bond, apparently. I glanced at Allison, who kept flicking her boring brown hair behind her ears. She stared intently forward at the proceedings in front of us.

What was she so interested in? The defendants looked like defendants: skinny and druggy-looking in one case, biker dangerous in another, and red-eyed alcoholic in the third. Two attorneys for the commonwealth handled the hearings, taking turns. One was a painfully young woman with shiny black hair styled like Allison's. Did they go to a barber and ask for the Boring Lawyer bob? The other prosecutor was the one who'd done my bond hearing, the one in his early thirties with messy dark hair like a surfer and a frayed shirt collar. I couldn't remember his name. Amity. Emery. Something. He did have impressive shoulders underneath his suit coat. I had to give him that.

I glanced at Allison again. Huh.

A bailiff led the third defendant away, shackles clanking. "Kira Grant? Matter of *Commonwealth versus Kira Grant*."

"That's us," Allison said moronically.

I rolled my eyes and stood, following her to the front to stand in front of the judge's bench like we had at the bond hearing. I got a better look at the prosecutor. Decent-looking, if you liked the sloppy look, which I didn't. I glanced at Miles, who'd stayed in the gallery seats. He smiled. Miles definitely won better-looking, though the fact that he'd played hide-the-salami with his skanky hygienist put a giant dent in his attractiveness at the moment.

"Are we ready, ladies and gentlemen?" the judge asked. She looked too annoyingly young to be a judge. Pearson, that was her name. "This is the preliminary hearing in the matter of *Commonwealth versus Kira Grant*. Counsel, please call your witnesses forward to be sworn."

Allison had explained that since the commonwealth carried all the burden here, we had no reason to let them have the opportunity to grill any of our witnesses—whoever they might be. As a result, we'd call no one. The sloppy-haired attorney called three people: a man in a tie I assumed must be from the hospital, the investigator who'd come to my house asking questions, and Summer. They all came forward to be sworn.

Summer glanced at me. I kept my face immobile, though she parted her lips as if she wanted to say something. As if I wanted to hear it. Benedict Arnold. Colluder. Obstructor. Traitor.

"Raise your right hands!" the judge said. She swore them in and, at Allison's request, sent all but the hospital guy into the hallway, where they couldn't hear what the others said.

Hospital Guy was quick. The attorney—Amaro, apparently—took him through what happened to Summer. She'd shown up at the hospital in extreme distress. She'd gone into full cardiac arrest and nearly died on the table. Once she was stabilized, they pumped her stomach when the symptoms indicated possible poisoning. She'd been monitored for more heart problems and kept for five expensive days. They sent her home with directions to come back every two months to check for damage to or weakness of her one remaining kidney for the foreseeable future—kidneys were poison magnets, he said. They'd analyzed the contents of her stomach. Lab tests, science-y crap, labs, blah, more labs, chemical nonsense, and bam: they found out it was aconite. Summer had been lucky to survive. No, aconite was not used in food, and poisoning with it was rare.

Allison followed up, not really disputing anything Hospital Guy said. No one planned to argue Summer wasn't poisoned.

I wondered when someone would ask the obvious question: What foul-tasting ingredient out of Satan's kitchen did Brandi Crane put in those god-awful smoothies before the poisoning? No one seemed to care about this, so on we went.

The judge excused Hospital Guy to go back to his high-paid hospital job. A bored-looking clerk called Summer's name.

Summer lumbered up the aisle from the back double doors. My daddy would have had a conniption fit if he'd seen that. *Ladies don't lumber,* he said. *They glide. And girls had better be ladies,* Daddy said. Summer nodded at the bailiff, and at the judge. I assumed since she worked for Social Services, she knew all the courtroom personnel. It annoyed me. I'd bothered to get dressed in this suit to curry favor, and she showed up in a maxi dress made out of a shower curtain and still made a better impression.

The Amaro man greeted her and got her into position in the center of our group.

"You're Summer Peerman?"

"Yes."

"Can you tell us whether you were present at Wolf Run Elementary School on June 2?"

"Yes, I was."

"Why were you there?"

"It was the last day of school for my son, Aidan. The PTA hosted a party for the fifth graders who were 'graduating,'" she said, making air quotes. My lip curled of its own volition. She'd told me she thought a fifth-grade graduation ceremony was stupid. It wasn't an achievement to graduate from fifth grade, she claimed. While I had to admit secretly that it was no achievement at all for my child, I hated to miss any chance to throw a party. And Finn's pictures had been adorable, at least before the incident. I was still mad I'd missed out on getting a chance to video him walking the halls to "Pomp and Circumstance."

"Did anything unusual happen at the party?" Amaro asked. Allison watched them both as if at a tennis game.

"Yes. I drank a smoothie from the refreshment table and was poisoned."

"Objection," Allison said, in a half-hearted tone. "She's drawing an impermissible conclusion."

"Rephrase, Counsel," the judge said, leaning back. "This is only a probable cause hearing."

Allison shot a look at the prosecutor. He bit his lip. Summer saved the situation. "I took a cup from the refreshment table, drank the contents, and then experienced a sensation, first in my chest. Everything went numb—first my mouth, then my face, my hands, my feet. That's all I remember before waking up in the hospital."

"Thank you, Ms. Peerman." Damn Summer for being an expert at testifying. The prosecutor flipped one of his pages and glanced at me. He had thick-lashed, deep-brown eyes. "Do you know the defendant, Kira Grant?"

"Yes. We're friends. Our sons are friends." Summer flicked her traitorous gaze to me. I stared back at her, not letting her see anything in mine.

"Was she present at the school on June 2?"

"Yes. She was in charge of the refreshment table."

"How did you acquire the cup you drank from?"

"I went up to the table with Aidan—my son—and a number of cups were already poured and sitting on the table. Three women were handing them out, as well, to keep the crowd around the table moving. Aidan spent some time dithering over which one he thought had the most in it and picked one and drank it. Kira handed me a cup. Aidan tossed his back and had no problems. I drank mine rather than take it to the kitchen to dump it out."

Typical. Aidan never had any problems.

"Why would you want to dump it out?"

Summer gave a charming wry smile. "The PTA smoothies are usually terrible."

"I see." Amaro smiled with her. *Oh, aren't we having fun?* "The defendant handed you the cup you drank from?"

Summer met my eyes again. "She did."

"Later, did the defendant visit you at home?"

"Yes, after I got out of the hospital, Kira and her children stopped by to bring a dessert. I was still home, recovering. We chatted about what happened."

"Did you know then what had happened to you?"

"Yes. They'd told me in the hospital I'd ingested aconite, and I told Kira what they'd said."

"Was Ms. Grant familiar with aconite?"

"She didn't say she was familiar with it when I brought it up. I said it was a plant, but I didn't make the connection to her garden. I think she changed the subject."

Not on purpose, but thanks for making me look shifty as hell.

"Did you tell her any more common names for it?"

"Yes. I told her it was also known as wolfsbane or monkshood."

"Were you aware Ms. Grant grows wolfsbane in her yard?"

She damn well should have been. I'd given her the tour at least five times.

"No. Not that specifically. She has a lot of flowers, but I'm not much of a plant person. To me, they're either pretty or they're not. I'm lucky to grow grass in my yard."

The prosecutor, the judge, and even Allison chuckled at that. Dammit.

"When you told her the common names, did she indicate any recognition?"

"No. She didn't."

"Did she say whether she'd intentionally put the plant substance in your cup?"

"She said she didn't."

I did not put that substance in your cup and you damn well know it. I'd always been brilliant at controlling my temper, but it was hard not to scream while others politely discussed me and my possible evil motivations right in front of me.

"Tell me, Ms. Peerman. Has Kira Grant ever lied to you before?"

Summer looked down at her hands, clasped before her. It took her a long time to speak. I couldn't remember a time when I'd lied to her. Or at least a time when she'd known I was lying. *Say no and get it over with.*

"On occasion."

Okay, when I said your dress looked hot and when I told you I loved your new sofa and a thousand other unimportant times, but sure, make me look like a lying evildoer.

"What has she lied to you about?"

"Objection," Allison said, heatedly this time. "Irrelevant to the question of probable cause."

"I'll sustain," the judge said, glaring accusingly at the Amaro man. "Move on, Counsel."

"That's all the questions I have," he said, red darkening his cheeks. I gathered it wasn't the done thing to end on a sustained objection. He scowled at Allison. Maybe he was one of those who hated being bested by a woman. Good.

"Cross?" the judge asked, checking her watch.

Allison stepped forward. "Yes, Your Honor. Ms. Peerman, you have been friends with Kira Grant for over six years?"

"Yes."

"Your friendship is the kind that is close enough to share playdates? You've kept her children for her and vice versa?"

"Yes. We've been close."

"You are not currently at odds over anything you're aware of right now?"

"No."

"And you weren't in any kind of disagreement on June 2?"

"No."

"Kira has not at any time indicated to you that she put poison in your cup either on purpose or accidentally?"

"No. She said she didn't."

"As you stand here right now, can you think of any reason, any reason at all, why Kira would be motivated to poison your drink?"

"Objection," the Amaro man said, looking at Allison in an odd way. "Calls for speculation."

"She's your witness, Mr. Amaro," the judge said. "If counsel for the defense wants to give free rein to the victim to speculate about any reason why the defendant might be guilty of the crime, I'm prepared to take it for what it's worth. I'll allow it. Go ahead."

Summer watched the judge, waiting for her to finish speaking. Amaro's lips tightened, red rising in his cheeks again. Maybe he wasn't experienced. Irritation intensified. Though it made absolutely no rational sense, it annoyed me that they'd assigned my case to an inexperienced prosecutor.

"No," Summer said. "I can't think of any reason she would do that."

I experienced a rare flicker of admiration for Allison. It had been ballsy to ask, and she'd gotten the victim of the crime to agree I had no motive to commit it.

"That's all the questions I have. Thank you." Allison made a quick mark on her legal pad and waited for the next witness. She was pleased. She worked hard to keep a smile off her face. Summer left, and the law enforcement guy strode up the aisle.

I remembered thinking he was a Neanderthal when he came to my house, and I saw no reason to change my opinion now. Bristling with confidence and righteousness, he weighed a bit too much and cut his hair a lot too short. His too-tight collar squeezed his neck over his unfashionable tie just enough to create a squishy roll.

I definitely did not like the smirk he gave me as he passed. We all had to pause for the judge to drink some water and sign a couple of papers a clerk brought in.

At my house, I'd been nothing but pleasant to Investigator Lucado. That's how he'd introduced himself, even though he was close to my age. I'd done the whole southern hospitality routine—got him a glass of sweet tea, offered him a snack. I answered his questions, but only the ones I knew either didn't matter or could be discovered by a quick Google search. I've watched a lot of *Law & Order* episodes. I knew the second he came to my door without calling first like a decent person that he considered me a suspect.

Under Amaro's questioning, Lucado went through all his credentials and how he got involved in the case, as if anyone cared. I assumed he was there to say I let him in my house and told him Summer and I were best friends and yes, of course Summer's poisoning came as a shock, and then how I smiled at him flirtatiously while telling him my husband would absolutely kill me if I talked anymore without asking our attorney about it. I even handed him a lemon–poppy seed muffin on his way out.

Which he ate. You'd think if he really believed I wielded poison as a lethal weapon, he'd have been a bit more careful, but at no time had he struck me as particularly bright.

Given that I already knew what he'd say, I zoned out while he talked about how they'd identified aconite in the cup Summer dropped and in an empty baggie found inside out in the trash in the school kitchen. Nowhere else. No fingerprints. A wasp buzzed near one of the fluorescent lights as if determined to electrocute itself. The courtroom stayed in constant motion: bedraggled sorts of the type I'd met in jail whispered with suit-wearing lawyers and uniformed cops. Groups formed, conferred in murmurs, and re-formed. The judge paid no attention to all the activity behind me. It drove me crazy. I wanted to turn around and tell them to sit down and shut the hell up.

"The defendant behaved very oddly when I asked her about her relationship with Ms. Peerman. Very oddly." Investigator Neck Roll raised his voice, cutting into my distraction.

What? Okay, he had my attention.

"Objection," Allison said, as if by rote.

Amaro didn't wait for the judge. "I'll clarify. What, specifically, did the defendant do or say to give you that idea?"

"Well. When I mentioned Ms. Peerman, she rolled her eyes a bit."

I did not!

"She continued smiling, as if she was trying not to laugh."

My mouth fell open. I'd done nothing of the kind.

"Your report said the defendant described the victim. How did she do that?"

"She said Ms. Peerman was a slow, plodding, fat woman."

Oh my dear Lord. He'd asked me to describe her physically. I'd said she was relaxed and a bit heavyset.

"Anything else?"

"She said she and Ms. Peerman got along most of the time, but on occasion they'd had major differences."

He'd asked me if we'd ever fought. I said four years before, we'd argued over whether the schools ought to make a big deal out of our sons' straight As. I thought they should proclaim it to the skies—after all, that is what the schools are for, right? Summer thought it might make the disadvantaged feel bad or some ridiculousness like that, and the schools should congratulate the boys in private. I couldn't recall any other arguments besides the one over Fiona, which I certainly hadn't mentioned to this lout. Major differences? Ridiculous.

"What did she say specifically they argued about?"

"She said something about their grades. I gather the Peerman boy is a better student than the Grant boy. I can't recall specifically."

The scream I'd fought down before battered again at the closed hatch. Finn and Aidan had identical grades. Neither had ever gotten a B. This low-intelligence cave dweller was making me sound jealous on Finn's behalf. I squeezed my hands hard enough for my fingernails to dent my palms.

"Ms. Grant allowed you to take gloves you saw on her porch?"

"Yes. When I arrived, I saw a pair of gloves on her porch floor and asked if she objected to me taking those in. She gave consent. The gloves were pink flowered and made to fit an adult woman's hand. They turned out to have alkaloid residue on them."

"Are there any other adult women in the defendant's household?"

"No. Only one other female, too small for those gloves."

It occurred to me that both Neck Roll and the prosecutor believed wholeheartedly that because the gloves had pink flowers on them, no man could possibly have donned them. I rolled my eyes, but there was no point in nudging Allison: all our suspects were women.

"One more question. Did you ask Kira about the aconite?"

"Yes. She denied knowing about it."

What? A second cold wave of rage swept over me. I squeezed my hands together again, this time feeling the skin break.

"Even after you told her the common names for the plants?"

"Even then. After Ms. Grant was arrested, we obtained a search warrant and discovered the plant known as aconite growing in her yard. She denied being familiar with the durn plant, and all the time it was growing right outside the very window where we sat."

I gasped. Holy Jesus on the cross. He'd made that up out of whole cloth. He'd flat out lied. Under oath. When he introduced himself at my door, he told me he wanted to ask me questions about Summer's aconite poisoning. I was sweet to him, but I wasn't about to let him ask me any questions about the actual event. I sent him on his way long before he could have gotten to questions like that. I glanced up, waiting for a lightning bolt to smite him into an ash heap.

What did you do when a cop lied to a judge? At a minimum, it seemed obvious I shouldn't nod along. I let my eyes widen and my outrage show. I elbowed Allison, not gently. "A word," I hissed.

Amaro thanked the witness and turned him over to Allison, who, if this were truly a hall of justice, should shank him in his sweaty neck right then and there. She considered me, then the judge. Apparently she planned to go with a less visceral response. "Your Honor, if I could have a second."

The judge nodded. Allison pulled me off to the side. The prosecutor stared after us as if tuning up his eavesdropping devices.

I didn't waste time. "He lied. I never said Summer was fat. He asked for a physical description. Summer and I never had major differences. And he never asked me about the aconite, so I obviously didn't say I'd never heard of it. He never asked me!"

Allison's lips tightened. "Okay. I believe you. He's done this before. He writes generic, vague reports and then fills in the details on the stand. Gives himself a lot of room. I'll do what I can."

"What do you mean?" I could feel my hysteria rising. Was this ordinary? Expected? Was our justice system this messed up? I felt naive for having believed in it, and I hated nothing more than feeling naive. "'What you can'? Can't you report him? Can a police officer just *lie*?"

"No. It's my job to prove him wrong."

She turned to Lucado, consulting her folder. I occupied myself trying to kill him with my brain waves alone, Darth Vader–style. What a spectacular superpower that would be. It would certainly have come in handy right now. It was *unacceptable* to have to stand here and take this.

Allison showed him a document, shoving a copy of it at Amaro without looking at him. She was angry. Good. He stared at it and didn't look up. "Investigator, this is your report of your interview with Ms. Grant?"

"Yes."

"You interviewed her only the one time?"

"Yes."

"Now, can you tell me where in your report you wrote that Ms. Grant described Ms. Peerman as 'fat'?"

"Right there. It says 'described the victim.' In a job like mine, I don't have time to write down every word someone says. I asked her to describe Ms. Peerman and that's what she said."

"Uh-huh," Allison said, in a scathing tone of disbelief almost worthy of me. "Now, sir, can you show me where you said Ms. Grant 'rolled her eyes'?"

"Same, ma'am. I don't write every single thing down. But I remember it like it was yesterday."

Allison didn't comment. She speared him with a glance. "Show me where it says you asked her about the aconite."

"I didn't write it down."

"You asked her about what amounts to the attempted murder weapon and you didn't bother to note that exchange or even that you had it?"

"No. I guess I forgot to write it. But I definitely remember asking her about it, because then when we found the plant in her flowers, it hit me she said that."

"But you didn't write it down."

"No. Listen, you probably don't know what it's like to be out there, doing the job."

I hated this man with nuclear-reactor-meltdown levels of hate.

He went on, doing the mansplaining I'd known was coming from the first neck-roll sighting. "It's tough out there. You gotta go with where your interview is taking you. You gotta be ready for the next question. Light on your feet. You can't write down everything or you miss things. I don't miss things. Like, for example, I didn't write down what color she had on or what she said when she opened the door, either. You can't write it all down."

"You didn't think your question about the poisonous plant was more important than what color shirt she was wearing?"

"I guess I didn't write it down. But I remember it."

Allison's voice got angrier and angrier. She glanced at the judge several times as if to make her point. The judge remained impassive. The prosecutor had enough humanity to be a bit wide-eyed. None of it mattered. Allison tried ten different ways but got nowhere. Neck-Roll Toad stuck to his story. She excused him, and the lawyers turned to the judge.

I didn't need her to rule to know I'd be going to trial for a felony.

"Counsel, we're running behind today. Save your arguments. I'm going to certify this matter to the circuit court for trial. I find probable cause exists given the evidence that the defendant lied to at least one witness about her knowledge of and access to the poison at issue in this case and that she had clear opportunity to commit the crime. Bond is continued until trial under the same conditions. Thank you, Counsel."

"Kira, can you wait for me a second? I have to say a few words to the prosecutor," Allison said. "Then we'll talk."

"What is there to say? That detective lied. The judge believed him because she knows him. Case closed. Good to know the justice system is this much of a joke."

"Case isn't closed. Not by a long shot. We'll start all over in the court upstairs. You'll see."

A twiglike woman in a garish suit approached us. "Hi, I'm Victoria Akers with Channel 12? We'd like to do an on-camera, if it's okay? Outside?"

Though I considered it—I'd always wanted to be on TV—I didn't know anyone at Channel 12 who'd conveniently cheated on a spouse. Allison had said no press, but surely this clueless child who phrased everything as a question could do little harm.

"No, thank you. No comment," Allison said, barely glancing at the girl. The TV reporter left, heading straight for Detective Toad. Dammit. Had Allison thought this through? If spin was about to be spun here, it would be so much better for me to do the spinning than Mr. Mendacity.

"Okay, go ahead and go home with Miles," Allison said to me, paying no attention to the reporter, who'd been—thank God—brushed off by the detective. "I'll call you later. We need to talk about your definition of *major differences*, by the way, but it doesn't have to be right this second." Allison's killer-death-ray eyes were all for the prosecutor. Part of me wished I could go over there and listen in, but Miles had been patient enough. Allison made a beeline for Amaro, to ream him out for putting a deceitful water buffalo on the stand, I assumed. I watched for a second as their faces grew red and they gesticulated with more animation than I thought might be usual for people who were in the business of fighting with each other.

"Kira, you ready?" Miles asked, holding my purse like a good little boy.

"Just a second." I'd always been a good observer of people. Something about the way the lawyers' hands flashed through the air made me certain I'd missed something important.

Then it hit me. It was what wasn't flashing. Neither Allison nor Amaro wore wedding rings. They were about the same age. They made a nice-looking couple . . .

Aha. That's how it was. My lawyer had some chemistry going on with her opponent. With *my* opponent. I remembered a legal show once making clear that opposing-lawyer sex was a huge no-no.

I filed it away. Let her have her little crush for now. As long as it didn't get in my way, I didn't object. No reason to torpedo it until I had to. If it became necessary, well, then, surely she'd understand I wouldn't hesitate. It might even be useful, somehow.

After all, my life was at stake.

CHAPTER TWELVE

ALLISON

"She's got a real affinity for the instrument," Hilde Leinenkruger said. Libby sat at Hilde's living room piano and tinkled away, so blissful she'd forgotten we were there. Hilde was a warm older woman with a German accent, a tangle of unrestrained gray curls, clunky homemade jewelry, and bright loose garments evoking the hippies my ex-husband had hated so much. I hadn't picked her for that reason, but it didn't hurt. She'd taught piano to my assistant, Maureen, when she was young, and I could find no better recommendation. Maureen played piano for her church choir.

"We don't have a piano, or room for one. I'm not sure how she'd be able to practice."

"Oh, you'd be welcome to bring her here, or to my church. It's right near your office. Someone is always there in the daytime, and I could let them know to expect you. It's not unusual not to own a piano. And at first, we'd be getting used to the instrument and to music as a concept."

We watched as Libby picked out the opening bars to "Joy to the World" on her own and sang along.

Hilde chuckled. "Well, maybe she's already done that part. She looks like she'd be an ideal student. When would you like to start? I can do evening hours if it would better accommodate your work schedule."

I loved this woman. I felt warmer in her house. Even her sofa hugged me. I wanted to lay my face against the fuzzy turquoise blanket draped across the back.

"Um. What are your rates?"

"Well, it's fifty dollars for an hour session. Most of my students come once a week."

Fifty dollars? That was more than two hundred dollars a month. Twenty-six hundred a year. I didn't have that much available cash, not with my student loans still unpaid and my crappy still-not-a-partner salary from Dan.

"Hilde, I'm sure Libby would love taking piano from you, but I'll have to discuss the cost with my ex-husband," I said, lying. And dying inside. "I'll call you next week, all right?"

"That's fine, dear. We'll figure it out. If I don't hear from you, I'll call you. I'd really like to teach Libby. She's a great kid. Lots of potential."

I bit my lip. Libby pretended to play the piano like a maestro—all crashing chords and tinkling high notes. There was drama, and yes, a musicality even I could hear in her fingers. "Come on, Liberina. We've got to go get some dinner, okay?"

"Nooo!" Libby crumpled, clutching the piano as if it were a life raft.

"Thanks, Hilde. Let's go, buddy."

Most of the time I was okay with doing the best I could for Libby—I'd been the latchkey daughter of penny-pinching parents myself. More and more, though, I worried that the best I could do wasn't at all what I'd envisioned—and wasn't nearly enough.

&

The next day, I wound along a gravel path through a huge trailer park I'd driven past for years but never entered. Tammy Cox had evaded my attempts to meet with her more than once but had finally given me consent to come and interview her. The common areas and the road were neat, but the trailers were ramshackle. Cheap plastic lawn furniture lay where it had blown during the previous night's storm. Faded children's toys crammed onto hand-built porches. The cars parked in the driveways weren't new.

Tammy's trailer was worse than most. Her grass hadn't been cut in a while. She flew a tattered American flag. Weeds grew between tangled shrubs and covered her front windows. I wondered how long it would be before the owner of the park would kick her out. I'd heard he had a low tolerance for failure to maintain.

Tammy answered the door. She was skinny to the point of emaciation and wore the tiny shorts they sold in the preteen section and a skimpy spaghetti-strap top with hot-pink bra straps showing. She sucked on a cigarette and smoke curled in a haze behind her, filling the trailer.

I hated secondhand smoke. It killed my grandmother. Still, I had no choice but to take a seat on the threadbare and somewhat sticky sofa. I tried not to breathe deep and made up my mind this interview would be over in less than thirty minutes.

"Can I get you something?" Tammy asked. "I got . . . uh, beer, some Mountain Dew?"

"No, thank you, Ms. Cox. I'm fine." It was eleven in the morning. The house was silent. "Where are your children?"

"Oh, the older one's off with her boyfriend somewheres. Caitlyn's out playing with her friend, I think. In one of the other trailers." Her hands shook from nerves or nicotine or both.

"Is Caitlyn the one you have at Wolf Run Elementary?"

"Yeah. She's going into second when they start up next week. She's about to have a fit to go back to school. I hate how they start in the middle of August now. Looks to me like they'd wait till after Labor Day like they used to. Leah, that's the older one, went there, too, before. She's thirteen."

Even though I pushed back at any resemblance to my own mother, I had difficulty with the idea of an unsupervised thirteen-year-old girl "off with her boyfriend."

"Are you ready to begin, Ms. Cox?"

She sat, birdlike, on the edge of a recliner. Her hands twitched. I was making her nervous. "Guess so."

"Can you tell me about your role on the PTA? What you do, why you joined? That sort of thing."

"Oh, I do it because back a few years ago, Leah begged me to. She wanted to show off her mama, she said, at the pancake breakfast. I don't do much except show up at the events. I'm a part-time hairstylist, you know. I see the PTA as a chance to get some customers. Almost all the women in this town come through the elementary school at some time or the other. I was the secretary this last year."

I glanced at her hair: thick and full and easily her best feature. "Does it work? Getting customers?"

"Well, yeah, some. Some of the mothers, the rich ones, they only go up to Lorenzo and Company up in Lynchburg. They wouldn't have no part of some lady doing hair in her kitchen here in a trailer park."

"Is Kira Grant in that group?" I asked, thinking of her spectacular movie-star hair.

Tammy snorted, stubbing out the cigarette and lighting another with shaking hands. "You've met her. What do you think? No, Kira'd die with a skunk stripe of gray down her part before she'd let me touch her hair in a trailer. She's the biggest bitch of them all, and that's saying something. She took one look at my tattoos the first day of school three years ago and gave me that look. Like she felt sorry for me and smelled a dead possum all at the same time."

"Do you and Kira get along at all?"

"Oh yeah. Kira's the polite sort, even if she's a bitch underneath. I'm no angel, either. I have to admit to having some fun with her. She thinks I'm a redneck, so I redneck it up as much as possible. You know.

Mention Hank Williams Jr. Say 'ain't' a lot. Ask her if she saw the NASCAR race. You should see the low-cut shit I wear to shock her at the events." She cackled deep and smoky, the mischievous spark taking years off her face. I grinned back despite myself.

"How about Summer Peerman? Do you know her?"

All the lingering amusement Tammy had been enjoying at Kira's expense vanished. "Summer's a piece of work. Kira's a regular old snob, no different from a hundred like her, but she won't bother me. Summer has stuck her nose in my damn business. I don't take kindly to people sticking their nose in my business."

All right, then. "I take it you do know her."

"Wish I didn't. My old bitch of a mother-in-law—ex-mother-in-law, that is—called up Social Services two years ago and told them a pack of lies to get Darrell custody of the girls. As if that old shitbag wanted custody. He don't, by the way. Spends his damn life in a tree stand hunting. But anyways. She told them I didn't watch the kids and I forgot to feed them and they had ringworm and some shit."

"And where did Summer Peerman come in? Had you met her before that?"

"Yeah, I'd seen her. Small town, you know. She showed up here one day and said she'd been assigned to investigate my parenting. Made me sign some damn paper said I agreed to feed my kids. Kind of insulting, don't you think, being asked to sign a contract that you're going to boil up a couple of hot dogs? Said Leah wasn't old enough at eleven, then, to watch Caitlyn if I went out to the store or to fix a meal, which is total bullshit, far as I'm concerned."

When I was eleven, I'd regularly gotten off the school bus to an empty house. At twelve, I'd earned money babysitting for a neighbor family of three kids under five. Times had changed, though. I'd already been lectured that I couldn't leave Libby in the car at a gas station when I went in for two minutes to pay. Tammy didn't look like the sort who'd be plugged into the ever more protective Rules of Good Mommies hotline, though.

"What did Summer say you had to do?"

"Said I couldn't leave Leah alone until she was thirteen. Said I had to cook dinner for them every night or take them to a restaurant. Hell. I started cooking supper for my three little brothers when I was nine. Leah was more than old enough to do the same. I figure there's a point around that age where if she never has to lift a finger, she won't never lift a finger. Summer said nope. In her opinion, it's my job to treat them like babies till they move out, I guess. Fine." Tammy took a long drag on her cigarette, making clear her scorn for that idea.

In between writing down what she said and lifting my pen from the paper, I had a small but worrisome epiphany. Was Tammy right? Were we raising a generation of kids who'd never learn to lift a finger? I knew Summer's directions to Tammy aligned with the societal ideals for proper parenting, but maybe we'd all gotten the whole theory wrong. Maybe a chain-smoking self-described redneck in a trailer had a better idea of how to parent than all the magazines and the experts.

I squelched the thought. I didn't have time to entertain an epic shift in my worldview at this moment. Besides, this particular parenting expert had just shared that she'd sent her thirteen-year-old daughter off with her boyfriend. Biology was a fact, not a theory. "So what happened? Was Summer okay with your contract?"

"Nope. She came and checked everything out. Had a lot to say about every damn thing. Junk food in the cabinets. Hadn't cleaned the bathtub good enough. I gave the girls Cokes and Mountain Dews instead of milk. I kept medicine in the bathroom where Caitlyn could reach. Car seat not the right size for her five-year-old butt. Leah's clothes were a size too small 'cause I hadn't been to the store yet and she grew about an inch a day that year." She rolled her eyes, but her hands shook. "You try to imagine someone checking behind you, watching every little decision you make for your kids. You got kids?"

"One."

"Would you pass that test?"

An irrational fear that Social Services might even now be compiling a complaint file about the many times I'd dozed off and let Libby have free run of the house pressed my lips together. "Did you pass that test?"

She stood and paced to the sink, where she stubbed out her cigarette and slid out yet another. A cat hopped up onto the counter and strolled lazily over a pile of dishes. Tammy petted it too hard with a distracted hand, and it yowled and jumped away. All this talk of Summer's investigation had agitated her beyond her control.

"No," Tammy said, sucking a long first drag on the new cigarette. "She scheduled a court date and said I was a neglectful parent. We went to court the first time, me with some court-appointed asshole who didn't give a shit about me. They scheduled another date for the next hearing. A week before that one, Caitlyn forgot her lunch at home and didn't have no money on her account. They called, from the school, but I didn't have my phone on. She didn't eat. Summer found out and told the court I'd failed to feed my children again. The court said I was a neglectful mother. Only reason Darrell didn't get forced to take the kids is he didn't bother to show up for court. Hunting season, of course."

"So what was the effect of that?"

"I had to be watched for a whole year, but the worst was I got fired from my full-time job, that's what."

"What job?"

"I worked at a day care. With kids. Once that shit is on your record, you're gone. The paper says 'a finding of abuse or neglect.' No more day care for me."

A mix of emotions held my pen steady. Tammy had a motive to do harm to Summer, which was good news for Kira. At the same time, I sympathized with Tammy, almost against my will.

"Did you find another?"

"Oh yeah, Summer woulda hauled my ass back to court if I didn't get another job. She'd have had no problem saying I was continuing to be neglectful for not earning money even though she's the one got me fired in the first place. I still do hair part-time, but I also have to clean. I got a job cleaning the mall, after hours. It's nasty, what those teenage shits do to the bathrooms there."

"I'm sure." I made the notes. "So how are things between you and Summer now?"

She took a contemplative drag on her cigarette before answering. "They're fine as long as she stays the hell away from me."

ॐ

Maureen announced Kira's appearance in my office, with both children in tow, three days later near closing. She hadn't made an appointment.

I didn't so much agree to let her in as not make any overt attempt to stop her. She swept in like a hurricane, her ducklings swirling around her. Kira pointed at a spot on the floor, and the children sat—the boy with a book and the girl with an iPod or iPhone.

"Kira. And this must be Finn and Fiona?"

The boy looked up. He was of slight build, and his glasses were crooked on his long nose. "Yes, ma'am. I'm Finn and this is my sister, Fiona," he said with perfect manners.

"What book do you have there? It's pretty big." Even though he was just entering sixth grade, he clutched a thick paperback.

He held it up: an adult-level fantasy with extravagant vocabulary I'd read only two years before. "Wow. That's a good book. I'm impressed."

"It's easy for me," Finn said, a hint of Kira's arrogance there somewhere.

With nothing to say to that, I turned to his mother. "So what can I do for you, Kira?"

"I'm here to help you," she said, setting down her expensive handbag and simultaneously making me feel like I was back in first grade with the never-satisfied Mrs. Van Loo.

I stared at her blankly. "Help me?"

"I need something to do. I'm going crazy, sitting at home, waiting for you to make some sort of progress. I can investigate something, or talk to people, or research things. Surely there's something."

"Uh. Um. Well, that's . . ." Not going to happen. Not usual. Not helpful. Possibly unethical. "Nice of you to offer, but I'm fine. I'm investigating and we've got plenty of time before trial."

"Nothing?"

I glanced around my office. Actually, I could use help in a thousand different ways—scanning old files into our online maintenance system, shredding old papers, cleaning the offices. Kira's pink linen blazer and the white sheath dress didn't exactly scream "work." I clapped a hand over the escaping giggle at a mental picture of her scrubbing the toilet Dan used. Besides, Kira in my office, going through other clients' files, was a major ethical no-no. "No, I'm afraid not. Maureen and I do a great job keeping things running here."

"I need to be doing something."

"What about your volunteer work or back-to-school shopping?" I said, wondering where in law school I'd learned my job would include advising rich women how to spend their hours.

She waved an annoyed hand. "Oh, those are easy."

"I'm sorry."

"Fine. I'll find something to do," she said, beckoning to her obedient children. "And I'd like a full written report of where you are in your investigation by Monday at five. Thanks so much!"

CHAPTER THIRTEEN

KIRA

It was absolutely amazing how often I left Allison's office with my mouth hanging open. I had extra time now that the children and I had been unceremoniously shunned from all participation in the activities of the community. I offered that extra time to her, pretty damn generously, I thought. All I would have asked in return was a teensy bit more hour-by-hour oversight of her work, and she blew me off.

Fine. If Allison wasn't taking this case seriously, I'd help her on my own. She probably was all wrapped up in idealistic ethics about truth and justice and that nonsense and would hesitate at checking things out the way I could.

I drove home with the volume up on the *Hamilton* soundtrack, let the children yell along with it, and gave them carte blanche in front of the TV and computer once we got home. That would keep them both quiet and away from me for hours. I needed time to think.

No matter how good she was at interviewing rednecks in trailers and overexcited young moms given to wearing dresses for six-year-olds, Allison would likely steer clear of the judge, and the judge, it appeared to me, was the key to this whole mess. A jury would not be deciding my innocence. The commonwealth hadn't requested one, and Allison, and then Dan when I went over her head for a second opinion, had recommended strongly against asking for one ourselves. A jury might get all emotional over poison in a school where there were elementary-age kids and what if that cup had fallen into the hands of a rosy-cheeked cherub and Dear God the Children. The judge could be expected to cut through all the hysteria and decide the case on the basis of the law and the evidence, said my lawyer. And her more experienced boss.

So the question of my freedom and the continuation of my normal lifestyle would be in the sole hands of Judge Christopher S. Turner, judge for the Forty-Second Circuit of Virginia.

I'd already done enough googling to know Virginia state judges ranked lower in prestige than federal judges, though I was fine with not being tried in federal court, where the sentences were stiffer. Among the state judges, a smaller hierarchy ruled, starting with the Virginia Supreme Court, then an appeals court, and then the circuit court judges. Generally, each county or city had one to three of these. Our county boasted only one: Christopher Turner.

I sat down and made myself some tea, starting out my search with an easy warm-up. On my iPad, I googled him. His picture sprang up with some biographical information. Not bad-looking. Age forty-seven. Born in Lynchburg. Went to the University of Virginia for undergrad and to Harvard for law school. He'd been a judge for nearly a decade, and before that a commonwealth's attorney.

Dammit. A former commonwealth's attorney would be sympathetic to that Amaro man.

I hadn't lied to Allison when I told her I was good at research. Few people had my skill at finding out all about people online—kind of a hobby of mine. Knowing who you're dealing with is the best way to keep the upper hand in any relationship.

I clicked further. Judge Turner had good reviews as a judge and had been easily reconfirmed by the state legislature time after time. A tediously vociferous website for an anti-child-predator group listed the record of every judge in the state for cases involving sexual crimes against minors. The group clearly expected all such defendants should be drawn and quartered without a trial, and they were harshly critical of every judge who'd merely put these folks in prison. Judge Turner, it seemed, came closer than most to doling out the cruel and unusual punishment the group fought for. Great. A harsh judge.

I sat back and stretched my spine. I'd already learned enough to know I couldn't leave this to Allison. It was too important. Judge Turner was the law-and-order sort: fond of putting people in prison, highly ethical on the bench, and young enough to want to continue for a while longer.

There'd have to be another way to attack this problem. While I thought, I spent a hundred bucks on a new UVA tie for Miles to wear to court. Couldn't hurt for Judge Turner to see a fellow Wahoo rooting for me. Even if said Wahoo was not actually a Wahoo and spat on the ground every time the University of Virginia came up in conversation. I might have to have sex with Miles to get him to wear the tie.

Perfect. Shopping always helped me focus. Within a few clicks, I had the name of the judge's wife—Laura Leigh Turner, formerly Laura Leigh Whitaker. You could always tell more about a man by what kind of wife he chooses.

I started with Facebook. Typical for the perfect social asset wife: Junior League, careful posts covering all political bases, a church mission trip to some godforsaken part of Appalachia. I flipped through the photos, and there they were. Laura Leigh and her Honorable husband, with two teenage sons. The men of the family were dark-haired, in the wholesome, apple-cheeked way of Superman or World War II recruits in a Steven Spielberg movie. Judge Turner's hair had begun to gray, but he was fit and aging well. Laura Leigh was dark blonde and younger than her husband—close to my age, I'd say. She'd had work done. That lack of cooperation between the brows and the huge white smile always gave it away.

Hmm. Her page supplied a wealth of information. The idiot sort who allowed her every interaction and location to be tagged, she'd helpfully provided the name of her hairdresser, her attendance at a benefit for flood victims, and that her sons were twins and seniors at the private Episcopal high school in Lynchburg. Laura Leigh ran the Junior League secondhand store for three hours every Thursday. And lo and behold, she ground coffee beans for the judge every Saturday morning so he could take his YETI cup to the tennis game he played at his country club.

Every single Saturday.

I had a friend who belonged to the Turners' country club. It had been far too long since I'd called her.

❧

The next morning, I left Fiona with the babysitter and took Finn to his new Saturday morning Japanese immersion class on the way to a certain country club for tennis with my dear friend Nicole.

Finn was in a mood.

I had little patience for moods when I operated at Peak Supermommy. Other than mine, of course.

"This is boring. I hate Japanese. I can't understand anything. If you'd let me take my phone, I could look up some words."

"If I let you take your phone, you'd sit in the corner and play your game with the blood moon and the zombies. You're supposed to be conversing."

Long-suffering sigh from the back seat. I never let Finn sit up front. He was too small to survive the airbag in the passenger seat, the imminent first day of middle school notwithstanding.

"Mom, the blood moon and the zombies aren't in the same game. The blood moon is in—"

"Anyway," I said, cutting him off. I'd swerve this car into a hundred-year-old oak tree before I'd listen to another two-hour lecture on the best strategy for whatever-it-was-called he played. "This is important, Finn. We've talked about this. You go to school with sports-crazed wildebeests. Your teachers are knuckle-dragging imbeciles. It's a miracle they taught you enough for you to get those test scores last spring. If we don't do half the education at home on our own, you'll never get into Yale. Granddaddy said on his deathbed how much he wanted you to go to Yale, remember?"

"Miss Towle was nice. I like my teachers."

"Oh, she was nice." Miss Towle was a bubble-headed baby factory, with a DUI they hushed up before the parents freaked out. "But she went to some college I never heard of. She doesn't have half your brains. We've got to do something with those brains, sweetie. You can't squander a gift like that."

"It's not fair. This is my last weekend before school starts and I have to do stupid Japanese. Who am I ever going to speak Japanese to?"

"You never know. You might grow up to be CEO of a Fortune 500 company. You might need to speak Japanese all day long. Besides, a diligent study of Japanese will make an impression on your college application. That and the Irish fiddle, and your chess game. We'll get you there."

"I don't even know if I want to go to Yale. It's cold in the north. And Aidan isn't going there."

Getting Finn into a decent college was my life's goal. He'd be going to Yale, even if he had to shiver in seven layers of clothes all winter. In six years, Aidan's college choice wouldn't be a factor for Finn. "Oh, sweetie. You'll love Yale. And if you want, I'll come and visit you every weekend. How's that?"

"What if you're in jail?"

My breath stuttered and restarted. The fear of being found guilty had begun to creep past my most stalwart defenses, showing up first in my nightmares and unaccustomed insomnia. "I won't be in jail, Finn," I said, as if to make it true. "I'm innocent, and I have a good lawyer. Don't you worry. The judge will see that. He'll do the right thing."

I glanced down at my bared cleavage and expanse of salon-bronzed, oiled leg. Oh, the judge would see plenty. He'd do the right thing, all right. I'd make him.

☙

"Nicole, I'm so glad I called you! It's been forever!" I cooed as I rounded the corner of the clubhouse.

Nicole Farthington was a card-carrying idiot. A rich idiot, but an idiot nonetheless. And for now, a useful idiot because she had agreed to play tennis with me on this beautiful Saturday morning and because she had no clue she was supposed to shun me for my association with the criminal underworld. If Nicole ever read the newspapers or any website other than Pinterest or Zappos, I had yet to hear about it.

We'd met in a breastfeeding class we'd taken before our oldests were born, and somehow she'd latched on to me far more firmly than either of my actual kids ever did.

"It has! And tennis is exactly what I needed. I'm so fat!"

Oh for God's sake. I forgot Nicole talked about only one thing, and her size-zero figure was that thing. Nicole was a walking, talking clothes hanger. She worked out hours of every day. She cleansed and dieted with the zeal of a Tibetan monk. Or whatever kind of monk it is who cleanses and diets.

"You look amazing, as always." She did. She frequently smelled bad, though, what with all the sweating and the excess methane production that results from relentless vegetable-eating. Nobody thinks about the poots when they see pictures of celery-thin Hollywood stars.

"Oh, you're sweet, but I could swear this tennis skirt is tight in the waistband. It must have been that half avocado I ate yesterday. I have no willpower."

Please. She wore hand-me-downs from her own eleven-year-old daughter. Idly I wondered if I had enough strength in my whole-avocado-powered muscles to snap her sticklike arm in half. Never mind. I needed her able to play tennis today.

"You look fab, though, Kira. Your hair is amazing! I love it blonde! It absolutely lights up your face. And I could swear you've lost some weight!"

Damn right. I'd stopped eating three days ago, right after I'd seen Laura Leigh Turner's perfect little figure on Facebook. I also had my colorist take me to a beautiful multitone Jennifer Aniston blonde, which did look pretty fabulous, though Miles had hated it. I'd dressed to kill today in my tightest V-neck athletic shirt and short shorts, which made my legs look a mile long. Nothing about my appearance was less than stupendous.

Nicole and I went to our court and began volleying as a warm-up. A pair of young women played on the court to my left. I spared their dewy skin one envious glance before returning to my mission. Only two courts lay to my right, and the one next to us was empty. Within ten minutes, all my chess pieces were in the right spots.

Judge Turner and another man arrived to play tennis on the court to my right.

God bless Nicole. She had nothing but air between her ears, but she knew everyone. "Chris! And Perry! It's been ages! Beautiful day for tennis, right?"

The men walked over to her, as did I, not willing to miss this introduction. Judge Turner's companion was short and bald. And Black. Hmm. I thought about Tattoo Girl in the jail. Judge Turner did indeed look like a judge who might be willing to stick it to a racist to prove he wasn't one. I knew a couple of possible racists I might be able to toss into his path. One particularly convenient one, as a matter of fact.

The judge was one of those guys who got better-looking every year. His dark hair sparkled with silver glints. The lines around his eyes only gave him more texture. No wonder Laura Leigh protected her figure the way she did.

I knew my own worth, however. I gave him the brilliant smile that had slayed legions of frat boys and dozens of my friends' Viagra-popping husbands. It worked on the judge, as it always did.

"This is my friend Kira," Nicole said. "This is Chris Turner and Perry Buffington. Old friends."

"Nice to meet you, Kira," the judge said, accepting my offered hand and lingering appreciatively. My first name clearly meant nothing to him. Even if he'd already opened my file, he'd have no reason to expect to find a felony defendant at his country club.

I gave his hand the slightest of pressure and smiled in the way I'd practiced to minimize my crow's-feet. "Nice to meet you, too. It's a perfect day to be outside—the scenery is lovely today," I said, making the meaning unmistakable.

The judge's eyes widened, and he grinned. Laura Leigh would be disappointed: no moral outrage there. Old Chris Turner liked the ladies as much as any other man. I shifted my hip enough to draw his attention to my practically perfect backside and the long leg beneath it. That worked, too. He took a long, slow gander at the goods.

God. Men were sheep. Yes, all men.

As if to prove it, Perry also took my hand, and we exchanged pleasantries. Perry, a restaurateur, had apparently gone to high school with the judge, where they'd been on the tennis team together. Though no doubt a lovely person, Perry wouldn't be determining the color of my wardrobe for the foreseeable future. *When hunting big game, don't waste ammunition on small birds,* my daddy used to say. I turned back to the judge.

"Well, gentlemen, we should let you get to your game. Nicole?"

Now came the hard part. I'd have to play a decent game of tennis in the heat of August knowing my ass had an audience, while remaining wholesomely attractive and not sweating too much. The waterproof makeup I'd bought yesterday better work. Nicole wasn't a pushover, despite her pencil shape.

Forty minutes later, I'd kept the judge's eyes on me by "missing" Nicole's shots toward the men's side of the court. I scurried over at least three times and let him get a good look at my toned backside as I bent to retrieve the balls from the ground. Through it all, I succeeded in remaining fuckable through judicious use of a face towel that reassured me my makeup wasn't running down my face. Time for the exit: tennis tended to sour once women passed the point of cute dresses and moved on to red faces and sweaty hair clinging to the neck. We gathered our things. The men paused in their much more athletic game to say goodbye.

"Leaving so soon?" Perry asked.

"Yes, I've got another engagement across town," I said. Leave them wanting more. Always leave them hanging.

"Too bad. We're about done here. Are you sure we couldn't interest you ladies in lunch?" The judge gestured at the clubhouse, where I knew for a fact the food all came from the same frozen-food company that provided Finn's school lunches.

"Kira? Are you sure you can't?" Nicole asked, though she had no interest in either man and God knew she never ate.

"No, I must go, but another time I'd absolutely adore it," I said, fluffing my hair and leaning forward to center the glowing girls. "Do you play every weekend?"

"We do," the judge said, sweat dampening the line between his pectorals.

I could swear he'd inched closer somehow. Smooth, Honorable Chris. Smooth. I gave him my most attractive smile and peered up at him through my eyelashes. "Wonderful. I'm looking forward to getting to know you better. It's so nice to meet new friends."

"Next week it is, then." He did that thing men do where they lower their voices beyond their natural pitch. Gratuitous oversell of the package—you could set your watch by it.

I slung my towel around my neck and walked away, knowing his eyes were still glued to my ass. I had no intention of being here next week. He'd never do anything untoward—he was the monogamous sort, but he still had eyes. He'd look for me. He would remember me. I'd practically sprayed hungry-cougar pheromones directly down the front of his shorts, then yanked away his lollipop right when his mouth started watering.

More importantly, I'd succeeded in making sure his first impression of me was not in a courtroom at the defense table wearing a dowdy suit. In the locker room, I admired my glistening cleavage once again. Take that, Laura Leigh.

And take that, little Allison, tiresome rule follower. Some rules are older than the legal system, and I knew all those rules like the back of my still-unfreckled hand.

Men had run the world for centuries, but their sexual desires would forever be their Achilles' heel. A clever woman didn't even need to gratify them—all you had to do was hand them just a little hope and you could walk away with your only slightly sweaty tits still covered and everything you came for in the palm of your hand.

CHAPTER FOURTEEN

ALLISON

The first cooling breezes of September marked six years for me at the MacDonald Group. I should have been well past the part of being a law firm associate whose role included carrying Dan MacDonald's briefcase.

I wasn't.

He'd checked my calendar for court yesterday, discovered I had a "free" morning, and ordered me to assist him as he defended a bank manager accused of embezzling. I could "keep track of the math," he said. I'd spent three hours frantically sorting, adding, and re-adding Dan's poorly organized trial exhibits.

The trial had ended with an acquittal. Afterward, Dan dragged me back to the judge's chambers to do his customary post-trial victory schmooze. He liked to bask in the praise, and he liked for me to see him basking in the praise, even when most of the praise originated from him.

Judge Turner had always been friendly to me in a formal kind of way. He and Dan ate lunch together on occasion. Dan was a huge believer in currying favor with the judge. As a woman, nothing resembling currying would be possible for me: not when the judge was a married man and I was single. For Dan, it meant camaraderie and even mentorship. For me, it would be straight-up impropriety.

Dan dived right in, greeting the judge with an outstretched hand. "That could've been a tough one, but the commonwealth gave it to the Ling girl to handle. Valerie must not have cared much about this one." He said all that with the perfect mix of humility, offensiveness, and braggadocio. Tiffany Ling was two years out of law school and the most junior of the commonwealth's attorneys. She'd done a good job, but her main investigator had been unavailable to testify. It had dented her case.

"Oh, now, Dan," Judge Turner said, winking at me. "You had a secret weapon with you. That must have been all the difference. Right, Ms. Barton?" He smiled in my direction. I thought there might have been a bit of sympathy there. Dan was pretty transparent.

"Oh ho!" Dan said, catching on quick. The door to the judge's chambers buzzed, and his assistant spoke to someone in the antechamber. Dan ignored it. "Yep, little Allison here's learning a lot. She's almost ready to graduate to the big leagues. Just last week I saw her make a clever argument in a DUI case."

Always the tone of surprise. The familiar low-grade irritation ate a bit more of my stomach lining, but I could kiss my legal career goodbye if I lost my temper in front of a judge. The judge's genuine smile grew pained and understanding. Though I knew the magnitude of Dan's legal reputation depended almost entirely upon him chopping everyone else's down to size, I was so tired of being his foil. His cute little mascot. The small insignificant thing that made him look bigger. Much longer, and I'd start to believe it myself.

Someone cleared his throat behind me.

Emmett, paper in hand. He'd heard all the "little Allison" stuff. He greeted me and Dan by name, carefully giving nothing away. "Judge, this is the order in the Jernigan matter from yesterday. I happened to catch Mike in the hall to get his signature."

"Thanks, Emmett." Judge Turner took the order, flipped the pages, signed it, and handed it back to Emmett to take it down to the clerk for filing. "Well, Dan, Allison. It's been a pleasure, but I've got a pile of case law to read before this afternoon."

Dan went out after checking to make sure I still had all the case files in his two huge litigation briefcases. He carried a slim file and a yellow notepad, enough to look the part of a busy lawyer as he crossed the courthouse square back to his office. My load weighed at least forty pounds.

Emmett trailed me silently until I made it to the relative privacy of the stairwell. "Here. Let me get those. I can carry them back for you."

I met his eyes, irrationally annoyed he'd seen me in my natural humiliated state. "Don't be ridiculous. You know you can't be seen carrying briefcases for me. And besides, if I can't do better than a 'clever argument in a DUI case,' clearly I haven't carried enough briefcases. These could really help."

"Don't say that, Allie. You're way better than that. He's a dick."

"I know."

"You've got to get out of there."

"I know that, too. And we both know the only way I can."

We stared at each other a second too long before I turned to flee.

❧

Starting kindergarten only increased Libby's desire for the piano lessons I couldn't afford ("In music class Mr. Kim lets me play 'Joy to the World'!"). She now had open disdain for sports balls, but I found myself at the vast fields owned by the Lynchburg Area United Soccer League on an unusually chilly morning at the end of September anyway. We had over a month to go before trial, but I still had important witnesses to interview. The wind whipped across the expanse of grass. Several parents waited in cars, clutching travel mugs. I stopped to ask directions of a man wrestling four folding chairs and a massive tent out of the back of a Subaru.

"Brandi Crane? I don't know her," he said, breathing a bit hard.

"Griffin Crane's mom? Do you know him? He's about eleven."

"Oh yeah," the soccer dad said, scratching his neck. "Everybody knows Griffin. He's one of the best kids we got. Coach Layne's got him, up at field eight. I expect his mom's up there. She usually is. Didn't remember the name of the mom."

"Oh. Thanks. So he's pretty good? Her son?"

"Yeah. Nimble as anything. He's easily one of the top two or three in that age group. My daughter used to play with him back when they did coed recreation. He could play the whole field all by himself."

"Is one of the other talented kids Aidan Peerman?"

"Yup. That's the one. Might be even better than the Crane kid. The Peerman boy doesn't play until the afternoon. Are you a scout?"

"Not a soccer scout. Thanks for your help. Field eight is over there?"

He nodded, an expression of faint disappointment at the lack of soccer clout I'd turned out to have, and I drove over to the far field. A fine drizzle had started. Wonderful.

At field eight, two young men who must be coaches unloaded soccer balls from a string bag and checked the net at one end. Three boys, at the awkward stage where their cleat-clad feet were as long as their calves, kicked a soccer ball to each other in warm-up.

At the sidelines, the first parents had set up chairs and rain covers and coolers, which to me seemed a bit much for an hour-long soccer game for eleven-year-olds, but who was I to say? One strawberry-blonde mother had established a fiefdom with three chairs, a cooler full of water bottles and Gatorade, a blanket, a sun shade, and a foam soccer ball she could wave at key moments.

Oh God. Maybe piano lessons for Libby were the cheaper option after all. I spared a moment contemplating a second job folding stock at Target to pay for all this paraphernalia. I tapped the woman on the shoulder.

"Excuse me. Do you know Brandi Crane?"

She stood up, vibrating with energy like a firecracker. "I expect so. I am Brandi Crane."

I stuck out my hand to her. She gave me a firm handshake. She was pretty, in an outdoorsy, windblown way. If she'd been born poor as Kira had said, it didn't show now. "I'm Allison Barton, and I'm investigating the case of Kira Grant and the poisoning of Summer Peerman. Do you have a few minutes to talk?"

She glanced at the field, assessing the progress. Only five boys had arrived so far. She brushed back a wisp of hair slipping from beneath a ball cap that bore the soccer organization's logo and gestured at a folding chair. "You're her lawyer, right? Word gets around, you know. That was slick, how you tried to sound all official. 'Investigating.' Ha. I'll talk to you, until the game starts. I never miss a minute of Griff's games. Have a seat."

"I hear he's pretty good," I said, settling into the chair. "Very good, actually. A man up at field four had heard of him."

"That right?" Brandi's face broke into a smile, showing off perfect white teeth. "Don't guess you know who it was?"

"No, I'm sorry, I don't. Which one is Griffin?"

Brandi pointed at the field, where a tall boy with dark hair did some kind of athletic hopping dance over and around his ball. It would rival anything at a *Riverdance* production. "Number twelve. That's Griff."

"Is Aidan Peerman on his team this season?"

"No." Brandi stiffened and let out a sniff. "Thank the Lord for small miracles."

To see her reaction, I pressed a bit. "Not a fan?"

"Humph. He's a right dirty player. He's roughed up Griff more than once, but they never call him on it. Gets whatever he wants from the coaches. They turn a blind eye to all of it."

Okay. The vibe from Brandi read as energetic hostility. An interesting mix. Possibly a dangerous one. I would not want to get between this mother and her cub. We'd come back to that topic, but first I had to gain her trust.

"You must be the team mom. This is quite the setup," I said, looking around at her blue-and-gold team color–coordinated cooler and chairs.

"No, but I do what I can. I'm just here to support the team. Some of these parents get a little nuts on the sidelines. Caleb Franklin's dad lost it last Wednesday when the ref didn't call the foul when Caleb had his leg cut up by some kid from Harrisonburg."

"Do you ever lose it?"

She narrowed her faded green eyes. "Oh, let me guess. You've been talking to Summer Peerman. She said I fussed at her kid, I bet. Well, it's not like that. She got in my face."

"Would you mind telling me about it?"

"Ha! Weren't nothing big. She cooked something up with the coach, got Griffin benched for three whole games, and got her kid primo playing time in the Roanoke tournament. Then when Griff got back in, Aidan threw elbows at him. I separated them and then she mouthed off at me, that's all."

"One of those guys?" I asked, gesturing at the coaches.

"Naw. This is Layne. Russell, the one from last spring, moved to Roanoke. Suspicious, if you ask me."

"What else did you say to Summer Peerman that day?"

Brandi gripped the handle of the foam soccer ball. "Nothing. I didn't say nothing. I corrected my kid after he got out of line on the field. I didn't touch that cocky little thing of hers. She was the one did all the talking." She narrowed her eyes. "She got in my face and said stuff about my kids. All my kids, even Joelle, who's an honor student. Uppity bitch. Acted like she knew they were going to jail. Acted like she was going to have them taken away from me, and you know she knows all those people up at the court. She meant it. What kind of bitch threatens kids with jail?"

"Right." Though Summer had freely admitted to crossing a line with that comment, there was a coded word in Brandi's diatribe that made me uncomfortable. I bit my lip, glancing at her son out on the field. He kicked a ball into the net over the practice goalie's head.

"Yeah. I was the bigger person, though. I didn't hit her. A little while after she said that hateful stuff about my kids, I went on Facebook and said a few things about unethical behavior of some state employees that ought to get fired for threatening people, but I didn't mention her by name."

Brandi had hit her kid in front of his coach and—at least judging from today's crowd—thirty parents, called another child a foul name, and tried in a passive-aggressive way to get Summer fired. I swallowed my horror. "What, exactly, did you put on Facebook?"

"If you want the whole ugly story, talk to your client. Talk to Kira Grant."

Stunned, I stumbled over my own tongue. "K-Kira?" Oh God, this was the first I'd heard that Kira had been in any way involved in the Summer-Brandi soccer incident. And adding Facebook to the mix couldn't possibly be good.

"Yeah, Kira. Within three days of my Facebook post, she got on there, posting about child abusers, crying about her concern for the safety of our community's children because she'd seen a post that 'confused the serious physical abuse of children with good parenting.' Got in a vague line about racists, all slick-like, as if I said a durn thing about Summer or Aidan being Black. And then she quoted me. Here. I still got the screenshots. One hundred and fifty-seven durn comments on her post, all of them claiming they never so much as swatted their kids on the butt or got switched as kids, when I went to school with half of 'em and I saw the bruises myself, and then someone identifying me as the person who posted the first thing. And a good fifty of them were parents at the elementary school. People I know."

She pulled out her phone and swiped pictures until she found what she wanted. "Here." Kira's post, dated less than a month before the poisoning, read as advertised.

> Lately I worry so much about raising my sweet children in a world so full of violence, hate, and poor judgment. A dear friend of mine told me that even now, in the last two weeks, she was subjected to a racist attack because of the color of her skin. Just this week, I saw a post here from someone I know in real life that confused serious physical abuse of children with good parenting. It said, "Let's be real—my mama used to make me go back for a second switch if the first one wasn't thick as her thumb. A swat isn't abuse and Social Services needs to stay out of our homes and let us make decisions for our own kids." The woman in question was seen abusing her child at an athletic field this spring. The days of switches and bruising are over. I'm concerned for the safety of all the children in our community if attitudes don't change quickly. Let's do better.

For two seconds, I tried to imagine Kira having the necessary idealism and sincerity to write such a post. I didn't buy her extreme concern for the children, remembering Kira's reaction to Summer's suggestion that she get help for Fiona. From the look on Brandi's face, she didn't buy it, either. I swiped farther. Brandi had taken screenshots of the comments as well. Most—though not all; Brandi had a handful of supporters—had bought it and piled on, ready to prove their own virtue through the difficult task of typing "Agree" and attaching enough exclamation points to show they really meant it.

I handed back the phone, feeling nausea flare in my stomach. I did not like finding out things about my client from hostile witnesses. It put me at a disadvantage.

"You see, right? Summer Peerman started it. Got in my face and tried to use her job to threaten taking away my kids. I'm the injured party. And then when I did a little venting on Facebook, she went and got with her buddy Kira to call me a child abuser. They planned it together to take me down. You know how many friends Kira has on Facebook? I'll tell you. Three thousand six hundred and twenty-two at the time she wrote that bullshit."

"That is a lot of Facebook friends," I said weakly. Kira had not mentioned this to me, though I doubted she spared a lot of attention for whether she hurt the feelings of people she considered beneath her. Brandi had clearly been stewing for months. "Did this Facebook deal affect you at all?"

"You kidding? Durn right it did. My pastor stopped me the next Sunday and asked if I needed help with my kids. My husband's coworker, busybody bitch, told him he needed to check behind me. My daughter Joelle, my second oldest, good girl. Straight As and Bs up at the high school. She's a senior now. Joelle had a boyfriend last spring, nice boy, a year older. He's got a real good job now, but he's got one of them social justice crazies for a mama. Him and Joelle were pretty serious, and I think he mighta married her when she graduates, but Kira's Facebook post caught his mama's eye and she put a stop to it. Told the boy he couldn't see Jo anymore because she comes from trash, is what she said. He listened to her and broke up with Jo. She's a mess now. Cried half the summer. Grades are slipping down to Bs and Cs already. She'd have been set for life if Kira hadn't posted that crap."

"I see." Brandi clearly didn't think it was possible the boy might have broken up with her daughter for any other reason.

"And also, I got a lot of trolls online. Hateful stuff. You wouldn't believe how much hate is out there."

"I absolutely would," I said with some relief, happy to contribute something that wasn't a hedge. "Well, I don't want to take much more of your time, Ms. Crane." Both teams had arrived at the field and were warming up in unison. A game appeared likely to break out any second. "You made the smoothies for the graduation party?"

"Yes, I did, and I already told the sheriff I didn't put any durn poison in them. Why in the world would I do that? My child was there. His friends were all right there. I was mostly in the kitchen, getting food ready, except for when I was talking to Griff or his friends. I wasn't working the refreshment table. And you can check. The deputies already came and did all kind of swabbing of my kitchen. They didn't find a thing. Not a drop of wolfsbane in my house."

"You know what aconite is?"

"Yeah. Wolfsbane. Monkshood. That stuff. Keeps the deer away."

"Are you a gardener?"

"You mean like Kira? Hardly. Those society ladies in that garden club of hers would stroke out and die if I showed up at one of their meetings after I grew up in Hale's Bottom. You gotta be kidding me. No, I worked for a landscaper when I was a kid. My daddy worked a crew. In the summers in high school, I wanted to work at Hardee's with my friends, but Daddy made me work with him. I remember the plants. Had to wear gloves to touch that stuff. Nowadays, I stick with trees and cutting the grass in the summer. I don't mess with all that picky flower stuff anymore."

She knew her flowers. She'd made the smoothies. She'd been at the event. And she hated both Summer and Kira. She had the means and opportunity she shared with Kira, and the motive Kira lacked.

"How did you feel when Aidan got the spot on the travel team over Griffin?" As I'd done with Kira, I asked my question and watched the reaction. I wasn't disappointed. Ugly emotion rendered her speechless for a second, but she got control back.

"I didn't like it much," she bit off, anger choking her voice.

"Did you threaten Summer Peerman? Tell her to enjoy it while she could?"

It took a few seconds for her to be able to speak. "I'm not talking to you anymore. That's enough."

I'd found reasonable doubt. Relief replaced the unease brought on by the unexpected Facebook bombshell. No need to prolong this interview. "All right, thank you, Ms. Crane. I appreciate your time. Good luck to your son today." I gestured out at the field, where the teams had gotten into formation for the kickoff. Or whatever they called it in soccer.

She gave me a level stare. "I know what you're doing, you know. You're going to go running off, make notes about how I know my poison flowers, how I fought with Summer, how I hate Kira, and you're going to make it look like I did it so you can get that bitch off. Well, I hope you can sleep at night, because I didn't do it. You see that boy out there? He's my baby. My biggest fear in the whole world is I'll die before I'm done raising him, and he needs me. All my kids need me. You think I'd risk jail, risk getting stuck off in prison, away from my kids, just to stick it to Summer Peerman or Kira Grant? Think again. They ain't important enough to me. Nothing is as important to me as my kids."

With that, she turned away from me, her gaze fixed on her child with a concentration so total and adoring it took my breath away.

CHAPTER FIFTEEN

KIRA

The dental practice of Miles Grant & Associates, DDS, sat in a dingy building in Lynchburg. I'd been after him for years to move to a better location, but Miles had gone to school with the guy whose dad owned the building. With Miles, a lifetime of acquaintance with someone equated to a lifetime of obligation.

I yanked the transmission into park and got the kids and their backpacks out of the car. They moved like turtles until I grabbed both their hands and dragged them behind me as I headed in.

"Good afternoon, Sandy," I sang through my gritted-teeth smile. As usual, Sandy wore her hygienist's coat over a tight V-neck sweater that showed off her tits—so huge and crammed together that Miles could probably stick his wandering joystick down in there and get his jollies just as easily as he could in her other orifices. Trust Sandy to make options available! She had a new hairstyle—even more like mine than before, down to the long bang in front sweeping off to the side. Did Miles show her pictures? God.

Well, I could exact momentary revenge, at least. "Gosh, Sandy, I so hate to do this to you, but my regular sitter is busy and I have an appointment. I can't take the kids. You don't mind watching them for a bit until Miles is finished up, do you?"

"Well, actually, Mrs. Grant, I have—"

Miles came around the corner. I had to admit it—he was good. He didn't even glance Sandy's way. "Hey, hon. What's up?"

"Sandy here offered to keep an eye on Finn and Fiona until you're done. Such a sweet thing to do. I have to go see Allison this afternoon. A checkup," I said, using code for him on the off chance he hadn't told this adulterous tooth scraper that his wife might soon safely be tucked away as a guest of the state correctional system. I wondered how she'd like watching the kids full-time if I went to prison.

Miles and Sandy exchanged looks.

"Hon, I've got one more filling to do this afternoon, and Sandy has a couple more cleanings." An older gentleman in the waiting room glanced between Miles and the kids apprehensively, as if imagining Miles drilling his molars with Fiona clinging to his leg. "I don't know if there's anyone who can—"

"Oh, I'm sure they'll be fine. Isn't Martha doing books in the back? Let them watch a video on your computer. Or do their homework. That would be even better. I've got to go or I'll be late. See you for dinner. Why don't you pick up something at the Thai restaurant?"

"Mommy! I don't like that spicy food! I want McDonald's!" Fiona screwed up her face as if I'd suggested she eat a live octopus.

Fine. I made a note to stop by Fresh Market for sushi for myself. Miles would give in and take them to McDonald's.

"Kira, I can't . . . You should have called. We're—"

"Gotta go!" I breezed out the door, leaving Fiona midwhine and Finn stony-faced after having been deprived of his iPhone after I picked them up from school. That's right, Miles and Sandy. Entertain them now that they're gameless. Appreciate my life for two hours. It won't even compare.

I promise you.

ॐ

Allison's office waiting room was as cheerless as usual. Her secretary, the heavyset woman who badly needed to bring her hairstyle into the twenty-first century, focused on her computer screen. I'd been waiting twenty minutes, and gleeful thoughts of Fiona terrorizing Miles's office and breaking one of Sandy's fingernails had only amused me for half of them. I glanced around. The secretary had lined her shelf with family pictures. Several featured a teenage boy in a football uniform.

"Is that your son?" I asked. The mere mention of him melted her. She sat back from the computer, pride glowing from every pore.

"Yes. That's Trevor." She touched the frame as if he were actually in it.

"He plays football?"

"Oh yes. He's played since elementary school." No doubt. She'd decorated her entire work area with Virginia Tech paraphernalia and whatever the high school mascot was.

"Don't you worry about CTE? You know, the brain damage thing where the professional players all commit suicide? I'd be terrified to let my son play football."

"Oh." She blanched. "Well, he . . . he never had a concussion, and . . ."

"You can't be too careful these days, can you?" I smiled at her. I'd probably let my courtesies slip a bit, but this whole football injury thing seemed like a no-brainer to me. I didn't understand how any mother who loved a child could allow it. "He's such a nice-looking young man."

Allison cleared her throat from her doorway. She wore a thunderous expression. She'd heard me. "Are you ready?"

I never do meek. I gave her a brilliant smile and gathered my things.

Allison took a minute or so to speak once she'd settled behind her desk. "I don't know what all was going on out there, Kira, but I won't tolerate people being rude to Maureen. Are we understood?"

Right. What on earth would she do to stop me? She could hardly bar me from entering the building. If she thought I'd embarked on some sort of preconceived plan to be rude to a person whose name I'd already forgotten, she'd far overestimated my interest in people of no importance to me. I had no intention of being rude to her secretary again, unless I happened to say something rude.

"Fine," I said, because we were wasting time, and the trial was getting closer every day. "Tell me about what you've discovered."

She twirled a pen in her fingers, her eyes still narrowed a bit. She'd give herself crow's-feet if she kept on like that.

"Right. I've gotten a pretty good handle on Tammy and Summer and Brandi, and I think I know how to use them as witnesses. I've got a call in to Ruthanne, the last of the women who were working that graduation party, but we haven't met yet. She says she's very busy with the PTA."

I would have snorted, except I don't snort. In public. "She has time for you. I know. I was the president before her. She has the one child, who is in school all day long now, and even if she spent three hours a day on PTA matters, she'd have time. She's avoiding you. Keep pressing."

I'd like to go jerk a knot into the cutesy printed dress hem of that sniveling coward. I'd always made PTA seem time-consuming to Miles so I'd have an excuse to justify hiring the woman to clean our house, but honestly. Seven or eight hours a week, max.

"Sure. Okay, let's recap where we are. Well, Tammy had some major issues with Summer. She told me all about Summer investigating her parenting, and how a finding of parental neglect two years ago affected her employment. She blames Summer for the things that are wrong in her life. It's not a lot, but it's a slight motive."

It was amazing how people's definitions of *slight motive* could vary. Tammy wasn't dumb. I knew plenty about her I'd never tell, starting with the fact she dialed her redneck up to eleven every time it suited her. I filed Tammy away for now; I had my reasons to direct this whole deal down another road. "And Brandi?"

"We might have something with Brandi. Brandi and Summer have issues with each other. Both told me about the incident at the soccer field, and how Brandi cursed at Aidan and hit Griffin, and how Summer mentioned her job at Social Services and implied Brandi's children were going to jail. Brandi stopped talking after I asked her if she'd threatened Summer. I can't prove she did it, but she looks a lot more likely than you."

"Good."

How it was possible for a woman as young as Allison to wear the exact disapproving expression of my elderly sorority house mother I'll never know, but she managed it. "I hadn't heard about the Facebook thing before, though. You want to tell me about that?"

Though I knew full well which Facebook thing, I made the "tell me more" face.

"You know, where you wrote a post about your worry at other people 'confusing serious physical abuse with parenting' or whatever? That one?"

Was she mocking me? Was she implying I didn't really care about child abuse? Her face gave nothing away. "Oh! Are you talking about that little thing with Brandi's post? Where she ranted about switching kids with sticks thicker than her thumb?"

"Yeah. That, and your response where you quote her post, don't mention her name, and add a vague sentence implying she was also a racist. Brandi showed it to me."

"There's no way anyone could be certain the sentence about the racist and the sentence about the child abuser referred to the same person."

"Oh, I saw that. You were careful. But they did refer to the same person, didn't they?"

I considered my words. "How long did you talk to Brandi?"

"I'd say about fifteen or twenty minutes all told."

"Was it enough time to get a sense of her?"

Allison squirmed a bit in her classic good-girl inability to criticize someone. "Well . . ."

"Did she tell you the truth about why she hates Summer and Aidan? Did she tell you it's because they're Black and she doesn't think her precious child should have to compete with a Black kid?"

"She didn't say that, no." Allison shifted. Maybe Brandi hadn't come right out and ranted about affirmative action—Brandi had a certain low cunning—but Allison's queasy expression made clear she'd gotten close enough.

Perfect. Time to cut the shit. "Over the year I've known her, I've learned Brandi has some problematic views on minorities. If she were asked in a lie detector test, I expect we'd find she honestly thinks people of color are not her equals, or that they're getting ahead because they're given advantages."

"Maybe. You could be right. She didn't go that far when I talked to her. But I'm not sure it matters—there's no dispute she hit her child in front of Summer and Summer got angry and made threats. That's enough to create some reasonable doubt that you were the poisoner when you don't have a clear motive. For what it's worth, Summer didn't think the soccer field incident had anything to do with race."

"Oh please. Were you born yesterday? Of course Summer would say that to you. You're a white woman she doesn't know. She probably worries you'll discredit everything she says if she even hinted someone was a racist. I think the real reason Brandi went off is she couldn't stand her son being bested on the soccer field by a Black boy."

That was a diplomatic but yet enlightened way to put it. Sometimes I impressed myself with my own power over words.

Allison's expression shifted between consternation, confusion, worry, and guilt. "Brandi did hint that Aidan had advantages."

"See!" Exultation fizzed through my veins. I had a racist—or close enough—that I could offer up as red meat to distract the legal system while I got safely away. "You know Aidan got the spot on the travel team and Griffin didn't. Which, by the way, had nothing to do with race. Aidan is better at soccer than Griffin. Brandi has no resources to process that idea, so she'd rather believe her child is a victim of affirmative action. She had motive, and opportunity, too, because she made the drinks. It's perfect!"

Because I'd always been scrupulously honest with myself, I checked my privilege. Yes, it was still there. Mentally, I patted it like you do when you make sure you still have your purse. I had all the privilege and had no plans to give any of it up, especially not now when it might help me avoid prison. I was white, rich by birth as well as by marriage, educated, intelligent, loved, healthy, and straight. Putting Brandi effectively on trial as my foil would require a public takedown of another person with less privilege than I had. Brandi was uneducated and born poor, after all. I probably should feel bad about that, but I didn't. She was also white, healthy, and straight and almost certainly a racist, which meant nobody would care about her underprivileged childhood. She'd be perfect.

Besides, nobody had charged Brandi with attempted murder. I was the one in legal jeopardy. I had to do whatever it took to get this nonsense to go away. To me this was as simple and obvious as the sun on a clear day.

Allison, the attack dog I'd hired, appeared a bit seasick. More like a puppy who'd eaten too much grass.

"What's the matter?" I asked.

"I don't love painting her as racist as well as hateful," she said carefully. How I'd love to knock her off her careful little perch. "I don't think we need to. Brandi has more known motive to hurt Summer than you do, given the soccer dustup and the travel team spot and the threat. Maybe she even has a motive to frame you after the Facebook thing, but I don't feel comfortable slinging around charges of racism as a tactic to gain an advantage for you, of all people. Racism is a serious thing. Calling someone a racist isn't a handy little grenade privileged white people should throw at each other like some kind of smoke-bomb diversion."

"Well, isn't that high-minded of you," I said, wanting to hit her sanctimonious face. "It is exactly the kind of grenade I'd like to throw, because it isn't a diversion! Brandi *is* a racist, and calling her one takes attention off me. Which, I'll remind you, is your *job*."

Allison's face was a blank mask now. "Also, as I said, I know you see it on TV all the time, but I can't prove Brandi poisoned Summer. Tammy could have done it, or Ruthanne, or a random stranger whose kids Summer removed. All I can do is point out their motives and opportunity. There's no hard evidence any of them did it."

"There's no evidence I did it, either," I said, more than a tad concerned I had to tell her this.

"I know that. Of course there isn't, but our position is that it's wrong to accuse you of it without any evidence. That's essentially what my argument will boil down to. You're suggesting our strategy would be to argue that not only did Brandi hate Summer and have obvious mother bear–type reasons to try to kill her, but also that she's a secret racist and racial animus on her part caused her to poison a Black woman and then frame the most convenient person standing by?"

"Yes!" I said, barely refraining from adding the "duh!"

Allison shook her head, still resisting. "You've been complaining the detective lied and made up stuff. If we argue Brandi is a racist and that's her motive, we could be making stuff up to bolster our case just like Lucado. If we do that, how are we any different than the commonwealth? How are we better?"

Um, *better*? Did she have a head injury? I'd been pretty clear. Fire with fire. "Yes. That is what I'm suggesting. And we don't have to be better—where is that in the rules? If they want to fight me in the dirt, I'm prepared to get muddy. We *do* know she's a racist. It's not a secret. You should have heard her mocking Linh Nguyen's accent at an event last year. The victim is Black. All the suspects, including me, are white. Race is part of this case. It's already there."

Surely she wouldn't make me point out she could be seen as failing to "zealously represent" me, which Google said all attorneys are required to do under their ethics vows. I did another internal eye roll at the thought of attorneys having ethics.

Though, looking at Allison hesitating, maybe I'd found the one attorney in Virginia who did. That would be spectacularly unfortunate. I had to admit, it was a bit concerning that my attorney seemed to think she'd been hired to defend me *and* meet some idealistic moral high bar. Just the first part, thanks.

"Let's wait a minute, Kira. I think we should stick with pointing out their lack of evidence and that there were others who could have done it. The prosecution has to prove their case. I think what they have falls short. All they have for motive for you is a four-year-old argument over school, and a brief break in your friendship with Summer shortly before the party."

Figured. She might not be an attack dog—more like those annoying little yappy dogs that are good at digging up bones. "Oh, that."

"Yes, that. The one where you stopped speaking to Summer because she suggested Fiona might be dyslexic."

"She's not dyslexic." Dammit. I did not want this ridiculous false idea getting around the community. Fiona would not be tarred with the special education brush.

"It doesn't matter if she is or not. What matters is you and Summer fought right before the party."

"I got mad because she interfered, took a week to calm myself, and then we made up. No big deal."

"Lucado didn't know about that argument when he testified at the preliminary, which means you didn't tell him. Which is interesting, even to me."

She gave me the stink eye, which annoyed me. "I forgot about it."

She didn't look impressed. "The commonwealth knows about it now—from Summer. I checked. They'll try to make it a big deal, but in my view, it still falls way short of a motive for murder. I might even be able to get the case dismissed without putting any defense witnesses on at all."

"Are you kidding me? You want to sit there and poke your little thumbtack holes into their witnesses? No. I've seen those witnesses. You do realize that detective could get up there and tell the judge I told him I hate Summer and decided to poison her because she didn't send me a Christmas card, right? He will say anything to get a conviction—this isn't the time to apply for the Nobel Peace Prize. We have to have a defense."

"I'm only talking out loud. Of course we'll have a defense."

"And Brandi the racist is it."

Allison bit her lip, still struggling.

Oh good God. "Here's what I think is going on," I said, knowing exactly the magic words to get her back in line. "Maybe you agree with Brandi. Maybe you think making fun of Vietnamese accents and ranting about how affirmative action is harming little white soccer players is just fine. Maybe you're one of those who thinks being *called* a racist is worse than *being* a racist."

Bingo. Her eyes widened in horror. She didn't answer me. She did that avoiding thing I hated where she wrote "notes" so she could think about her answer.

I lost patience. She'd get there, but I didn't want to wait. Time for the nuclear option. I did pay the bills around here. I stood up and went to the door, leaning out to where the football-worshipping secretary typed. "Oh, hello there! Would you buzz Dan and ask him to come in here as a special favor to me?" I turned to glare at Allison, my message to her communicated loud and clear. "Allison would appreciate it, too."

"Sure," the woman said. She picked up the phone. "He said he's got a minute and will be right over."

I sat with the debutante's grace I'd practiced for years, leaving the chair closest to the door for Dan. Allison's lips made a thin line. I held in a giggle.

It didn't take long, and the silence between me and Allison didn't bother me at all.

Dan and Miles's younger brother had known each other at the same private high school in Lynchburg where the judge sent his sons. The alumni recognized each other everywhere they went. I'd never met him before, but I'd heard Dan was male-model handsome and a predator, and I was not disappointed.

"The beautiful and clever Kira Grant!" he boomed, filling up the room with his charisma. I stood. Allison didn't. "Well, aren't you lovely? Miles has an unerring eye for the best of women."

Didn't he, though.

Dan reached for my hands, pulling me uncomfortably close. I did my professional simper and acceptance of the compliment, all the while waiting for him to let go of my hands. For an attractive man, his hands were sweaty, and the sweat began working into my palms like lotion. Fortunately, when I pulled, they slid loose with a tiny but audible "slurp." I wiped them discreetly on the cheap upholstery of Allison's office chair.

"Dan, Allison and I were talking about defense strategies for my case. I know you must be familiar with it." I filled him in on my theories about Brandi and her usefulness as a straw man. Allison sat silent, her eyes hard.

"Well, I'd say that sounds great! That's a perfect defense."

"Allison says she'd prefer not to use the race angle."

He swung her way, all drama as if he were in front of a jury. To her credit, she stared back, unfazed. "Do what? You may as well toss your law degree in the trash if you pass up an opportunity like that. A case like that with a defendant that looks like this?"

Though it hardly surprised me when he sketched my shape in the air like an exaggerated Kardashian, I did feel a flash of irritation and a moment of pity for Allison. It wouldn't be easy biting your tongue around a pig like this.

"Pretty white lady defendant with a clean record, much-loved minority public-servant victim, poison at an elementary school, and an alternate white-trash suspect who whines about advantages? It's an absolute movie script. A gift. You'll go that way, and that's an order. Might get some national press in here in addition to the local. Case like that would bring in a lot of business for both of us."

"Dan, it's ugly. The Crane woman might well be a horrible person, and she has more motive than Kira, but I can't prove she did it. There's no physical evidence. I can't put her near the cup with the poison in it. Her kitchen was clean of aconite. Kira's the only one whose house had any trace."

I heard the skepticism, and I didn't much appreciate it. I stared at her, realizing something I hadn't up to this moment. "You think I'm guilty. That's it, isn't it? You don't care about whether there's evidence. You're protecting her! You can't bring yourself to take her down because you think I did it."

Allison's face was unreadable. Dan broke the silence with a loud guffaw.

"Hon," he said to Allison. "If you thought you could defend an attempted murder case without pinning the attempted murder on somebody else by whatever means necessary, you must have been living under a rock. Damn, anyone who's seen any TV at all knows that much, and you've got a damn law degree. Use your brain. Throwing someone under the bus who might be innocent is the name of the game. It's what the commonwealth does. It's what they did do, right here." He turned to me. "Right, sweetheart? Of course you didn't do it. You couldn't even conceive of it, could you?"

I had good control over myself and my emotions, but the times when I came the closest to slipping were when someone idiotic questioned my intelligence. Of course I could conceive of it. Anyone with any brains who's ever been wronged could at least *conceive* of it. I gave him a huge grateful-puppy smile and made myself pat his hand. I needed him to view me a certain way. "Of course I didn't put anything in the cup. And you're right as always, Dan. It would never have crossed my mind to poison Summer."

"See?" he asked, punching the air for emphasis. "She didn't do it. Likely the white trash soccer lady did. Even if she didn't, you've got to argue she could have. Women don't usually kill anyone outside their families, and the judge knows that. You're going to need a lot more motive for her than just having a spat and a couple of dumb threats. Go on in there and throw some pig's blood on her. You need her to be a racist, too. That's a motive. People can understand it. The press is rooting for you. For Kira. It's as close to a slam dunk as a criminal case comes."

Allison sat there like a belligerent kitten, gritting her teeth, looking stubborn as hell. The little bitch. Well, let's have a reminder of who's in charge here and what you have to lose. I knew how much she needed this case. And it would be fun for me, too. I never could resist a little fun.

Dan got up to go, thinking we were done. *Sit down, Pretty Boy. We aren't done.*

"Dan," I said, giving my eyelashes the tiniest flutter. "Allison seems to be having a really tough time embracing this defense. I'd absolutely hate the idea I'm making her uncomfortable. I'd like to transfer this case to you as lead counsel, if you're willing. You seem so much more . . . well, in tune with me. So understanding. Of my needs. Is that all right with you?"

Dan practically had an orgasm right there. "Absolutely! I think that's wise. I'd be honored, Kira. You'll have to excuse Allison. She's still learning. Takes years to learn effective trial strategy. Shall we repair to my office, discuss things? I might even have a glass of wine."

"Oh, I so wish I could," I said, my skin crawling. Was he envisioning me spreading my legs on his desk inside of half an hour? With his secretary typing outside? Ew. "Unfortunately, I've got to run. I'll come in tomorrow."

I stood and gave a crocodile grin to Allison, who sat there shell-shocked. She didn't move. Dan threw out about ten more compliments and moved in for some serious arm and hand fondling. Eventually I shook him off and he left.

I slung my purse over my arm and turned to Allison, still sitting there silent. "You understand I have to do what is best for me, I assume."

She nodded, on autopilot. "Good luck, then," she managed.

"Thank you." As if it were an afterthought, I said, "I'd noticed you and Mr. Amaro have some kind of little flirtation going. I guess you're free now to act on it. Consider it a gift from me." I stood in the door frame, aware that a frame always made me look willowy and tall. Allison's eyes widened. "Maybe some lawyer-lawyer sex might loosen the poker that's up your rear end. Can't hurt to give it a try."

I waggled my fingers at her and walked out, taking great pleasure in all the fiery wreckage I'd left behind.

CHAPTER SIXTEEN

ALLISON

I went home in a stupor, not even able to distract myself with Libby. Steve had her tonight. I stopped at the package liquor store and bought myself some rum.

She'd ditched me.

Kira had ditched me, and she'd implied I was more horrified by Brandi being called a racist than by Brandi being a racist. Unease made the potato chips I ate midafternoon turn to a greasy lump in my stomach. Surely it couldn't be that.

I got out of the car clutching my bottle, doing an honest search of the mental waterproof box where I tried to keep my ethics and personal decency dry. I fought a constant battle to keep them fresh as well, and I didn't always win—I could be as clueless a white lady as anyone else—but I'd never hesitated to call out racism before. This time, though, I had a problem with *Kira* wanting that defense, and *why* she wanted it. Kira didn't want to call Brandi out to right a societal wrong—I'd bet my mortgage that Kira didn't give a shit about ridding the world of racism—Kira wanted to use Brandi to shore up her own privilege.

I'd stood up to her and lost the best chance I'd ever had at forging a career of my own. I would be stuck carrying Dan's bags and taking his sloppy seconds forever, and when Maureen and I got old enough to lose whatever looks we had, Dan would toss us out on the street.

In my silent kitchen, I mixed up a rum and Coke—mostly rum, not much Coke—and tossed it straight back. My hand shook a bit mixing the second.

Maybe I should try teaching at a community college. Maybe it would be better to walk away while I still could. Before Libby discovered my job required me to slither around in the putrid-smelling liquid at the bottom of other people's psychological trash cans.

I scrolled social media, not able to digest any of it. A clock ticked in the living room, loud in the house without Libby. The Coke ran out. How drunk was I? Tired of looking at photos of happy vacations and immaculate bookcases, I pulled up my list of contacts, needing someone to talk to.

Suddenly, it all struck me as hilarious. Drunkenly hilarious, but hilarious nonetheless. All of it: Kira the queen of the PTA in her pristine linen almost literally getting into bed with Dan and his Italian suits and perfect hair and secret excess perspiration problem. The absolute balls of her to suggest she'd done me a favor to free me up to be with Emmett.

Well, why the hell not? I pulled up his contact. I waved my glass in the air as if toasting invisible people. I'd touch this screen and call his number right now. I had permission, didn't I?

Oh shit, I'd moved my finger too close. His number lit up and the call went through. In one ring, there was the telltale click of the answer. I had half a second to hang up.

"Allison?"

Too late. I stood to pace as I talked, but nope—too unsteady. I toppled back onto the sofa. "Emmett! So, funny thing happened on the way to the courthouse today—Kira Grant fired me and hired Dan! Isn't that hilarious?"

"Um. Sure. Hilarious." His voice was warm but alert. "Where are you right now, Allie?"

"I'm home. On the sofa." I put my hand over my head to confirm this fact. Yup. The sofa. "And I might have been drinking."

"I can tell," he said, chuckling cautiously.

Needing to vent out loud to an actual person instead of my car's rearview mirror, I said, "You'd be drinking, too, if you had to deal with that woman for even one minute."

"Kira?"

"Yes, Kira Grant, queen of the bitchfaces. Evil hag. I hope she has wrinkled knees, horrific varicose veins, and her shining pink scalp is showing by the time she's fifty. And that she goes to prison for twenty years. So make it happen, okay?"

Emmett laughed. "I thought innocent people never went to prison. You're not hinting she's guilty, are you?" His light teasing eased a lot of the stress that had tightened my neck muscles.

I rubbed the muscles as they loosened. "She's guilty as sin. Of being a terrible, terrible person. If I had enough energy, I'd go throw eggs at her house."

"You wouldn't, because you know it's illegal and I'd have to have you arrested. And you're not going anywhere, are you?"

"You'd stop me if I did something dumb, wouldn't you? You did that, you know, back in law school." I had no idea where the memory came from. I'd been out with a bunch of classmates at a bar and had gotten separated from my group. Steve had been somewhere else; I didn't remember where. A hulking, stubbly medical student had backed me into a corner, looming over me in a way that had begun oozing over the line into threatening. Emmett had come over, pretended to be my boyfriend, and told him off. Then he'd walked me home and waited while I locked the door behind him.

"In law school? I don't remember you ever doing anything dumb."

"You saved me once. At Dunleavy's Bar. From the elephantine med student I thought wanted to eat me for lunch. Do you remember?"

"Oh right. Big guy, buzz cut, right? I'd seen him there before." Emmett cleared his throat, an unsure note creeping in. "I never knew for sure if you wanted me to interfere. If you'd rather have stayed. I kind of agonized about it—maybe I was too presumptuous."

"You weren't." Recklessness loosened my tongue. "This is going to sound bad, because I was with Steve then, but . . . back then I would have rather been with you pretty much all the time."

"Back then?" His quiet voice was like velvet. There was a long pause. "And now?"

I gripped the phone so tightly I hit a side button by accident. "Now?" I stalled, waiting for him to save me. Or for bravery to kick in.

He didn't save me. He outlasted me, waiting in silence for an answer.

I took a deep breath. "Now. Um, now . . . nothing has changed. Except now there's no Steve." I dug my hands into the sofa, wishing the cushions would swallow me while he came up with a response.

"You know, it might not be the worst thing in the world if you're off that case, because . . ."

Meaning buzzed and crackled. "Because?"

"Because now we're not on opposite sides. And I can keep it that way when other cases come in, if I want."

"And do you want?"

A thousand years of agony passed before he said anything more.

"Yes." He swallowed. I heard it. "Very badly."

More silence, as a delicious golden warmth swirled in my belly. "Well, then."

"Well, then."

"Where are you?" I asked, dying of joy.

He actually groaned. "I'm at my parents'."

That dumped a metaphorical bucket of cold water over my head. I laughed. "Oh. Then I'm guessing you're tied up tonight."

He laughed, too, a naughty edge to his voice. "Tied up? Not at the moment, but I'm always open to negotiation."

"Oh my God. Stop!" I said, mortified but so turned on. "You know what I mean."

"I do," he said, his chuckle now open and free. "Just playing. Can I see you tomorrow night, though? Say, dinner at seven? And then . . . whatever?"

The soaring sandcastle I'd built out of anticipation flattened into frustration, but only temporarily. I could ask Steve to keep Libby a second day. He owed me. "I think we could. See you tomorrow night, Emmett. I want . . . too."

❧

The next morning, I arrived at work—with actual makeup on—to find Dan pacing in my office. He did not look pleased.

"Kira Grant called me at home last night to say she'd reconsidered. She said you'd done a good job on the bond hearing and the prelim and she'd talked to her husband and they'd agreed it wouldn't be a good idea to change horses midrace. She says as long as you're willing to work with her on the defense, she'll stay with you and the firm."

"She what?"

"What the fuck, Allison? Did you call her and beg? What kind of bullshit is this?"

"She wants me?" Mind games. My thoughts raced forward, wondering what her endgame was. To screw with Dan? To play with me and with Emmett?

Oh God. Emmett. Date. With Emmett.

"That's what she says. And you'll agree and you will put on whatever defense she wants. She helpfully explained she and Miles Grant have lots of friends who'd love referrals here, but only if we were 'cooperative.' She listed their names. It's every damn family with money in the area."

Oh shit. What if I didn't want Kira? "I need to think about it." I was in over my head. I couldn't keep pace with Kira's anarchist chess game.

Dan laughed, hysteria edging his voice. "Oh no, you won't. No thinking at all. Here's how it's going to be. You'll take her back or you'll pack up today and get out. If you lose this case, you can pack up then. I'll lodge a bar complaint against you. You'll never practice again."

Bills and lessons and day care and car payments swam in front of my face. I didn't have enough savings and therefore no choice. Neatly trapped, I gave him a tight smile of assent. "Fine. I'll let the commonwealth know."

I gave Hailey the message. Two hours later, Emmett sent me an email from his official work account: Seriously?

I responded with only two words: I'm sorry.

It took me three days to regain even a hint of productivity. Four before I could manage politeness during an actual phone conversation with Kira instead of terse emails. The court docket never stopped, though, so I found myself waiting for a child-support matter in the hallway of the juvenile court on Friday afternoon. I stared unseeingly at my client notes while pondering Deep Thoughts about Right and Wrong.

Emmett came out of the Commonwealth's Attorney's Office down the hall from the juvenile court and sat beside me on the bench. He smelled like chocolate. A rush of loss wrung me out.

I squelched the feeling without mercy. No possibilities here. Not anymore.

"Do you have court?" I was a curious professional, nothing more. On Fridays, the juvenile court had a civil docket: child support, contested custody cases. I knew the prosecutors generally spent the day catching up from the rest of the week. Emmett had no files or legal pads in his hands.

"No. I saw you from the window and wanted to ask you something."

"What?"

"Do you think Kira Grant might consider a plea deal?"

I let out a breath. Holy crap, a plea. I never thought I'd hear that word in the same sentence as my client's name. Valerie must have had a temporary break. "A plea?"

"Yeah. This case is ugly, the local reporters are checking in once a week for developments, the school would like it to be over, and I think we might be able to come up with something that would work for your client if she's willing to think about it."

"Is Valerie on board?"

"Yes. Since when do I get to make plea offers without Valerie signing off?"

"Right." He didn't. As the elected commonwealth's attorney, Valerie made all the decisions and ruled that place with an iron fist. And if Valerie had authorized him to talk plea bargains, then they'd acknowledged their case had flaws even a mendacious detective couldn't paper over. This was good. Very good. "I can ask her. We haven't talked about it."

"Not at all?"

"No. She says she didn't do it."

Emmett scoffed. "Don't they all say that?"

"No, actually, most of them are pretty honest."

"You saying she's not honest?" he teased.

I smacked him on the arm as he grinned. It was far more solid than the average attorney's arm. Thank God, we were feeling our way back to something like normal. "Nope, smart-ass. I'm not saying that at all. I don't know if she'll take a plea. I frankly can't imagine her agreeing to admit guilt or accept any sentence. But I'll ask."

The laughter left his face as he glanced down at his arm where I'd touched him. "Do that. Let's get this case out of the way. I've never received a more depressing phone message than the one you left."

I met his eyes, which were closer than usual, and noticed the lighter brown around his iris. Oh God, I wanted to get this case over with. He opened his mouth as if to say something more, then closed it.

A surge of desperate confidence powered my lungs. Talking about things wasn't an ethical violation. "Emmett, the other night—"

A courtroom door banged the wall and we jumped, breaking the eye contact. The loudspeaker went off. "Matter of Isaiah Markham. Isaiah Markham and parties to the courtroom."

I stood, vaguely thankful for the interruption. I hadn't been sure exactly how the question I'd started would end. "That's me. I'll see you, Emmett."

❧

After another week of dissembling, rescheduling, texts full of smiley faces, and protestations of extreme busyness, Ruthanne Dillard finally agreed to meet me at the elementary school at the end of her child's school day. I jumped at the opportunity, because it meant I could pick up Libby at the after-school program early and surprise her.

Because of my work hours, Libby stayed after kindergarten for what the school called an "enrichment program" and I called "babysitting." It consisted of outside playground time and board games in the cafeteria—the same cafeteria where Summer Peerman had drunk a poisoned smoothie. I staggered in as close to five thirty each evening as possible, in concert with other haggard and bedraggled working parents, to pick her up.

Picking up a child at the actual school release time was a wholly different affair. A line of cars snaked through the parking lot, with adorable ponytailed mothers at the wheel interspersed with an occasional grandparent. I stared with wonder. What lives did these people have that they were available to wait in this line for forty-five minutes at three in the afternoon every day? Familiar worry that I'd made bad choices for Libby by staying in my demanding job flared. I ignored the line and pulled into an empty parking space. Ruthanne had said we could meet at the office.

To get inside the building, I had to buzz a small camera thing at the front door that reminded me of the one I'd had on my apartment building in law school. I assumed the schools intended it to prevent school shooters from getting in. The buzzer provided no more security here than at the apartment building: before anyone could answer, a woman walking out held the door for me.

Ruthanne fit the description Kira had given me so closely I had to swallow a giggle. She was tall and thin with the long-limbed natural grace of a model, but she couldn't have dressed less like a model if she'd tried. An adult model, anyway. She wore a yellow sundress printed with pink flowers and bordered by ruffles. A pink satin headband held back her long, wavy brown hair. At her neck, she wore a broken locket like the one in *Annie.*

She did look like a seven-year-old. Her seven-year-old, I suspected.

"You didn't give your name to the office to get in? Ooooh. You really should have. The security system saves lives. It's so important!" Her shocked face made me rethink my scoffing at the security system. Maybe it worked by fooling people into thinking it worked.

"You must be Ruthanne Dillard," I said.

"I am. And you're Allison Barton? Come on, you've got to sign the office visitor ledger."

Though this seemed patently ridiculous given I'd come to meet a parent, not a teacher or student, and all the students these precautions were intended to protect were even now getting in cars and onto school buses, I did as she said.

Once all the rules were followed, Ruthanne took me to an empty classroom with a hand-painted sign on the door that said **Parents Love Our Teachers!!** A neat line of red glitter and heart stickers edged the poster board. I took one look at Ruthanne's dress and decided she'd made the sign. As if the room were her home, Ruthanne offered me a small plastic chair. We sat, our knees awkwardly higher than our waists.

"So, Ruthanne, I understand you're the president of the PTA now?"

She preened. "Yes, since Kira wasn't . . . able to do it any longer, I took over. We met over the summer, and she gave me all the records and the plans and the budget materials."

"Do you enjoy it?" I knew she must. On Libby's first day of kindergarten, she brought home a "Welcome to School" gift bag with pencils, a tiny notebook, three or four nut-free healthy snacks, a homemade magnet that said **BOOKS ARE OUR FRIENDS!** and a couple of the "achieve-mints" Kira had warned me about. These last were peppermint Life Savers wrapped in decorated paper and renamed. The whole thing, for eighty kindergartners, must have taken Ruthanne days to put together.

"Oh, I love it. My little Aurora is in second grade with Miss Thompson, and it means so much to participate in her education this way. Her teacher allows me to sit in with her a few times a week, and I eat lunch in the cafeteria with her nearly every day. I've always been crafty, and there are such great ideas for visual motivation on Instagram and Pinterest these days."

The case of *Commonwealth v. Kira Grant* had taught me there were many different kinds of mothers in the world. In front of me right now was the kind that scared me the most—the kind who insisted it would be safer if the umbilical cord stayed intact and who planned to dominate every minute of her child's life until Princess Aurora didn't know how to find her way out of a paper bag without an assist.

That was what I told myself, anyway, to make myself feel better. Deep down I feared that my motherhood was a slapdash thing made of patchy papier-mâché next to Ruthanne's hand-grooved organic teak.

"My daughter is in kindergarten, and so far I've been very impressed with the activities offered by the PTA. I appreciate all you do." I clicked my pen and poised it over my legal pad. "Last year is what I'm most interested in, though. You were on the PTA then?"

"Yes. I was the treasurer."

"Who else was an officer of the PTA?"

"Kira was the president, Brandi Crane was the vice president, and Tammy Cox was the secretary. Dr. Rickman, the principal, is a nonvoting officer, but he hardly ever comes to meetings."

I wrote it all down, though none of the information was new. "You know of course I'm here about the poisoning. Tell me what you were doing that day."

Ruthanne spun her wedding ring around her finger like a talisman. "Well, it was a crazy day, even before the poisoning. We'd all done Field Day, and all the different awards days, and this was the last day of school. Aurora slept badly, so of course I slept badly, and then I burned her egg and avocado sandwich for breakfast . . ."

Avocado sandwich? Libby ate the same bowl of Honey Nut Cheerios every morning and wouldn't recognize a weekday hot breakfast if it bit her in the nose. Yup, I'd never keep up with this Jones.

Ruthanne continued, blissfully unaware of my shortcomings. "Anyway, I got to school frazzled, Aurora was upset over losing her teacher for the summer, and I started working on setting up the outside tents and overseeing the bouncy castles."

"The bouncy castles?" I asked, dumbfounded.

"Yes, the fifth-grade graduation is a big deal. It's a real achievement for these children, and we try to make it special for them. They have a daylong party to celebrate. They play games outside in the morning and have a dance party later; there are the bouncy castles and then refreshments and a slideshow of all the pictures of them throughout their years at school. That takes place right before they walk the halls for the last time and the younger children applaud."

For the time being, I'd swallow my thoughts on whether graduation from fifth grade was in fact an achievement and narrow in on what she'd said. "The PTA does all that? With how many people?"

"Not as many as you might think. We have the four officers. We have some regular participants, and an occasional helper. I'd say no more than twenty parents helped that day, and most of those only for setup or takedown. It's so sad how many parents don't realize or care that showing up for our children is half the battle. It's the officers who really do the work." She gave me a coy look. "You say your daughter is in kindergarten here? You should come out. We'll be having our Breakfast with Santa in December. We'll need all the help we can get: pancake flipping, Santa pictures, decorations, craft table. Someone always has to be on glitter patrol."

I shifted guilty eyes to my notes. "Right. Well, we'll have to see how the case goes. It might be a bit awkward with PTA officers as witnesses given that the trial is right before Thanksgiving." I wrote something down to give myself something to do with my hands. "Does Summer Peerman volunteer?"

"Not anymore. Her son's in middle school now. She did, though, when she could, but she works," Ruthanne said with a tinge of judgment I didn't appreciate. "She can't be there for her child during the day."

Uh-huh. No, Summer Peerman stayed busy all day watching out for abused children. If anyone got a pass, Summer should. "Did she help the day of the fifth-grade graduation?"

"I think she may have helped set up in the gym in the morning before work, but she spent the refreshment hour talking to other parents. She was kind of the center of attention, even before the poisoning. I think she was supposed to do cleanup, but obviously . . ."

"Center of attention? Why?"

"Aidan—that's her son, super nice boy—had won a bunch of awards the day before at the assembly. He placed first in the big race at Field Day. He got perfect scores on all the state standardized tests. It's rare to get one perfect score, let alone three. And I think he may have won the Outstanding Fifth-Grade Student award. That's the big award the school gives, for grades, scores, and behavior. People were congratulating Summer and Aidan. That poor child, that he had to watch what happened to his mother. I imagine Aurora witnessing something like that and I start to cry."

Dear Lord, she actually welled up. "Right. So the refreshments were near the end of the party?"

"Yes. All we had to do was serve the smoothies and the snacks and then the teachers would take over and handle the graduation walk. It's timed, or was supposed to be timed, to send them out the door at the end of the last school day."

"Tell me about your involvement with the smoothies."

"I really didn't have any. Brandi insisted on the smoothies. I didn't vote for smoothies—I'd been planning to bring a fruit plate, but since we had smoothies, that would've been too much fruit. So I had to do vegetables and I hate that, because the children are so messy with the dip. I also did a cracker plate, with cheese cut in fun shapes, and pigs in a blanket."

I knew I should not, but I couldn't stop myself. "Wow."

She laughed self-consciously. "I love to do things like that. A lot of moms nowadays don't have time to do things . . ."—she swallowed the *right* like a good girl—"like I do."

"So who handled the drinks?"

"Brandi made the smoothie batch the night before and brought it in. It was a lot of work, but I totally get it. Her youngest child was graduating, and she wanted to do something special for him." Ruthanne's expression drifted into some happy fantasy of the no doubt over-the-top thing she'd do for little Aurora.

"Griffin, right?"

"Right. Anyway, they argued in the kitchen over the smoothies."

"Who did?"

"Brandi and Kira. Kira didn't want anyone pouring the smoothies at the refreshment table out of the milk jugs Brandi brought them in; she said it didn't look nice. So Brandi and Tammy poured all the smoothies from the jugs into the pitchers we use for this kind of event in the kitchen. Then the pitchers went out to the table in the party area, and Kira and Tammy poured them into the cups from the pitchers. I helped some, but I had to keep an eye on the food table and greet people. Outreach to parents is so important to keep the PTA going, you know."

So far, her version coincided with the others', with the exception of the pitchers detail. The pitchers would have made it far more possible to get the aconite into the right place. But how? They'd tested everything, and nowhere had there been a mention of aconite residue in a pitcher.

It had to have been one of the four officers of the PTA who poisoned Summer Peerman.

"Can you think of any issues the other ladies had with each other, or with Summer?"

"Summer? Well, she and Kira were best friends, I think. Their sons are best friends, anyway. You should see the way those boys ran around the school during our meetings. I don't know of any issues Tammy or Brandi had with Summer. Tammy and Kira had a problem, though. I don't know if I should say any more." Ruthanne drew in her legs and arms as if surrounded by a miasma of contagion.

"What kind of problem did Tammy and Kira have? You should know things like this always have a tendency to come out during litigation."

"Well, okay. Last winter, I found a discrepancy in the PTA account. We were off by three hundred dollars. I keep careful records, and Kira used to be an accountant, and so we don't make mistakes. We did—or I should say, Kira did—some pretty aggressive digging, and it turned out Tammy had taken the money to pay her car payment. Things at her house were tight, she said, since she'd lost her job. She put it back right away. I was all ready to forget it, and I thought we had."

"I assume it didn't get forgotten?"

"No. A couple of months later, Tammy told me privately Kira had threatened to charge her with a crime—and so that's why Tammy had been doing the worst jobs for the PTA. Kira said if she didn't, she'd talk to the prosecutors. Once, I guess, Kira had Tammy come out to weed her garden. She paid her, but only half what she'd have to pay normally. For some reason, Tammy was convinced if she got charged with a crime, she'd lose custody of her children. Tammy loves those girls."

"Tammy weeded Kira's garden?" The one where the monkshood grew?

"Yeah. Once. Mostly she did the gross stuff for PTA." Ruthanne wrinkled her nose, managing to look adorable. "The Sam's Club run. Cleaning out our closets. Ugh. Everyone hates cleaning out the closets. Oh, and even on the day of the poisoning, I walked into the kitchen and found Kira and Tammy having some kind of standoff."

"A standoff? What do you mean?"

"Well, I'm assuming. They were standing there, staring at each other. I could feel the tension. Like an argument had just ended."

This could be nothing, but it could be something. "Tell me more about that. You mentioning it makes me think you thought it was odd."

"Yes, I guess so. I'd come in to get the cheese shapes out of the fridge last minute. You know—I didn't want to take a risk on a child eating spoiled cheese. Kira was standing still with two full pitchers of smoothies in her hands. Tammy was across the room by the trash can. They were staring at each other, like they were saying something without saying something. Tammy kind of smiled, but not like, happy smiling. It felt . . . I don't know, tense. And different."

"Different? Different how?"

"Look, I don't have a clue what had happened. I say 'different' because usually Tammy takes it when Kira orders her around like a servant. That day . . . it was like Tammy had something on Kira instead of the other way around. Like the opposite of the way Kira kind of reminds Tammy of the money theft with one look."

"What made you think so?"

"Only their body language. Kira looked . . . I don't want to say *guilty*, because of the poisoning, you know. Less . . . in charge, or something."

Something had happened there, but what? "Did an argument happen between them after you left the room?"

"No. Kira followed me right out to start pouring the drinks. There wouldn't have been time."

I glanced over my notes, trying to make sure I'd covered everything. "I'm guessing Kira never reported Tammy's theft?"

"Not that I know of."

If Tammy lived her life afraid of losing custody of her kids because of Summer's official investigation, and Kira had threatened her with a charge that would have put the nail in her DSS coffin, the motive for killing Summer and framing Kira for it would be obvious for anyone to see.

Add that to Brandi's equally credible motivation, and I had more reasonable doubt than I knew what to do with. Emmett's offer of a plea deal looked worse and worse all the time. If ever there were a criminal case to take to trial, this might be the one.

"Thanks, Ruthanne. You've helped a lot."

"You know, it's funny," she mused. "You asked me whether the ladies had problems with each other, and that's the only thing I can think of. For the most part, we get along fine. All four of us are doing PTA because we love our children more than life itself and want to make the best of their school years. Even though they have flaws, I'd stake my life on it. We all love our children and want them to be happy."

She bit her lip.

"What else, Ruthanne?"

"Well, this sounds terrible, but I have to change my answer. We all want our children to be happy. That's definitely true of me and Tammy and Brandi."

"And Kira?"

"Kira wants hers to be amazing."

CHAPTER SEVENTEEN

KIRA

My cell rang—Allison the back-in-her-place lawyer. I blew on my nails one last time and glanced at the salon worker doing my pedicure. "Hello? This is Kira."

"I can't talk long, but I wanted to let you know the commonwealth approached me about whether you might be interested in a plea deal."

The woman at my feet—Miri, I think she said her name was—didn't appear to be listening, but I'd have to be careful about what I said. My usual salon had politely informed me I was no longer welcome. They had to think of their clientele, they said. I'd be damned if I'd lose this one, too. I hardly planned to start sloughing off my own foot calluses. "Which means what, exactly?"

"You'd plead guilty either to the attempted murder or to a lesser crime, and the commonwealth would agree to a lighter sentence than what you'd get if you were convicted at trial."

Like hell. I wouldn't plead guilty in a million years to something I didn't do, yet this was as good a test as any as to whether my lawyer packed heat or slept with the light on. It wasn't too late to change horses. Again. "And what do you think?"

"I think, first, that the mention when we're still six weeks from trial is evidence they aren't sure they can convict you. Secondly, I think you can think about it for a while because I haven't heard specifics yet. Once they tell us what crime and what sentence they're proposing, we can get a clue how weak they think their case is. Valerie doesn't plea-bargain much. This is a good sign."

"So we don't need to do anything at this point." The pedicurist scraped a toenail cuticle too close. "Ow."

"What? No. We don't need to do anything until we hear what they're offering. I wanted to let you start thinking about whether you'd be interested. I'll be ready for trial. I've got material to work with. We're strong on reasonable doubt."

"Well, then, it sounds like we've decided. Go on and tell them no."

A pause. "Let's let them wonder for a while. Sometimes if they're counting on ending the case with a plea bargain, they hold off on preparing the way they ought to. Waiting to tell them will let us keep going while they sit."

"And your experience with the . . ." I glanced at Miri, minding her own business at my toes. "With this particular one? Will he fail to prepare?"

She let out a tiny sigh. "I'll do my best to let him think we're interested as long as possible. I've got to go. They're calling my case. Think about it, okay?"

"Fine." I hit "End." I'd think about it. I spared a moment to wonder idly whether Allison had taken advantage of her short stint of freedom to bang the prosecutor.

I could have stayed with Dan MacDonald. Yet when I got home and thought about Dan's hand sweat moisturizing my palm, or, worse, my thigh under the counsel table, I wanted to peel off my skin. I didn't want a lawyer I'd have to flirt with and hold off like a horny high school quarterback. It would have been exhausting. Allison had sucked up her *Teen Beat* fetishizing of the Amaro man long enough to do a decent job on my bond hearing and my preliminary hearing. She could get through the trial. I had ways of getting her back in line if she drew too many hearts on her yellow legal pad.

"Everything okay?" Miri asked, massaging my feet.

"Yes. I think everything is great."

❧

After school I waited in the pickup lines, glowering at other parents who took care not to meet my eyes. Finn complained about his science teacher, and I made a mental note to look at his homework and to write an email to the teacher explaining that Finn was an A student. Grades, like so much else in life, were all about the perception. Fiona cried and said her kindergarten teacher had made her miss recess for taking too long on her word-study worksheet.

The kids picked up the devices I depended on to keep them quiet in the car as I drove home. The news that school hadn't gone well did not improve my mood. Why did it feel like only my sheer force of will kept Finn and Fiona from falling off the ladder of success? The stress of engineering their lives consumed me: my jaw ached at night, my back muscles were tight, and stress eczema broke out across the backs of my knees no matter how much cream I put on them. They were only eleven and five—I worried my body wouldn't hold out until Fiona left home. I hated how little control I had over what they did inside the school building, how much they cared, what their goals were, or whether they even had them. Mothering is a shit job: the only measure of success is the success of the offspring, and dammit, they would be successful if it killed me. It would be nice if they helped me out a bit.

Miles's car sat in the driveway—both unusual at 4:00 p.m. and less than desirable. With him home, I'd have to interact with the family instead of plunking the kids down in front of the TV and going off to my room to read.

In the garage, I nagged Finn and Fiona to get all their things—backpacks, completed work, the cuddly toy Fiona took with her in the car every day—while cataloging in my mind all that had to be done. Homework, homework check, laundry, dinner, dinner cleanup, heartworm medicine for the dog . . .

Miles bounded out of the house, moving faster than I'd seen him move since he played lacrosse on his fraternity lawn. Before I could open my mouth, he'd swept me up into his arms and spun me around as if we were in some Rodgers and Hammerstein musical. Finn stared with wide eyes. Fiona put her index finger in her mouth and dropped the handful of artwork she'd brought home.

"What on earth is going on, Miles?"

"It was Martha! All the time it was Martha!" He hugged me close, providing me with the first close-up whiff of his aftershave I'd had in a long time. "Go on in the house, kids. Get started on your homework. Mommy and I have to talk."

They went, though not before Finn's eyebrows pinched together.

"You want to talk here, in the garage?" I glanced around. The stepladder leaned crazily against one wall. The lawn mower, still encrusted with grass, had left black scuff marks on the unpainted drywall. The garage was Miles's domain, and I made an ostentatious point of not neatening it up.

He glanced around but, as usual, didn't register any of the mess. "Here is fine. Kira, listen. I figured it out!"

"What are you *talking* about?"

His blue eyes burned feverishly. "I've been spending hours, Kira. Hours and hours combing through the practice's books. Money has been disappearing. At first I went to the auditors, but they couldn't find anything. They said everything appeared in order. But something was wrong. The insurance payments were off, and I couldn't figure out how. Eventually I called a forensic accountant. Lady by the name of Linda Price."

Linda. When I'd called the unknown number on the cell phone bill, the voice mail had been for a Linda.

Miles continued, the words spilling over each other. "Linda and I have been going over everything, after hours so Martha wouldn't know, and at last we figured it out. Martha! I'd suspected all along, but it turns out Martha was working together with a man at the auditor's office. That's why it took so long. The auditor was in on it. We called the state police."

"You've been going over your books? Every night? Late? You expect me to believe that, Miles?"

He flushed, the light going out of his eyes. "Yes. That is what I've been doing. I have not been having an affair with Sandy. Or Linda Price. Or with Martha, God forbid."

I kicked a chip in the concrete floor.

"I'm not cheating on you, Kira. I've never cheated on you. I fell in love with you that day at the tailgate, and I still love that same girl." He grazed his fingertips down my upper arms, his face naked and raw.

He was telling the truth. He had to be. He knew I could check on this embezzling story and that I would. I bit my lip. Ugh. I didn't enjoy surprises.

"Do you believe me?" he asked, his voice low and intimate.

"Yes," I said, and dammit, I did. Now I had to decide whether his fidelity mattered anymore. Whether I needed a new reason to push him away, or no reason at all.

"Okay, then." He put one hand at my low back and the other in my hair and pulled me close, his lips meeting mine.

It had been a while since we kissed this way. I'd been in a fury at him—at a lot of things—for nearly a year, but of course once I'd realized I needed his visible support for my case, I'd let him back into my bed. We'd done it once a month, maybe twice a month, just often enough to keep him around, and always in the dark, in our bed, with elevated efforts at skill on my part but with lowered returns. How believable the ruse had been I didn't know, or care.

Until now, oddly enough. His kiss, the first romantic one not assured of the imminent reward of sex in months, undid things inside me. It made me want more, to remember the tall blond college boy everyone had wanted but who only had eyes for me. We'd had good sex, then, at the beginning. Maybe we could again.

"Maybe after dinner the kids can watch TV," I said with a tentativeness I despised.

"Maybe dinner can be late," Miles said, trailing his lips along my jawline.

"I think dinner can be late."

❧

In bed that night, I flicked through the internet as Miles slept beside me, breathing like a thirty-year-old Hoover vacuum cleaner. Whatever temporary insanity had made me respond to him had blown away like dust in the wind, and I'd gone right back to wavering over what to do about Miles. During our predinner interlude earlier, he'd told me he loved me more than he'd ever imagined loving another person. I couldn't reciprocate, so I'd put my mouth somewhere distracting.

If I stayed with Miles, I didn't have to work, which meant a fair amount of time to myself now that both children were in school. I knew my alimony rules: feminism had done me no favors there. The days of lifetime support for women were over. If we divorced, I'd be expected to support myself. I'd have to return to work as an accountant, and I'd gouge out my eyes and live on disability first. Being an accountant was exactly as boring as a million sitcoms portrayed it. The other accountants were worse: tediously earnest and uniformly homely.

All that argued for staying. Besides, staying meant I kept the house, with its wide porches and subway-tiled bathrooms, my kitchen with the marble counters and farmhouse sink, and most important, the garden I'd labored over for years. Staying meant no messiness with custody disputes, no unpleasant explanations to family and friends in the annual Christmas card, and the continued ability to judge other couples for not sticking it out.

Staying meant Miles, though, forever, and there might be too much water under the bridge. I glanced at him, lying facedown, his cheek mashed into the pillow toward me. He'd aged, but so far it wasn't awful. His skin had spots it hadn't had at twenty-five. His hair still glinted gold, but there wasn't as much of it as before. The lines around his eyes only made him look more distinguished, damn him. Though his abdomen no longer resembled the washboard it had been when he'd been in the habit of flaunting it on the lawn of his fraternity during endless Frisbee games back in college, it hadn't gone flabby like those of his friends.

I had no idea when I could expect to be allowed to retire from the field of regular marital duties, but it couldn't be long. Another ten or fifteen years, at most. Men in their sixties couldn't possibly expect it weekly. Besides, soon I'd be able to plead menopause, or pre-menopause, or whatever. Miles was hardly the type to question anything to do with woman problems. For example, he still believed periods lasted a full seven days.

I could probably do without the sixty-decibel dragon-snoring, and Lord knows nobody looks good sleeping with their mouth open that far.

In any case, it hardly mattered now. I had a prison sentence to avoid, and I needed Miles around until I'd squared everything away.

I got lost in the research of conviction rates and first-time offender sentencing and the chances on appeal. I remembered a dim time before the internet, but I shuddered at the thought. We were fumbling through life blind back then. I followed a rabbit hole of links into the not-quite-dark web about escaping to countries without an extradition treaty until the first yawn escaped me.

Miles let out another gusty breath. Maybe he had sleep apnea as well as a peanut allergy. Something old-man was definitely happening in the nasal passages over there. I set the alarm and stretched out. As I closed my eyes, he produced a loud and juicy fart.

My God, surely nobody could expect me to sleep next to that forever.

CHAPTER EIGHTEEN
ALLISON

"Hello?"

"It's Emmett." His voice was cold and professional. A business call. "Valerie has authorized a plea deal for Kira Grant."

I bit my lip. Half of me hoped it would be amazing and Kira would jump at it. I could be done with this case. The other half of me hoped it would be terrible and make the choice easy. I didn't think she would take any deal short of dropped charges and a personal apology from Emmett, Valerie, each and every deputy in the sheriff's office, and Summer Peerman herself. "And? What are you offering?"

There was a pause. "She's charged with attempted murder. Carries twenty years to life. We'd be willing to let her plead to attempt to poison, which is only a class 3 felony and carries five to twenty. We'd agree to a ten-year sentence, seven of those suspended, and she'd be banned for life from any building owned by the school system."

Well, that made things easy. She'd never take it. For a second I tried to imagine Kira serving three years anywhere, let alone the state prison for women. And Kira might consider the school banishment worse anyway.

"I'll tell her and we'll let you know."

"You never called me to let me know whether she'd be interested in any deal. You know, when I asked you before."

Yeah, on purpose. I'd let him think it was a possibility for two extra weeks and now we were inside a month until trial—a blink of an eye in the legal system. Hearing the actual offer also gave me a pretty good idea what the commonwealth thought of their case: not super strong, but reasonably muscly. "She hadn't decided yet."

"Are you going to recommend this deal?" he asked. His voice got warmer.

I stiffened my spine. "I'm not going to tell you, Emmett. As you said, we're not working on this case together. I'll let you know when she decides."

"Unfortunately, I can't let the offer hang out there forever. We're running out of time. I'll give you until Friday afternoon. If you take it, you save us both a lot of work. If you don't, well, then, I'd better get moving."

"Get moving?"

He sighed. "Get moving. With the case preparation. You know my job is to take you down." He sucked in a breath as he realized what he'd said.

We were not in Kansas anymore. "Fine. We'll let you know."

❧

I took my half-finished coffee out to Maureen's area and perched on the edge of her credenza. She looked up with a smile. Maureen was the best part of working here. She'd seen a lot in her life, and she never judged. Every morning, she listened to my worries and offered advice on how to handle Libby or Dan or Steve or anything else that caused the tension headache between my eyes. Time with her wasn't billable, but it had probably saved my sanity more than once.

"Sorry I didn't catch that call," she said. "I was pouring coffee. Who was it?"

"Emmett Amaro from the commonwealth."

She laughed. "I know who Emmett Amaro is."

Of course she did. And by saying it that way, I'd only emphasized it. She'd know I had a thing for him. "They're offering a plea deal for Kira Grant. Three years to serve, conviction of a class 3 felony."

"She'll never take that."

"No. And I'm not going to recommend it. I'll tell her, of course, because I'm obligated to, but . . ."

Maureen rolled her eyes dramatically. "I don't envy you, to have to tell her they think she should live without hair-care products and high heels for three years. It'll take you fifteen minutes to calm her down." Her face softened. "Do you want me to do it? I can pass along the message as easily as you can."

"No way. I wouldn't do that to you."

The phone rang. Maureen answered it. "The MacDonald Group. How can I help you?" She listened for a minute as the expression on her face grew troubled. "One moment." She hit the "Hold" button.

"What?" I asked.

"It's a reporter from the *Washington Post*. She wants to talk to you about the Grant case. Should I say you're out?"

Washington and its famous newspaper lay a four-hour drive north from here. I had to admit curiosity. "I'll take it. Here. No need to transfer." I took the phone as she released the call from hold.

"Hi! This is Clarissa Rogers from the state section of the *Post*," chirped a young-sounding voice. "You're Allison Barton, attorney for Kira Grant?"

"Yes," I said, worried I'd already said too much. I did not have practice talking to reporters.

"I've reviewed the records and the local coverage and Ms. Grant is charged with attempted murder for poisoning cups of drink at an elementary school?"

"She is charged with attempted murder. And is innocent of any crime until proven guilty beyond a reasonable doubt."

"Okay, 'allegedly poisoning,' then. We've gotten a tip that there's a new development in the case. Do you mind if I read to you some of what I have for an upcoming story and you can confirm or deny?"

Oh holy shit. She already had a story. Who had she gotten it from? Emmett? Kira herself? "I'd be interested to hear what you have."

"Basically, in a nutshell, I have that Ms. Grant was the PTA president, that her own son was in the room, that there were eighty fifth graders and their parents also in the room, and that the woman, Summer Peerman, took the cup, drank aconite, and went into a medical emergency on the floor. The plant used grows in Ms. Grant's yard. Is all that correct?"

Yes, and nothing new, but I wouldn't help her out by confirming it. "Why don't you tell me what else you have?"

"My understanding is all the women working the refreshment table were white and the victim is Black. And there had been some arguments over affirmative action between the victim and one of the other women. Can you confirm your defense will be that that woman did the poisoning as racist revenge?"

Shit. Shit. Shit. She knew. Either this Clarissa was a budding legal genius with astonishingly astute online skills, or she'd gotten a tip from someone I'd spoken to. Given that she'd mentioned race as a motive, I'd put money on Dan or Kira herself. "Clarissa. I appreciate you checking your story with me. I feel confident, however, that my client would not appreciate me talking to the press. My reply is 'no comment.' Thanks for calling." I hung up.

Maureen stared.

"They know. They know everything. The crime. The charge. Even the defense Dan wants me to go with. The race angle is going to be in a national newspaper. This isn't going to be any helpful puff piece like the local one. Emmett will see it, and it will help him prepare."

"They probably won't be the last to call. The other state papers, the local TV. Do you want me to keep track and tell them all 'no comment'?"

I nodded, unable to speak. As I stumbled toward my office, Dan opened his door and hollered down the hall. "Allison!" he boomed. "A word?"

Might as well. This morning couldn't get much worse.

Dan's office did not resemble mine. The firm had paid for the furnishings in both, but mine had a hand-me-down desk and mismatched chairs from the used office furniture store, my diploma and bar admission certificates on the walls, and a potted plant I'd brought from home.

Dan's, on the other hand, had an antique desk befitting the White House, a massive bookcase filled with gleaming law books I knew he'd never cracked open, a thick persian rug, upholstered client chairs, drapes, and a framed oil painting of a distant scene of foxhounds in pursuit.

"Sit," he said, pointing at one of the chairs.

I sat.

"Just got off the phone with Valerie. I called her to check on the specifics of a plea deal for Kira Grant." He reclined majestically in a butter-soft leather chair.

"Dan. You're way out of line. This is not your case. It's mine. You don't need to be talking pleas with the commonwealth."

"Oh, easy now, hon. I know Emmett called you first thing. Class 3, ten years, seven suspended, three to serve. You tell them no. See? I didn't tell Valerie where to stick it. I left it for you to do that. You did tell him to stick it, didn't you?"

"No, not yet, Dan. I haven't had the chance to tell Kira. You know ethically I can't reject a plea deal without telling my client."

He made a dismissive sound. "She's going to reject it. You're wasting time. Now you'll have to call Emmett back."

"Still, ethics require it. And I'm not going to tell Emmett no, assuming Kira says no, until the deadline. Why should I give him four more days to prepare?"

Despite himself, Dan looked pleased. "Well, that's some good thinking right there!"

I could do without the tone of surprise, as if I were a chimpanzee who'd managed to type a word.

"Thanks, Dan," I said, standing. Near the door, I turned and said, before I lost my courage, "And hey. Leave off handling my case, okay?"

I took off down the hall before he could respond, thankful I'd be so buried under an avalanche of work for Kira's case that I'd have an excuse to avoid him for the next month.

❧

Friday afternoon, I shut down my computer at four forty-five. I'd sent Maureen home at four, because her son played football every Friday night in the fall and Maureen never missed a chance to help out the school athletic boosters. I had no idea where Dan or his three assistants were—all was quiet in his part of the building.

Kira, as expected, had turned a fire hose of outrage on me when I relayed the official plea offer to her. How dare they think she'd be willing to trade three years of her life to avoid a trial when she would be completely vindicated at that trial? Didn't I know that being a convicted felon would mean she couldn't *vote*?

It went on in that vein for the approximate amount of time Maureen had predicted. Innocent or guilty as sin, Kira was as far from an easy client as I'd ever had. She hadn't been humbled at all by her weekend in jail; somehow she'd only become more entitled. She viewed me as the hired help and frequently treated me as such.

Most criminal clients weren't amoral or evil. They were regular people who'd grown up in unstable homes, usually without role models to show them the right way. Too often, no one had cared when they drank too much or tried illegal drugs or hung out with the wrong crowd. From there, one desperate mistake followed another, trapping them in the unending cycle of the criminal justice system.

Kira did not fit that pattern.

I dialed the commonwealth's office number with five minutes left before the deadline.

I let it ring and ring, wondering if everyone had gone home. Just when I was about to hang up, someone answered.

Surely I'd misidentified the voice. "Valerie?"

"Yes. Who's calling?"

"Uh . . . ," I stammered, unprepared to tell Valerie Williams herself that Kira had expressed a clear desire to consign the commonwealth and its offer to hell. "This is Allison Barton. Is Emmett there? I need to advise him of my client's plea decision."

"He's gone for the day, sweetheart." I was not fooled by the endearment. Valerie called everyone sweetheart: male and female, old and young. "I authorized the plea offer. Tell me and I'll let him know."

"Okay. Kira Grant rejects the plea deal altogether. She wishes to go ahead with the trial." I left off the expletives Kira had directed me to pass along.

"I wish you could get her to change her mind. This trial'll be ugly. No secret how nasty all these PTA women were to the victim, and what your defense has to be. Your society lady ought to realize she won't be the same person on the other side." Valerie sighed. There was a pause. "And neither will you."

For a second I had to entertain the notion that Valerie cared about me. No. Impossible. "I know. The alternative is so unacceptable to her that she'll risk it."

"All right. I'll tell Emmett. He'll be unhappy." Damned if she didn't sound wistful. I hadn't known Valerie had a wistful setting.

I know that, too, I didn't say. "Thank you. You have a good weekend, okay?"

"You, too."

I moved the phone toward the base to hang it up but caught her still speaking.

". . . and good luck to you."

Still shaking my head, I gathered my things to leave. It was Steve's weekend with Libby, so I had an extra-large "go home" pile to carry.

The outer office door opened, jingling the bell on the doorknob back. Dammit. I'd forgotten to lock it, and now I'd be stuck dealing with a walk-in.

Emmett ventured into my office, as if surprised no gatekeeper had wrestled him to the ground.

"Are you closed? Where's Maureen?"

"Gone to the football game. Looks like everyone left early but me. I just left a message for you with Valerie. Herself. Since when does she answer phones?" I set my laptop case and purse on my desk.

"Valerie does a lot of things. I actually came over to find out your answer."

It wasn't a long stroll from Emmett's office to mine. Still, it was odd he hadn't called instead.

"The answer is no. She won't take the deal."

He sagged slightly. "I thought that might be the case, but I hoped otherwise."

"She says she's not doing time for something she didn't do."

He slumped into one of my chairs. I perched nearby on the edge of the desk. He loosened his tie and ran a hand through his hair. "So I guess we're going to have to do this?"

"I guess we are."

"I'm tired already just thinking about how much work I have to do in less than a month. You, too—not like this is our only case."

A wave of weariness swept over me at his words. I'd counted when I was packing up my Friday piles: I had twenty-eight court appearances for other clients between now and Kira's trial, one of which was a full-day personal injury jury trial. Putting the finishing touches on Kira's case would have to get done in my free time at home. "Did you get a call from the *Washington Post*?"

"Yeah. I said 'no comment.'" He met my eyes. "Interesting legal theory she said you have."

"I said 'no comment,' too. She didn't get any of that from me. I don't know where they're getting their material. Someone is talking."

He squinted at me and smiled, a tired smile. "Between you and me, Valerie was angry I didn't comment."

"I'm sure. The press has been a good friend to her for a long time." After her daughter was raped decades before, she'd become an activist, and that platform and access to the media had gotten her elected to her position. Dan had told me a million times that Valerie continued to court them, trying, mostly successfully, to get them to print lurid details of crimes and rumors about defendants' past crimes that wouldn't be admissible at trial so the potential jury pool could be swayed. Don't let anyone tell you prosecutors are angels.

Emmett sprawled lower in the chair. "Don't you get tired of the lying? The deceit? The fact we work so hard on behalf of terrible people? I don't mean Valerie, by the way. She thinks she's doing right. Or this client of yours, specifically. I'm sure she's a lovely person," he said, raising a sardonic eyebrow. "But good God. Some of the victims are worse than the defendants. Do you know the vast majority of people live their entire lives without ever seeing the inside of a courtroom?"

I relaxed a bit more. I missed having someone to talk to about these things. The pace of my practice meant I hardly had time for my law school friends in other cities, and none of my nonlawyer friends would have a clue what Emmett was talking about. "Yes. I'm tired. And I've only been at it six years. Are we stuck here, Emmett? Are we going to be doing this dance with each other, dragging terrible people behind us into court for the rest of our lives?"

"I don't want that. I want to travel. I want to see the Great Wall of China. I want to sail around Cape Horn. Hell, it would be nice to be able to take a whole week off to go to the beach."

I let out a long sigh of delight. "Oh, that would be so nice. I'd love to see the world. I've even—" I shifted my weight on the desk edge and knocked my name plate off the corner. I bent to retrieve it.

Emmett bent at the same time, too close. I caught a whiff of his hair: almost like pine and leather. We managed to avoid knocking heads, but we both reached for the name plate and ended up with our hands touching.

I swallowed hard. Emmett moved his hand, sliding it slowly into place, until his fingers interlocked with mine. He stood, not breaking the contact. The name plate lay forgotten under my feet. He took my other hand and tugged me closer.

"Look at me, Allie."

My gaze went up, with halting movements, past the broad white expanse of his shirtfront, past the small V of his collar where his tie hung loose, past the faint shadings of his dark end-of-the-day stubble and into his eyes. The intensity there made my throat dry up. "Wh-what do . . . ?"

His unwavering stare burned. His lips parted. I think mine did, too, but I couldn't swear to it.

I couldn't swear to much of anything right then.

We should not be doing this. We should not be touching. We should not be here alone. We should not . . .

Without warning, he grazed one thumb along my jawline. I swallowed and inched closer. He lowered his head, bringing his lips toward mine. He paused there, a hairbreadth away, waiting for permission. My lips parted into a surprised-but-not-surprised O, then they made the decision and sought his. His kiss was both unbelievable and predestined, somehow.

I didn't like to think about how long it had been since I stopped looking at Emmett as only a friend. Years, possibly. So many minutes and hours I'd spent wondering about how his lips would feel on mine.

As the kiss deepened, he slid his hands to my lower back, anchoring me against the desk with his body. His hips pressed mine and invited me to dangerous places. Suddenly desperate, I clutched his shoulders, kissing him back, giving him everything. One of his hands tangled in my hair, tilting my face to get a better angle.

Alarm and worry and desperate desire mingled and overwhelmed me until I could do nothing but kiss him and kiss him and keep kissing him. God, he was as good at it as I'd always known he must be. His hair was as silky and thick as I'd imagined. His neck was hot to the touch under my hands. His lips were soft and knew me. And his tongue. It knew exactly how to move, and I imagined it moving elsewhere.

Things grew more frantic, desperate. Our bodies collided, tight against each other, so tight, heat burning me full length. I pushed papers off the desk like they meant nothing to make room for us and pulled him down with me, needing this, needing him. Our mouths were everywhere, leaving trails of fire as our hands kept returning to each other's cheeks to remind ourselves this was real.

Oh my God, this is real. I felt him realize it at the same time.

With almost simultaneous gasps, we separated, breathing hard.

For a moment, there was no sound but our ragged gasps for air. Neither of us moved. I imagined what we must look like: twin images, disheveled, horror-stricken, unsatisfied.

"Oh God, Emmett. The case. We . . . we can't. We're not allowed . . ."

"No. We're not. It's so wrong. I don't really know what I was thinking." He backhanded his lips and ran a hand through his hair, his eyes wide. The motion made me raise a hand to my own hair, only to find it a rat's nest. I pushed myself off the desk, needing air. Suddenly there wasn't enough air.

"I can't believe . . . we . . ."

"Oh shit," he said, closing his eyes. "Allison, you can report me. You should report me. That was my fault. I'd been wanting . . ." He trailed off, leaving that tantalizing sentence unfinished.

"Don't be ridiculous. I'm not going to report you. And it wasn't only your fault. I'd been wanting, too." I moved behind my desk, putting the furniture between me and my insistent desire to take him down in a whole different way than legal opponents normally did, right here on the cheap office carpet. My body, even now, vibrated with unmet need.

He backed up a step, too, eyes still wide. "I'll get the case moved to Sunil. Or Tiffany. Somebody. We can't go in there after this, like nothing . . ."

His dismay was beginning to damage my self-esteem. Um, not necessary to act as if I'd given him the bubonic plague. "Again, ridiculous. We kissed. We shouldn't have. We won't do it again. The trial's too close anyway. We'll go in there and do our jobs." I straightened my rumpled collar, slung my purse and jacket over my shoulder, and picked up my "go home" pile.

Emmett lingered by the door, a safe distance away, tucking in his shirttail where it had come loose. "That should sound like a really great plan. Except . . ."

"Except?" I turned off the lights and preceded him toward the lobby door.

He was quiet as we exited the building, then held out his hands for my pile of files to free my hands to lock the door. I let him, feeling oddly like crying. We paused, ready to go our separate ways. I waited for him to finish his sentence.

"Except . . . my God, Allie. Except I want to do it again."

TRIAL

CHAPTER NINETEEN

KIRA

Daddy used to say clothes make the man. If that's true, then clothes *are* the woman. Clothes tell you everything you need to know about any woman you've ever seen. Of course, I bought the most amazing suit Saks had to wear to my trial. I glanced at Allison, seated beside me and surrounded by boxes, folders, and paper. She wore the same black pantsuit I'd seen a million times. She hadn't even gotten her hair done. I wanted to poke her with frustration, but I settled for curling my lip when no one could see.

"All rise! The Circuit Court of Noble County is now in session. Honorable Judge Christopher Turner presiding. God save this commonwealth and this honorable court."

Right. As if God gave two shits about what happened in this pedestrian courtroom. There was a massive scraping as the audience behind me stood. We'd drawn a lot of spectators. A number of people from the press had asked me for comment—denied, of course—on the way into the courthouse. The crowd of cameras and stick-thin on-the-scene girls had grown. Miles had cringed, ducking his head. It made me want to jam one of my stilettos into his instep, though such a move would probably not have done me many favors in the stories they'd write today. I'd refrained and held my stomach in and my breasts high for the cameras.

Judge Turner, in a black robe, entered the courtroom from a small door behind the elevated bench and sat, dropping his file on the desk. He peered down at me, taking his first perusal of his defendant.

I tried not to giggle.

It took Chris a beat or two to make the connection between the Kira Grant in a penitent's business suit and the Kira Grant whose shining cleavage he'd ogled at the tennis court way back in August, but he got there. His eyes widened and his nostrils flared, but no sound came out of his mouth—nor would it. I'd neatly trapped him with his own appreciative gaze. His storied career would come to a screeching halt if he held up an attempted murder trial to announce his recusal on the grounds that he'd noticed the defendant had spectacular tits during a chance encounter three months before.

I gave him my best sober commiseration smile. The sunny sorority girl one wouldn't work here—I'd been cautioned against appearing unconcerned with the severity of the tragedy that brought us all here.

He blinked, cleared his throat, and we were in business. Not for the first time, it annoyed me that people had no idea how brilliant I was.

Because we had no jury, Judge Turner—Chris, to me—asked Amaro to stand and give his opening statement. It was predictable: I grew the plant. I'd clipped some with my gloves on and idiotically left the gloves where they'd caught the eye of law enforcement. I'd put the plant in a smoothie I made sure Summer drank. When he got to my supposed motive, I couldn't restrain myself from an eye roll massive enough to bring on a migraine.

Apparently, I'd snapped and decided to poison Summer because Summer had suggested Fiona might be dyslexic. I'd taken offense at her criticism of my parenting, and then I'd feared the wrath of Summer's employer, Social Services, for failure to treat my child's learning disability. I stared at Amaro. I hadn't suspected him of being a scriptwriter for *Law & Order* in his spare time. Creative. I'd give him that.

Allison watched Amaro avidly but gave away no reaction to the things he said. I wrote her a note instead with my thoughts on what utter bullshit he spouted. She didn't look at it.

Amaro wrapped up by saying I'd lied about my familiarity with wolfsbane, and I'd had the opportunity to place the substance in the cup. He sat.

Allison stood, with only a single sheet of notes, some of which she'd written during his opening.

"Good morning, Your Honor. I'm not going to waste anyone's time here. There was poison in Summer Peerman's cup. What happened to her, in front of her terrified child, was horrific. No one disputes those facts. What we will be disputing is who is responsible for that terrible event.

"The commonwealth bears the burden of proving, beyond a reasonable doubt, that Kira Grant, and only Kira Grant, is guilty of attempted murder, and that she, and *only* she, put poison in a cup with the intent to cause harm to Summer Peerman. In order to do that, they'll need you to believe she went out to her own lovely yard, where she grows an unusual and memorable plant she's shown to many people, and cut some wearing her own gloves. Then, you'll have to believe she casually discarded those gloves on her own porch in plain sight of anyone visiting. On top of that, you'll have to believe she took this poisonous plant to her son's school with plans to put it in the cup of her best friend in the world, in the presence of her own child and dozens of other people, over a weeks-old disagreement over child-rearing."

Allison paused, with a level of drama I hadn't known she possessed, and caught the eye of the judge. "I think you'll agree that's going to be difficult. The commonwealth may be able to prove opportunity here. There's no dispute she grows the plant. They'll call witnesses who'll no doubt say they were there, they were in the PTA with my client, they remember the smoothies and pouring them out for the kids, but not one of them will say they saw Kira put anything in anyone's drink. Was she there? Yes. Did she hand the victim the poisoned cup? Unfortunately, yes. But did she put the poison in? No. Because she didn't. You won't hear a single person say they saw her do it. She herself denied it—to law enforcement, to the victim herself, and to everyone who's ever asked her. Kira has no criminal record—not shoplifting as a teen, not even reckless driving. Nothing."

Well, to be fair, I would have had multiple shoplifting convictions if the CVS near my house in high school had ever caught me. I didn't volunteer that little tidbit, however.

"What the commonwealth can't prove is motive. That's because there isn't one. There's no way a woman with as many advantages as Kira—and as much to lose—risks her family, her happiness, her very freedom over . . . what was it, Mr. Amaro? Some argument over parenting choices? Kira and Ms. Peerman were friends. They argued, and then they made up. At no time did Ms. Peerman ever threaten Kira with her position as a Child Protective Services worker. That motive is flimsy at best and laughable at worst."

Despite myself, I was impressed. I'd never told Allison that Summer hadn't threatened me. She'd come up with that on the spot. Maybe I'd underestimated her.

"Furthermore, she's about the only woman at the PTA refreshment table who doesn't have a motive to hurt Summer Peerman. Summer had made some enemies. One woman had a public spat with her about playing time for their sons on the soccer field, culminating in Ms. Peerman's son getting the primo spot over his rival on an all-star team. Another had actual history—as in litigation with—Ms. Peerman's employer, the Department of Social Services. Motives, Your Honor, abound.

"It so happens, however, that the commonwealth is unable to find one for Kira Grant. Their case is all theory, no evidence. Thank you."

Well, well, well. Turned out I'd hired a bulldog after all. I gave her a nod to acknowledge I was pleased. I glanced at Miles, sitting in the front row wearing the orange UVA tie I'd bribed him to wear with sexual favors. He gave me a discreet thumbs-up. She'd done well, judging from the resentful glare the Amaro man gave her.

"Thank you, Counsel," my pal Chris said. "First witness, Mr. Amaro?"

Amaro got the boring people out of the way first. A botanist from Richmond talked about wolfsbane and its poisonous properties. I noticed she never referred to it as aconite or monkshood. Wolfsbane sounded worse, I supposed.

Hospital Guy came back to discuss how the alkaloid poisons found in wolfsbane were found in Summer's stomach and the inside of the cup she'd dropped, but not in any other cup at the party or in any of the milk jugs Brandi had brought. He said the amount she'd ingested would have killed anyone under 120 pounds.

Some forensic scientist, so young she could have been Floppy Child's twin, testified that no alkaloid residue had been found in the kitchens or anywhere else on the property of any other woman at the refreshment table, but trace amounts had been found on a pair of pink flowered gardening gloves left on the floor of my porch. Amaro showed her the gloves in a bag. I felt a twinge of loss. Those gloves had been my favorites.

Ruthanne—in a blue polka-dot sheath dress and matching headband—testified about the party, the smoothies, the staffing of the refreshment table, Brandi's milk jugs and the pitchers to which we'd transferred the sludgy purple liquid (my description, not hers), and the immediate aftermath of the disaster. Allison asked the experts no questions and Ruthanne only two: did she put the aconite in the cup (no), and did she see me put aconite in the cup (no). When she was finished, we took a lunch break.

Given the glaring going on between them, I assumed Allison and Amaro wouldn't be sharing a table for two at lunch and sucking on a single strand of spaghetti. I spent my break chattering on about Finn's fiddle lessons and Fiona's eczema issues to Miles, ignoring his despairing silence and the fact that tears welled up in his eyes whenever he met mine. I took the high road and ignored it rather than slapping him across the face.

Back in the courtroom, the audience had grown and now included the commonwealth's attorney herself, the one who ran for election every four years. I knew her face. The trial resumed with little fanfare. Now that he'd set the scene, Amaro called the victim. Within minutes, Summer lumbered up the aisle. She glanced at me and bit her lip. I hoped that was a good sign.

Nope. Summer and her expert testimony skills didn't help. Both attorneys were solicitous of her, and we quickly heard again about her experience at the party and how I'd brought her a pie and indicated I didn't know what aconite was.

This time Amaro anticipated Allison's questions. "Do you know who poisoned the cup, Ms. Peerman?"

"No."

"Did you see anyone adulterate the cup?"

"No."

"Tell us about how you ended up with that actual cup, if you could."

"I went up to the table with my son. I headed in Kira's direction, because she was a friend, and I didn't know Ruthanne. Tammy was filling cups and sliding them into rows, not handing them out. I didn't really want to take a cup, because I've had smoothies at PTA events, and they never taste good."

For a second, the echo of the friendship that used to exist between me and Summer flared. We'd laughed about Brandi's smoothies. Summer once said they tasted like what you'd get if you pureed your crisper drawer with an envelope of Kool-Aid. She'd made me laugh. It was too bad, really, that things had gone the way they had between us.

Before getting too maudlin, I glanced back into the audience, looking for Brandi. No sign of her. I supposed she had to wait somewhere else because she was a witness. What a pity. Wouldn't have hurt her to hear from someone other than me that her smoothies tasted like a vacant lot.

"So how did you end up with one?"

"Aidan was sugar-buzzed. They'd been playing all day, bouncy castles and such, and cupcakes in his classroom, and he had a bit of last-day-of-school hyperactivity going on. He darted ahead of me to the table. Aidan grabbed a cup of smoothie from farther down the table. Kira handed me one, like as a joke. We'd joked before about not being fond of the smoothies. Aidan tossed his first cup back and reached for another. I stopped him and tried to give him the cup in my hand since I didn't want it, but he changed his mind and waved it away. I think the aftertaste may have hit him. He ran off with a friend. I was left holding a cup and I would have thrown it away, but Brandi came out of the kitchen when her son called her and would have seen me. We'd had enough drama, so I drank it to get rid of it."

"So that was the poisoned cup?"

"Yes."

"You were going to give it to your child and he almost drank it?"

"Yes." She glanced at the judge. "Thank God they tasted bad enough he didn't want seconds."

"I have only a few more questions," Amaro said, looking almost guiltily at Allison. "Can you describe the nature of your friendship with Ms. Grant? How close were you?"

"Objection to relevance!" said Allison, standing up beside me.

"The defense has indicated that Ms. Peerman was the defendant's 'best friend in the world' and implied that the relationship mitigates against motive," Amaro said, shoulders squared.

"I'll allow a little leeway here, Counsel. We'll see where it goes." The judge sat up straighter.

There was a long silence. Long enough that something twisted down deep inside me in a way that felt distinctly like pain.

"I would imagine that Kira thought of us as closer than I did," Summer said, biting her lip and looking at me.

"Why do you say that?"

"Because her friendship was always on the surface only. She never tried to get to know me deep down. She's white, obviously, and she used to assume things she didn't have the right to assume. Like . . ." Summer searched the air, as if the memory would materialize.

"Like the time she asked why I'd want to go to the beach. Like it was a joke. She said she used to lie out in the sun for a whole vacation when she was a teenager to get half the 'tan' I started out with. As if her reason to go to the beach was the only reason."

Oh my God. She'd read the paper. Was she trying to co-opt my plan to throw the judge a racist to blame? Was this some strategy she and Amaro had cooked up to paint *me* as the racist?

"She used to compliment me," Summer went on. "Said I never got bothered when other people said stuff or was oversensitive. I was so easy to talk to, she said. She never asked if I was actually bothered. She was content to assume that because I never said anything, that I wasn't. It's hard to feel really close with someone who isn't interested in . . . in your *story*. In what matters to you. Oh, she was my friend. I'll stand by that. Just not as close a friend as she might have thought."

My stomach felt hollow and stunned. Like being hungry and finding out they've dropped the last plate of dinner in the kitchen. I didn't want to process that feeling, so I refocused on anger. Who did these commonwealth assholes think they were? Was the fact that I was a bad friend, according to Summer, supposed to mean I wanted to murder her? I would absolutely love to see the dictionary definition of *bad friend* right about now. Summer's face would be under it.

"Have you ever outright argued with Ms. Grant?"

"Only twice that I can think of."

"Tell us about the first time."

"It was about four years ago. We'd gotten together for drinks. Kira was angry the school hadn't recognized Finn for his straight As that year. Aidan, too. I said honoring the straight-A kids in their grade would hurt two children in particular, who struggled mightily but never got straight As. It got surprisingly heated, but the wine might have been to blame."

Actually, the school was to blame. They never hesitated to recognize athletic achievements. Summer's argument would mean we shouldn't award MVP or varsity letters lest we destroy the already-teetering confidence of the unathletic, and I hadn't yet seen anyone marching in parades to shore up the self-esteem of the uncoordinated and the scrawny.

"How did this fight resolve?"

"We yelled at each other a bit, and then after we cleared the air, everything was fine."

Everything was fine because I knew there was no point in arguing such an obvious point with someone so blind.

"And the second argument? When was that?"

"In May, I think. About three weeks before the graduation party."

Oh, Summer. Don't you dare. Fiona doesn't need your pity.

"What happened?"

"I don't know. This was different. Kind of odd. I watched Fiona, Kira's younger child, for an afternoon. She had some distinctive issues with her reading. With her understanding of letters. Kira had mentioned before her concern about Fiona being slow to read. When Kira came to get her, I asked if she'd thought of getting her tested for dyslexia. She went off." She shuddered.

"Went off? Can you describe it?"

Summer shook her head. "Well, I don't know. I'll try. Kira is always controlled. Very calm. Self-possessed. But that day—after I said the word *dyslexic*, she went into a rage."

I jabbed Allison in her frumpy thigh. *Do something.* She jumped up. "Objection."

My pal Chris nodded. "Ms. Peerman, be more specific. You can't describe emotions another is feeling. It's speculation."

"Okay," Summer said, understanding how to screw me immediately, damn her. Yep, this friendship she thought was so flawed was over. "Her face turned red. Like, really red. Her eyes widened. She clenched her fists and her jaw, and her voice lost all hint of warmth. She ordered Fiona out of the room and then turned and kind of growled out, 'You will keep your fucking nose out of my business.'"

"She cursed? Is that unusual for her?"

"Yes. I've never seen her that upset. I've never heard her use a curse word before. She told me once her father made her do a sheet of math problems for every curse word he heard."

Good thing she couldn't hear the inside of my fucking head, then.

"After that, what happened?"

"She didn't talk to me for a week. Snubbed me once at school, in the pickup line. And then she just started up acting normal out of nowhere."

"And how long was this before the fifth-grade graduation party?"

"About three weeks."

"That's all the questions I have for this witness." Amaro sat down. Summer waited for Allison to begin speaking. She stood, slowly.

"Ms. Peerman, you're not a doctor, are you?"

"No."

"You're not a psychologist, or a learning specialist, or a school counselor, or in any way qualified to make an official diagnosis of dyslexia, are you?"

"No."

"This argument you had in May. You offered an unsolicited parenting opinion, did you not?"

"I did."

"Kira didn't touch you, did she?"

"No."

"She didn't threaten you, did she?"

"No."

"She didn't tell you to watch what you drank three weeks later, did she?"

"No. Obviously not."

"You never suggested to her that Social Services would investigate her if she didn't get Fiona checked out for dyslexia, did you?"

"No. That wouldn't reach the standard of abuse or neglect. I could have been wrong. We never investigated Kira for anything."

"Oh, and the argument before that, the one, what, four years ago? Let's dispense with that right now. Do you have any reason to believe Kira would be motivated to poison you because of your argument over academic honors for first graders, four years ago?"

She considered. It occurred to me what a risk Allison had taken to ask that open-ended question. Then I realized it only appeared risky. If Summer said no, then it would seem like she believed in me. If she said yes, then she'd look crazy to believe a four-year-old argument over something so dumb had motivated an attempted murder.

"No," Summer said.

"Thank you, Ms. Peerman. That's all the questions I have."

Summer got off the stand and headed for the doors. The commonwealth's attorney—Williams, that was her name—got up to put an arm around her and walk her out. A show of support for the victim that the judge wouldn't miss. Clearly she thought as much about optics as I did. Damn her.

The judge stretched. "Next witness, Mr. Amaro? We have time for maybe two or three more."

I checked the clock above the empty jury box. It was only two thirty.

"Investigator Joseph Lucado."

Great. We could spend the next hour enjoying the spectacle of Neck-Roll Toad flinging feces at the wall. The back doors of the courtroom opened, and the toad himself entered. Somehow he'd managed to get an even less flattering haircut than he'd had at the preliminary hearing.

He took his seat. Amaro underwent some kind of body language change, almost as if he were warding off a blow. Beside me, Allison tensed.

Amaro took him through his name, his title, his experience. He told the same lie about me describing Summer as fat. He told the same lie about me telling him I'd never heard of aconite. I controlled my anger; somehow knowing it was coming made it easier.

Amaro glanced at Allison. "You have in your notes here that Ms. Grant said during your visit that she and the victim had been friends for a long time?"

"Yes. She said that."

"She told you about an argument they had?"

"Objection. Leading."

"Sustained," Chris-the-judge said, with a half yawn. He leaned heavily on an elbow as if trying to stay awake. I bet he'd wake up if I stood and did a little bend and snap.

"Did you and the defendant discuss any arguments she'd had with the victim?" Amaro asked. I couldn't understand why Allison had objected if rephrasing the same exact sentence fixed everything. It reminded me of the ridiculous rule on *Jeopardy!* where the contestants had to say "What is" before every answer.

"Yes. She told me about an argument."

Amaro looked at Allison again. I really didn't much like this solicitous thing they had going on. What was this? "This argument concerned the way the school treated the kids' grades?"

"Objection!" Allison said, flushing red with anger. "Leading!"

"You're leading your witness, Counsel. Sustained. Watch yourself. I give a certain amount of leeway to law enforcement witnesses, but don't push it."

Now I saw. Amaro had telegraphed a message to Mendacious Toad. By breaking the rules. Allison was outraged. She muttered something to herself, too low for me to hear.

Amaro rephrased like a good little *Jeopardy!* robot. Toad said the answer right. He got in all the evidence he needed: plant found at my house, in my garden, gloves on my porch, nothing found at Tammy's, Brandi's, or Ruthanne's houses related to aconite.

"Oh, one more question, Investigator," Amaro said. "When you asked the defendant about arguments with the victim, did she admit to only one?"

"Yes. Only one. An old one years ago. About grades."

"She didn't tell you about storming out of the victim's house weeks before the poisoning?"

"Not a word."

Amaro turned him over to Allison. She stood, back straight, hands clenched.

"Investigator Lucado, do you recall testifying at the preliminary hearing in this matter?"

"I do."

"You noted in your report you asked about an argument between Ms. Grant and the victim?"

"Yes."

"This is a copy of your report, is it not?"

"Yes. That's it."

"In the report your words on this topic were 'said she and victim had been friends for a long time and last argued over their sons' grades.' Is that an accurate reading of your report?"

"Yes."

"Can you take a look at this document and tell me what it is?"

He turned over some paper in his meaty hands. "Looks like a transcript of the preliminary hearing."

"At the preliminary hearing, when you were asked about this, your answer is found on page seven. Can you read us that answer?"

"I said, 'She said something about their grades. I gather the Peerman boy is a better student than the Grant boy. I can't recall specifically.'"

"Do you have any reason to believe that transcription is not accurate?"

"No."

"Your Honor, we move for the admission of both of these documents: Investigator Lucado's original report, and the transcription of his testimony at the preliminary hearing."

"If there's no objection from Mr. Amaro, they'll be entered."

Lead-the-Witness Prosecutor didn't object.

"So at the earlier hearing, you guessed, is that right?" Allison asked Lucado. "The part about the Peerman boy being a stronger student?"

"I wouldn't say—"

"Would it surprise you to learn that both boys have perfect straight-A averages from kindergarten to this very moment?"

"Uh. Well, she said—"

"Would you like to see their report cards?"

"I only know what—"

"No? Well, let's move on. In fact, Investigator, Ms. Grant didn't say anything about one boy being a better student than the other, did she? No one did. Because they're identical students. You were speculating at the preliminary hearing."

"I wasn't—"

Allison's questions came rapid-fire. She gave the investigator no time to dissemble. It was a performance, and a good one. "When Mr. Amaro questioned you just a minute ago about this, you agreed with him that the argument was about the way the school treated the grades, not what they were, correct? Should I have it read back?"

The court reporter, otherwise as unremarkable as a thumbtack, lifted her head, a gleam of excitement at the opportunity to do something other than type lighting her dull eyes.

"No. No, I said that."

"Today you say the argument was about how the school treated the grades, correct?"

"Yes."

"At the preliminary hearing you said the argument was about one boy being a better student than the other?"

He saw the trap and wanted to fight. His neck roll turned red. In the end, though, he had no choice. "Yes. That's what I thought it was about then."

"So two different stories about this argument, both under oath," Allison said. She made sure to meet the judge's eyes as she said "under oath."

"I do the best I can to remember what witnesses said."

"Uh-huh." Spectacular contempt for him just dripped off her. "Do you recall also testifying at the preliminary hearing that you don't write everything down?"

"Yes, I explained then I can't write everything down, but my memory is good, and—"

"I think we've established your memory might not be as good as you think, Investigator, haven't we?"

Lucado goggled but said nothing.

"Either that, or the part where you swear to tell the truth, the whole truth, and nothing but the truth doesn't mean much to you."

"Objection!" Weak sauce from Amaro, but I supposed there were obligations.

"Withdrawn. No more questions." Allison turned her back on Lucado.

My meek little lawyer had squashed the toad.

CHAPTER TWENTY

ALLISON

After Emmett rested the commonwealth's case, Judge Turner overruled my motion to strike the case, which meant he thought Emmett had done enough to require me to put on a defense. It was 4:00 p.m.: time to break for the day, and we'd return tomorrow. That meant I had a bit of time to work before I had to pick up Libby.

I knew I'd done about as well today as ever before in a trial. Kira and her husband had gone, but not before effusive praise from Miles and a quick "I hope it goes as well tomorrow!" from Kira. I'd hidden in one of the underused courthouse conference rooms after the recess, so I wouldn't have to risk running into Dan at my office. The blank beige walls, a utilitarian table and chairs, and the low buzz of the fluorescent lights gave me a modicum of peace.

Emmett had stalked off without a word, out the back of the courtroom toward the stairway that would take him to his office, to lick his wounds.

Today had been the hardest day in court I'd ever had. Every point I'd scored was his direct loss, and I'd scored more points than he had. Courtroom law didn't work like a tennis game or chess, fairly played and then shaken off. Every objection sustained, every judge's lecture, every wrong question asked, every bad answer elicited: it was personal.

It all made you look stupid and incompetent and in front of an audience of the media and the bar. Every lawyer had heard the bailiffs and the court reporters giggling over How Embarrassing It Was last week, or worse, The Time When That Thing Happened years ago. No lawyer was immune, though of course we didn't hear the laughing when it was about us. We all knew it happened, though. Judge Turner had been a revered prosecutor in the city of Lynchburg before he took the bench. His opinion mattered.

Never before had it bothered me to beat up an opponent. Most of the time I had a client I liked or a lawyer on the other side I didn't, and in criminal cases, Valerie's avenging-angel zeal made it fun to win. But something had changed. Emmett no longer stood in for Valerie. He was just Emmett. I'd probably killed whatever had happened that afternoon in my office. Since that day, we'd behaved ourselves. We'd never discussed it, and we'd made damn sure never to be alone together even for a minute.

None of that had kept me from lifting my head when anyone said his name, freezing to listen when I heard his voice, staying tuned perpetually to some kind of Emmett-frequency only I could hear. Alone at night, after Libby had gone to bed, my imagination grew torrid. I dreamed about him naked, me writhing over him in the sheets.

A knock startled me. I closed the folder I'd stared at for fifteen minutes. "Come in."

The object of my obsession filled the doorway but made no move to step into the room. He stood for a moment, starting and stopping a sentence at least three times. I waited.

"Look. You had a great day today. I admit it. You ran circles around me." His face was cold. Uninterested. Maybe I'd only been a toy to him.

My skin went numb. What if the kiss, the ice cream, the . . . *wanting*, all of it, was some kind of massive distraction attempt? Romance the out-of-her-depth single mom and keep her off balance, prevent her from preparing her case adequately and litigating it articulately once in court? He'd told me I should report him after the kiss. Maybe he'd been telling the truth. He stood here now, detached and emotionless. He'd chased a hundred beautiful women or more—as easy for him as breathing. I didn't fit the pattern. Weren't we trained as lawyers to watch for the thing that didn't fit the pattern?

The realization woke my self-loathing, and with it, an absurd desire to lash out. "Thank you," I got out.

God, I was stupid.

"I should go," he said, his eyes unreadable.

Not so fast, bud. I had some things to get off my unremarkable chest. "You let Lucado lie again. You encouraged him to lie. Leading questions, much?"

He had the grace to drop his eyes and look a bit embarrassed. "Yes, they were leading questions, but I wasn't encouraging Lucado to lie. I was trying to stop him from lying. I care about the truth, you know. I trusted the victim's version of that argument more than his."

None of that diminished my level of upset. Emmett was supposed to be one of the good guys. "Stop him from lying? You tell yourself that, Emmett. You were trying to get him to tell a consistent story with Summer's and make him a more reliable witness, and you know it."

"Believe what you want," he said, his tone implacable.

"There's not a single member of the bar in a ten-county area who doesn't know he's the bad apple. The worst liar in law enforcement. You know it, too."

He didn't deny it. "For what it's worth, the new sheriff isn't a fan of Lucado's general attitude and is encouraging his retirement."

I gave him a dramatic eye roll and pressed my lips together. Even if that were true, it wouldn't do a damn thing to help me now.

Emmett hadn't appreciated my theatrics. The lines of his body knotted tight and anger roiled off him. "You know I never want a liar on the stand."

"Well, then you know what to do about that." I jumped up, slamming my folders together. "Try not calling a liar as a witness! Or maybe tell him beforehand, 'Hey! Let's try to get our falsehoods down to fewer than two a minute, okay?'"

He took a step closer, and his eyes flashed dangerously. "I don't choose the investigator. The fact that he fudges his reports ended up helping you today, not me. I've got to dance with the one who brought me, Allison, just like you. Or hadn't you noticed you're sitting next to a cold-blooded killer?"

"Oh, stop." Blood rushed through my veins, though I couldn't chalk it all up to anger. He'd implied I was acting as consigliere for a murderer, and yet. And yet. "You have no damn idea who poisoned that woman. It could have been any of the four or anyone else. It could have been some sick psycho who put poison out there, without even knowing where it would land, like the Tylenol killer. Just walked by and dropped it in a cup. You can't prove otherwise."

"It wasn't a random sick psycho, and you know it."

I did know it. That was the worst part. Ruthanne had no reason, it would have been impossible for Tammy to hide traces of aconite in her mess of a trailer, and somehow, Brandi's up-front hatred was too clear for her to have risked her kids when she'd be so obvious a suspect.

Kira had done this, somehow. I just couldn't figure out why.

"What I know is you rested your case, and you didn't prove it wasn't some sociopath."

He closed his eyes, a telegraph of exhaustion. "Okay. We'll agree to disagree. Let's stop before we prove what jerks law has turned us into. I only came in here to compliment you."

My fury evaporated like that. He'd had a spectacularly shitty day in court, and he had in fact come to find me for that purpose. Oh God. I was an asshole. A killer-defender asshole. "Emmett. I . . ."

"Don't," he said, holding up his hands. "I'll see you tomorrow. Hang on to that anger. You'll need it."

❧

I crept into my office, an index finger over my lips so Maureen would stay quiet and Dan wouldn't hear me come in. She shook her head sadly, then said in a normal voice, "Dan's waiting to talk to you in his office." She lowered her voice. "Sorry. He does seem pretty happy, though."

I made a vague "kill me now" hand motion and went straight there. Better to get it over with.

"Well, well! I hear you cut Lucado down to size! Nicely done, nicely done!" Dan had gotten into his bottom right drawer early this afternoon, I saw. His cheeks shone red. He gestured at the chair across from him. I sat, knowing I'd be here awhile. "Did I ever tell you about the time when I caught a forensic scientist who'd falsified a lab test on the stand? Beautiful moment. First year in practice. The guy was a true-crime fan and desperate to bring down my guy. I got two independent lab tests and I got him."

I mustered up an impressed expression, but I was so tired.

"You'll have a great moment like that one day, hon. Your day is coming. Today sounds like a nice start, though." He scanned me from head to toe and back. "That what you wore to court today?"

I glanced down. I wore a black pantsuit with a cream silk blouse and burgundy patent heels. The shoes were new. Here we go. "Yes. Why?"

"Wear a skirt suit tomorrow. And don't button the blouse up so high. And maybe think about a how-to video on makeup. That's one of a million advantages you girls have that the rest of us don't. Judges like to see some leg. You're not bad-looking, but you need to maximize what you have going on there."

"Dan, this conversation is not appropriate. It's not for you to tell me what I should wear. And I am not planning on making sexual overtures to the judge." I stood, the relief of righteous anger washing over me.

Dan guffawed. "Oh please. Trial law is all about appearance. I expect you told your client how to look, didn't you?"

Dammit. I had, of course. I'd told Kira to look nice but not too rich, attractive but not too sexual.

He kept laughing. "If you didn't, you're committing malpractice. Did I tell you about the time when I had a custody case over a little girl? I represented the mama. Dad claimed Mama had been letting the little girl sneak off to screw her boyfriend. Fourteen years old. Girl turned up to testify in a T-shirt that read 'Slut.' Kind of ruined my case."

I would have liked to have seen it. Dan usually told only stories in which he appeared as a titan of legal prowess. It figured he'd make an exception for The Time When a fourteen-year-old "slut" had ruined his case. "Thanks, Dan, for the tips. I've got a long night of work, and I've got to pick up Libby first."

I'd grown to dislike Kira so much that I'd forgotten how much more I disliked Dan. I needed to win this case. This win was my ticket out. Renewed energy—panic, more likely—fired my synapses. I raced back to my office and made three trips out to my car with all the case materials. I had twenty minutes to pick up Libby before the late fees set in, but I'd be awake all night going over this case.

Kira insisted on taking the stand.

I'd lost at least six nights of sleep to my growing certainty that my client had purposefully handed out a poisoned cup and that anything she'd say on the stand would therefore be a lie. If I found out she was lying, I'd be faced with the choice of withdrawing on the spot, which was what the ethical rules required, thereby cluing in the judge that she was lying and ensuring her conviction, or letting her talk and knowingly suborning perjury.

I didn't know for sure what she would say. I told myself *belief* in her guilt wasn't the same as *knowledge* of her guilt. A threadbare ethical blanket to be sure, but it covered me.

As usual, I rolled in to the after-school day care with no more than five minutes to spare. Another mother, wearing hospital scrubs, gave me a tired smile as we met at the doors. Libby raced up to me with a piece of construction paper onto which she'd glued butterfly antennae and a prodigious amount of glitter.

"Mommy! You're here!"

A flood of peace relaxed me as she hugged me and hung on. Glitter transferred itself all down the front of my not-sexy-enough black suit, but I didn't care. For a few minutes, I could just be a mom. Loved by her child no matter what I wore, what I said, whom I sat next to in a courtroom. Unable to do wrong. For a minute, I envied Ruthanne Dillard or Brandi Crane or even Kira, able to spend as much time as they wanted with their children.

"How was your day, buddy?"

"Good! Mrs. Quinn let me be the line leader! 'Cause the bee with my name on it stayed in the Green Fields of Good for a whole week!"

"That's great. I'm proud of you. How about we get pizza?"

"Can it be cheese?" Libby did not like food touching other food, up to and including pepperoni.

"Sure." We walked out to the car, hand in hand. I didn't know how much longer she'd let me hold her hand in public, but I hoped it would be forever. Nothing felt better.

"Mommy, did you win your trial?"

"Not yet, buddy. It's not finished yet. I have to do the rest of it tomorrow."

"When it's done, can you come to my class and do an art project?"

"Maybe." I checked the buckle of her car seat, then started the engine.

"Oh! I forgot! There's a new girl in my class. She used to be in Miss Gonzalez's class but now she's in mine."

"That's good. Make sure you're nice to her. What's her name?"

"Fiona."

Oh God.

As far as I knew, Wolf Run Elementary boasted only one kindergartner named Fiona.

And I knew her mother well.

CHAPTER TWENTY-ONE

KIRA

I hate school mornings. I want to kill everybody on school mornings.

School mornings when I also had to show up in court to be tried for attempted murder somehow managed to be even grimmer than usual. I gave up trying to sleep at five and showered and fixed my hair. Of course we only had one working shower today, because apparently the second one leaked. Something about the grout failing. Miles called somebody, but they couldn't come for days. Fiona got a bath the night before, but I still had to shuffle three people through the shower in time to leave the house by seven thirty for the early middle school start time.

I dumped kibble in the dog's bowl, but he was nowhere to be found. Ungrateful beast. I started unloading the dishwasher, only to find Miles had shoved two dirty plates in with the clean late last night, rendering the whole load suspect. I ran it again with my teeth grinding themselves into dust, then went upstairs to wake my family, none of whom had heard of alarm clocks. I thought about trying to make the bed with Miles still in it. I shoved his shoulder instead and headed for Finn's room.

"Finn! Get up now. Your 'five more minutes' is up. Go get in the shower and I'll have breakfast ready. Go." I stood there, waiting. Nothing. No movement. I stomped into his room and yanked the blanket off him. "Finn. Time to get up. We don't have time to dawdle today." He reached sleepily for his glasses.

Allison had said she thought we might finish the trial today and get a ruling by nightfall. She said if I was found guilty, I'd be taken to jail right then. I could be in jail this time tomorrow. I wouldn't have the chance to wake Finn or kiss Fiona again. Something inside melted my temper away. I sat on the edge of his rumpled bed and rubbed his shoulder, reaching to squeeze his warm hand. Such a good kid. The vessel for all my hopes and dreams. Love for him choked me, robbing me of speech. My purpose on earth was to act as his shield and sword.

Like Aidan had done, the day of the poisoning.

My feelings toward Aidan had been uncomplicated—and negative—until that day. He was bigger, stronger, and more popular than Finn, and there'd never been a single thing I could do about it. But that day, in the bouncy castles, Jacob Zimmerman made a game out of knocking Finn down over and over as they bounced, laughing and calling him foul names. Finn fled from the inflatable thing, straightened his glasses, and let out a tiny, heartbreaking sigh. The Zimmerman lout had done this kind of thing before; the truth was written in the defeated slump of Finn's skinny shoulders.

My blood boiled and I moved toward that little turd to tell him a few things that would ruin his sleep for a couple of months, but Aidan saw it, too. He got there first and shoved Jacob in his chest to get his attention. Using his ridiculously large vocabulary, Aidan made clear that he wouldn't tolerate anyone being mean to his friend Finn, and if Jacob didn't like it, then Jacob could find a new sport, because Aidan would never pass him the soccer ball again. Jacob apologized quickly, aware he'd be reduced to eating lunch with the nose-pickers if he didn't.

I hadn't had to do any defending at all.

It meant I'd had to change direction on a dime when it came to Aidan, but I'm adaptable.

"Five more minutes," Finn mumbled now.

"No, sweetie. Time to get up." I hauled him bodily into my arms, causing a start of surprise. I didn't do this often enough anymore. He slumped against me, and a memory flashed of sleeping on the sofa with him as a newborn, a warm bundle on my chest. Now he was all bony limbs and musty prepubescent smell. I held him long enough for him to begin struggling away. I kissed his forehead and gave him one last squeeze. "I love you, Finn. You know I'd do anything for you, don't you?"

He nodded and shuffled off to the bathroom.

"Fiona, sweetie. Time for school." She sat up when I entered her room, her beautiful hair like minted gold in the earliest rays of the sun. I ran my hand down the shimmering length and kissed her on the top of it. She'd always been easier to wake in the morning than Finn. "You've got a new teacher, remember?"

I'd finally convinced Miles to let me persuade the school to switch Fiona from Miss Gonzalez's class to Mrs. Quinn's. The latter was an experienced teacher with a motherly, easygoing manner. Miss Gonzalez had actually emailed us and suggested Fiona needed special services. I hated that the switch had coincided with the day of my trial, but it seemed to have gone well yesterday. She'd made friends but of course couldn't remember any of their names. I carried Fiona downstairs, her growing weight a bit too much for me.

In the kitchen, a wild-haired Miles poked in the cereal cabinet, waiting for Finn to relinquish the shower. "Have we got any Kashi?"

"*We* are out of Kashi. Eat something else." I mentally cursed myself for the sarcastic tone. "We" needed Miles today. He'd be the first witness for the defense in a matter of hours. I slipped behind him and put my arms around him and squeezed. He turned and kissed me. I did my best to pretend I didn't notice the morning breath.

"Oh, Miles," I said, the ghost of the flirtatious girl I'd been creeping in, "tell me everything is going to be okay. I can't bear the thought of . . ." I gestured around the familiar kitchen and at Fiona, knees pulled up in the armchair in her nightgown while she buried her face in her blanket and stuffed animals.

"It'll be more than okay. You've got a great lawyer. She did a heck of a job yesterday. We've heard all the commonwealth's evidence. If that's all they've got, then they've got nothing. Eh. It looks bad for them, and we haven't even heard all the other motives the other women have."

He patted my shoulder. "It'll be fine."

❧

Miles stood at the front of the courtroom, resplendent in his navy suit and another orange tie. He held up his right hand.

"Do you swear to tell the truth, the whole truth, and nothing but the truth, so help you God?"

"I do." He took his seat in the witness chair. He looked so handsome I almost forgot he'd left his stinky running shoes on my driver's seat all night.

Chris-the-judge had seemed to recognize Miles when they called his name. Figured. Miles was a dentist, a professional, the one who'd gone to the right schools and belonged to the right clubs. A guy who lived a life not much different from Chris's. A man whose name was important to know. A man. I swallowed my resentment, because today, that clubbiness would only benefit me. Chris sat up taller on the bench, the way guys do when they sense the presence of other alpha males.

Poor Amaro. Apparently he didn't inspire that level of respect on the part of Chris-the-judge.

Allison, now wearing a skirt suit, unfashionable pantyhose, and some seriously dark circles under her eyes, rose to question him. "Can you tell us your name and how you know Kira Grant?"

"I'm Dr. Miles Grant. I'm a dentist," he said, looking at the judge like I'd told him to. Chris nodded and actually smiled. "I'm Kira's husband."

"Do you have children?"

Amaro stood. "Objection to relevance."

"I'll allow some leeway here, Counsel," Chris said. Amaro had clearly been expecting that. He sat, unflustered.

"Yes. We have two children. Finn is twelve, and Fiona is five. They're in school right now."

"Do you recall the last week of school this past spring?"

"I do."

"Can you tell us about it?"

Miles went into a speech about the PTA activities and my dedication and love for my children. Though I knew Allison had essentially written it for him, I let myself pretend he'd given me a real compliment. They were rare enough.

"Did you attend any of these events?"

"I was on my way to the school for the part where they walk the halls when I heard about what happened to Summer."

"Right. Let me ask you about the day before the last day. Do you remember the day before the graduation?"

"They had the awards ceremony. I went to that. Finn won so many awards, and it was a big deal for him. Kira cried."

I hadn't, actually, but he might have thought I did. Other mothers had.

"And after the ceremony?"

"I congratulated Finn and went back to work."

"What time did you get home?"

"I didn't. I met Kira and the kids at O'Charleys for a celebratory dinner and then a movie. Some animated thing."

"Had your house and the garden been unattended that day?"

"Yes. Kira was at the school for PTA all day. Then she had to pick up Fiona from the babysitter. When I got to the restaurant, Finn was still wearing his medals from the awards ceremony."

"Would another person have had an opportunity to go onto your property and cut some monkshood?" Allison glanced at the judge.

"I'd think so. We have a fence, but it doesn't lock. It's a big yard on a quiet street, and most of our neighbors work all day."

"And you and Kira? What did you do between nine that night and when you left the house again the next day for work and school?"

"Not much. We put the kids to bed and watched some TV together and then went to bed ourselves. Kira was exhausted. In the morning, we rushed out the door like we usually do. Nothing at all unusual."

"Was Kira with you the whole time after your workday?"

"Yes."

"Did you see her go out to the garden at any point that evening?"

"No."

"Out of curiosity, Dr. Grant, has Finn ever received a B?"

"No. Well, not in elementary school. I understand he's teetering on the edge of a B in math now he's in middle school."

He was. The fear of a B made me crazy, especially now that he refused to let me do all his math homework for him. I'd already begun taking him to a college professor for intensive tutoring. That next report card figured almost as prominently in my nightmares as prison.

Allison asked him questions about my garden and what I grew and how many people had been invited to see it over the years. He estimated at least a hundred people had seen the monkshood in that time, which, let's be honest, was generous, including Tammy and Brandi for PTA meetings.

As if Miles could pick either woman out of a lineup where they wore name badges, but I'd take it.

"And one last question. The day before the graduation party, the day of the awards assembly, how long do you think your house was unoccupied and its garden unattended?"

"At least twelve hours. Actually, fourteen. From about seven in the morning until nine at night."

"Thank you."

Amaro did a half stand. "No questions."

Thank you, Miles. That went exactly as we discussed. Nicely done. He stepped briskly off the stand and veered off track to touch my shoulder. I smiled my brave smile up at him. His eyes glistened. Wow. Previously unsuspected talents.

As he left and we waited for Tammy to take the stand, I glanced at Allison. On the surface, nothing was amiss. She made notes and shuffled papers and opened and closed folders as she always did, but something was missing. Aha. She wasn't doing that little-lost-puppy-dog thing with the Amaro man. They acted as if they weren't in the same room. Most likely, Amaro had had his manly feathers ruffled by our win with the toad yesterday. Bad deal for Allison—being a tough lawyer in a man's courtroom would dent her romantic prospects. No man wanted a ballbuster. Good deal for me, though. Ballbusting worked perfectly fine for me.

"Your name?"

"Tammy Cox." Tammy, as usual, wore clothes that had fit her when she was in high school in 1995. It was hard to believe she'd been skinnier then than now, but it had to be true. Her threadbare V-neck showed off every ridge and strap of her bra, which she barely needed. Though I thought we were all glad she'd worn one.

"Ms. Cox, were you an officer of the Wolf Run Elementary School PTA last year?"

"Yes. I was secretary." She was shaking—no opportunity for cigarettes in far too long—and her voice was so quiet the judge had to ask her to speak up. She kept glancing my way. I never broke eye contact. *Know who is boss here, Trashy Tammy. Remember, I know what you did.*

"Were you present on June 2 at the fifth-grade graduation party?"

"Yes."

"Can you tell us about that day?"

"Well, I didn't have no kids at the party—I got one in the middle school and one was in first grade. So Kira said for me to wash the pitchers and scrub the kitchen and all the tables and change the garbage bags while she watched some dance party or some such in the morning."

"I take it you're not a fan of Kira?"

"Kira and I get along, but we ain't friends. If you know what I mean."

"Have you ever done any tasks at her house?"

"Yeah." Maximum sullenness. "I weeded her garden once."

"How long ago was that?"

"Early this spring sometime. April, maybe."

Allison had said this would be a careful dance with Tammy. If everything went perfectly, Allison would get Tammy to admit to not liking me, but prevent her from telling the court I'd blackmailed her into doing the shit jobs and weeding my garden. According to Allison, judges frowned on defendants who persuaded people to do things by holding the threat of criminal prosecution over their heads. Who knew?

I'd admitted readily to Allison that I'd blackmailed Tammy with her theft from the PTA coffers. If you asked me, I'd been kind. Legally, I should have reported the theft, but DSS would have taken Tammy's kids away. My solution was win-win. Someone had to do the nasty PTA jobs. Why shouldn't it be the person who'd tried to steal from it? My conscience was clear as a mountain spring.

On that score, anyway. Tammy and I had other history that did not need to make any appearance in this courtroom—for both our benefits.

"How did the smoothies get into the building?"

"Brandi brought 'em first thing. She and I spent a long time cramming them into the fridge."

"They were served later?"

"Yeah. After she come back, Kira said we had to pour them all into the pitchers I'd washed. Looked nicer, she said." Tammy made a sour expression I'd seen before. It didn't improve her looks.

"Did you see Kira put anything into any milk jug, pitcher, or cup of smoothie?"

Tammy blinked. "No."

"At any point prior to the time Summer Peerman fell onto the floor, did you see anyone, anyone at all, put anything into the cups?"

"Yeah."

I froze. Allison froze. What? What was she doing? Holy crap. We'd fended off Mendacious Toad. If Tammy the Half-Naked Criminal tried to go off script, I'd make what Allison did to the toad look like a warm squishy hug.

"What did you see?"

"I saw a boy, Joshua something, big kid, spit in a cup and then hand it to another one."

The courtroom let out its collective breath. I started breathing again.

Allison managed a laugh. "Did you see any other person put anything other than saliva into a cup at any point that day?"

"Nothing but them nasty smoothies."

"Summer Peerman, Ms. Cox. Are you a fan of hers?"

"We had our differences."

"More than differences, wasn't it?"

"We had our differences."

"You've been in this courthouse before, haven't you?"

Amaro stood. "Objection. Leading."

"I'll rephrase," Allison said. Given that Tammy was cooperating so nicely, you'd think she'd look a bit more fiery, but Allison went about things as if she were working an ordinary shift at Walmart. "Have you ever been involved in a case in this courthouse before?"

"Yes."

"Was Summer Peerman involved in that same case?"

"Yes." Tammy's teeth began to chatter. She probably thought we'd be morphing this case into some Social Services nightmare.

"Was this an abuse and neglect proceeding?"

"They only said neglect. On the paper. That's all." She shot past fear all the way to naked, shaking terror. Her voice went all high and thin, which, combined with the smoker's raspiness, produced a very weird sound indeed.

"Neglect of your two daughters?"

"Yes." Her voice cracked. Allison had her.

"How did that finding affect your job situation?"

"I got fired the next day."

"Who was the social worker who asked the court to make that finding?"

"Summer Peerman." In her skinny face, her eyes were huge, like one of the caged dogs in the mournful animal cruelty ads on TV.

"Did she have the power to remove your children?"

"So she said. If I did anything wrong."

"Was she still watching you?"

"Yes."

"How did you know she was watching you?" Amaro waited for an objection opportunity, but Allison was careful and methodical.

"At Field Day she said she was."

Allison let a pause stretch long. The courtroom was silent. "And how long before the poisoning was that?"

"Four days."

And perfect. God, Allison had a gift for the dramatic ending. Funny she didn't have a bigger reputation in Lynchburg. Everyone I knew thought Dan was the one you wanted.

Amaro stood up. He didn't look at her. She didn't look at him. There was so much not-looking it started to get awkward.

"Ms. Cox, I apologize. A few questions."

Tammy looked up at him mutely, still shaking like a leaf.

"You didn't put the wolfsbane in the cup, did you?"

"No." Her voice was so unsteady she had to say it twice. "No."

"You weeded the defendant's garden."

"Yeah."

"Out of the goodness of your heart, or for money?"

She stared at him with defeated eyes. "Little of both, I guess you could say."

"Would you recognize wolfsbane in a garden?"

"No."

"Thank you, Ms. Cox." Amaro pivoted as if heading back to his table. Then he pivoted back. "Oh, Ms. Cox. One more. When you weeded the garden, did the defendant warn you about the poisonous properties of that plant?"

"No."

"She didn't tell you it could be dangerous merely to touch it with your bare hands, did she?" Amaro held up his own hands as if to remind her what hands were.

"No. She didn't say nothing about that."

"Thank you."

As I suspected, Tammy wasn't the sort to be bothered much by a few lies under oath.

CHAPTER TWENTY-TWO

ALLISON

Q: What do they call a dozen lawyers at the bottom of the ocean?

A: A good start.

There's a seed of truth in all those jokes. I'd had bad moments as a lawyer, but I'd rarely felt worse than I did after questioning Tammy Cox. I'd made her relive her terror of the removal of her children. Fear had been rolling off her in sickening waves. I'd almost made it seem as if such a thing could happen at any moment, while she sat here under subpoena, with an ambush outside in the hall. What kind of job was this? The ethical rules required me to represent my client "zealously." The rule applied even if it meant smashing to smithereens the psyche of an impoverished single mother who loved her children, and on behalf of a wealthy woman who had everything.

Emmett had given me a look, only one look, as I passed when he stood to question Tammy. Anger flared again—prosecutors like to pretend they're on the side of truth and justice, but they had to do plenty of low-down things, too. They've taken apart many an innocent witness on the stand. I'd seen it done.

And now I had about ten seconds to decide if I'd made it to the bottom of the sea or if I wanted to start digging in the silt. Not that it was a real decision: Summer had forced the issue. I'd have to put Brandi Crane on the stand and call her a racist.

Summer's testimony had made Kira look thoughtless at best and uncaring at worst. Not long after I met her, I'd wondered how much worse Kira's blatant lack of concern for other people would come across to a friend of another race, and even though I could have guessed, it had been easier not to *know*. With a pang, I considered how nice it was for me to have the choice not to know. Summer didn't.

No matter—I knew now. And so did the judge.

I wavered. Brandi had to testify: she made the smoothies and argued with Summer over the travel team. I could go over the argument about soccer and not get into the Facebook post or publicly allege she was a child abuser. And a racist. Without that, I was 80 percent sure she'd still say enough to establish reasonable doubt—and of course I'd established Tammy also had motive and opportunity to poison Summer. I'd already destroyed one person today. Did I need two?

Kira had been clear from the beginning. The judge needed to have someone to blame other than Kira, and he'd be more likely to do that if Brandi looked worse. If I chose not to pursue that line of questioning, and Kira got convicted, that choice would be the centerpiece of her malpractice case against me. And Dan would make sure I defended that malpractice case unemployed.

There was no choice at all. There never had been.

"I call Brandi Crane."

Brandi came into the courtroom, waved at her soccer prodigy son and a teenage girl seated in the gallery, took her oath, and sat. She gave her name and said she'd been present at the graduation party. I got her to give me a brief history of her involvement in the PTA and the plans for the fifth-grade graduation party.

"Did you have anything to do with the refreshments at that party?"

"I made the smoothies at home and brought them."

"Why did you do that?"

"My youngest, Griffin—that's him sitting right there," she said, pointing, "was graduating and this was my last thing with the elementary PTA, and I wanted to do something for him. He loves those smoothies." I turned, despite myself. Griffin, though a big kid, had a baby face and an electric smile.

Oh God.

For Kira, I asked, "What did you put in the smoothies that day?"

"Oh, I hate to say my secret recipe."

"Truth, Ms. Crane," I said with surely the last smile that would grace my face today. I could practically hear Kira memorizing the recipe to mock it later.

"Okay, then. Strawberries are the base. Beets for color. Coconut water and honey. And spinach and flaxseed for the vitamins. And radishes. Only a couple radishes. They give it a little kick. They're so healthy."

Dear God. Radishes. No wonder Summer Peerman couldn't taste the wolfsbane.

"Were all the milk jugs the same? Did you put different ingredients in any of them?"

"No. It was all the same."

"Do you know what wolfsbane is?"

"Yes. My daddy ran a landscaping company. I used to work for him in the summers. It's an ornamental plant found in some gardens. Poisonous."

"Were you aware Kira had it in her garden?"

"I'd seen it there, yes."

Every question got harder. I hated to do this.

"Did you and the other ladies pour the smoothies into the cups from the milk jugs?"

"No. We poured it into the PTA pitchers first, then they carried those out to the table."

"Did you see Kira put anything into the smoothies? Anything at all?" In her pretrial interviews, she'd said the same as the other two ladies: no. She hadn't seen Kira put anything into a cup.

"Well, I was mostly in the kitchen, so I don't know." Instantly, my gut went into overdrive. Sweat dampened my underarms. The train, just like that, had gone off the tracks.

"What do you mean?"

"At one point, I went out to talk to my boy. Kira was at the table pouring smoothie from one pitcher to another pitcher. To consolidate them, she said, and keep it cold. There were three people at the table, and four pitchers, which seemed odd to me. I didn't see what she did with the first emptied pitcher."

Oh shit. Bad. Bad. Bad. *Four* pitchers for three people? The rookie mistake sank like deadweight into my stomach: I'd never asked anyone how many pitchers. How many had been tested for aconite? I glanced at Emmett, who looked like he'd been cattle-prodded. He was flipping madly through his file. Dread dried my throat, but there was nothing to do but press on.

"That's not what I asked you. Did you see her put anything into the liquid?"

"No."

Brandi stared me down with the tiniest of smirks. She knew exactly what she'd done with the four-pitchers thing. She'd done it on purpose. It didn't even matter whether it was true. She'd given a method. An extra pitcher. A way Kira could have accomplished it.

All of a sudden I didn't feel so bad any longer. I might be a terrible person, but so was my client, and Dan, and Lucado, and probably the judge. Brandi Crane might be a racist, had definitely hit her child, and was terrible, too. The courtroom tainted everything and everyone who entered. We'd all go straight to hell together. There'd be a line for entry longer than the ones at Disney for Space Mountain. Despair at the awfulness of everyone overwhelmed me. The thin strap tethering me to social convention snapped.

"Are you and Kira friends?" I changed my tone, lost any last hint of conciliation.

She sat up straighter, understanding we'd quit the small-talk portion of the proceedings. "I wouldn't say so, no."

"Did Kira post anything about you on Facebook?"

"Objection. Leading." Emmett stood, watching me.

Judge Turner steepled his hands. "Rephrase, Counsel."

I advanced past the counsel table, closing in on the witness stand. "Have you and Kira ever had an online dispute?"

"Yes. She called me a child abuser on Facebook."

"Did she name you?"

"No. She quoted one of my posts."

"Go ahead and tell us, Ms. Crane. What was your post about?"

"It was about what happened at a soccer game. My son got involved in a fight. I went over and corrected him with a swat. Summer Peerman threatened me with a child abuse report to Social Services." Brandi raised her chin a bit. She knew punches were coming. Not dumb, this one. She squinted her eyes at me, enough to let me know she was pissed.

Well, great. That made two of us. "May I approach?" I asked the judge. He nodded. "Let me see if I have it here. Can I show you this printout? Is this from your Facebook page?" I closed the last distance to the witness stand and got right in her personal space to show her the exhibit.

She took the paper, snatching it out of my hands, her body language clear she didn't like me this close to her. Good. She was getting angry. Angry people didn't govern their tongues well. They made the best hostile witnesses. They tended to say things they wouldn't otherwise. "Yes. This is the post I wrote." She shoved it back at me.

I held up my hands, refusing to take it back and making clear I wanted nothing to do with touching it. Out of the corner of my eye, I caught Emmett's acknowledgment of what I was doing. "Careful, Ms. Crane. Can you read it again and make sure it's what you wrote?"

"It is."

I asked for and received permission to have a copy admitted as evidence.

"Can you read it aloud?" I studiously avoided facing the audience where her children sat.

She bent her head and read. "'For those people who like to stick their noses in other people's business and talk big about calling the cops on me for swatting my child for fighting, let's be real—my mama used to make me go back for a second switch if the first one wasn't thick as her thumb. A swat isn't abuse and Social Services needs to stay out of our homes and let us make decisions for our own kids.'"

More than one person behind me in the gallery clapped. The judge banged his gavel. "Quiet in the court."

"Is that the post Kira quoted from?"

"Yes. I got sixty-two likes on it." A snorting laugh sounded from the gallery.

"Was Kira one of them?"

"No."

"Did she quote your post approvingly?"

"No. She called me a child abuser." Brandi stared down Kira at the table. Kira, God bless her, managed not to sneer back.

Now or never. "Did she call you anything else?"

"She hinted I was a racist."

"And are you?"

"Objection!" Emmett shook his head, dismay written all over him. He'd read the *Washington Post* story. He knew we'd get here. His expression made me more determined. He'd put Lucado on the stand to lie. Emmett was in line for the rocket ship to hell along with all the rest of us. God, I'd give anything for a cool glass of water right now, but even the water in this courtroom was fetid and sour.

"It goes to motive, Your Honor," I said, part of me hoping the judge would sustain the objection and end this quicker. "The victim in this case is a person of color."

"Get there quick, Counsel. Answer the question, Ms. Crane."

"No. I'm not a racist. I believe everyone should be treated equally."

I took a second to consult my notes, trying to figure out where to go next, when Brandi spoke up without a question pending.

"I'm sure Kira thinks I'm a racist because I get tired of Griffin losing opportunities because he's white. Which is the opposite of equal," she said.

"Losing opportunities?" I was dumbfounded and stammering. My God. She dived right in. Kira had been right all along. Brandi's anger at Summer had been race-based, and what's more, she was dying to vent it.

"Yeah, lady," she spit at me. "You tell me with a straight face he's not losing opportunities. My boy is the best player on his soccer team and got benched for no reason. A Black kid gets his position and plays it for three games, and then he's the one who got the all-star travel team spot instead of my kid. Soccer's a pretty white sport—all the time we're hearing about how we need more Black kids in soccer. That coach probably figured somebody'd accuse him of being a racist if he sent only white kids to the all-stars. Well, to me, picking kids to advance because of their skin color only is racist, too, that's what I say."

I forced myself not to look at the gallery, where Griffin Crane could hear every word his mother said. "Did you speak to the coach about it?"

"Yeah. He claimed it had nothing to do with race." She followed this remark with a brief sniff, which made clear what she thought of that. "Of course he said that. Everyone says that. It's never true. Everybody's afraid of looking racist nowadays. They all bend over backward to make decisions based on race while screaming to the sky that race has nothing to do with anything."

I let her rant echo in the chamber for a few seconds. She'd said enough—more than enough—to give herself a motive, but we had a whole array of motives to discuss. "You said Summer Peerman was there when you . . . what was it you said? Swatted your child for fighting?"

"Yes."

"What is your understanding of Summer Peerman's job at that time?"

"She works for Social Services. She takes people's kids away."

"What if any conversation did you have with Summer that day on the soccer field?"

"She threatened me with a Social Services report. Must be nice to go swanning around, judging other people's parenting all the time. Must be nice to be perfect."

"What did you say to her?"

She stared me down. I excelled at this part of questioning a witness—we both knew where things were going, but because of the formality of the courtroom and the intimidation of the judge's presence, she wouldn't get there until I let her. It allowed for drama. It enraged the witness, helpless against the inevitability of the reveals. All that emotion worked in court. I tried not to think about the fact that my career required me to manipulate other people's emotions as a blood sport. "I didn't argue. She was ugly to me. She got in my face and said stuff about my kids."

"When, in relation to the graduation party, did this argument occur?"

"A long time. A month, maybe. More."

"What's the name of the boy who took your son's spot on the travel soccer team?"

Her lips twisted, caught in the trap she'd seen coming a mile back. "Aidan Peerman."

"And who is his mother?"

"Summer Peerman."

"The same Summer Peerman who got poisoned at the party?"

"Yes."

"The party for which you made the smoothies for the refreshments and then helped serve them?"

"Yes, durn it, you know it's the one." Brandi Crane was ready to flee.

"When did you find out Aidan had made the travel team and Griffin did not?"

"Middle of May."

"The poisoning took place on June 2. Was it about two weeks before?"

"Yes," she growled, looking guilty as hell.

I headed back to my table without releasing her. I turned back in time to see her getting up, seriously disgruntled. "Oh, Ms. Crane, I have one more question for you." Watch me, Emmett. Two can play at the leading-question game.

"When you found out about the travel team spot going to Aidan Peerman, you told Summer Peerman to 'enjoy it while you can'?"

Her face went white with rage. Emmett jumped up to object, but she spoke first. "I durn well did. She thinks she's so special. So perfect and right. Well, that ain't the way the world is. You gotta enjoy stuff while you can, because you never know when your time in the sun is up."

Dear Lord. "Thank you. No further questions." I turned my back on her.

"But I didn't poison her!" Brandi yelled behind me. "I didn't do nothing to her!"

There was a buzz behind me. People talked and got up to leave. The door opened and closed. The judge banged his gavel again. "Quiet! Quiet in the gallery or I'll clear the courtroom!"

I sat and had time only to whisper one question in Kira's ear. "Four pitchers?"

She nodded.

Emmett stood, the expression on his face thunderous. "Ms. Crane, you didn't put anything in those smoothies other than the edible ingredients you told us about, did you?"

"No!"

"You don't like Kira Grant or Summer Peerman, is that fair to say?"

"Yes, it's fair. They're hateful to me."

"Is that enough reason to try to kill one of them?"

"No. They have to live with their sorry selves. I didn't do nothing to those smoothies."

"Four pitchers went out of the kitchen with only three women to pour them at the table? You're sure it was four?"

Dammit. He'd seen what that might mean.

"Yes."

"And the pitchers and that there were four was Kira's idea?"

"Yes."

"Have you ever engaged in an act of violence against a person of another race?"

"No. Nothing. My boy was in the room. If I'd wanted to kill Summer Peerman, I'd have durn well done it out of sight of my kid! I promise you that."

"Are you a racist?" Emmett's questions came like drumbeats, one right on the heels of another. He wanted her off the stand, and no wonder.

"No, I ain't. I only believe in fairness."

"Thank you."

Brandi got up and stalked out, red-faced. She stopped in the aisle, beckoned her children, and they left. Before she turned away, I saw the track of a tear on the cheek of her teenage daughter.

I hardened my spine. We'd arrived at the big moment. "Defense calls Kira Grant."

Another wave of buzzing from the audience. In the language everyone knew, a defendant has the right to remain silent. Anything she says can and will be used against her—including her testimony in her own trial. In the end, the choice belongs to the defendant, and the choice to testify was rare.

Kira stood, elegant as ever in an indigo suit and nude heels. She looked amazing. She swept her now dark-blonde hair back and strode confidently to the stand. She took her oath with her head held high and stated her name. I took her through her background and her family and some of the various things she did for the community: PTA, former swim team mom, Garden Club, church choir. It never hurts to get in that your defendant sings in a church choir.

"Let me ask you right off the bat, Kira. Did you put aconite in the smoothies in an attempt to poison Summer Peerman?"

"No. Absolutely not."

"Do you now or did you then have any desire to injure Summer Peerman?"

"No. Never. She was my best friend."

"'Was'?"

"Yes. She used to be." She offered the judge a sad, sweet smile. "She was right; I thought of her that way. During the time since I was charged, the prosecutor hasn't allowed me to have contact with her. I've lost my friend, but worse, my son, Finn, has lost his best friend as well. Summer's son, Aidan, is important to Finn. In fact, earlier on the day of the poisoning, Aidan defended Finn from a bully. I'd had no idea up to that point what a good kid he was."

Kira had never before mentioned this heartwarming tale, not even during our practice sessions. Distant mental alarms went off. Her expression didn't quite match the story. She looked pleased—with herself, not Aidan. Something was significant here, and I was missing it.

I had no time to ponder it now, but the disquiet burrowed deep. *Up to that point.* What changed about Aidan that day? I searched my notes.

"Is Finn a good student?"

"An excellent student. Straight As in elementary school. Straight As so far in middle school. He got two perfect scores on the statewide tests they gave last year. In math and reading," she said, as if to negate what her husband had said about the boy struggling in math.

"And you have another child?"

"Fiona. She's in kindergarten. We have yet to see what kind of student she'll be, but she is a sweetheart of a child."

"Did you and Summer argue about her as Summer described?"

"Summer did suggest I have Fiona tested for a learning disability, but I wouldn't agree I got that angry. I was very stressed out that afternoon, and it had nothing to do with Summer. I had no idea Summer thought I wasn't speaking to her. I see now there was a lot that Summer didn't tell me about how she felt. It certainly wasn't intentional or because I was angry or anything. I was extraordinarily busy that week."

"What kind of things did you and Summer do together?"

"We had coffee every now and then, or went out for a movie or drinks if we could manage it. More often, we got together when our boys were playing together. We babysat for each other. She kept Finn for the three days when I was in the hospital having Fiona. Not long before the graduation party, I kept Aidan for a weekend so she could go to the beach with her sisters."

"You heard the investigator say you called Summer fat. Did you call her fat?"

"No. I believe he asked me about her physical appearance. I said she was on the heavyset side and easygoing."

"Did he ask you about the aconite plant?"

"No. He never said one word about the aconite, or wolfsbane or monkshood, or even a rosebush. He never asked me one word about plants at all."

"So he's not telling the truth when he says you denied knowing about it?"

"He's not telling the truth. He never asked me. And it's not in his notes."

"Why did they find aconite residue on your gardening gloves?"

"Because I'd cut some flowers from the hydrangeas for a table bouquet for my dining room several days before the graduation party. The hydrangeas are next to the monkshood—sorry, that's what I call it—and I must have pushed the monkshood aside to get to a particularly attractive mophead. I pulled off the gloves on the porch to answer my cell and then totally forgot about them."

I got permission to approach and showed her a photo. "Can you tell me what is in this picture?"

"It's a picture of the east side of my house. That's my garden."

"Did you take this picture?"

"Yes. Around the end of June."

"What does this picture show?"

"It shows the monkshood in my garden as an accent plant among the hydrangeas. You can see the hydrangeas are on the downswing—this was a bit after the graduation party. At that time of year, the monkshood hadn't yet bloomed, but the hydrangeas were only beginning."

I got the picture admitted as evidence. "How long have you grown monkshood?"

"Oh, years. Miles and I moved into this house when Finn was tiny—not yet walking. I started right away on the garden. It's looked pretty much like this for at least five to seven years. I love to garden. I used to be vice president of the Garden Club before I got arrested."

"Have you shown the monkshood to the Garden Club?"

"Oh yes, and a number of brides, and of course every single member of the PTA. Including Brandi and Ruthanne and Tammy. Summer's seen it, of course. I love entertaining. Everyone I know has been to my house."

"You've also heard Tammy and Brandi testify here. Did you know about their issues with Summer?"

"Well, I knew about Tammy's issues with Social Services. She'd mentioned it a time or two. I didn't know for sure Summer was the worker on her case, because Summer is so circumspect about her cases, like the law requires, but I did know Tammy didn't care for Summer. It wasn't hard to put two and two together."

"And Brandi?"

"My son doesn't play soccer, so I wasn't present when she and Summer argued. I so hated to hear about Griffin being hit by his mother on the soccer field. He's a sweet boy, and it must have been humiliating for him. I did see Brandi's post on Facebook and I did quote from it, but I was careful not to use her name because of her children. My post was about asking for a world for our children in which we could end the sometimes violent discipline our parents and grandparents perpetuated."

Unease tensed my shoulder muscles, already tight. Kira on the stand was an entirely different person from the one I'd met before. She came across as sweet and sunny and respectful and honest and everything I'd never seen any sign of before. She'd erased all evidence of the entitled arrogance I thought had been her resting default. How?

Such an astonishing personality transplant certainly helped my case, but it didn't bode well for the truth. The truth, apparently, was whatever Kira wanted it to be. The amazing amount of things Kira may have secretly resented about Summer Peerman without Summer's knowledge expanded on into infinity in my worried brain. I needed to get her off the stand, and quickly.

"Did you call Brandi a racist in your Facebook post?"

"Oh no! I was totally shocked to hear her say the things she said today. I had no idea. In my post, I talked about how I worried about the world my children live in and said I'd heard about a friend being subjected to a racist remark, but I wasn't referring to Summer or Brandi with that sentence. It was a different friend." She smiled so sweetly it would melt anyone's heart.

Oddly enough, mine stayed quite frozen.

"Your post talked about discipline—did that part refer to Brandi?"

"Yes. That part did."

"One last question. Can you explain the four pitchers thing?"

"Oh sure! Brandi was stationed in the kitchen, pouring her smoothies into them. I assigned three of us out at the table to handle the crowd—me, Ruthanne, and Tammy. The PTA owns four pitchers, so I thought it was a no-brainer to use them all. That way we could keep the drinks pouring as fast as possible, and allow for one of the pitchers to go back and forth to the kitchen for refills. I assure you there was no nefarious motive."

"Thank you, Kira. Mr. Amaro may have questions."

She turned this new sunny smile toward him.

Mr. Amaro definitely had questions. Emmett stood up with an alacrity that brought to mind the wolf outside the three little pigs' houses from the story I'd read Libby last night.

I sat, pressing my damp hands together between my knees, praying.

"Ms. Grant, you're a garden expert, correct?" Emmett peered at his papers, as if only now discovering this fact.

"Well, I don't know if I'd say 'expert,'" Kira said, with a pretty dip of her head toward the judge, who hung on her every word, "but yes, I know my plants."

"So you're familiar with the properties of wolfsbane, and the danger that can come from ingesting it or even touching it bare-handed?"

"Yes. In fact, I never allow my children to play outside without supervision in part because of that."

"You live in a subdivision, do you not?"

"Yes."

"There are other children there, yes?"

"I suppose so. Yes."

"Do you supervise all of them, too?" Emmett looked ready to pounce.

Kira blocked him. "Well, no, but we do have a fence around the yard."

"Tammy Cox weeded your garden for you, didn't she?"

"Yes. She did."

"Without gloves?"

"I don't know. She didn't ask to borrow mine. I assume she brought some."

"You didn't say a word to her to protect her from the wolfsbane, did you?" The coil and the spring for the pounce came again. Again, foiled.

"Not that day. I had her weed the rosebushes."

This flummoxed Emmett. He hadn't been expecting that. Nor did I think he would bother to recall Tammy to confirm it. Kira was betting on that, too. Oh God. She might be lying, but I didn't know for sure she was lying and I didn't want to know. "Where are the rosebushes?"

"They're in the backyard in a separate plot. Not in the beds around the house. Rosebushes are deciduous," she said, and then for all the world like she wanted to help Emmett out, added, "You know, they drop their leaves. They're not pretty in the winter, so I have them a bit out of sight. There's nothing poisonous in that part of the yard." Kira gave him her most helpful smile, then added, almost as if it were an afterthought, "Of course Tammy had gotten the full tour of the whole garden during PTA meetings. She would have seen the monkshood then."

I couldn't read Emmett's expression. He was either shaking with frustration at being thwarted or filled with grudging admiration for her adroitness. "The investigator asked permission to take gloves from your porch?"

"Yes."

"They tested positive for aconite, didn't they?"

"Yes. I normally put away my gloves, but the phone rang and I forgot them. If I were guilty, it would have been pretty foolish of me to leave them out, right? I mean, I'd have burned them the same day if I'd used them to try to poison Summer, wouldn't I?"

Judge Turner raised a considering eyebrow. Kira had made clear her intelligence to the judge. Not getting rid of—and then handing over—those gloves would require spectacular stupidity in a guilty person.

"You testified that the PTA owned four pitchers?"

"Yes. I bought them myself two years ago. Blue glass."

"Ms. Grant, you heard the experts testify earlier. Do you recall hearing that they inventoried the kitchen at the school and tested everything for aconite residue?"

"Yes."

Emmett held up a stapled document, then showed it to me. A lab report on the kitchen contents admitted without objection early in the trial. I'd never thought to ask what *wasn't* on it. I nodded at him, feeling sick.

"Are you aware that only three pitchers were found at the crime scene?"

Kira smiled at him, completely unruffled. "No surprise, really. I would imagine that whoever did this got rid of the one with the poison in it, if that's what they used. To throw attention off the PTA." My God. The way she could think on her feet. The random-stranger theory I'd liked so much had shattered at my feet like a blue glass pitcher, but she'd handled that curveball like an MVP.

"You were the one who handed the cup to Summer, did you not?"

"Yes. I handed cups to dozens of people. Tammy and Ruthanne filled them and slid them into place and I handed them out as fast as I could."

"It would have been difficult, would it not, for someone other than the PTA ladies to poison the cup?"

"Yes. I'd say it would be almost impossible."

"Then tell me, Ms. Grant. You can't explain why yours was the only home to show any traces of aconite of the four ladies present that day, can you?"

"No. I can't explain," Kira said, almost cheerfully, still flushed with pleasure at having fended off every one of Emmett's attacks. He pivoted, as if to sit down. Behind him, Kira continued. "But I can say only an imbecile would pick a poison from her own garden, dump her garden gloves on her own porch floor, mince the monkshood tiny enough not to be noticeable, and then hand a special cup directly to the victim. And I'm far from an imbecile."

There, at last, was the touch of arrogance—and the alarm bells grew louder in my head.

That was the last seminormal thought I had that day.

ꕥ

I didn't remember how Kira got off the stand. Emmett must have stopped asking questions. Judge Turner must have released her. She must have returned to the table somehow.

Time stopped.

Mince the monkshood, she'd said. A nice, alliterative phrase.

The problem was that no other witness had used it before her. No one—not the botanist, not the medical professionals, not the forensic scientist—had said what form the monkshood had been in when it went into the cup. It could have been diced, juiced, pureed, whirled through a Cuisinart. I'd seen cooking shows. *Minced* was a specific term.

Why would Kira use that word unless she'd been the one doing the mincing? How else could she know?

And yet. She'd said only an imbecile would hand the cup directly to the victim. Kira was many things—most of them frightening—but most definitely not an imbecile. And yet she had handed the cup to the victim.

But what if Summer hadn't been the victim she'd intended?

During our first appointment, Kira had told me that the amount of poison in the cup had been too small to kill a person of Summer's size. I'd filed it away as a self-satisfied comment on Summer's weight.

My stomach lurched.

The dose had been too small to kill someone who weighed as much as Summer. But not someone who weighed less. The expert witness had said it would have killed someone below 120 pounds. The elementary school cafeteria on the last day of school had been full of people who weighed less than 120 pounds. Fifth graders often did.

The dots snapped together, and a new theory showed itself to me whole.

It was so horrifying it couldn't be true.

Time started up again with an attention-grabbing throat clearing from the bench. "Ms. Barton, do you have more witnesses?"

It took me a second to make the words come out. "No, Your Honor. The defense rests."

CHAPTER TWENTY-THREE

KIRA

That, ladies and gentlemen, is how you testify at your own criminal trial. Daddy would have been so proud. I'd pretended he was here, watching me be the perfect southern girl: attractive, kind, accomplished but humble, smart but respectful, and above all, sweet.

I made my way back to the table, my heels managing to make my backside sway. Without looking, I knew Chris-the-judge's eyes must be on it.

He cleared his throat. "Ms. Barton, do you have more witnesses?"

"No, Your Honor. The defense rests." Her voice was a croak. I glanced at her. She was white-faced. Something was wrong. She'd better not get sick before we got all this done. We were too close to our goals to ruin everything with projectile vomiting.

"Anything else from the commonwealth before closing statements?"

Amaro stood, shuffling papers. His hair looked even more unruly than usual. Way past "surfer cool" to something more like "run over by a lawn mower." "No, Your Honor."

"Fine. It's four o'clock. I've got a matter I've got to hear before the end of the day, and these folks have been patiently waiting. You can give your closing statements in the morning. I'm sure you'll appreciate the time to prepare them."

Neither attorney appeared pleased by this news. This trial had been expected to be a day and a half and now it had stretched into three. I'm sure they had lawyer things to shuffle—not that I cared. Noise broke out in the courtroom as the audience for my trial departed and the people for whatever came next moved into place.

Amaro swept his things into his arms and stalked out.

Allison turned to me, gathering her folders, grim as death. "Where did Miles go?"

To make himself useful, I hoped, though it was odd he hadn't waited for me. "I saw him dash out as I was coming off the stand. Finn has a fiddle lesson, and Fiona needs picking up from the babysitter."

She smiled, though it didn't reach her eyes. Allison had done a hell of a job on this case, but she was in the wrong line of work anyway. She didn't love it. She'd signed on to become a throat cutter without considering the inconvenient fact that she hated the sight of blood. "My ex has my daughter as well. I wonder . . . do you have a few minutes to talk?"

You'd think her dog just died. Ladies, I'm here to tell you the weight of the world isn't an attractive accessory. "Absolutely. I'll take you out for a drink."

She glanced at me, as if wondering if she was allowed. God. Get a spine.

"We'll make it a working drink. I'd like to hear about your closing statement, and I plan to drink wine while listening. You're free to take the moral high ground and drink water if you think the bar association will be watching, but to be completely honest, you look like you need straight whiskey."

This time she actually laughed, a tinge of hysteria to the sound. "Okay. You're right. Whiskey's not my drink, but I could do with a bit of tequila."

❧

Twenty minutes later, Allison had dropped her stuff at her office and made her way to the little Mexican restaurant across the way from the courthouse where they had a full bar. I ordered a pinot grigio and paid for Allison's margarita. She was young. Of course she'd order a margarita. She'd lick the salt off the glass, too, I had no doubt whatsoever.

We sat awkwardly at first. Allison struggled for the words for whatever she'd wanted to say. I broke the ice.

"So I hear our daughters are now in the same class," I said. Never too early to begin sussing out the competition.

"Yes. As of yesterday, I think," Allison said, on autopilot.

"Do you have a picture of her?"

"Um. I think so." Allison hesitated, then fumbled in her disorganized bag and came up with her phone. The child was plain and unformed, like her mother. Brown hair. Brown eyes. But she had promising bone structure. She might be a beauty one day. Maybe she'd inherited cheekbones from her father. Only time would tell. Fiona would never best anyone on the academic playing field, but surely she'd be the most beautiful girl in her grade. I did the expected compliment thing and handed back the phone.

"So, that new defense of yours," Allison said, running her finger along the glass rim and, yes, licking off the salt.

"What new defense?"

"The 'I am not an imbecile' defense. Did you make that up on the spot, or did you plan that?" I didn't like the stubbornness in her eyes: the look of someone who is trying to grow a brain.

"I thought it was fair. I'm quite obviously bright. Amaro's argument seems to be that I have the intelligence of a learning-impaired squirrel. I pointed out the fallacy in it."

"God, Kira. Nobody doubts your intelligence. It's just that smart people do dumb things sometimes."

The unmitigated gall. I fought the snarling rage that leaped forth back onto its leash. "Do they?" I managed, grinding my teeth. "Do tell."

"'Minced' monkshood? Your testimony was too cute by half. But maybe nobody noticed but me." Allison took a gulp of her margarita, as if it would fuel her bravery, then met my gaze. I gave her my best freezing glare to shut down this line of thought. It didn't work; she soldiered on, damn her. "You didn't intend to poison Summer. You meant to poison someone else."

For a second there was nothing but silence.

A stew of emotions almost burst forth. I tried to name them as I forced them down: fury at her effrontery and righteousness, grudging admiration for her puzzle solving, and most of all, a desperate desire for her to appreciate the intellect she was poking at as well as the beauty of the entire story. It would feel good to tell her what really happened. The relief of revelation would be incredible. First, I'd need to confirm some parameters. "Let me ask you a question first. The commonwealth has rested. You've rested. Can any more evidence come in?"

"No. Only the closing statements, which can't introduce new evidence. They summarize the old evidence."

"One more question. Tell me about the attorney-client privilege."

She stared at me, a faint wrinkle appearing between her eyes, the human equivalent of the yellow caution light. "What you tell me is secret. Unless you tell me I can speak, I can tell no one what you've told me." A pinprick of fear showed itself in her gaze. "Um, that doesn't apply if you tell me you are planning to kill someone. Or commit substantial bodily harm. I'm required to report those things."

I laughed. "Oh no. I'm not planning to hurt anyone." It was the truth, for the moment, at least. "So if I tell you the truth, you can't reveal to anyone what I say?"

"No. I can't," she said, glancing around wildly for help. The flight instinct had taken over. "But never mind. Forget I asked."

Talk about never asking a question you don't want to hear the answer to. I almost laughed at the trapped-animal expression on her face. "No, no. You'll always wonder if I don't tell you. Now that I know I'm safe, I can."

"Really. You don't need to."

"Yes, I kind of think I do. I'd hate to be the only one to appreciate how spectacularly the whole system failed to find the truth."

"Failed?" she asked, in a dramatic whisper, like she hadn't quite found enough air in her lungs to power the simple word.

I nodded. "Let's take these drinks outside where we can talk." She followed me like a sheep out to the deserted area where the restaurant kept cast-iron tables for outside dining. A bit of chill hung in the air.

"It was Tammy," I said, with all the appropriate fanfare. God, I'd been waiting so long to say it.

Allison hadn't expected that. She choked on her drink and turned red. "T-Tammy? Are you saying Tammy poisoned Summer?"

"Yes. She put the monkshood in Summer's cup. As I've said all along, I did nothing wrong. I'm completely innocent of this crime."

God, it was a relief to say so. Cleverness felt so much better when it could be appreciated. Up to this point, Tammy had been the only one with even a glimmer. I thought back to how close things had come. Tammy caught me that day, in the cafeteria kitchen throwing away the baggie with the cut-up monkshood in it after I'd changed my mind. She'd ducked behind me, doing that thing she does where she invades my personal space so she can force me to breathe a walloping lungful of her cigarette odor, and stared at the baggie in the trash.

"Well, even a redneck like me knows you rich ladies smoke your pot at home, after you get the kids safely to bed, so I know that ain't drugs," Tammy had said, wide-eyed with delight at catching me off guard.

I wouldn't tell Allison how terrified I'd been in that moment, of all moments, when I'd decided not to do it and was washed clean of all sins, that Tammy would realize what I'd done. What I'd *almost* done, I should say.

My terror had been a self-fulfilling prophecy. Tammy, long accustomed to watching my face for reactions to her mentions of Hank Williams Jr. and Mountain Dew and tobacco dips, saw the fear. It only took her a few seconds to figure it out.

"No, it ain't pot," she said. "You're scared as shit. This stuff is too green. Recent cut. From your garden, I expect. You old bitch. Who were you going to poison?"

Obviously I couldn't tell her. Not everything, anyway. "Yes, it's from my garden. It was in my pocket after I worked in there yesterday. I just found it and needed to dispose of it."

She cackled, her smoker's cough sounding like demons trying to escape, and reached into the trash.

I raised my hand. "Don't touch it. It's poisonous to the touch. Leave it."

She straightened but didn't move. "Oh sure. The old poisonous-plant-in-your-pocket problem, huh? Happens all the time. When you pull weeds, you always cut 'em up this tiny and bag 'em neatly in a Ziploc? You put it in your pocket yesterday and found it today. Sure. You normally wear those fancy linen pants for gardening? And two days in a row, on top of that? Right. Totally normal. Well, well, well." Her smile gleamed, wide and elated. She'd been looking for a way to get me all year after the blackmail.

I grabbed two pitchers and opened my mouth to remind her I could still charge her with embezzling the PTA funds, but Ruthanne walked in before I had the chance. Tammy didn't matter. She had nothing on me. I'd poisoned no one and had no intent to poison anyone. No intent by the time she saw me, anyway. Tammy couldn't touch me. I'd admitted nothing, and possession of monkshood was hardly illegal. Marijuana would have gotten me in a lot more trouble than this.

Ruthanne considered us, one at a time. I cleared my throat and assumed command. "It's almost time, ladies. They'll be here soon. Stations!" I walked away from the trash can and never saw the monkshood again.

After that, things spun quickly out of my control. Time to explain everything to Allison, who ought to be reassured to know she'd been defending a completely innocent person this whole time.

The blotchiness of Allison's complexion turned frozen with shock. Her words came out in an inarticulate gabble before she found her voice. "*Tammy* put that stuff in . . . But . . . but Brandi . . . and you said . . . I don't . . . Wait. How do you know, and *why on earth* wouldn't you have told me before now? Don't you think it would've been helpful information all this time?"

Before I could stop it, a giggle burbled free at the sight of her sputtering and frothing. She reminded me of a freshly caught trout. "Sorry, but you do look funny. Well, first off, this can't come as a surprise to you. You were right all along about Tammy's motive—she wanted Summer out of her way because she was afraid Social Services would take her kids. At Field Day, Summer asked Tammy how her girls were. I heard it. I assume Tammy took it as a threat."

Still sputtering, Allison managed, "But . . . but how? That's still only a guess."

"It's not a guess. I saw Tammy in close proximity to the monkshood right before Summer was poisoned."

"Y-you . . . you what? You told me Brandi . . . you wanted me to take Brandi apart in front of her kids and half the reporters in Virginia." She shuddered. "Why in the hell wouldn't you have told me about Tammy the first time we met?"

"Well, because in a way, Tammy couldn't have done it without me. She caught me throwing it away. She tried to touch it, and I told her it was poisonous. She couldn't know what I'd planned to do with it, but as soon as Summer got sick, I knew what *she'd* done. It wasn't as if I could mention her name to the police: she'd have been delighted to take me with her to jail as an accessory."

"You brought it?"

"Obviously. She must have fished it out of the trash. We were all wearing food-serving gloves, of course. No fingerprints."

"Summer wasn't the person you planned to kill, was she?"

"No." I really shouldn't be enjoying this so much.

"Was it Summer's son? Aidan?" Allison's whole body was frozen like she needed this answer before her heart could beat another time. It annoyed me. How could someone be as smart as she clearly was and still think that good deeds were rewarded and the meek would inherit the earth?

I took a sip of my wine, thinking of the best way to tell this so she'd appreciate my genius and have her pure little ideals dismembered at the same time.

"Your daughter is only in kindergarten, so you don't really understand yet what's at stake. Public schools are too focused on sports and simple high school graduation rates. Not enough of the graduates go to college, or top colleges, I should say. On occasion, a good student will get turned away from one of the better colleges for failing to have studied a 'rigorous' enough program. Oh, parents can help. Every entrant to Harvard or Yale needs a spectacular out-of-school extracurricular. Fiddle, say, or chess. Or excelling in a sport. But that only gets you part of the way there. You've got to be tops academically. There's only one path to the Ivy League for public school kids, and it requires the child to have taken every Advanced Placement course available, to qualify for every one of the limited gifted programs they offer, to have straight As in everything, and, from our schools, to be the valedictorian."

"Oh my God, Kira. And Aidan . . . at the awards assembly . . ."

"Do you want to hear this, or not? I was my high school's salutatorian. Came in second to Amy Louise Bailey. My daddy got very angry when I didn't get into Yale. Daddy said I would have if I'd been valedictorian instead of just the salutatorian. William & Mary should have been my safety school, he said. If I'd concentrated on beating Amy Louise instead of doing cheerleading, the world would have been my oyster."

I didn't like to remember his cold dismissal. I'd been a legacy, and I still hadn't gotten in. Daddy hadn't spoken to me for a month after the rejection came. Mama, as usual, was afraid to buck him, and so she ignored me, too. Daddy's love felt like oxygen to me, and for a few horrible weeks, I thought I'd lost it forever. I shuddered. Allison sat perfectly still, only her blinking letting me know she was still breathing.

"My son, Finn, was brilliant right from the start. Memorized whole books at two. Read all the Encyclopedia Brown books in first grade, by himself. Blew the curve out of the water on the entrance test for the gifted program Wolf Run offers." I patted her cold hand. "Look for the information coming home in Libby's backpack. They do the testing at the end of kindergarten."

She pulled her hand back like she'd been burned. Fine.

"Daddy had cancer and died the year Finn was in second grade. Mama'd already gone into a nursing home for early-onset Alzheimer's—didn't use her brain enough, Daddy used to joke. His last words to me were about Finn. 'Get him into Yale,' he said to me. 'Fix your mistake.' He left money for Finn to go. The will says if Finn doesn't get into Yale, the money goes to charity. It doesn't matter about the money, really. Miles makes enough to pay for college. It's about Yale. Finn needs to go there. It's our family school, and he's so bright, so gifted. Destined to do amazing things. Anything less would be wasting him. And to go to Yale, he has to be the valedictorian."

Allison was quick, I had to give her that. She'd probably been the Amy Louise Bailey some other woman still hated after all these years. "And Aidan is competition for valedictorian."

I rolled my eyes. "I kept thinking he was a fluke, that kid. He joined Finn in the gifted program early. Summer and I got to be friends in part because we shared a desire to help our sons succeed, but I never thought Aidan would be real competition. Who could compete with a kid who could read all the Encyclopedia Brown books so early?"

Allison only blinked. Her margarita sat untouched on the table, condensation dripping away.

"Anyway, I kept waiting for Aidan to get a B. Anything so I could have some peace that Finn's perfect grades were enough, but it never happened. Aidan spent the weekend with us occasionally. Each time it worried me more: he's so articulate and so . . . so *interested* in everything. Finn would sit there and play video games, but Aidan had . . . a *thirst*, almost, for knowledge. I'd thought for a while I might need to do something about it, but then came the awards assembly."

"Kira. Stop. I don't want—"

"You do. So listen. Finn and Aidan got all the same awards at first. Straight As for the year. Straight As for all of elementary school. The President's Award for academic achievement. All that I expected. But then they got to the testing results. Fifth graders take three statewide tests: math, science, and reading. Finn got perfect scores on the math and the reading and missed two questions on the science. He got two medals for the perfect scores. So did Aidan. And then Aidan did what no kid in twenty years has done at Wolf Run. He got a third medal for the science score. Three perfect scores. He'd beaten Finn."

"Holy shit, Kira. You make it sound like a judgment from God. It was only one day. Two questions! Maybe Finn didn't sleep well the night before the science test."

"You're not listening to me. Finn's path to valedictorian wasn't clear. Aidan was not a fluke. Teachers weren't favoring him. He really was that smart. He'd be competition for Finn all the way through high school. And if Finn's not the valedictorian, he will never get into Yale. Look at the statistics. Only two kids from our high school have gone to Ivy League colleges in the past twenty years. Both were valedictorian."

Allison's horror-struck face worked. "Then why not move him to private school? Or a prep school where they send dozens of kids to the Ivy League? If it's that important? Instead of . . . instead of . . ."

"There aren't a lot of competitive private school options here, Finn would never survive boarding school, and besides, I can't get Miles to consider it. His mother taught public school, and he says he isn't paying tuition."

"So divorce him! Get a job and pay it yourself! My God! Are you saying your solution was to poison Aidan Peerman? To get him out of Finn's way?"

"Well, yes, but I didn't. I changed my mind. When it came down to it, I couldn't hurt him. He stood up for Finn that morning. He faced down a bully for him. If Finn is safe from bullies, he'll do so much better academically. I'll have to think of another way to get him into Yale—maybe I can persuade Miles to change his mind, too. There's still time."

Allison stood up, all drama from head to toe, as if we were in a high school production of *Julius Caesar* and I'd stabbed her on the Ides of March. Spare me. She had a client accused of poisoning someone and I'd just told her—truthfully—that I was entirely innocent of the crime. I had changed my mind. Seen the light, even. She was a criminal defense lawyer. Surely the luxury of having a completely innocent client was rare. You'd think she'd appreciate it.

"So how were you going to . . . h-how did Tammy . . . ?"

Good thing she'd been more articulate in court. This goggling and gasping thing she was doing right now would hardly have impressed the judge. "Brandi guessed correctly. It did have to do with the four pitchers thing. I'd planned to start an argument between Ruthanne and Tammy as to who would take the first empty pitcher to the kitchen to fill it, then dump in the stuff while they were distracted, but obviously I didn't do it."

"How did Tammy do it?"

"I honestly don't know. My guess is she waited until a pitcher was almost empty, dumped the stuff in, and then filled up the cup too high so she'd know which one it was. She must have taken the poisoned pitcher out to her car after everything went crazy. Everyone thought it was a heart attack at first. She'd have had time to get rid of it."

"You handed Summer the cup."

"That wasn't a coincidence, was it? Tammy slid it under my hand to give to the next person, who was Summer. Aidan already had taken a cup off the table. Tammy didn't like me much, either—why not kill two birds with one stone? Poison her Enemy Number One and let Enemy Number Two hand off the actual poison. Tammy is trashy, not stupid. I had no idea that cup had poison in it until Summer started gasping. I absolutely hate that Tammy and I are in this situation—locked in perpetual silence because we know what the other has done. I mean, Tammy. A redneck. Ugh."

Poor Allison still hadn't quite gotten the whole picture yet. "So you did cut the stuff. Out of your own garden. Why would you give them your gloves? Why didn't you burn them? My God."

"Oh, the gloves? I did burn the blue ones I used to clip the monks-hood. I forgot about the pink gloves. What I said on the stand was all the truth; can you believe it? I did cut hydrangeas with those and forgot all about them. I probably have ten pairs."

Allison looked queasy. "And Aidan. He almost drank that cup any-way. Summer tried to give it to him!"

"Oh, I know! And if he'd taken it, I wouldn't even have been guilty of doing it. I didn't even know there was poison in it! It's too perfect that his life was saved because Brandi's smoothies are so disgusting he didn't want seconds." That made me giggle.

"Oh my God," Allison said, like a broken record. "Kira, you're sick. You need help."

"Thank you so much for your thoughts, but if I were you," I said meaningfully, "I'd stick with legal advice." She could quit with the drama any second. In the end, no harm done. Summer was fine—well, mostly fine. Her kidney likely wouldn't fail. Maybe middle school would prove too much for Aidan and he'd drop off the grid. Maybe he'd fall in with those boys Finn said believed being a good student was uncool. I may have been a bit hasty. We'd have to see how it went. I had a few more years to arrange things before Finn entered high school.

"I don't know what to say. I'd like to withdraw from representing you, if you'd consent."

"What? With only closing arguments to go? The judge would think something funny was going on. He'd think I'd fired you and that would make me look nutty. No, ma'am. I need you to finish the job."

"I can't." She sounded like a robot. "I have to withdraw. I'll ask the judge if you won't release me. I can't possibly . . . not after . . ."

"Oh, you can. You're in a better position now than you were—you know I'm absolutely not guilty now. And you'll get in there and finish the job, unless you want me to tell the judge you've been banging the prosecutor."

On cue, my Teenage Dream lawyer turned bright red, confirming my guess. No surprise. She'd been obsessed with him all along, and she was the sort who needed the permission.

I laughed. "If you could see your face. My goodness. You *have* been banging the prosecutor, or near enough, anyway. Sorry, but I'm not releasing you. I need you. I will recommend you to my friends, of course, assuming I get acquitted. And I should. I don't think your boyfriend proved the case, but even if he did, you did a great job with the reasonable doubt thing. I feel good about it."

"Um. Okay." On autopilot, she literally backed away as if I'd attack her.

For God's sake. We'd come all this way. Did she think she could somehow magically disassociate herself with me at this late date? So virtuous, young Allison. Almost as if she didn't spend her days representing carjackers and drug addicts and thieves. My daddy used to say, *You lie down with dogs, you're gonna get up with fleas.*

I figured out long ago we're all sleeping with dogs, and the flea scratching is what eventually kills us.

Suddenly I couldn't stand another second of looking at her round little face. "Fine. I've got to go see what atrocious dinner idea Miles has allowed the kids to conceive. I'll see you in court tomorrow morning at eight thirty."

I'd be shocked if Chris found me guilty. I was, after all, completely innocent. It annoyed me to have to stay silent about Tammy, but no irreparable harm had been done. Nobody died.

Yet.

CHAPTER TWENTY-FOUR

ALLISON

As soon as I got out to the parking lot, I threw up. I'd never drink another margarita again in this lifetime. Inside the car, I wiped my mouth, locked my doors, and drove. Somewhere. Anywhere.

I wanted to call Steve's house to check on Libby, because all of a sudden, everything felt unsafe and terrifying. I knew I was too upset to talk on the phone; Libby didn't miss anything and she'd hear it in my voice. I pulled over at a gas station and texted him, then sat, tapping my fingers on the steering wheel until he wrote back.

Steve: She's fine. Doing a puzzle on the floor. What's her bedtime on school nights again?

Me: Eight. With book. Tomorrow's Friday. Make sure she turns in her homework packet.

Steve: Right. Where would I find the packet?

I lost the ability to deal with him. Tossing the phone back in my purse, I shifted the beat-up car out of park and drove on.

My client was not guilty of the crime. Accessory, at most. But she'd considered far, far worse—seriously enough to bring the murder weapon to a school. And the circumstances that gave rise to her blithe original plan to murder a child—a child!—in front of his mother and all his classmates hadn't changed a bit. Miles had testified Finn was teetering on the edge of a B in middle school math. If he got it, who knew what Kira would do?

I'd had clients who'd done bad things before. Kira was different. Her face had been so earnest and rational as she'd told me her reasons for plotting to murder a child. Oh, she'd claimed to be unable to do it at the moment of action, but I didn't think for a minute Aidan had earned more than a temporary reprieve. Dear God. I touched the brakes, scanning for a place to pull off in case I threw up again.

She lived that perfect life—clothes, hair, house, garden, kids, clubs—and nobody had a single hint that inside, she was as rotten as a four-day corpse in the summer sun. Nobody but me, and I could never tell a soul. I'd never understand how she'd allowed what sounded like a Greek tragedy–type daddy situation to ferment into this level of sociopathy, all the while running PTA fundraisers and feeding her kids chicken nuggets and arranging hydrangea bouquets, without anyone catching on. Where the hell was her husband? Did he pay her no attention at all?

Summer had seen it without recognizing it. She'd said Kira was hard to know. Even I'd noticed something felt a bit off. I'd wondered about secret alcoholism or a secret lover or secret abuse as a child, but in a million years I'd never considered that Kira's secret was a total and complete breakdown of all societal norms. To target a child, her own son's best friend—what kind of person can do that? What kind of mother can do that?

Oh God. A mother. Of a child. Of a child in Libby's class. What would happen if Libby and Fiona became friends? There were only eighteen children in Mrs. Quinn's room. The odds were good; I'd never be able to keep them apart. My mouth went dry, and my stomach heaved again. What if Kira decided Libby was in Fiona's way? What then?

If everything went the way I expected it to the following day, I'd give a closing argument and Judge Turner would find Kira not guilty and send her home to her family. I could taste the victory in this case, only this time it tasted like radish-flavored poison. Emmett knew it, too; I'd seen it on his face as he left the courtroom. I hadn't felt bad, because I needed this victory more than he did. But now . . . I'd done my job too well. If I won tomorrow, I'd be sending a potential child killer back to the PTA, back to keeping Aidan for weekends, back to plotting murder every time he used a big word.

And I couldn't tell a soul who she really was, if she was acquitted. The duty of an attorney to keep the confidences of a client was perhaps the most bedrock responsibility of all. Even if I told, the information couldn't be used in court. It was inadmissible. Kira could not be convicted on what she'd told me.

If I disclosed what she'd said, I'd be disbarred. Forbidden to practice law altogether and for all time. I still owed money on my law school loans and had no education that would be useful in another job.

I could not tell.

I couldn't withdraw from the case, either. Without Kira's permission, I'd have to petition the court at the start of the day. The judge would, indeed, smell a rat. He would suspect Kira had fired me, making her look petty or . . . I held back a hysterical giggle . . . crazy. Kira would allege malpractice against me. Dan would help her. While I might risk it if I thought it would make a difference, it wouldn't. All the evidence had already come in. Both sides had rested. There'd be no point to withdrawing.

All I had left was the closing argument.

I made a U-turn and headed home.

❧

The judge sat forward a bit. "Ms. Barton? Are you ready for your argument?"

Kira gazed at me beatifically, resplendent today in a burgundy jersey dress that clung everywhere and soft brown knee-high boots. She wore a simple scarf with fall leaves on it. Somehow the ensemble communicated a definite subliminal message of "Let me go outside; don't incarcerate me." No doubt she'd planned it.

"Yes, sir." I rose to my feet. I'd gone home last night and rewritten my closing argument. I'd done all I could do.

Subliminal messages, indeed.

"Your Honor, this has been a longer trial than any of us anticipated, so I'll keep this brief. As you know, the burden in this case is on the commonwealth to prove the defendant guilty beyond a reasonable doubt. To find the truth. To prove its case, and in this matter, the commonwealth has not done it. There's no truth here. We heard from the sheriff's investigator. His reports are brief and distressingly free of any useful information. He found his narrative and he stopped there. He made up answers and never asked any of the right questions at all.

"Instead, there are only possibilities. It's possible, maybe even likely, Kira put the poison in the cup. But 'likely' isn't 'beyond a reasonable doubt.' It's also possible Brandi Crane put the poison in the cup, or Tammy Cox, or Ruthanne Dillard. All four ladies had access to those smoothies, to the cups, and to the four pitchers. We heard about an awful lot of transferring of liquid between jugs and pitchers and cups. The chaos of all the traffic back and forth between the table and the refrigerator. Anyone could have slipped poison into that single cup.

"We've heard a lot about the victim, and her relationship with Kira. We heard a lot more about her relationships with Brandi and Tammy. What we never heard is conclusive evidence that Kira would have had any reason to harm *Summer*. There is, in fact, a total lack of convincing motive to harm Summer. The commonwealth says an argument over parenting is the reason, but never showed how, if it happened like they say, Summer Peerman's death would benefit Kira Grant. Not a single word did we hear about how this poisoning would benefit Kira Grant.

She and Summer argued. They made up. It happens. It's not a motive to kill. That's reasonable doubt."

I glanced at Emmett, praying he'd hear this next part. It was the part that mattered—the only part that mattered.

"It may well be the cup wasn't intended for Summer. It probably wasn't—the amount of poison was lethal only for a much smaller person. A person the size of a fifth grader. Kira would have known that. She knew all about wolfsbane. If she'd intended to kill Summer Peerman, she'd have gotten the amount right. Kira would know how much poison to give a person to kill him."

Emmett kept his impassive listening face. The judge's brows drew together, but probably only because he thought this might well be the dumbest closing argument a defense lawyer ever gave.

I was not getting through. I hadn't really expected them to get it, but this was all I could do. Despair began to weight my limbs.

"I'll wrap this up by saying that criminal matters are simple. The commonwealth must prove its case beyond a reasonable doubt, and the commonwealth did not do it. There's all kinds of doubt here. My head is swimming with doubt, in fact. We don't know what really happened, but I can say this: the truth about how the poison came to be in the cup in Summer Peerman's hand hasn't been told in this courtroom. And that, Your Honor, is reasonable doubt. Thank you." I sat.

Kira poked my thigh, hard. "It's an *odd* choice for a defense attorney to point out to the court that her client knows how to poison people properly."

"I have an *odd* client."

She ground her teeth at me but said nothing.

"Mr. Amaro, do you have a rebuttal?" Judge Turner asked.

Emmett's brows were lowered as he flipped pages of notes. The prosecution always goes first, but because they carry the burden of proving the case, they can choose to save some time for a rebuttal after the defense argument. His closing had been exactly what I'd expected:

a concise, well-worded argument that Kira had committed the crime beyond a reasonable doubt because of the missing pitcher, her access to the murder weapon, the gloves on her porch when none of the other women's houses turned up traces of aconite, her unique ability to understand the plant's effects, and her lies about her knowledge of aconite. It had been weak on motive: only the argument over the dyslexia, and the fact that she hadn't mentioned it to the investigator.

I held my breath.

"No, Your Honor. No rebuttal."

He hadn't gotten what I'd tried to tell him. He hadn't caught my hints, not even the desperate emphasis on "fifth grader." I glanced up at the judge, now my last hope. He pinched the bridge of his nose and rested his eyes on Kira.

"Well, I have many other matters scheduled this morning. There's one piece of evidence I'd like to review again before I rule. I'll plan on being back here with y'all at eleven thirty. Thank you, Counsel."

He stood, setting off a creaking and scuffling as everyone in the courtroom hustled to stand as well. The clock read 10:02. Almost ninety minutes to kill. An annoying time frame: too long to hang around here and do nothing, but too short to get anything substantive done at the office. The gallery was noisy as the spectators exited. Kira gave me one oblique glance and went out alone. I didn't see Miles, who'd arrived with Kira this morning pale and drawn. I gathered my case file to haul back to the office—for the ruling I would need only a blank legal pad.

Emmett stood at the opposite table, doing the same. I tried not to look at him. I didn't want him to see the terror and the wretchedness in my eyes. As I was about to rush off, I dropped a folder, cutting off my escape by giving him time to come over to the defense table.

"Hey," he said, too close. "You tried an excellent case. I knew you would. I'll be honest. You ought to win this one. I hope it helps, Allie. With getting out of . . ." He glanced to the back of the courtroom. Dan stood there talking to a new lawyer, an attractive woman only a year out of law school. His face was flushed with pleasure as if he'd delivered the closing argument himself. "You know."

Oh God. Six feet away from Dan stood Summer, talking with the court reporter. I bit my lip. Everything in me wanted to rush up to Summer, beg for forgiveness, and tell her to move to another town. Or at the very least, never to let her child into the Grant house for even a minute. Never to accept a batch of cookies Kira might make. Never to go anywhere with Kira alone. Short of moving, however, there'd be little Summer could do to protect Aidan from Kira because of Finn. They were in the same grade.

Libby and Fiona were in the same grade, too. My knees felt shaky and sapped. I gripped the table, suddenly needing its support.

Please, God, let this woman be convicted.

"Are you okay?" Emmett's face was written with concern. "Something's wrong."

I met his eyes, full of kindness. No agony of defeat there. I tried to sound normal. "No. I . . . I haven't been sleeping. I felt . . . a little faint, right there. I think I'd better go back to my office and eat something. Maybe take a thirty-minute nap. God knows I won't get anything else done."

"Right. Yeah, I'm tired, too. You're a tough opponent," he said, trying to make me smile.

I tried to give him the smile, but the muscles at the corners of my mouth felt too weak. "You ever wonder if we should have run for office? Maybe join the mafia? Sometimes I think it would be more honorable."

"Allie. What's going on?" He took hold of my shoulders, real worry in his voice.

Oh God, it reminded me of that day in my office. And yet we were so far away from that day in my office. "Nothing. Nothing new. I'll see you at eleven thirty."

"See you." He went out. No one stopped him to congratulate him. Another ominous sign.

I stood at the table for another minute more, watching Summer talk to a woman I didn't recognize. Right. She knew everyone because of her job.

For a second, everything became crystal clear. The rules of ethics binding my profession of six years, nine if you counted law school, proclaimed clearly that I could say nothing at all to Summer to warn her. I'd be disbarred if anyone found out I warned her.

Yet, my law school diploma wouldn't make me feel better if Kira killed Aidan and I'd said nothing. There were risks that had to be taken. Being a decent person was more important than being a decent lawyer. And besides, Summer wouldn't likely report me to the bar for warning her about danger to her child.

Before I could change my mind, I scooped up my folders and dashed to the back of the courtroom. "Ms. Peerman. Do you have a second?"

Summer looked up from her conversation. She exchanged glances with the woman she'd been talking to, and her easygoing face shuttered into professionalism. "Excuse me."

The other woman patted her arm, and Summer followed me out to the hallway, where at least one local camera crew cooled their heels and possibly four or five others I took to be reporters scribbled on notepads. Phones and tablets weren't allowed in the courtroom. I took a second of pleasure in knowing the reporters had been inconvenienced by the rule.

I gave Summer a meaningful glance. "I have to go to the bathroom."

She caught it. "Right. Me, too."

In the mercifully empty bathroom, I didn't waste time. Anyone could walk in at any moment. "You never heard this from me. I'll deny I ever said it. Stay away from Kira. Keep your family away from Kira. Take whatever steps you need to take. From everyone involved in this case, actually."

"What?" she asked, though she understood what I was saying. I saw the knowledge she'd always had but hadn't admitted to herself take hold.

"Be careful, Ms. Peerman. I'll see you at eleven thirty."

And then I ran away to the safety of Maureen and my silent office.

CHAPTER TWENTY-FIVE

KIRA

Where the hell was Miles? After the closing statements, he was nowhere to be found. If there'd been an issue with one of the children at school, I'd have a text. Nothing. Any second now Chris-the-judge would emerge from his little door with his Hotly Anticipated After the Break decision, and I needed Miles to be visible by my side.

He'd been near mute since yesterday. Was he really that terrified that I'd go to prison and leave him, alone and unqualified, in charge of raising our children? Well, no matter. That would happen only over my dead body. Or someone's.

The courtroom buzzed and whispered. I'd attracted a whole crew of reporters and newspeople. When I came out of this courtroom, there'd be cameras. I'd spent a good thirty minutes of the gap time on my makeup and hair and brushing my teeth. Neither Tammy nor Brandi had showed today once released from testifying, but Ruthanne sat with Summer in the front row behind the prosecutor. Summer's mother, whom I'd always liked, kept shooting me ominous glances from her other side. Aidan would be in school, safe behind a security camera that would never stop me from coming in if I ever changed my mind again.

"All rise." The bailiff didn't go into any long nonsense about God saving the judge and all that this time. I guessed he was obligated to invoke the Almighty only once a day.

Chris-the-judge made his big entrance and looked straight at me as he sank into his seat. I'd swear he had a twinkle in his eye. I straightened my back as if in respect to the court, all the while knowing it threw my jersey-clad breasts into better prominence. I smiled my brave smile. Allison, damn her, sat there like a slug, pretending I didn't exist.

"All right, I'm ready to give my ruling. Before I do, I'll say this. What happened at that elementary school is a horrible thing. I've got children of my own, and I'll be honest, I'm outraged and sickened that a person would put lethal poison in a cup in a room surrounded by eighty fifth graders on their last day of school. Only a truly depraved person would do such a thing. This cup happened to end up in the hands of Ms. Peerman, which was terrible for her, but fortunate overall, because the amount of poison used here would have killed one of those children if they'd gotten hold of it."

We'd have to agree to disagree on our definitions of *depraved*, Chris.

"In any case, the burden here is on the commonwealth to prove its case beyond a reasonable doubt, and so it is up to me to decide if they have carried their burden. Will the defendant please rise?"

Allison and I scraped back our chairs and stood, two feet apart but as if we occupied completely different air.

In the half second before the judge's next sentence, images flashed: Miles feeding the kids frozen junk without me at the table. Finn being allowed to quit fiddle and Japanese to play video games all day. Fiona, her beautiful hair uncombed, with no one to read to her. The orange jumpsuit and dirty mattress of jail.

I sucked in my breath and held on.

"I find in the matter of *Commonwealth versus Kira Grant* that the commonwealth has not proved its case beyond a reasonable doubt. Therefore, I find the defendant not guilty."

The courtroom let out a collective gasp, which covered the exhale of my brief moment of terror. Really, they shouldn't have been surprised. I had a talented lawyer I had the means to pay a good chunk of money for. I was rich, white, attractive, and connected. I didn't look like a criminal, so I hadn't been treated like a criminal. People: this was the way things worked. Go to the jail and ask for Tattoo Girl if you want to check. She'll tell you how it is.

As a reward I gave Chris one of my most brilliant sorority smiles, and then did a little blinking show and a discreet wipe of a tear I was surprised to find was real. Out of the corner of my eye, I caught a glimpse of Allison's stoic expression and a similar one on the Amaro man's face.

"You are free to go, Ms. Grant. Thank you, Counsel. Please move out of the courtroom as soon as possible so the bailiffs may go to lunch."

Everyone in the courtroom stood as the judge took his leave. Allison turned to me and gave me a tight smile that did not reach her eyes.

"Congratulations. Before you leave, let's chat, okay?" She pointed at a nearby conference room. I followed her.

"Actually—" Miles leaned around the door frame, pale and red-eyed. "I need to speak with Kira in private first," he said to Allison. "Do you mind?"

Allison nodded and went out to wait in the hall. Miles closed the door behind us and took a while before turning to face me. I tried not to tap my foot.

When he turned, there was nothing left of the sunny boy I'd married. "I'm leaving you, Kira. Today. Now, in fact."

The words reverberated in my head—so far from what I'd been expecting that they made no sense at first. "What? Leaving me? Are you crazy? I'm innocent. Did you not hear the judge?"

"I heard him. I also heard you." He turned away, both hands to the sides of his head, paying no attention to the state of his hair. "How many times, Kira? How many times have you told me . . . ?"

"Told you what? What on *earth* are you going on about?"

"Meat loaf."

"What?"

"Spaghetti sauce. Soup. Even once a chocolate milkshake."

"Now I know you've gone crazy." Ah. A mental break. There were places I could put him. He'd lost his marbles, babbling on about meat loaf. Good God.

"No. Far from crazy. Fiona doesn't like vegetables. You hide them in her food. When I cook, you yell at me for not mincing them up small enough to hide them from her. 'Mincing?' I asked. 'What does that mean?' You remember this conversation, Kira?"

A cold chill slipped down my spine. "*Mincing* is a common word. It's a cooking term. Read a cookbook sometime. It's everywhere."

"Maybe," he said. "You're an expert at it, though. You mince vegetables so tiny and so obsessively it's like they've done something to you. And . . ."

"And?"

"And I saw you that night, in the kitchen. Late. The night before the last day of school. I was stressed out about fitting Finn's graduation thing into a busy day, and I woke up sometime past midnight. You'd been pissed all day because Finn didn't get a perfect score on that stupid test. You didn't hear me when I came to find you because you were doing whatever you were doing with the knife and the cutting board. I could tell you were angry and I'm not a masochist, so I didn't bother you. I thought you were cutting stuff up for Fiona's food the next day. I went back to bed, and honest to God, I put it out of my mind. But then you said 'mincing,' and I remember seeing . . ."

"You have no idea what you saw." Sirens went off in my head. To think that all this time, he'd seen. He'd known.

"No. I don't. Not for sure. But I also remember buying you blue flower-print gardening gloves for Mother's Day, and they're missing. The ones in the evidence bag were pink. We're missing a cutting board, too. And probably a knife. You're so neat. Everything in its place. I've always loved that about you."

A tear trickled down his face. Disgust roiled my stomach.

"Fine. Go, then. I was planning to leave you anyway. It's been . . . problematic, shall we say, to have to consult you about the children's schooling and lessons. This will be easier. And don't think you can go running to the judge or that prosecutor. Double jeopardy means I can't be tried again."

"I know that, Kira. And you won't have to consult me about the children anymore—I'll be taking Finn and Fiona with me when I go."

With him? He'd lost his damn mind. I laughed, a rough, ugly sound. No need to maintain any pretty illusions around him anymore. "You will not. No judge would give you custody. I'm their primary caretaker."

He stared at me with tired eyes, patiently waiting for me to understand that he had far more than enough rope to hang me.

It didn't take long. The knowledge fell into place with an almost audible snap, and a switch in my brain flipped from reason to something more primal. My vision darkened and blurred. Blood roared in my ears. My muscles understood everything they needed to: their function was to hurt, to smash, to destroy.

I launched myself at him. The sounds that came out of my mouth weren't even words. He held me off easily by my forearms and waited out the minutes or hours it took for sanity and reason to return.

"Careful. You'll ruin your clothes." Miles set me away from himself once I'd stopped struggling. Tears ran down my face, and each breath scratched and clawed its way in and out. I could not best him this way. I had to think of a better one.

"You need help," I said. "Serious, white-coated, syringe-shooting help."

"No, Kira, not me. I know how you think. I loved you so much, for so long. You had no reason to kill Summer—but I know exactly how you feel about Aidan being smarter than Finn."

"He's not . . ." I choked it off. When the *fuck* had he started paying attention? Or had he been, all along, and I was the one who'd been missing things? "You have no proof."

"I have enough that you are going to give me custody of the children, amicably, just as soon as I can get the paperwork written up. Either that or I'll tell the police, or better yet, Social Services, about what I saw. And you know it."

I did know it. Everything would happen exactly the way he described it. I closed my mouth, desperately trying to think of a way to talk him off this ledge. I came up with nothing. Miles would not change his mind. He was unmovable.

He was the obstacle.

Unless.

Unless there were no Miles.

If he keeled over while we were still married, before he went to see a lawyer about a custody arrangement, before he told anyone what he planned, I would be the beneficiary of his sizable life insurance policy. The policy hadn't even been my idea. He'd said he worried about what would happen to me and the kids if he got in a car accident or something. I'd have to hurry.

Life insurance money would allow me to put Finn at a school with a better Ivy League admission record. It would allow me to separate Finn and Aidan. All without having to be a drudge in an accounting firm all day long.

"All right," I said. "I need to talk to Allison. We can discuss arrangements this afternoon. I'll meet you around one? Shall I let you know where after I see when I can get out of here?"

He narrowed his eyes, disconcerted by my easy acquiescence. "Okay. Fine. One o'clock it is."

"Now get out of my sight." I couldn't help squeezing my fists into bloodless balls of frustration.

He gave me a sad smile flavored with a strange note of recognition. Allison came in, rubbernecking at Miles as he passed her on the way out.

"Is he okay?" she asked, closing the conference room door.

"He's fine," I said, needing to get to work. "Will this take long? Your fee should be paid in full."

"No," she said. "My office will be in touch if there are any issues with the fee. I wanted to ask you a question."

"Yes?" I said, already knowing where she was going. I sat, demonstrating the grace a lady uses to seat herself. I'd noticed how Allison sort of threw herself into chairs.

She sat there, mouth working. It took all my restraint to wait politely.

"How could you do it?" she said.

"I didn't do it."

"How could you even think of doing it?" Allison asked. "Didn't you care about Aidan even a little? He's a child. A good kid. You were there for his first day of kindergarten."

"He's not *my* child."

"He's *a* child!"

I leaned back. How could I put this so she'd understand? "You have your daughter. Do you love her?"

"Of course."

"How much do you love her?"

"Wh—? As much as anyone ever could. How can you ask me . . . ?"

"Would you die for her? If it were only the two of you and one of you had to die, would you volunteer?" I already knew the answer. Any decent mother would give it, and Allison surely had nothing to live for except that child.

"Yes. I would volunteer."

"So would I. I'd die for Finn. I'd let someone cut off my arm if it would help him. My children are my life's work. I don't see it as a stretch."

"You must be joking. I'd die for Libby, but I wouldn't kill someone else's child."

I almost rolled my eyes. People were so sure of their virtue until they realized it was a cup full of mirage water that disappeared as soon as they tried to drink it. "Wouldn't you? What if it were between your child and another? You're in a tsunami and you have a child by each hand. Only one of them is yours. A huge wave is coming and you can't hold on to both or you'll all drown. Do you let your own child go? Or the other one?"

She backed away, agitated. Yup. She'd toss that other kid out to sea in a second if it were between her child and another. Just like anyone would. The veneer of civility in all of us is so very, very thin.

"It's not the same," Allison sputtered, from the top of her high horse. "Finn's life wasn't at stake. Isn't at stake. If he doesn't go to Yale, he'll be fine. Most people live long and happy lives without the Ivy League."

I hid my recoil at the image of Finn covered in grease and rolling out from under a car. "Ah, but there's the difference. To me, Finn's life is always at stake. That's what it means to be a mother. We give them life at birth and we stand guard over those lives every day after that. All day, my every breath is focused on giving him the life he's supposed to have. We sacrifice ourselves, our dreams, our lives, for our children, and the only thing we expect in return is the pleasure of watching them live the lives they deserve. One way or another."

I couldn't help it. I let out a burble of a laugh. One way or another, indeed. Actually, it was a good thing the poisoning thing had failed. At long last, I'd thought of a much better way. Poison would have a nice symmetry to it, but Miles had a serious peanut allergy. We actually worked to keep his food from killing him. It would be easy to just . . . hide some in his food. An accident. Anywhere, really, where I wouldn't be the primary suspect. Maybe he'd be willing to have our one o'clock custody discussion in a restaurant instead of at home. The key was to make it happen before he got custody paperwork organized and alerted anyone that I'd have a motive.

Allison shook her head. "You're sick."

"Maybe. Or maybe I'm the only sane one." I rose gracefully, though I suspected Allison was beyond the point where she could appreciate me modeling grace for her. "That's it, then? No other business to attend to?"

"Kira. If you try anything to hurt Aidan or Summer, I will quit my job, turn in my bar card, and do everything I can to help convict you."

Such drama. But I didn't have time for more of this if I was going to prepare for lunch.

"I already told you. The Peerman family is safe. Now. I expect the press is waiting to interview us." I stood, and with my hand on the doorknob, I assessed her. Ugh. "Comb your hair. It's sticking up at the crown. And for God's sake, try to pretend like you're pleased. We're going to be famous!"

I flung the door open, ready to take on the world.

Summer Peerman stood there with a tiny woman in a cardigan and pink-beaded braids I'd never seen before. I glanced at Allison, but she was clueless.

"Kira," said Summer. "I want to introduce Carrie Johnson-Mendel. She's a coworker of mine. We've just received a CPS complaint concerning Finn and Fiona and your parenting of them, relating to the events of this trial. Carrie will be handling it because I'd have a conflict, so I'll leave you to it."

"What?" My mouth dried up. Already? Miles knew me better than I thought. Better, apparently, than I knew him. "Wh-what did you say?"

"I just wanted to introduce Carrie. If now is good, she'll have paperwork to discuss with you. I can't be here for that part." There was real sadness in her smile, the bitch. I envisioned claw marks on her face. "And Kira—there's part of me that wishes we could turn back the clock. You know, to a time when none of this had happened."

Carrie pulled out a chair for me and sat across from it. She watched me, her dowdy Behavior Police badge hanging around her neck, waiting for a reaction she could type up in that little report she'd no doubt begun writing in her mind.

My mind, on the other hand, whirled with death and dismemberment and revenge, but I could do nothing but paste on my smile. "Well. The world spins on."

Summer bit her lip, then left. I glanced at Allison. "You should stay. You handle domestic matters as well, right?"

There was a long pause. Allison took her time deciding. I watched her blink at least four times and knew what she would say before she said it.

"No, Kira. Not this time. I'm afraid I can't take on a new matter right now. I'd be happy to give you some names of attorneys who might be willing to work with you." She picked up her yellow legal pad as if it had grown lighter. Before she disappeared into the hall, she turned. "Oh, and Kira? May justice be done."

Somehow I took my seat for the inquisition, even though white-hot rage blurred my vision. Pinpricks of light burst everywhere: stars exploding in a dying universe that only I could see.

CHAPTER TWENTY-SIX

ALLISON

Safe in the hall, with a closed door between me and Kira Grant, I started breathing again. Summer stood waiting, as if she knew she'd knocked me for a loop. A Child Protective Services complaint about Kira? Probably overdue, but who had filed it? Brandi? Tammy? The kindergarten teacher who'd been slandered for failing with Fiona? The list of people who would love to stick it to Kira was long.

"You didn't . . . ?" I stuttered, thinking of what I'd said in the bathroom. "Not from anything I said, right?"

"No. It's not your complaint. It was filed by someone else."

I would never know, and soon I wouldn't have to care. "Thanks. For that."

Summer gave me a quick nod and hurried down the hall.

Once I escaped the gauntlet of reporters and well-wishers in the courthouse, I skirted the building by crossing the lawn. Maureen's car sat in an almost-empty lot. I made it all of three steps into the area where she sat, typing as usual, before she noticed.

"Oh lordy. Your face. What happened? Did you lose?"

"No. She was acquitted."

"Was she a bitch to you?" God bless Maureen, ready to throat-punch Kira if she'd been a bitch to me.

"No. If only that were the worst thing about her."

"Huh?"

I glanced at her. Maureen was too pure a person to have to view the contents of my head right now. "No, she wasn't a bitch to me. Well, not more than usual."

"Then what?"

I put my folders down on the service counter. "Did you ever do something amazing, and then find out you've been working on the wrong side?"

"Are you telling me . . . ?"

"Nope. I'm telling you I don't think I'm cut out for being a lawyer."

Maureen came around the counter and hugged me. "You are. Don't you quit. You'd have to be without a soul to be unaffected by the things you see in this office. Since I've worked here, we've had that custody case where the dad showed the mom's sex tape to their ten-year-old, the drug dealer who asked if he should 'get rid of the witnesses,' and the man who woke up with his wife standing over his private parts with a crossbow. You've probably heard a lot worse."

"But Maureen, I don't feel good about myself a lot of the time. I don't want to help some of these clients."

"Look at it this way. When you represent them, you do your best to give them their fair day in court while showing them how to follow rules. If you weren't around to do it, then someone else much shadier than you will represent them. If all lawyers were like Dan, what kind of justice system would we have? What kind of judges would those lawyers become? Way I see it, people like you are vital. Hang in there. Don't quit."

I smiled, the first real one all day. For a second, her words helped me remember why I'd gone to law school in the first place: to make the world a fairer place. To preserve and protect the rule of law and the justice system. "Thanks. On the plus side, I got a lot of attention afterward, with the press. They were all asking me what kind of cases I handle. One or two reporters even asked for my card. Phone should be ringing tomorrow. Enough to ditch this Popsicle stand. You have any major issues with no longer being an employee of the MacDonald Group?"

She grinned and sat down at her computer again. "I've already found two office leases to show you."

"Good. Because we're doing this."

❧

At the end of the workday, Maureen buzzed me. "You have a walk-in. I'm sending him in and taking off for the day. See you tomorrow, okay?"

A walk-in? "Wait, Maur—"

I should have known. It was Emmett, already shed of his coat and tie.

He flopped into a client chair. "I thought you might come up and see me after the verdict."

"I felt weird about it. I probably wouldn't be Valerie's favorite person today."

"No, probably not." He leaned back, letting the exhaustion from the trial show. "For what it's worth, you were always going to win that trial. You had the facts and you worked harder."

"You're not even upset," I said. How could it be possible when upset was only the bare minimum of what I felt?

"No. Win some, lose some. I'm only tired. And, like I always do after a trial like this, I'm wondering what percentage of people in the world are assholes. Seventy-five percent? Eighty?"

I smiled, mostly because it wasn't funny. "I don't know. I worry being a lawyer makes it seem higher to me. Are people worse? Or do we have X-ray vision?"

"Both, probably. I don't know. That Brandi Crane was a piece of work. Nice Facebook post of hers. Good digging there, to find it."

"Yeah. Though how about the people in the gallery who clapped for it?"

"I know. Libby goes to that school, doesn't she?"

"Yeah. I made a mental note to sign up for the Wolf Run PTA right away," I said, as facetiously as I could. "I can't wait to hand out radish smoothies with that bunch."

Emmett cracked up, the laughter melting away the tension in his shoulders and neck. "Oh yeah. The faces of those other women talking about the taste of those smoothies! And I can see you getting a headband like that one lady now. Does she always dress like she's a kid?"

I nodded, laughing. "Yeah. You should have seen her face talking about her cheese tray. I spent way more time than I should have picturing her sitting by her TV, using a paring knife to carve hundreds of blocks of cheese kids were only going to chuck at each other and squish under their flip-flops."

"That woman definitely eats, sleeps, and breathes PTA." Emmett's smile was free of tension for the first time in months.

My laughter drained away. "Actually, I'm going to move Libby to the other elementary school. It's not like I could ever participate at Wolf Run after this."

"I can see that could be an issue. The Dillard lady would drive you batty." Emmett met my gaze, eyes kind and direct. "Your client's youngest kid goes there, too, doesn't she?"

I stared at him. What had he guessed? I played it off. "Libby doesn't seem to care much about school one way or another at this point. She just wants to play the piano."

"I didn't know that. Do you play? I feel like I'd have known if you did."

"No. I don't have a piano, or any money for one. Or for a teacher. So piano lessons are on hold for now."

"No way. Bring her over to my house. Believe it or not, I took piano into my college years. My mom insisted on moving my piano everywhere I've lived, and that's a lot of places, given law school and everything. I could teach her the basics for now."

I gazed at him. I'd never suspected him of being a dedicated piano student. "Seriously?"

"Sure."

I bit my lip. No other way to ask this than straight out. "Will we run into your latest girlfriend there?"

Emmett shifted awkwardly in the chair. "Um. No. No girlfriend in a while."

"Really? Why's that?"

"Because I've had a trial with you. No time for anyone else." He grinned. "You know. All those bond hearings and closing arguments. All foreplay, every minute of it."

"Oh." Heat rose into my cheeks. "Oh."

"Don't know if you've noticed, Allison, but the trial is over. No more ethics rules keeping us apart."

"Um. Yes. Yes, it is."

"And we have no other cases together, either. I swapped everything else with Sunil."

"You did?"

"Yup. And assuming things go the way I hope, I'll ask Valerie to wall me off from anything you're involved in going forward. I don't think it'll be a problem. She likes you." He stood up and came around my desk, resting on the edge, his muscled thighs inches from me. "Are you going to let me talk all night, or are you going to come here and shut me up?"

I stayed where I was, a huge smile breaking free. "I do like to listen to you talk."

"Well, then, maybe I should say something that matters. Go out with me."

My breath caught. "N-now?"

Laugh lines appeared, bracketing his mouth. "Yeah, now. I've been staying home lately, wishing you were around to talk to. Now would be great." He broke off, a sheepish expression making him look years younger.

"Really. Well, as a matter of fact, I do have a fair bit of time alone in the evenings myself."

"For the record, talking isn't *all* I want to do."

"That's a relief. I do like to watch TV, too," I said in my best serious deadpan.

His laugh rumbled, warm and suggestive. "That *is* a relief. Come up here. With me." He grabbed my hand and pulled.

I stood and went willingly into his arms, where, for now, I could lay my head and rest. His kiss was gentle and wholehearted and flavored with spearmint and fatigue. We touched foreheads and leaned on each other.

"Are you okay?" he asked me, rubbing my back with one hand while tipping up my chin to look in my eyes. "You didn't look as . . . thrilled as you might have after the verdict."

The echo of the kiss turned sour on my tongue. No, I wasn't thrilled. I'd set an aspiring murderer loose. I'd placed a sociopath back on the street, and there wasn't a damn thing I could do about it.

The hint of sour turned to ice, freezing my veins to blue icicles. Kira was free to kill anyone she wanted—a Social Services investigation might slow her down, but it couldn't fix what was broken inside her. I'd made it possible, and I couldn't tell Emmett. I could never tell him. Even if it didn't violate attorney-client privilege, even if I trusted him enough not to turn me in to the state bar, Emmett had tried to do the right thing—lock up a dangerous criminal—and I'd thwarted him. It was my greatest legal achievement—and the worst thing I'd ever done.

Yet this was my job—what my profession's ethics required.

I wanted a relationship with Emmett. I wanted to be with him, to sleep with him, to share my fears and my dreams with him, but Kira would always be part and parcel of any "story of us" Emmett and I ever forged. There would be no forgetting her—exactly how she would want it.

Maybe I could look at it another way. Maybe—against all the odds given the decomposing thing that remained of her soul—Kira could be responsible for the growth of this one good thing.

We lived in an ugly world. Even the most beautiful garden hid dirt and worms and rotting things, but Emmett must know that, too. Maybe now, six years in, I'd finally learned what all lawyers know. We protected the secrets of some of the worst people on earth, and we did it while following every rule ourselves.

I met Emmett's eyes, and something passed between us: shared exhaustion, maybe, or even joint complicity. I told myself he did know what I couldn't say.

I kissed him once more and pulled him by the hand to the door. He squeezed mine back.

"I'm fine," I said, flipping off the lights. "I've got to pick up Libby. Let's go get some ice cream."

ACKNOWLEDGMENTS

When my children were in elementary school, I was a PTA officer. The women of this story bear no resemblance to any of the wonderful parents I knew there, for the record. PTA parents are invaluable and know the secret: showing up for your kids makes a huge difference in their lives. Thank you to everyone who has ever hosted a pancake breakfast or sold cookie dough to raise money for playground equipment or bought Goldfish in bulk at Sam's Club or hired a bouncy castle to celebrate the transition to middle school. You are heroes.

I have also been a small-town general practice attorney, and I have endless gratitude for my fellow attorneys and the judges, commonwealth's attorneys and staff, bailiffs, Sheriff's Department investigators, legal assistants, and Department of Social Services caseworkers I worked with on a daily basis. You are out there protecting the rule of law. Because you are all so lovely in real life, I had to create villains straight out of my imagination.

Thank you, as always, to my parents, Bob and Nancy Button, who taught us that parenting is about doing the best you can to teach the right values and then trusting that everything will be okay.

A million thanks to the Den, my group of writing partners who read and critique everything I write: Elly Blake, Jennifer Hawkins, Mary Ann Marlowe, Kelly Siskind, Summer Spence, and Ron Walters. Your daily—sometimes hourly—support means everything.

Thanks for the support of my friends, family, coworkers, and community who have treated me like a Big-Time Author, especially Mary Louise and Frank Wright, Geoff Button, Kari Sorenson, Audrey Button, Pat Davis, Cathy Moore, Meghan Crowther, Dawn Osal, Sherry Harding, Brooke Wright, Ronna Johnson-Davis, Frank Rogers, Clif Tweedy, Mary Amiss, Beth Worth, Jordan Wellborn, and Michelle Hazen.

Thanks to my team at Thomas & Mercer and beyond—the amazing Elizabeth Pearsons, who pulled me, Allison, and Kira out of the slush; editors Caitlin Alexander and Grace Doyle, who made it better; the meticulous Sara Brady and Tara Quigley Whitaker, who found all my misplaced commas; cover designer Shasti O'Leary Soudant and production editor Laura Barrett, who made it pretty; and Sarah Shaw, who helped me and the book find an audience.

My eternal thanks to my agent, Sharon Pelletier, who spotted the 280-character Twitter pitch for this manuscript one happy day in June 2019, signed me up as a new client, and helped me shine up this story and share it with the world.

Thank you to my sons, Austin and Matthew, who have never once needed me to employ any Kira-like tactics to ensure their success. I love you and I'm so proud of who you are.

And last, but far from least, thank you to my husband, Frank, who knows I write in the cracks of a very busy schedule and takes the boys hiking when deadlines approach, listens to me brainstorm, and reassures me that I'm a good mother even at the moments when I feel like the opposite. I love you.

ABOUT THE AUTHOR

Photo © 2018 Lindsey Hinkley Photography

Kristin Wright is a graduate of the University of Michigan Law School and has simultaneously been a small-town general practice lawyer handling criminal defense and the vice president of the elementary school PTA. She lives in Virginia with her husband, sons, and two beagles. For more information about the author visit www.kristinbwright.com.